The Crime of Father Amaro

First published in 1874 in Portugal as *O Crime do Padre Amaro*

First published in Great Britain by Max Reinhardt, London 1962

A hardback version of this edition first published in 1994
as *The Sin of Father Amaro* by Carcanet Press Limited

First published in paperback in 2002 by

Carcanet Press Limited
Alliance House
Cross Street
Manchester M2 7AQ

English translation copyright © Nan Flanagan, 1962, 1994, 2002

The right of Nan Flanagan to be identified as the translator of this
work has been asserted by her in accordance with the
Copyright, Designs and Patents Act of 1988

A CIP catalogue record for this book is available from the British Library

ISBN 1 85754 684 9

The publisher acknowledges financial assistance from
the Arts Council of England

Printed and bound in England by SRP Ltd, Exeter

EÇA DE QUEIRÓS was born in 1845 at Póvoa de Varzim in northern Portugal, the son of a magistrate. After studying law, he travelled widely and entered the diplomatic service. Married, and with four children, Eça was known as a good host, a raconteur, wit, dandy, aesthete and bon viveur. He served as consul in Havana, Newcastle, Bristol and Paris, where he died in 1900.

Eça's travel articles, essays and short stories first brought him to the notice of Portuguese critics. His early novels, *The Crime of Father Amaro* (1876) and *Cousin Bazilio* (1878), won him recognition as a writer of European stature. While Eça's most significant literary influence was the French Naturalist tradition of Flaubert, Balzac and Zola, his novels have their own distinctive voice: urbane, exact, amused and ironic. Eça's exposure of the greed, pretensions and hypocrisies of his society is tempered by a warm sympathy for human frailty and a poignant sense of the fragility of happiness. His enjoyment of everyday life and his sense of the unpredictability of individual destiny give his novels an enduring immediacy.

Also by Eça de Queirós from Carcanet

EÇA DE QUEIRÓS

The Crime of Father Amaro

Translated from the Portuguese
by Nan Flanagan

Chapter I

IT WAS Easter Sunday when it became known in Leiria that José Migueis, the Cathedral paroco, had died of apoplexy in the early hours of the morning. He was a full-blooded, overfed man, known among the clergy of the dioceses as the Prize Glutton. Carlos, the apothecary, who detested him, used to say as he watched him coming out after his siesta, with his cheeks all swollen and congested with blood: 'There goes the boa-constrictor digesting his food. One day he'll burst.' As a matter of fact, he did burst—after a fish supper, at the same time as a dance was going on in the house opposite. (Dr Godhinho was celebrating his birthday and the polka was stepped out with great noise and hilarity.)

Nobody regretted him and few people attended his funeral. He was of the peasantry and had the manners and thick wrists of a ploughman, a hoarse voice, long hairs in his ears and a rough manner of speaking. He was never liked by the devout; he belched in the confessional, and as he had always lived in country districts or mountain villages he didn't understand certain niceties of devotional exercises; so, from the beginning he lost nearly all his woman penitents, who passed over to the polished, sweet-tongued Father Gusmão who affected interest in their scruples. As for the sanctimonious churchgoers, contemptuously known as *beatas*, who had remained faithful to him, when they spoke of visions or scruples José Migueis scandalized them by growling: 'Nonsense, you mock the saints! Ask God to put some sense into your heads!' The excesses of the fasters irritated him still more: 'Eat and drink, you miserable creatures!' he would bawl at them. He was a Miguelista and the papers and opinions of the Liberals filled him with an irrational fury: 'Get the stick to them. Get the stick to them!' he would cry, waving his enormous red umbrella.

In his later years his habits became sedentary, and he lived a solitary life with his old servant and his dog Joli. His only friend was the precentor, Valladares, who then governed the bishopric, as two years before the senhor bishop, Dom Joaquim, had retired to his estate in Alto Minho, moaning and groaning with rheumatism. The paroco had a great respect for the precentor, a dry individual with an enormous nose, very short-sighted and an admirer of Ovid, who always pursed his mouth when speaking and delighted in making mythological allusions.

The precentor thought highly of the paroco, calling him Friar Hercules.

7

'Hercules on account of his strength,' he laughingly explained, 'friar because of his gluttony.'

At the burial, he himself sprinkled the coffin with Holy Water; and as he was accustomed to offer him snuff every day from his gold snuff-box, when, according to the ritual, he threw the first clod of earth on the coffin, he leaned across to the other canons and said in a whisper: 'This is the last pinch he'll get from me!' All the chapter laughed heartily at the precentor's joke. Canon Campos told the story that night as he was taking tea in the house of Deputy Novaes; it was received with screams of laughter, all declaring with respect that his excellency was a great wit.

Some days after the funeral, the dog Joli appeared wandering round the Square. The servant was in hospital with malaria and the house was all barred up, so the poor abandoned dog howled with hunger from door to door. He was a small, extremely fat water-dog with a vague resemblance to the paroco. Being accustomed to the cassock and avid for a master, he no sooner spied a priest than he followed behind him, yelping low and pitifully. But none of them wanted the unhappy Joli, and they drove him off with the tips of their umbrellas. The dog, his suit rejected, howled all night on the streets. One morning he was found dead by the wall of the Misericordia. The driver of a dung cart picked up his body, and José Migueis was definitely forgotten.

Two months later the news spread in Leiria that another paroco had been appointed. It was said he was a very young man who had not long left the seminary. His name was Amaro Vieira. His choice was attributed to political influence, and Leiria's opposition paper *The Voice of the District* wrote bitterly of the matter, citing Golgotha, court influence and the reactionary views of the clergy. Some of the clergy, who were incensed by the article, spoke angrily about it to the precentor. 'Yes,' said the precentor, 'there was favouritism. It was the minister of justice himself, Brito Correia, who wrote to me confirming his appointment. He even remarked that the new paroco was a fine, good-looking fellow. So that now,' he went on, enlarging the idea and smiling with satisfaction at his cleverness, 'after Friar Hercules perhaps we are going to have Friar Apollo.'

In Leiria there was only one person who knew the new paroco: Canon Dias, who had been Amaro's master of moral during his first days at the seminary. 'At that time,' said the canon, 'Amaro was a thin, bashful young fellow, full of pimples. I can almost see him now in his shabby old cassock, with a yellow face like someone with worms! All the same, he was a good lad, and very sensible.'

Canon Dias was well-known in Leiria. Lately he had been getting fat—his protruding stomach pushing out his cassock, and his little grey

8

head, his swollen, puffy eyes and thick lips calling to mind old stories of sensual, greedy monks. Uncle Patricio, commonly known as The Ancient, a shopkeeper in the Square, a strong Liberal who growled like an old mastiff if he passed a priest, used to say when he saw the canon crossing the Square, leaning on his umbrella, weighed down after a good meal: 'What a rascal! It might be King Dom John V. himself.' The canon lived alone with an old sister, Josepha, and a servant, who was often seen in the street wrapped in a dyed black shawl and dragging her felt slippers after her. Canon Dias had the reputation of being rich: he enjoyed the rents from property on the outskirts of Leiria; he gave turkey suppers and his wine, duque 1815, had quite a good reputation. But the salient fact of his life, the fact commented on and whispered from ear to ear, was his long connection with Senhora Augusta Caminha, commonly called Senhora Joanneira as she was a native of St João da Foz. Senhora Joanneira lived in the Rua Misericordia and kept lodgers. She had a daughter Amelia, a girl of twenty-two, good-looking, well-built and much sought after.

Canon Dias displayed much pleasure at the appointment of Amaro Vieira. In Carlos the apothecary's, in the Square and in the Cathedral sacristy he extolled his record at the seminary, speaking of his prudent habits and his obedience, even praising his voice, which he described as having such a rich timbre that it was a joy to listen to it: 'To put a little sentiment into the Holy Week sermons, it will be just the thing,' he said. He emphatically predicted a happy future for him, a sure canonship and perhaps the glory of a bishop's mitre.

At last, one day he received a letter from Amaro Vieira, who was in Lisbon. He showed it with great satisfaction to the coadjutor, a silent servile creature.

It was an afternoon in August when they were both walking along by the side of the Ponte Novo. The construction of the Figueira Road was in progress: the old wooden passage over the River Liz had been demolished, and already the much vaunted new bridge with its two large stone arches, strong and sturdy, was being used. Just then the work was suspended on account of expropriation; the muddy road of the Marrazes district, which the new road would incorporate, could still be seen; layers of pebbles covered the ground; and huge cylinders of stone, used to grind and work over the macadam, were dug into the dark muddy earth soaked through from the rain.

Around the bridge the view is wide and tranquil. At the end where the river issues low round hills can be seen, covered with the dark green branches of the young pines; below, among the great trees, are the houses, giving the melancholy scene a character more alive and human, with their joyful whitewashed walls shining brightly in the sun, and, in the evening, the smoke from the chimneys tingeing the always clear and limpid air with blue. In the lowlands, where the river drags its way along between two rows of pale willows to the sea, stretch the first fields of the plains of Leiria, large, fertile, and full of light. From the bridge little of the town itself is to be seen: just an angle of the Jesuit-style masonry of the Cathedral, a corner of the cemetery wall covered with wallwort and the dark green needles of the cypresses; the rest is hidden by the solid mass of bristling wild vegetation, among which the castle ruins stand out with a grand historic air, silhouetted against the sky and enveloped in the evening by the circling flight of owls.

At the foot of the bridge a sloping path descends for a little way along the edge of the river. A tranquil secluded spot covered with old trees, it is known as the old poplar avenue. There, walking slowly and speaking low, the canon consulted the coadjutor about an idea he had got from the letter, an idea which to him appeared perfect, absolutely a master-thought! Amaro urgently requested him to arrange a rented house for him, cheap, well situated, and if possible furnished; or perhaps, better still, rooms in a respectable lodging house. 'One can well see, my dear master,' wrote Amaro, 'that the latter would suit me best. I certainly don't want anything luxurious; a bedroom and a small parlour would be enough. The important thing is that the house should be a respectable one, quiet and central, and that the owner be well-intentioned and not too exacting; I will leave all to your good judgement and ability, and you may rest assured that your kindness will not fall on barren ground. I wish above all that the woman of the house should be orderly and clean-tongued.'

'Now listen to my idea, friend Mendes. It's to put him in Senhora Joanneira's house!' resumed the canon with a satisfied air. 'It's a good idea, isn't it?'

'A splendid idea,' said the coadjutor in a servile tone.

'Yes, she has the room below, the small parlour attached and another room which will serve as a writing-room. She has good linen and good furniture.'

'Beautiful linen,' said the coadjutor with respect.

The canon continued: 'It would be a good arrangement for her: giving the two rooms, food and service she can well ask for six tostões a day. Besides which she will have the honour of having the paroco in the house.'

'It's on account of Ameliazinha that I'm doubtful,' timidly considered the coadjutor. 'Yes, there could be comments. A young girl. They say the paroco is a young man. You known, senhor canon, how people's tongues wag.'

The canon had stopped. 'Nonsense!' he exclaimed. 'Doesn't Father Joaquim live under the same roof as his mother's god-daughter? And Canon Pedroso, doesn't he live with his sister-in-law and a sister of hers, a young girl of nineteen? There's no sense in your objection.'

'What I would like to say——' the coadjutor attempted to explain.

'No, I see no objection whatever. Senhora Joanneira can let her rooms to whom she likes. After all, she keeps a lodging house. The Secretary of Education, wasn't he there for a few months?'

'But a clergyman——' insinuated the coadjutor.

'There is a further guarantee, Senhor Mendes, a further guarantee!' exclaimed the canon. Stopping, he continued in a confidential tone. 'After all, it suits me, it suits me more than anybody, my friend!' There was a short silence. Then the coadjutor said, lowering his voice: 'Yes, senhor canon, you are very good to Senhora Joanneira.'

'I do what I can, my dear friend, I do what I can,' said the canon. Then with a sudden tender intonation and laughing paternally: 'She is so good that she deserves it all.' He stopped, and turning up the whites of his eyes continued: 'Now the day I don't appear in the morning on the stroke of nine, she is in a fever! "Oh, woman!" I say to her, "you worry unnecessarily." But then that's how it is. When I got colic last year, I got so thin, Senhor Mendes, and she couldn't do enough for me. When a pig is killed the best parts are for the holy priest—that's what she calls me.' He spoke with a slobbering satisfaction, his eyes shining. 'Oh, Mendes,' he continued, 'she is a precious woman.'

'And a pretty woman,' said the coadjutor respectfully.

'That she is,' said the canon, again stopping. 'One can see she is no kitten! But she hasn't one grey hair, not even one. And what lovely skin. But it is here, Mendes,' he said, passing his fat hand under his chin, 'that she is so perfect. Then she is such a clean, fresh woman. And how she thinks of me! Not a day passes that she doesn't send me her little present—a plate of rice, a dish of jelly, a beautiful black pudding! Yesterday, she sent me an apple tart. If you could have seen it! The sauce was like a cream! It was so good that Josepha said: "It is so perfect that it might have been cooked in Holy Water."'

Then, placing his spreadout fingers on his chest: 'These are things that touch one's very heart, Mendes. It's not for me to say, but there is no one like her.'

The coadjutor listened in envious silence.

'I know well,' said the canon, stopping again and dragging out his words, 'I know well that there is talk here and there . . . But it is a great calumny! The fact is that my friendship with these people dates from the husband's time. You know that well, Mendes.'

The coadjutor nodded affirmatively.

'She is a good moral woman, that's what she is, a good moral woman,' exclaimed the canon, digging the point of his umbrella forcefully into the ground.

'People's tongues are full of venom, senhor canon,' said the coadjutor in a whining voice. Then after a short silence he whispered in the canon's ear: 'But the affair must be an expensive one for you, senhor canon!'

'Indeed you are quite right, my friend! You can imagine how it is since the General Secretary left her and the poor woman has had her rooms empty: it is I who have kept the pot boiling for her, Mendes.'

'She has a bit of a farm,' considered the coadjutor.

'Just a small corner of land, my dear senhor. When she has paid the taxes and the necessary labour there isn't much left. So, I say, the paroco will be a godsend to her; with his six tostões a day and what I give her she will be able to manage. And it will be a great relief for me, Mendes.'

'It will be a great relief for you, senhor canon,' repeated the coadjutor.

They both stood silent. The evening fell clear and limpid; the sky overhead was a pale blue, the air was still. Just then the river was shallow; little patches of sand shone bright and dry, and the low water flowed with a soft murmur, babbling and wrinkling over the pebbles.

Two cows driven by a young girl appeared on the muddy road, which was lined on either side by a row of bramble bushes, and faced the old poplar avenue. They entered the river slowly and, stretching out their necks, skinned from the halter, drank lightly and noiselessly, from time to time lifting up their friendly heads and looking round with the passive tranquillity of satisfied beings. Threads of water dribbling from their mouths shone in the light. With the sinking sun the water lost its clear reflected light and the shadows from the arches of the bridge lengthened. From the hills a hazy twilight mounted, the blood-and-orange-coloured clouds telling of the hot day that had passed. They made a rich apron over the sea.

'It's a lovely evening,' said the coadjutor.

The canon yawned, and making the Sign of the Cross over his gaping mouth said: 'Let us go back, it is nearly time for the Angelus.' As they were ascending the Cathedral steps, the canon stopped and said: 'Then we'll install Amaro in Senhora Joanneira's house. It will be a good job done for everybody.'

'A good job,' said the coadjutor respectfully.

They entered the Cathedral making the Sign of the Cross.

Chapter II

A WEEK later it was known that the new paroco was to arrive from Chão de Macas by the coach which brought the evening post. So from six o'clock onwards Canon Dias and the coadjutor were walking up and down the Fountain Square waiting for Amaro.

It was now the end of August. In the macadamized path which stretched along the river one caught a glimpse of the bright-coloured clothes of the women as they walked to and fro between the two rows of old poplars. In the row of poor dwellings at the side of the Archway, the old women sat at their doors, spinning; the dirty, ill-nourished children played on the ground, showing their nude, swollen bellies; and the hens went round voraciously picking among the dirt and filth. Round the fountain all was noise; vessels were dragged over the stones, servants abused one another, soldiers in dirty uniforms and enormous laced down-at-heel boots waved their malacca canes and made love; girls with fat-paunched pitchers on their heads walked in pairs swinging their hips; two lazy officers, with their uniforms un-buttoned and hanging loose over their stomachs, chatted together as they waited to see who might arrive. The coach was late. When twilight descended a flame from the lamp in the saint's niche over the archway became visible. From the hospital windows in front lights appeared one by one, throwing out a dull glow.

It was already dark when the coach, with all its lanterns ablaze and drawn by two emaciated white horses, plodded across the bridge and drew up beside the fountain below the Inn of the Cross. Uncle Patricio's assistant ran through the Square with a pile of *The Popular Daily*. Uncle Baptisto, the owner of the coach, his black pipe hanging from the corner of his mouth, unharnessed the horses, swearing tranquilly. A man wearing a high hat and a long ecclesiastical coat got up from the cushion beside the driver, stamped his feet to bring the life back to them, then carefully descended, grasping the iron rails.

'Oh, Amaro!' the canon, who had approached the coach, exclaimed, 'oh, you rogue you!'

'Oh, master,' said the other joyfully. They embraced one another, while the coadjutor, all bent, stood holding his biretta in his hand.

A little later the people in the shops saw passing across the Square, between the canon with his slow corpulent gait and the long-shanked figure of the coadjutor, a young man with his priest's cloak hanging

13

from his slightly stooping shoulders. They knew it was the new paroco; and it was said afterwards in the apothecary's that he was a fine figure of a man. João Bicho walked in front of him with a small tin trunk and a carpet bag; he was humming the hymn *Praise Be to God*, and, as he was tipsy, staggering from side to side.

It was nearly nine o'clock, and the night was closing in. Most of the houses round the Square were shut and their inhabitants already sleeping; from the shops below in the Arcade, the dull lights of the paraffin lamps showed up sleepy figures at the counters, persistently chatting. The gloomy, tortuous streets, each with its one large, wan light, appeared uninhabited. In the silence the Cathedral bell drearily tolled for the souls of the Faithful Departed.

As they walked along Canon Dias slowly and heavily explained to the paroco what he had arranged for him. He hadn't got him a house, as then it would have been necessary for him to buy furniture, pay a servant and incur numerous other expenses. It had seemed to him that rooms in a respectable lodging would be best; it would certainly be more comfortable; and (his friend the coadjutor here could confirm this) there wasn't another house in the town to compare with that of Senhora Joanneira. It was clean and airy, and no unpleasant smells came from the kitchen; the General Secretary of Education and the school inspector had lived with her; and as to Senhora Joanneira herself (friend Mendes here knew her well), she was a godfearing woman, strict in the performance of her religious duties, a thrifty housewife, and full of little kindnesses. 'There you will be as if you were in your own house: you can have your stew, a second helping, your coffee . . .'

'We'll see, master; and the price?'

'Six tostões a day. My God, man, it's a gift! You will have your bedroom and your little parlour.'

'A nice little parlour,' commented the coadjutor respectfully.

'And is it far from the Cathedral?' asked Amaro.

'Just a few steps. You could run and say Mass in your carpet slippers. There is a young girl in the house,' the canon continued in his leisurely voice. 'She is the daughter of Senhora Joanneira, a girl of twenty-two, pretty and high-spirited, but good at heart . . . Here is your street.'

It was a narrow street, squeezed in by the walls of the old Misericordia, and lighted by one dismal lantern at the farther end. The houses were mean and low-built.

'Now here you have your palace!' said the canon, knocking on a narrow door.

From the first storey two old-fashioned, iron-railed balconies projected, chock-full of rosemary, which grew and spread from four

14

wooden boxes, placed in the corners; each of the very small upper windows also had a little iron-railed balcony; and the wall, because of its irregularities, reminded one of a battered tin.

Senhora Joanneira was waiting for them at the top of the first flight of stairs; a delicate looking, freckled servant was holding aloft a paraffin-oil lamp, to show them their way in. The figure of Senhora Joanneira stood out plainly against the light thrown on the white-washed wall. She was tall, fat and very pale. Her black eyes already had wrinkles round them; her frizzy hair, tied with a scarlet ribbon, was getting thin on the top and at the parting; but one caught a glimpse of plump arms, a copious neck and clean neatly arranged linen. She had a pleasant easy-going air.

'Here, senhora, is your lodger,' said the canon, mounting the stairs.

'I have great honour in receiving the senhor paroco! Great honour! You must be tired, I'm sure. Have the goodness to come this way. Be careful of the little step.'

She showed them into a small parlour, painted yellow, with a huge cane-bottomed sofa against the wall, and in front a folding table, opened and covered with a green felt cloth.

'This is your parlour, senhor paroco', said Senhora Joanneira, 'you can receive your friends or retire here.' 'Here,' she added, opening another door, 'is your bedroom. You have your chest of drawers, your wardrobe . . .' She slid the drawers backwards and forwards and praised the bed, punching the mattresses to show their springiness and softness. 'And here is a little bell which you can ring if you want anything. The keys for your chest of drawers are here . . . if you would like another bolster to make your head higher . . . I've only given you one quilt but if you'd like more . . .'

'It's all right, all is very good, my dear senhora,' said the paroco in his low suave voice.

'If there is anything at all you want we will be only too pleased to get it for you.'

'My dear woman,' interrupted the canon jovially, 'what he wants now is his supper!'

'The supper is all ready; the broth has been on the fire since six o'clock in order to make it more appetizing.' She left the room to hurry up the servant, calling out as she reached the stairs: 'Come on, Ruça, get a move on! Get a move on!'

The canon sat down heavily on the sofa, and taking a pinch of snuff, said: 'Be content, my friend, this is the best I could do for you.'

'I'm satisfied in every way, master', said the paroco putting on his felt slippers. 'When I think of the seminary! . . . And of Feirão where the rain used to come in on my bed.'

Then, from the direction of the Square, came the sound of a bugle.

'What is that!' said Amaro, going to the window.

'Half-past nine, the tattoo for the soldiers.'

Amaro opened the window. At the end of the street the light was slowly dying. The night was black, and over the whole town had fallen the hollow silence of a vault.

After the bugles had ceased, a long muffling sound of drums came out from the barracks; below, a soldier who had delayed in some alleyway of the Castle came running beneath the window; and from the walls of the Misericordia came the persistent puling cry of an owl.

'This is gloomy,' said Amaro.

But Senhora Joanneira called from above. 'You can come up, senhor canon! The soup is on the table.'

'Come on, come on, you must be dropping with hunger, Amaro!' said the canon, lifting himself heavily out of the sofa. He detained the paroco for a minute by the sleeve of his coat: 'Now you are going to see a chicken prepared by Senhora Joanneira. It will make your mouth water.'

In the middle of the dining-room, covered with dull wallpaper, the brightness of the table, with its snow-white cloth, the china, the shining glasses reflecting the strong light from the lamp with its green lamp-shade, gave an air of joy to the whole room. From the tureen came the savoury odour of the soup: in a large dish a plump chicken, smothered in white juicy rice, and surrounded with large sausages, had the succulent appearance of a dinner fit for a morgado. In the glass-doored cupboard, placed a little in the shade, shone the brightly coloured chinaware; in a corner underneath the window stood the piano, covered with a faded satin cover. There was frying going on in the kitchen; and a pleasant smell came from a basket of newly washed linen. The paroco rubbed his hands with glee.

'This way, senhor paroco, this way. It may be a little cold over there,' said Senhora Joanneira, as she proceeded to close the window shutters and bring him a box of sand for the cigarette-ends. 'And the senhor canon will take a glass of jelly, won't he!'

'I will to be sure, just for company's sake,' said the canon jovially, as he sat down and unfolded his table napkin.

Meanwhile, Senhora Joanneira, while she bustled about the room, had time to observe and admire the appearance of the new paroco. As he sat with his head bent over his plate, silently blowing on the spoon to cool his soup, he appeared well-made; he had jet-black hair, slightly

16

curly. The face was oval, the skin brown and fine, the eyes big and black, with long eyelashes.

The canon, who hadn't seen him since the seminary days, found him stronger, more manly.

'You were a pitiful sight in those days.'

'It was the good air of the mountains which strengthened me', the paroco replied. He then recounted his sad life in his last parish in Feirão in the heights of Beira, during the bitter winter months, with no other company than that of the shepherds. The canon filled their glasses, lifting the decanter high to put a froth on the wine:

'Drink it up, man! drink it up! You didn't smuggle in anything like this in the seminary.'

They then spoke of the seminary.

'What became of Rabicho, the bursar?' said the canon. 'And do you remember Carocho who stole the potatoes?'

They laughed and drank, in the joy of their reminiscences, calling to mind the stories of those times, the rector's catarrh, and the master of plain chant, who one day let fall from his pocket the obscene poems of Bocage.

'How time passes, how time passes!' they said.

Senhora Joanneira then put on the table a deep dish of baked apples.

'Hurrah!' exclaimed the canon, 'I'm going to help myself to some of these. Lovely baked apples are things I never refuse! You are an excellent housekeeper, my friend. Our Senhora Joanneira is an excellent housekeeper.'

She laughed, showing the stoppings of two of her large front teeth. She went to fetch a bottle of port wine; then she put on the canon's plate, arranging it with an excess of devotion, a cut, prepared apple, drowned in powdered sugar; and patting him on the back with her soft fat hand: 'This is a saint, senhor paroco, this is a saint! Ah, I'm indebted to him for many favours!'

'Let her talk, let her talk,' said the canon, beaming with a slobbering smile of contentment. 'A good drop!' he added, taking a sip of his port. 'A good drop!'

'Yes, it is some we've had since Amelia's last birthday, senhor canon.'

'And where is she, the little one?'

'She went to Morenal with Dona Maria, and from there they naturally went on to the Gansosos' house to pass the evening.'

'The Senhora here is a property owner,' explained the canon, referring to Morenal. 'In fact she is an estate owner.' He laughed good-naturedly, his eyes lighting up with tenderness as they ran over the plump body of Senhora Joanneira.

'Oh, senhor paroco, he's only talking, it's just a small piece of land,' she said.

Then seeing the servant leaning against the wall, shaking all over with a fit of coughing, 'Oh, child,' exclaimed Senhora Joanneira, 'go and cough outside! Good heavens!'

The girl went out, holding her apron to her mouth.

'She appears to be ill, God help her,' observed the paroco.

'She is very sickly, very!' said Senhora Joanneira. 'The poor soul in Christ is my godchild and an orphan. I'm afraid she is tubercular. I took her in just out of pity, and also because my other servant had to go to hospital. The brazen-face got into trouble through a soldier!'

Father Amaro slowly dropped his eyes—and munching crumbs of bread between his teeth, he asked if there had been much sickness in the parish that summer.

'A little colic from eating green fruit,' murmured the canon. 'They ran over the melon beds and then they blew themselves out with gallons of water. Of course, the usual fevers.'

They then talked of the malaria in the Leiria swampy districts.

'Now I have much better health,' said Amaro. 'Praised be to Our Lord Jesus Christ, I am healthy, yes, I am!'

'May Our Lord Jesus Christ keep you so. No one really knows the value of good health except those who have lost it,' exclaimed Senhora Joanneira. Then she recounted the great sorrow that she had in the house, a sister of hers, half idiot and paralysed for the last ten years, who was now going on for sixty. Last winter she had caught a cold, since then, God help her, she had been fading away. 'A while ago, just at the end of the afternoon, she took a fit of coughing, I thought she was going; but it passed, and we were so relieved.'

She continued talking of this trouble, afterwards of her little Amelia, of her dear friends the Gansosos, of the rise in prices—sitting with the cat in her lap and monotonously rolling the crumbs of bread into little balls with her two fingers. The canon heavily closed his eyes, and everything in the room seemed to be gradually going to sleep; the light from the lamp began to fade.

'Now, good people, it is getting late,' said the canon turning in his chair.

Father Amaro stood up, and lowering his eyes said grace.

'Would the senhor paroco care for a night-lamp?' said Senhora Joanneira attentively.

'No, senhora, I never use one. Good-night.' He slowly descended the stairs, picking his teeth.

Senhora Joanneira brought out the lamp to light up the stairhead.

But after the first steps the paroco stopped and turning said very graciously: 'You know, Senhora Joanneira, tomorrow is Friday and a fast day.'

'Yes, yes,' chimed in the canon, who was wrapping himself in his glossy silk cloth cloak and yawning, 'you will dine with me tomorrow evening. I will call here and we will go together to the precentor and to the Cathedral and make a few more calls. Listen, I have some sleeve fish for tomorrow, which is a miracle as we hardly ever get fish here.'

Senhora Joanneira immediately put the paroco's mind at ease. 'It's not necessary to remind me of the fast days, senhor paroco. I am very scrupulous about these things.'

'I spoke,' said the paroco, 'because unfortunately so few people trouble nowadays to keep the fasts.'

'You are quite right,' she intercepted. 'But as to me! Heavens, my soul's salvation comes before all!'

Then the door bell below rang violently.

'That must be the little one,' said Senhora Joanneira. 'Open the door, Ruça.'

The door opened and there was a sound of voices and laughter.

'Is that you, Amelia?'

A voice was heard saying: 'Good-bye, good-bye', and there appeared, almost running, lightly lifting up her skirts in front as she mounted the stairs, a beautiful girl, tall, strong, well made, with a white scarf round her head and a twig of rosemary in her hand.

'Come on up, my dear,' said her mother. 'Here is the senhor paroco. He arrived this evening almost at night fall. Come up!'

Amelia stopped, a little embarrassed, turning her eyes to the top of the stairs where the priest was standing, leaning against the railings. She was breathing heavily after running; her face was all aflame and her lively black eyes were shining; she gave a feeling of freshness and of walking through green meadows.

The paroco descended, keeping close to the banisters in order to let her pass; lowering his eyes he murmured, 'Good-night!' The canon, who came down heavily behind him, took the centre of the stairs in front of Amelia:

'These are nice hours for a young girl to keep; you rogue, you.'

She gave a little laugh and shrugged her shoulders.

'Now go and put yourself under God's protection, go!' he said, slowly patting her face with his fat, hairy hand.

She went running up the stairs, while the canon, after going into the parlour for his umbrella, went out, saying to the servant who was holding the lamp over the banisters to give him light: 'It's all right, I can see, don't catch cold, girl. Then you are to be up and ready at eight, Amaro! Go to bed, girl, good-bye. Pray to Our Lady of Pity to cure that cough of yours.'

The paroco closed the door of his room. The bed had been turned down, and the fresh white sheets had the pleasant smell of newly-washed linen. Over the head of the bed hung an old faded print of Christ on the Cross. Amaro opened his breviary and falling on his knees at the side of the bed made the Sign of the Cross; but he was tired and yawned copiously; then from above, on the other side of the ceiling, breaking across the ritual prayers which he mechanically continued to read, came the tic-tac of Amelia's little boots as she moved about the room, and then the noise of her shaking her starched skirts as she undressed in preparation for bed.

Chapter III

Amaro Vieira was born in Lisbon in the house of the Marqueza d'Alegros. His father was valet to the marquez; his mother was a chambermaid, almost a friend, of the marqueza. Amaro's father had died of apoplexy, and his mother, who had always been so healthy, succumbed a year after to consumption of the throat. Amaro was then at the end of his sixth year. He had an elder sister who from childhood had lived with a grandfather in Coimbra, and an uncle, a well-to-do grocer, in Estrela, a suburb of Lisbon. The senhora marqueza, who had become attached to Amaro, kept him in her house, tacitly adopting him, and now began very scrupulously to look after his education.

The Marqueza d'Alegros became a widow at forty-three, and for the greater part of the year retired to her estate at Carcavelos. She was a passive individual, indolently kind, with a chapel in the house and a reverent devotion to the priests of St Luiz, the best part of her life being taken up with the affairs of the Church. Her two daughters, educated in the fear of the heavens and the preoccupations of being chic, were, at the same time, fanatically pious and followers of the mode; talking with equal fervour of Christian humility and the latest fashions from Brussels. A journalist of those days used to say of them: 'Every day they think of the toilette in which they should enter paradise.'

The senhora marqueza made up her mind from the beginning that Amaro should become a priest. His yellow face and thin body asked for the destiny of a recluse for which he had been chosen: he was already attached to the things of the chapel, and his great delight was to nestle at the feet of the women, to cuddle in the heat of their meeting skirts and listen to them talking of the saints. The senhora marqueza didn't wish to send Amaro to college, as she felt that he would suffer from the contact with evil company and from the impiety of the times. Her private chaplain taught him Latin, and the eldest daughter, Dona Luiza, who had a hooked nose and read Chateaubriand, gave him lessons in French and geography.

Amaro was, as the servants described him, 'a warmed-up corpse'. He never played, never jumped about in the sun. He became very nervous and subject to fears, so at night they let him have a night light and put him to sleep at the foot of the children's old nurse. The other servants made him girlish; thinking he was a pretty boy they hugged him amongst them, kissing and tickling him; he rolled among their

21

skirts, making contact with their bodies, with little cries of enjoyment. When the senhora marqueza went out, amid peals of laughter from the women they dressed him in their clothes; he, with his languid disposition, abandoned himself, half naked, weakly closing his eyes and feeling a burning patch on each cheek. Besides this, the servants used him in their intrigues with one another; it was through him they made their complaints. With this he became tricky and very untruthful.

When he was eleven he assisted the priest at Mass, and on Saturdays he cleaned the chapel. On this day he felt the importance of his task, and loudly sang the *santissimo* as he worked. Locking himself in, he devotedly arranged the saints on a table in the full light, greedily kissing them and lisping tender holy words to them.

Though he grew, his appearance didn't change; he still remained thin and yellow; he never gave a hearty, natural laugh and continued going about with his hands in his pockets. He was extremely lazy, and it took them all their time to wake him up in the morning from his unhealthy sleep. Already a little round-shouldered, he became known among the servants as the Jack Priest.

One Quinquagesima Sunday morning after Mass the senhora marqueza dropped dead of apoplexy. In her will she left a legacy for Amaro and recommended that he should enter the seminary at fifteen and, when the time came, take Holy Orders. Her chaplain, Father Liset, was entrusted with the pious task of seeing her wishes carried out.

Amaro, who was then thirteen, was sent to his aunt and uncle in Estrela. The grocer, an obese man, was married to the daughter of a poor public employee who had accepted him just to get away from the meagre food and housework and get a chance of going to the theatre. Amaro didn't find there the feminine, affectionate surroundings which he had enjoyed at Carcavelos. His aunt hardly noticed him and the grocer took Amaro on as a painful necessity, using him to serve in the shop. They both detested him; his aunt called him Onion while his uncle called him Donkey. They even begrudged him the thin slice of beef which he ate for his evening meal. Amaro became still thinner and wept every night.

He knew that when he was fifteen he must enter the seminary. His uncle reminded him of it every day and he came to look forward to it as an escape.

No one consulted either his inclination or his vocation. They pushed him into a surplice, and with his passive, easily-dominated nature, he accepted it, as one accepts a uniform. On the other hand, he didn't find the idea of being a priest a disagreeable one. He had given up the perpetual praying practised in Carcavelos; but he kept his fear of hell, though he lost his fervour for the saints. However, he thought of the priests who came to the senhora marqueza's house as clean, fine people, well treated, who ate with the gentry and took snuff from gold snuff-boxes; and that profession would suit him, in which one spoke softly with the women and received presents from them on silver trays. One day they had had a visit from a bishop who had been a priest in Bahia, and had even travelled to Rome. He was very jovial; and in the salon, with his anointed hands smelling of eau-de-cologne, he leant on his gold-headed cane, surrounded by rapturous women wearing ecstatic smiles, while with his beautiful voice he sang to entertain them: *Sweet little mulatto of Bahia, born in Capuja.*

A year before Amaro entered the seminary his uncle, dispensing with his services at the counter, sent him to a master to improve his Latin. For the first time in his life, Amaro was free. He went alone to school, walking through the streets. He saw the town, he saw the infantry exercising; he lurked round the doors of the cafés, read the theatre handbills. He began especially to notice the women—and because of all he saw a great sadness entered his soul. His dreariest hour was when he returned from school and night fell. His room was in the attic, and had a little skylight in the tiles where he would prop himself up to look out at a part of the town below. He lost himself in vague imaginings, and suddenly from the depths of the blackness of the night feminine forms appeared by pieces, a leg with a little calamanco boot and a very white stocking, or a rounded arm, bare to the shoulder . . . Then below, in the kitchen, the servant would begin to wash the dishes and sing: she was a fat girl, very freckled; he had a longing to go down and rub against her or to sit in a corner and watch her as she washed the plates; he brought to mind other women whom he had seen on the roads, in boots down at heel, noisy starched skirts, hatless; from the depths of his being came a languid desire to embrace somebody, in order not to feel so alone. He considered himself unfortunate and meditated suicide. His aunt called from below: 'Now, why aren't you studying, you rogue?'

Then, feeling wretched, he would lean over his Livy, his head nodding, rubbing his knees one against the other, aimlessly opening and shutting the leaves of his dictionary.

He began to feel a certain disinclination for the priest's life of celibacy. The other boys in the school had already filled his unhealthy mind with curiosity and corrupt thoughts with regard to women. He smoked in secret and got yellower and thinner.

He entered the seminary. At the beginning, the long corridors of sweating stone, the dull lights, the narrow rooms with high rails instead of walls to ensure that the students were under constant vigilance, the black cassocks, the forced silences, the sound of the bells, filled him with a mournful, terrifying sadness. But he soon made friends; his pretty face was pleasing. The other boys began to address him by the familiar 'tu', and during the recreations and Sundays walks to admit him into the conversations in which they recounted stories of the masters, calumniated the rector, and perpetually lamented the melancholy life of the cloister; because nearly all spoke with longing of the free life they had left: those who came from the country couldn't forget the clear fields on which the sun beat down, the time of the *esfolhadas* (when whoever was lucky enough to find a black corncob could kiss the girls) and the cattle which they led home to be milked, while the sweet meadows exhaled vapour; those who came from the little towns lamented the tortuous, tranquil roads, where they made eyes at the neighbours' daughters, the happy bright market days, the grand adventures of the time when they studied Latin. They found nothing to make up for this in the flagged playground with its few trees, its high overpowering walls, and the monotonous game of ball: they choked in the narrow corridors and in the Saint Ignatius room where they made their morning meditations and studied their evening lessons; they were envious of all, even the most humble, whose destinies were free.

And in the refectory, in front of the meagre helpings of vegetable soup, when the rector with his loud voice began monotonously to read the letters of some Chinese missionary or the bishop's pastoral letter, how many longings there were for the family dinner—the good slices of fish, the pig-killing season, the lumps of fat pork sizzling and jumping in the pan, the appetizing smell of the *sarrabulhos*.

Amaro hadn't left beloved ones; he had come from his uncle's brutality and his aunt's bored face, smothered with powder; but little by little he began to think of his journeys to and from school, of the times when he leaned against the shop windows contemplating the nudity of the dolls.

Slowly, however, the customs of the seminary were turning him, with his colourless nature, into an indolent sheep. He regularly learned his allotted tasks; he fulfilled his ecclesiastical services with the prudent exactitude; and silent, timid, bowing very low before the lecturers, he succeeded in getting good reports.

He never could understand those sanctimonious ones who loved the seminary, who wore their knees out with constant praying, meditating, with bowed heads, on the texts of *The Imitation*; or when in the chapel, turning up the whites of their eyes and almost fainting with rapture; or those who even during recreation or during the walks read pamphlets such as *Praises of Mary* and delightedly complied with all the rules: ascending to heaven one step at a time, as recommended by St Bonaventure. To them the seminary gave a foretaste of heaven; to him it only offered the humiliations of a prison, added to the tediousness of a school.

Nor could he understand the ambitious ones: those who aspired to be bishops' train-bearers, and in the sumptuous episcopal palaces to lift up the ancient damask curtains; or those who after being ordained wished to live in the towns, to hold services in aristocratic churches and in front of the devout rich. There were still others who dreamt of destinies outside the Church: the army, or the full life of the farmer. And all, except the few devout ones, whether aspiring to the priesthood or to secular careers, wanted to leave the narrow life of the seminary in order to eat well, to earn money and to know women.

Amaro seemed to want nothing definite.

'I don't even know,' he used to say in a desolate tone.

Meanwhile, listening with sympathetic interest to those who considered life in the seminary fit for galley slaves, he became very perturbed by these conversations with their impatience for a free life. He had fits of nerves: in bed till dead of night he twisted and turned but couldn't sleep, and in his dreams silently burnt like a red hot iron the desire for a woman.

In his cell was a picture of the Virgin, reposing on the sphere and crowned with stars, her gaze wandering towards the Immortal Light a she crushed the serpent under her heel. Amaro turned to her as a refuge, saying *Hail Marys* to her; but in pausing to contemplate the print, he forgot the sanctity of the Virgin, seeing in front of him only a pretty blonde girl; he loved her; he sighed for her and as he undressed he turned and looked lewdly at her over his shoulder; in the daring curiosity of his imagination he even lifted the chaste nails fixing the blue robes of the Virgin and supposed delicious forms and white flesh. Afterwards he was afraid and thought he could see the eyes of the Tempter shining out in the dark room; he sprinkled his bed with Holy Water; but he didn't dare to reveal these deliriums when he went to confession on Sunday.

How many times, at the recommendations, did he listen to the master of moral, in his hoarse voice, speaking of Sin, comparing it to a serpent as, with unctuous words and broad sweeping gestures, slowly delivering the mellifluous pomp of his pauses, he counselled the students to imitate

25

the Virgin by treading on the ominous head of the serpent! And next it was the master of mystical theology who, while he slowly took his pinches of snuff, told them it was their duty to vanquish their natural desires! And quoting St John of Damascus and St Chrysostom, St Cyprian and St Jerome, he explained the anathema of the saints against women, who were, according to the expressions of the Church, Serpents, Darts, Children of Lies, Doors of Hell, Sources of Crime, Scorpions.

'And,' he concluded, 'as our own Father, St Jerome says'—loudly and ostentatiously blowing his nose—'Paths of Iniquity, *iniquitas via.*'

Even the books Amaro studied were preoccupied with Woman! What being was this then, who, in spite of all the theology, was enthroned over the altar as Queen of Grace, and afterwards cursed in brutal terms? What power was hers, that the legions of the saints when they met her fell into a passionate ecstasy, acclaiming her the queen of all the regions of the heavens—and then ran away from her, with sobs of terror and cries of hate accounting her the universal enemy, and hiding themselves from her like hermits in dreary deserts and cloisters, going there to suffer from the evil of having loved her? Without beng able to define them, he felt these perturbations continually weakening and demoralizing him; and before making his final vows he failed in his efforts to quieten them.

He felt the same rebellion of nature taking place in the other boys around him: the studies, the fasts, the penances could subdue their bodies, could give them mechanical habits, but inwardly their desires moved silently like a cradle of serpents. Those who suffered most were the full-blooded type, as sadly and as straitly pressed down by the rules as were their great plebeian pulses by the cuffs of their shirts. When they were alone their nature burst forth and their desires gained force, provoking disorders. With the lymphatic natures the repression produced great sadness, soft listless silences. Nature revenged herself by turning the repressions into the desire to indulge in petty vices: to play with an old pack of cards, to read a romance, to obtain by devious intrigues and delays, a packet of cigarettes—what enchanting sins!

In the end Amaro almost envied the studious: they, at least, were content. He himself sometimes had sudden ambitions to learn science; but in front of the vast folios he felt an insuperable tedium. Still, he was devout: he said his prayers, he again had unlimited faith in certain saints and an agonizing terror of God. But he hated the cloistered life of the seminary! It seemed to him that he could be good, pure, and have more faith if he were only free to run the streets or to walk in the peace or the fields, anywhere outside those dreary walls. He grew thinner, he

26

had terrible sweats and in his last year, after the heavy services of Holy Week, as the hot weather began, he entered the infirmary with a nervous fever.

At last he was ordained, during the Ember days of St Matthew; a little while later he received, while still in the seminary, the following letter from Father Liset, the former chaplain of the Marqueza d'Alegros.

'My dear son and brother in Jesus Christ,

Now that you are ordained, I feel in my conscience that I must give you an account of the state of your affairs, as I would like to fulfil to the end the task which the late lamented marqueza left on my weak shoulders, assigning to me the honour of administering the legacy which she left for you. Though I know that worldly goods will be of little importance to a soul vowed to Holy Orders, still, one must remember the old saying: "Good accounts make good friends." I would have you know then, my dear son, that the legacy of our dear Marqueza—for whom an eternal gratitude must rise up in your heart—is entirely exhausted. I take advantage of this occasion to inform you that after the death of your uncle, your aunt after going bankrupt, gave herself up to a new mode of life of which I as a priest could not approve: falling under the force of her passions she formed an illegal union, thus losing her possessions at the same time as her virtue; now she has established a boarding-house in 53 Rua dos Calafates. If I touch on these unclean matters, so improper that such a tender young Levite as my dear son may not even know such things exist, it is because I wish to give you a complete account of your respected family. Your sister has, as perhaps you know, made a good match in Coimbra, and though I'm sure you will agree with me that in marriage money is not the principal thing, still in the case of future necessity, it is important that you, my dear son, should be aware of this fact.

Our dear rector has written to me suggesting that we should try to send you to Feirão, in Gralheira. So I am going to speak to some important people who, in spite of the fact that I am but a poor humble priest, who only begs mercy of God, have the extreme kindness to listen to me. Thus I hope to obtain my request. Persevere, my dear son, in the path of virtue, of which quality I know your chaste soul is full, and I believe happiness is to be found in this our holy ministry when we learn how many are the balsams which flow from its bosom and how many are the alleviations which the service of God gives.

Good-bye, my dear son and new colleague. Believe me, my thoughts will always be with you, the ward of our late lamented marqueza, who most certainly from the heavens, where I am sure her virtues have exalted her, will supplicate the Virgin, whom here on earth she loved so much, for the happiness of her dear ward.

Liset.

P.S. Your sister's husband's name is Trigoso—Liset.'

Two months afterwards, Amaro was appointed to the parish of Feirão, in Gralheira, in the heights of Beira-Alta. He was there from October till the end of the snows.

Feirão, a parish of poor shepherds, was at that time of the year almost uninhabited. Amaro passed a very lazy time, sitting at the fire ruminating on the tediousness of his position, listening to the wind howling outside in the mountains. In the spring the two districts of Santarem and Leiria, populous parishes, with good ecclesiastical revenues, became vacant. Amaro wrote to his sister recounting his poverty in Feirão; she sent him, accompanied with advice as to economy, twelve moedas to go to Lisbon to put in a petition for a move. Amaro left immediately. The clean-swept, bracing air of the mountains had strengthened his blood; he returned robust, more erect, better disposed towards everybody, and with a good healthy colour in his brown skin.

When he arrived in Lisbon he went to 53 Rua dos Calafates, the house of his aunt: he found her looking much older, with her hair twisted up in an enormous bun tied with a red ribbon, and her face still smothered in powder. She had turned religious and it was with a holy joy that she opened her arms to embrace Amaro.

'Ah, how lovely you look! How splendid! What a difference! Oh, Jesus! how you have changed!'

She admired his cassock and his tonsure; and recounting her troubles to him with exclamations about the salvation of her soul and the rise in the cost of living, she led him up to the third storey, to a little room which looked out on to an interior patio.

'Here you will be as comfortable as an abbot in his cell,' she said. 'And it's so cheap! Ah, I'd like to take you for nothing, but—I've been so unhappy Joãzinho! Oh, excuse me, Amaro, I always have my Joãzinho in my head!'

The next day Amaro went to St Luiz to look up Father Liset. He had gone to France. He then thought of the youngest daughter of the Marqueza d'Alegros, Senhora Dona Joanna, who was married to the Conde of Ribamar, Councillor of State, a man with much influence, a faithful reformer since the year 1851 and twice minister of the Crown.

On the advice of his aunt, Amaro, immediately he had put in his petition, went to the house of the Condessa of Ribamar, Rua Buenos Ayres. There was a coupé waiting at the door.

At that moment, from a folding door covered with green baize, over a stone step at the end of the flagged patio, the senhora condessa appeared, dressed in gay colours.

'The senhora condessa doesn't remember me?' said Amaro, bowing and advancing with his hat in his hand. 'I'm Amaro.'

'Oh, Amaro,' she said, surprised when she heard his name. 'Oh, Holy Jesus, look at him now! He is a man! Who could think it!'

Amaro smiled.

'I could never have believed it!' she continued, gazing wonderingly at him. 'Are you in Lisbon now?'

Amaro recounted his appointment to Feirão and the poverty there.

'With the result, senhora, that I've come to beg a favour of you.'

She listened to him, leaning forward with both hands placed on her long-handled bright silk sunshade, and Amaro felt coming from her a perfume of powder and a freshness of cambric.

'Then don't worry,' she said, 'make your mind easy. My husband must speak of this. I myself will see to this for you. Listen, when can I see you? . . . Wait, tomorrow I go to Contra, Sunday, no . . . It's best to leave it till a fortnight today. A fortnight today I'm certain to be here.' And laughing with her large shining teeth: 'It seems only yesterday that you were translating Chateaubriand with my sister Luiza! How time flies!'

'And senhora your sister, is she well?' asked Amaro.

'She is well. She is on her estate at Santarem.' She gave him her hand and then jumped lightly and gracefully into her coupé, with a swing which revealed a profusion of white petticoats.

Amaro now had nothing to do but wait. In his room in the evenings with the window open to the heat of the night, stretching himself on the bed in his shirt sleeves and stockinged feet, he smoked cigarettes and ruminated on his future. Every minute his mind turned with renewed joy to the words of the condessa: '. . . Make your mind easy. My husband must speak of this.' And he already saw himself priest in a nice town, living in a house with an orchard, and a garden full of cabbages and fresh lettuces, tranquil and important, receiving dishes of dainty pastries from his rich parishioners.

At this time he was in a very peaceful state of mind. The excitements from which he had suffered on account of the repressions in the seminary, had now calmed down, as he had had relations with a big fat shepherdess in Feirão, whom he used to love to look at on Sundays as she hung from the bell rope, rolling from side to side and swinging her Saragossa tweed skirts, her face bursting with health. Now serene, he punctually paid to the sky the prayers which the ritual demanded and carried a body quiet and satisfied, with a strong determination to get the best out of life.

At the end of a fortnight he went to the condessa's house.

'She isn't in,' said a groom.

Rather worried, he returned some days later. The green baize folding doors were open: Amaro entered and walked very slowly, very bashfully up the large red carpet fixed with metal rods. The heat was intense; the proud aristocratic silence filled Amaro with terror; he stopped a moment with his umbrella suspended from his little finger, hesitating. He thought of turning back, when he heard from behind a green baize folding door a man's loud, deep laugh. He took out his handkerchief and removed the dust from his shoes, then, pulling down his cuffs and blushing furiously, he entered the room. It was a large salon upholstered in yellow quilted damask; a soft full light came in from the french windows which gave on to the veranda and through which one got a view of trees in the garden. In the middle of the room three men stood talking. Amaro advanced and muttered: 'I hope I'm not disturbing you.'

A tall man, with a greying moustache and gold-rimmed spectacles, a cigar hanging from the corner of his mouth and his hands in his pockets, turned round in surprise. It was the senhor conde.

'I'm Amaro ...'

'Ah,' said the conde, 'Senhor Father Amaro! I know well who you are! So pleased to see you. My wife has so often spoken of you. So pleased to see you.'

Turning to a short stout man, almost bald, who was wearing unusually short white trousers: 'Senhor, this is the person of whom I spoke to you.' Then turning to Amaro: 'This is the senhor minister.'

Amaro made a cringing bow.

'Senhor Father Amaro,' said the Conde of Ribamar, 'was brought up as a child in my mother-in-law's house. Born there, I believe.'

'The senhor conde is right,' said Amaro, remaining apart, his umbrella clenched in his hand.

'My mother-in-law, who was very religious, and every inch a lady—her like doesn't exist today!—made a priest of him. I believe there was even a legacy ... Anyway, here is the priest. From where do you come, Senhor Father Amaro?'

'Feirão, excellentissimo senhor.'

'Feirão?' repeated the minister, finding the name strange.

'In the mountains of Gralheira,' the other informed him in an aside. He was a thin man, squeezed into a blue frock coat, with very white skin, superb coal-black whiskers and a wonderful head of hair pasted down and shining with pomade, the parting extending in a perfect line to the nape of the neck.

'In fact,' resumed the conde, 'a horror! In the mountains, a poor district, with no distractions and a terrible climate.'

'I've already put in a petition, excellentissimo senhor,' Amaro timidly hazarded.

'Good, good!' affirmed the minister. 'It must be arranged,' he added, rubbing his cigar.

'It's not only just,' said the conde, 'but it's a necessity! The young and active men must be in the difficult parishes, in the towns. That appears obvious! But no: now take, for example, the town of Alcobaça, at the foot of my estate. They have put an old gouty priest there, an ancient rector of a college, in fact an imbecile! It's because of such things that people lose their faith.'

'It's true,' said the minister, 'but, on the other hand, appointments to good parishes must be the reward of good services. The stimulation is necessary.'

'Quite,' replied the conde, 'but services to religion, vocations, services to the Church, not services to the government.'

The man with the superb black whiskers made a sign of dissent.

'Don't you agree with me?' asked the conde.

'I very much respect your excellency's opinion,' replied the other, 'but if you'll allow me—yes, I must say that the town parishes are a great help to us in election crises. They certainly are a great help!'

'Yes, but——'

'Listen, your excellency,' said the other, anxious to give his opinion. 'Look, your excellency, at what happened in Thomar. Why did we lose? On account of the attitude of the priest. Nothing else.'

The conde rushed in to defend his former statements. 'But pardon me, it mustn't be so; religion and the clergy are not election agents.'

'Excuse me,' said the other, attempting to interrupt.

The conde stopped him with a firm gesture, and speaking slowly and gravely, in a tone full of authority and vast understanding: 'Religion can and must help to establish the government, operating as one might say as a curb . . .'

'Yes, yes!' murmured the minister slowly, spitting out bits of chewed tobacco from his cigar.

'But to descend to intrigues,' the conde continued slowly, 'to under-hand plotting—you'll pardon me, my dear friend, but that isn't the work of a Christian.'

'But I'm a Christian, senhor conde,' exclaimed the man with the superb whiskers. 'Yes, I'm a good one. But I'm also broadminded. I understand that in a representative government—yes, I say with more solid guarantees——'

'Listen!' interrupted the conde, 'do you know what it does? It discredits the clergy and discredits politics.'

'But are, or are not, majorities a sacred principle?' cried the man with the superb whiskers, accentuating the adjective.

'They are a *respected* principle,' said the conde.

'Much more than that! Much more than that, excellentissimo senhor!'

Father Amaro listened without stirring.

'My wife would surely like to see you,' said the conde, leading him to a curtain which he moved: 'Enter,' he said. 'Here is Father Amaro, Joanna.'

It was a drawing-room with walls covered in white satin wallpaper and furniture upholstered in fine bright coloured cashmere cloth. In the recesses of the windows, between the large folds of the milk-white damask curtains, tied almost at the floor with silk cords, light feathery flowerless shrubs in white vases lifted up their fine foliage. The fresh half-light gave to all the whiteness a delicate impression of clouds. On the back of the armchair a parrot was perched, firmly standing on one black foot, twisting and turning his green head to scratch himself. Amaro, very embarrassed, with lowered head sought protection round a corner of the sofa, from which point he could see the fair frizzed hair of the condessa which swelled on her forehead, and the shining gold rims of her eyeglasses. A fat boy was sitting in a low chair in front of her, resting his elbows on his open knees; he occupied himself in balancing, as a pendulum, his tortoiseshell pince-nez. The condessa had a little dog on her lap and with her hand, dry, fine, and full of blue veins, she stroked its hair, white as cotton.

'How are you, Senhor Father Amaro?' The dog growled. 'Quiet, Joia. Do you know that I've already spoken about your affair? Quiet Joia. The minister is here.'

'Yes, senhora,' said Amaro, still standing.

'Sit over here, Senhor Father Amaro.'

Amaro sat down on the edge of an armchair with his umbrella clutched tightly in his hand—and then noticed a tall woman standing near the piano, talking to a blond boy.

'What have you been doing these days, Senhor Amaro?' said the condessa. 'Tell me one thing: what became of your sister?'

'She is married in Coimbra.'

'Oh, she's married!' said the condessa, twisting her rings.

There was a silence. Amaro, with eyes cast down, put his hand to his lips in a wandering, embarrassed gesture.

'Then Senhor Father Liset is away?' he asked.

'He is in Nantes, a sister of his has just died there,' answered the condessa. 'He's always the same: always so pleasant, so sweet. He is such a virtuous soul!'

'I prefer Father Felix,' said the fat boy, stretching his legs.

'Don't say that, cousin! Jesus, what a shock for the heavens! How can you make such a statement. Father Liset commands such respect! He has a different way of saying things, he's so benevolent, so gracious. It's easily seen that he is a delicate soul.'

'Yes, I know,' said the fat boy, 'but Father Felix——'

'Now cousin, don't say that! I know that Father Felix is a person of much virtue, that's certain; but Father Liset is more devout.' And with a fine, delicate gesture she found the word she wanted: 'Finer, more distinguished. In fact he mixes with different people.' And smiling towards Amaro: 'Don't you think so?'

Amaro didn't know Father Felix, and couldn't remember Father Liset.

'Senhor Father Liset must be old now,' he ventured.

'I think so,' said the condessa. 'But very well preserved! And what vivacity, what enthusiasm in the cause of the faith. Yes, he is something out of the ordinary.' Turning towards the lady who was standing near the piano: 'Don't you think so, Theresa?'

'I'm coming,' said Theresa, absorbed in what she was doing.

Amaro fixed his attention on her. She seemed a queen, or a goddess, with her tall, strong figure, the magnificent line of her shoulders, her high firm bosom; her black hair, lightly waved, stood out against the whiteness of her clear cut face, which bore a resemblance to the dominant profile of Marie Antoinette.

'Were the people in your parish very devout, Senhor Amaro?' asked the condessa.

'Very, very devout people.'

'That is where one can still find real faith, in the villages,' the condessa considered in a pious tone. She then complained of being obliged to live in the town, in the slavery of luxury. She would love to live always at her estate at Carcavelos, and pray in the little old chapel, and talk to the good simple folk of the country.

Theresa walked slowly to the window and looked out into the street, and then went to sit in a *causeuse*, with an abandon which put into relief the magnificent sculpture of her body. She turned lazily towards the fat boy: 'It's time we were going, João.'

The condessa then said to her: 'Do you know that Senhor Father Amaro was brought up with me at Bemfica?'

Amaro turned red. He felt Theresa looking him over with her beautiful eyes, which were like black satin covered with water.

'Have you just come from the provinces?' she asked, yawning a little.

'Yes, senhora, I came from there a few days ago.'

'From a village?' she continued, slowly opening and closing her fan.

Amaro, watching the precious stones shining on her fingers, replied, affectionately clinging to the knob of his umbrella: 'From the mountains, senhora.'

'Just think of it!' broke in the condessa. 'It's a horror! Always snowing. They say the church has no roof and all the people are shepherds. It's a disgrace! I asked the minister to see if he could be moved. You ask him also.'

'What's this?' said Theresa.

The condessa then recounted that Amaro had petitioned for a better parish. She spoke of her mother and of the friendship she had for Amaro.

'She would die for him.' Then turning to Amaro: 'Do you remember the name she gave you?'

'I don't remember, senhora.'

'Friar Pasty Face. It was funny. How yellow Father Amaro was in those days. He was always stuck in the chapel.'

Theresa, going towards the condessa, said: 'Do you know who this senhor is like?'

The condessa looked attentively at Amaro and the fat boy gazed at him through his monocle.

'Doesn't he remind you of that pianist of last year?' continued Theresa. 'Just now I can't remember his name.'

'I know,' said the condessa, 'Jalette. Yes, he's a good bit like him. But the hair, no.'

'That's obvious, the other hadn't got a tonsure.'

Amaro became scarlet. Theresa got up, and dragging her gorgeous train after her, seated herself at the piano.

'Do you know anything about music?' she asked, turning to Amaro.

'One learnt it in the seminary, senhora.'

She ran her fingers for a minute over the bass notes and played a bar of *Rigoletto*, the desolate rhythm of which had the forlorn sadness of loves which are ending and of arms which unlock in last good-byes.

Amaro was lifted out of himself. He envisaged a vague, superior existence, of romance taking place over luxurious carpets, or in padded coupés, with airs from the operas, melancholy and in good taste, and love scenes of exquisite enjoyment. Buried in the elasticity of the *causeuse*, listening to the aristocratic lament of the music, he called to mind his aunt's dining-room and its smell of fried onions: he was like the vagrant who, tasting a rich sweet, fearfully prolongs his pleasure, thinking that he must soon return to hard bread and the dust of the road.

Meanwhile Theresa, brusquely changing the melody, sang an old English air from Haydn that fully describes the sadness of parting:

> *The village seems dead and asleep,*
> *When Lubin is away!*

'Bravo! Bravo!' cried the minister of justice, who had just appeared at the door, softly clapping his hands. 'Very good, very good! Delicious!'

'I have a favour to ask of you, Senhor Correia,' said Theresa immediately getting up from the piano.

The minister approached with gallant haste: 'What is it, my dear senhora? What is it?'

The conde and the man with the superb whiskers entered, still disputing.

'Joanna and I have a favour to ask of you,' said Theresa to the minister.

'I've already asked, I've already asked twice!' said the condessa butting in.

'But my dear senhoras,' said the minister seating himself comfortably and stretching out his legs to their full length, with a self-satisfied look on his face: 'Now what is it that you want? Is it something serious? My God! I promise, I solemnly promise to do what I can.'

'Good,' said Theresa, playfully smacking him on the arm with her fan. 'Then which is the best parish vacancy?'

'Ah!' said the minister, beginning to understand, and looking at Amaro who sat with head hanging and blushing furiously.

The man with the superb whiskers, who was standing playing circumspectly with the trinkets of his watch chain, came forward full of information.

'The best vacancy, senhora, is Leiria, capital of a district and seat of a bishopric.'

'Leiria,' said Theresa. 'I know it, aren't there some ruins there?'

'A castle, senhora, originally built by Dom Diniz.'

'Leiria is excellent!'

'But pardon me, pardon me!' said the minister. 'Leiria, seat of a bishopric, a town—Senhor Father Amaro is a young priest.'

'Listen to that, and Senhor Correia himself is not young?' exclaimed Theresa.

The minister laughed and bowed.

'Say something, you,' said the condessa to her husband, who was affectionately tickling the parrot's head.

'It seems to me useless, poor Correia is already vanquished. Cousin Theresa called him a young man!'

'But pardon me,' protested the minister. 'It doesn't seem to me to be exceptionally flattering; after all, I'm not so very old.'

'Oh, you shameless fellow!' cried the conde. 'Don't you remember how we were already conspiring together in 1820!'

'It was my father, you calumniator, it was my father.'

All laughed.

'Then it's settled, Senhor Correia,' said Theresa, 'Father Amaro goes to Leiria!'

'Good, good, I give in,' said the minister with a gesture of resignation. 'But it's a tyranny!'

'Thank you,' said Theresa giving him her hand.

'But my dear senhora, I find you in a strange mood today,' said the minister, fixing his eyes on her.

'I feel happy today,' she answered, dreamily looking at the floor for a minute, and giving little pats to her silk dress. She then got up, and abruptly seating herself at the piano, again played the sweet English air:

> *The village seems dead and asleep*
> *When Lubin is away . . .*

Meanwhile the conde had approached Amaro, who stood up.

'The business is settled,' he said. 'Senhor Correia will arrange all with the bishop. In a week from now you will be nominated. You can go home with your mind at ease.'

Amaro bowed, and servilely advanced to thank the minister who was near the piano: 'Senhor minister, I am very grateful to you.'

'It's the senhora condessa you must thank. It's the senhora condessa,' said the minister smiling.

Amaro, bowing low, approached the condessa and said: 'I thank you, senhora condessa.'

'Thank Theresa! I think she wants to gain some indulgences.'

'Senhora——' he said as he went forward towards Theresa.

'Remember me in your prayers, Senhor Father Amaro,' she said. And she continued, with her dolorous voice, telling the piano of the sadness of the village at the absence of Lubin.

A week later Amaro knew of his appointment. He often called to mind that morning in the house of the Conde of Ribamar—the minister in his very short trousers, buried in an armchair, promising him his appointment; the calm clear light coming in from the garden; the tall blond boy. That sad air from *Rigoletto* was continually passing through his head and always pursuing him was the whiteness of Theresa's arms. His temples beat with the idea that one day he could confess that divine woman and feel her black silk dress rub against his old lustre cassock in the intimacy of the dark confessional.

One day at dawn, after many embraces from his aunt, he left for Santa Apolonia, with a porter carrying his tin trunk. The morning broke. The town was still, the street lanterns dying out. Now and then a dust cart rolled past, shaking the stones; the streets seemed interminable; here and there a sharp voice called out the daily paper and the employees of the theatre ran with their pots of paste, sticking up posters at the corners.

When he arrived at Santa Apolonia the splendour of the sun had turned the sky behind the mountains of Outra-Banda to orange; the river extended motionless, striped with currents the colour of lustreless steel; and already some *faluas* with their white sails were slowly passing by.

Chapter IV

IN TOWN next day all were talking of the arrival of the new paroco, and the news had already gone round that he had brought a tin trunk, that he was tall and thin, and that he had addressed Canon Dias as Master.

Senhora Joanneira's friends—or at least her most intimate friends, Dona Maria of the Assumption and the Gansosos—called at her house first thing in the morning, to find out if all these statements were correct. It was nine o'clock; Amaro had just gone out with the canon. Senhora Joanneira, radiant and important, with her sleeves tucked up, as she had been busy with her morning's housework, greeted them from the top of the stairs, and immediately, with much excitement, she gave them an account of the arrival of the new paroco, his nice manners, and all he had said . . .

'But come with me, I'd like to show you his things.'

She took them to see the priest's room, his tin trunk, a shelf that she had had fixed up for his books.

'It's very nice, it's all very nice,' said the old ladies, walking slowly and respectfully round the room, as if they were in a church.

'What a rich cloak!' observed Dona Joaquina, feeling the cloth of the long bands which hung down from the coat-hanger. 'It is surely worth a couple of moedas!'

'And his lovely white linen!' said Senhora Joanneira lifting up the lid of the trunk.

The group of old ladies leaned in admiration over it.

'What consoles me is that he is a young man,' said Dona Maria of the Assumption sanctimoniously.

'Me also,' said Dona Joaquina Gansoso authoritatively. 'For one to go to confession and see the snuff dropping from the priest's nose all the time as with Raposo, heavens! It was enough to disturb one's devotions! And that brute of a José Migueis! No, may God grant that I die amongst young people!'

Senhora Joanneira continued showing them the other wonderful possessions of the paroco—a crucifix which was still wrapped up in an old newspaper, a photograph album, where the first photograph was one of the Pope blessing the Christian world. They all went into raptures: 'We've never seen anything nicer,' they said, 'we've never seen anything nicer!'

When leaving they kissed Senhora Joanneira several times, while congratulating her on having secured the paroco as a lodger; she was now almost an ecclesiastical authority.

'Can you people come tonight?' she called from the top of the stairs.

'Yes, certainly!' shouted back Dona Maria of the Assumption, already at the street door, tucking up her cloak. 'Yes, certainly! Then we can observe him at our ease!'

Libaninho, the most active religious fanatic in Leiria, appeared about midday; as he ran up the stairs he called out in his squeaking voice: 'Oh, Senhora Joanneira!'

'Come on up, Libaninho, come on up!' said Senhora Joanneira, who was sitting at the window sewing.

'So the paroco has arrived, has he?' asked Libaninho standing at the door of the dining-room, showing his fat, lemon-coloured face and his shining bald head; he waddled towards Senhora Joanneira with little mincing steps. 'Then what is he like, what is he like? Is he a nice man?'

Senhora Joanneira again began the glorification of Amaro: his youth, his air of piety, his lovely white teeth . . .

'Praise be to God! Praise be to God!' said Libaninho, slobbering with tender-hearted devotion. 'But I can't wait, I'm due at the office. Good-bye, good-bye, child!' And patting Senhora Joanneira on the shoulder with his podgy hand: 'You grow a little fatter every day! Listen, yesterday I said the Hail Mary which you begged me to say for you, you bothersome woman!'

The servant had entered.

'Good-bye Ruça! You are so thin: try praying to Our Lady, Mother of Men.' And spotting Amelia through the half open door of her room: 'Ah, but you are a lovely flower, Amelia. In the grace of your beauty I know one who could gain a place in the heavens!'

And hurrying, moving his buttocks from side to side, and giving out sharp little 'hems', he rapidly descended the stairs yelping: 'Good-bye, good-bye, little ones!'

'Oh, Libaninho, you'll come tonight?'

'Ah, but I can't, child, I can't,' he exclaimed whiningly. 'Don't forget that tomorrow is the feast of St Barbara and that she has the right to six Our Fathers.'

Amaro had gone with Canon Dias to visit the precentor, presenting him with a letter of recommendation from the Conde of Ribamar.

'I knew the Conde of Ribamar very well,' said the precentor. 'In '46 in Oporto. We are old friends. I was then a priest in Santo Ildefonso. Ah, how long ago was that!'

Reclining on the old damask armchair, he recalled with pleasure incidents of those times: he told tales of the Junta, he spoke with appreciation of its members, imitating their ways of speaking (this was a speciality of his excellency), their mannerisms, their petty arguments —above all Manoel Passos whom he described passing in the New Square, in his long dark coat and his wide-brimmed hat, saying: 'Cheer up, patriots! Xavier will keep his seat!' The members of the church council laughed heartily. There was great cordiality amongst them. Amaro left feeling very flattered.

Afterwards he dined with Canon Dias, then both went for a walk along the Marrazes Road. A soft thin light spread over the whole countryside; on the hills in the blue of the sky was an aspect of repose, of caressing tranquillity; whitish fumes came from the houses and one heard the melancholy tingle of the bells as the cows were led home. Amaro stopped near the bridge, and said as he looked all round at the peaceful landscape: 'Well, I think I'm going to have a very good life here.'

'You're going to have a magnificent life here,' affirmed the canon taking a pinch of snuff.

It was eight o'clock when they entered Senhora Joanneira's house.

The old friends were already in the dining-room. Amelia was sitting at the lamp sewing.

Dona Maria of the Assumption was dressed, as on Sundays, in black silk: her golden wig, tinged with red, was covered with black lace-work; her bony hands, encased in mittens and shining with rings, solemnly reclined in her lap, and from the brooch fastening her collar, to her waist, hung a heavy gold chain laden with little filigree rings. She sat up very straight and ceremoniously, with her head a little to one side and her gold-rimmed spectacles fixed on her hooked nose; she had a large hairy mole on her chin; when she spoke of religious subjects or miracles she stuck her chest forward and smiled a silent smile which revealed her enormous teeth covered with green scum and dug into the gums as if with a wedge. She was a widow and rich and suffered from chronic catarrh.

'Here is the new paroco, Dona Maria,' said Senhora Joanneira.

She got up, all flustered, and made a curtsy with a wag of her hips.

'There are the Senhoras Gansosos, of whom you must have heard,' said Senhora Joanneira to the paroco.

Amaro timidly saluted them. They were two sisters. They had the name of having money, but were in the habit of taking lodgers. The elder one, Dona Joaquina, was a dry individual with an enormous broad forehead, two lively little eyes, a turned-up nose and very tight lips. Wrapped neatly in her shawl, with her arms crossed, she kept up a continual flow of conversation, in a sharp dominating voice; she was very self-opinionated. She spoke badly of men and gave freely to the Church.

Her sister, Dona Anna, was extremely deaf and never spoke; with her fingers crossed over her lap and her eyes cast down she sat tranquilly twirling her thumbs. A strong woman, perpetually dressed in a black dress with yellow stripes and an ermine tippet round her neck, she slept all the evening, only making her presence felt by emitting an occasional sharp sigh. It was said that she had a fatal passion for the postmaster. All pitied her and admired her ability in making paper frills for cakes.

Dona Josepha, the canon's sister, was also there. She was nicknamed the Peeled Chestnut. She was a little withered creature, crookedly formed, with shrivelled, cider-coloured skin and a hissing voice; she lived in a state of perpetual irritation, her small eyes always alight, her nervous system eternally contracted, her whole attitude full of spleen. She was dreaded by all. The malignant Dr Godinho called her the Central Station of the intrigues of Leiria.

'Then you walked far, senhor paroco?' she asked vehemently.

'We went almost to the end of the Marrazes Road,' said the canon, seating himself down heavily behind Senhora Joanneira.

'Don't you think it's pretty, senhor paroco?' asked Senhora Dona Joaquina Gansoso.

'Very pretty.'

They then spoke of the beautiful walks of Leiria and of the many lovely views. Senhora Dona Josepha liked to walk along by the river best of all; she had heard it said that even in Lisbon there was nothing to equal it. Dona Joaquina Gansoso preferred to walk up the hill to the Church of the Incarnation.

'One can pass the time well there.'

Amelia said smiling: 'As for me, I like that little bit at the foot of the bridge, below the weeping willows.' And cutting the cotton with her teeth: 'It's so melancholy!'

Amaro then looked at her for the first time. She had on a tight-fitting blue dress, which showed up her beautifully formed bosom to advantage; her full white neck was visible over a turned-down collar; the enamel of her teeth shone between her fresh red lips, and it seemed to the priest that the little soft downy hairs gave the corners of her mouth a sweet, subtle shade.

There was a short silence. Canon Dias, his lip hanging, was already closing his eyes.

'What happened to Senhor Father Brito?' asked Dona Joaquina Gansoso.

41

'Perhaps he has a migraine, the poor holy man,' Senhora Dona Maria of the Assumption piously suggested.

A young fellow who was near the sideboard then said: 'I saw him today riding on horseback towards the Barrosa Road.'

'Sir!' said the canon's sister, Dona Josepha Dias, with acidity: 'It's a miracle that you noticed him!'

'Why, senhora?' said he, getting up and approaching the group of old ladies.

He was tall and dressed all in black: from his well-formed face, with its fair skin, his small jet-black moustache stood out, falling down at the corners of his mouth. He was continually nibbling it.

'How can you ask!' exclaimed Dona Josepha. 'You, who don't even lift your hat when you pass a priest!'

'Me!' he exclaimed.

'They say that of him,' she affirmed in a cutting voice, adding with a malicious laugh: 'Indeed, senhor paroco, you could very well put Senhor João Eduardo on the right road!'

'But it seems to me that I am not on the wrong road,' said he laughing, with his hands in his pockets. Each moment his eyes turned towards Amelia.

'That's funny!' exclaimed Dona Joaquina. 'Now, because of what this senhor said in front of me today about the saint of Arregassa, he will never get to heaven!'

'Now listen to that!' shouted the canon's sister, turning brusquely towards João Eduardo. 'Now what has he to say about the saint? Perhaps he thinks she is an impostor?'

'God preserve us!' said Dona Maria of the Assumption clasping her hands, and fixing a look full of pious terror on João Eduardo. 'Do you mean to say he said that? My God!'

'No, Senhor João Eduardo,' the canon gravely affirmed, waking up and folding his red handkerchief. 'No, he is incapable of saying such a thing.'

Amaro then asked: 'Who is this saint of Arregassa?'

'Heavens! Then you've never heard her spoken of, senhor paroco,' exclaimed Dona Maria of the Assumption, surprised.

'You surely must have heard of her,' affirmed Dona Josepha decisively. 'Why, they say that the Lisbon papers come here full of the subject!'

'It is, as a matter of fact, a very extraordinary thing,' pondered the canon in a profound tone.

Senhora Joanneira stopped knitting and taking off her spectacles said: 'Indeed, senhor paroco, you can't imagine the wonder of it, it is the miracle of miracles.'

'Yes, it is! Yes, it is!' they all chimed in.

The old ladies drew closer together in a silent pious understanding.

'But then?' said Amaro full of curiosity.

'Listen, senhor paroco,' began Dona Joaquina, straightening her shawl and speaking with great solemnity: 'The saint is a woman who lives in a district near here and who had been twenty years in bed——'

'Twenty-five,' remonstrated Dona Maria of the Assumption in a whisper, tapping her on the arm with her fan.

'Twenty-five? But listen, I heard the senhor cantor say twenty.'

'Twenty-five, twenty-five,' affirmed Senhora Joanneira, and the canon supported her, gravely nodding his head.

'She is paralysed all over, senhor paroco,' broke in the canon's sister, bursting to give information. 'Her body is devoid of flesh, only her soul remains. Her arms are like this!' she added holding up her little finger. 'In order to hear what she is saying it is necessary to put one's ear to her mouth!'

'Then if she lives she is sustained not by earthly power but by the grace of God!' said Dona Maria of the Assumption mournfully. 'It's pitiful! One can't get her out of one's mind . . .'

A troubled silence now fell among the old ladies.

João Eduardo, who was standing at the back of the company with his hands in his pockets, chewing the ends of his moustache, laughed and said:

'Listen, senhor paroco, the truth is—the doctors will tell you—it is a nervous disorder.'

This irreverence shocked the devout old ladies; Dona Maria of the Assumption crossed herself as a precaution.

'For the love of God!' bawled Dona Josepha, 'the senhor can say this to whoever he likes, but not in front of me! It is an affront!'

'It is bad enough for God in his anger to strike him dead with a flash of lightning,' gasped Dona Maria of the Assumption, very terrified.

'Now, I also would like to state,' said Dona Josepha, 'that he is a man without religion and lacking in respect for all sacred things.' And turning towards Amelia she added bitingly: 'If I had a daughter I wouldn't give her to him!'

Amelia reddened; João Eduardo also coloured, and then bowing, he said sarcastically: 'I'm just telling you what the doctors say. And as for your other remark, I might inform you that I have no desire to ask the hand in marriage of any of your family. Nor have I any wish to marry you, Dona Josepha!'

The canon gave a deep chuckle.

'Out of my sight! Heavens!' she shouted furiously.

'But what has the saint done?' Father Amaro asked to pacify her.

'Everything, senhor paroco,' said Dona Joaquina. 'She is bed-ridden, she knows the right prayers for all occasions, the person for whom she pleads gains God's grace and all who have faith in her are relieved of all their sufferings; and when she takes communion she begins to raise herself up and remains with her whole body in the air and her eyes gazing fixedly towards the heavens, till the onlookers are in terror.'

At this moment a voice at the door of the parlour called out: 'Long live the company! I see there is a brilliant gathering this evening!'

The intruder was an extremely tall fellow, with a yellow face and sunken cheeks, a matted mop of frizzed hair, and a Don Quixote moustache; when he laughed his mouth was like a dark cave, as nearly all his front teeth were missing; his sunken eyes, surrounded with deep furrows, wandered upwards with a look of ridiculous sentimentality. He held a guitar in his hand.

'Well, and how are things going with you these days?' they asked him.

'Badly,' he replied mournfully, as he took a seat. 'The pains in my chest are still there and I'm coughing continually.'

'Then the cod-liver oil is doing you no good?'

'What good is cod-liver oil?' he answered hopelessly.

'A voyage to Madeira, that would be just the thing for you!' said Dona Joaquina decisively.

He laughed with unexpected joviality:

'A voyage to Madeira! That's a good one! Dona Joaquina has grand ideas! A poor manuscript copier with eighteen vintens a day and a wife and four children! A voyage to Madeira!'

'And how is Joannita?'

'Poor soul, she is all right! She is healthy, thanks be to God! Fat, and always with plenty of appetite. It's the children, the two eldest ones are always ill, and now, to add to our troubles, the servant is ill in bed! It's the devil! But one must have patience,' he concluded, sadly shrugging his shoulders.

Then turning towards Senhora Joanneira and giving her a pat on the knee: 'And how goes it with our Mother Abbess?'

There was a general laugh: and Dona Joaquina informed the senhor paroco that that young man, Arthur Couceiro, was the funniest fellow and had a beautiful voice. In fact for singing popular songs there was no one in the town to beat him.

Ruça had entered with the tea. Senhora Joanneira, holding aloft the teapot, said as she poured out the steaming drink: 'Come on, come on, children; this is the best tea money can buy. It came from Sousa's stores . . .'

Arthur passed round the sugar with the time-worn joke:

'Sweets to the sweet.'

The old ladies sucked up the tea from their saucers, and carefully picked out the pieces of toast, and as they ate they munched loudly; in order to protect their clothes from the droppings from the saucers and the grease of the butter, they cautiously spread their handkerchiefs over their laps.

'Now won't you take a little tart, senhor paroco?' said Amelia, holding the plate in front of him. 'They are made by the pensioners in the Rua Incarnation and are lovely and fresh.'

'Thank you.'

'Come now, take this one, it's an angel cake straight from heaven.'

'Ah, yes! it is from heaven,' said he, smiling all over his face. And as he took the cake with the tips of his fingers he looked directly at her.

Senhor Arthur was in the habit of singing after tea. Over the piano was a candle to light up the piece of music, and Amelia, immediately Ruça had cleared the table, settled herself down at the piano and ran her fingers over the yellow keys.

'Now what would you people like today?' asked Arthur.

There was a volley of requests: *The Warrior, The Nuptials in the Tomb, The Miscreant, Oh Never More* . . .

The canon, from his corner, heavily named his song: 'Come on, Couceiro, with *Uncle Cosme, My Rascal.*'

The women reproved him: 'Heavens! Why that? Senhor canon! How can you suggest such a song?'

And Senhora Dona Joaquina Gansoso called out emphatically: 'None of those. Give us something sentimental, in order to show our senhor paroco what Arthur can do.'

'Yes, yes!' they cried in chorus, 'let it be something sentimental. Yes, Arthur, something sentimental.'

Arthur cleared his throat, then spat, and suddenly putting on a doleful face, he mournfully lifted up his voice and sang:

Good-bye, my angel! I leave without you . . .

It was a song of the romantic times of '51, called *The Good-bye!* It told of the last farewell of two lovers in a wood, on a pale autumn afternoon. Afterwards, the hero, who had inspired this fatal love, now abandoned, wandered lonely and distracted to the seashore, where there was a forgotten sepulchre, in a distant valley, and pure white virgins came to cry with him in the silvery light of the moon.

'How lovely, how lovely!' they all murmured.

Arthur sang to draw tears, with a vacant wandering look; but in the

45

intervals, during the accompaniment, he smiled all round—and in his dark mouth one saw the stumps of his decayed teeth. Father Amaro, as he sat under the window smoking, contemplated Amelia, who was absorbed in that morbid sentimental melody. Against the light her fine profile had a luminous line; the curve of her bosom stood out harmoniously; and he followed the motion of her eyelids, with their long eyelashes, going up and down with a soft movement as they met the music-board. João Eduardo stood at her side, turning over the leaves.

And Arthur, with one hand on his chest and the other in the air, in a movement at once desolate and vehement, poured out the last verse:

> *In the end, I will finish with my unhappy life*
> *And the rest in the darkness of the tomb!*

'Bravo! Bravo!' they exclaimed in chorus.

The canon commented in a low voice to Amaro: 'Ah, as a singer of sentimental songs there is no one to beat him.' Giving a loud yawn he added: 'My dear son, the sleeve-fish that I ate today are continually growling inside my stomach.'

The time for a game of lotto had now arrived. They all picked out the cards they were in the habit of using and Dona Josepha, her eyes alight with greed, vigorously shook up the great sack of numbers.

'There is a place here for you, senhor paroco,' said Amelia.

It was by her side. He hesitated, but they had moved up to make room for him, so he went to sit down, blushing a little and timidly twisting his collar.

For a minute all were silent, till the canon, in his sleepy voice, began to call out the numbers. Dona Anna Gansoso peacefully slept in her corner, lightly snoring.

With the shade from the lamp the heads were in a half-shadow; and the crude light, falling on the dark shawl which covered the table, showed up the cards greasy from constant use, and the dry withered hands of the old ladies in their different clawlike attitudes, mixing up the glass counters. Over the open piano the candle burnt with a straight high flame.

The canon called out, making the traditional jokes: 'One, Head of a pig!—Three, Funny Face!'

'I require the twenty-one,' said a voice.

'The three,' murmured another with delight.

The canon's sister called out voraciously:

'Shuffle up those numbers, brother Placido! Go on!'

'And bring me the forty-seven, which I'm still hunting,' said Arthur Couceiro, as he sat with his head between his clenched fists.

At last the canon made the winning number. And Amelia looking round the room said:

'Why isn't Senhor João Eduardo playing? Where is he?'

João Eduardo, who was in the recess of the window, came out from behind the curtain.

'Take this card and go on and play.'

'And as you are already standing you can take the entries and be the receiver,' said Senhora Joanneira.

João Eduardo went round with the china saucer. In the end, when he counted, he was ten reis short.

'I've put my money in, I've put my money in!' all exclaimed, very excited.

'It was the canon's sister who couldn't spare a copper from her vast pile,' said João Eduardo, bowing. 'It appears to me that Dona Josepha hasn't entered.'

'Me!' she yelled, furious. 'What a thing to say! I was the first to enter! God forbid! I distinctly remember putting in two pieces of five reis each! What kind of man is this?'

'All right then. It must have been I who forgot. There you are; I'm putting it in,' said João Eduardo, as he muttered between his teeth: 'A religious woman and a thief!'

The canon's sister whispered to Dona Maria of the Assumption: 'I'd like to see if he'll escape punishment, the blackguard. He is wanting in the fear of God!'

'The only one who isn't enjoying himself is the senhor paroco,' someone observed.

Amaro smiled. He was tired and inattentive, and sometimes forgot to mark; Amelia, touching his elbow, said: 'How is it you are not marking, senhor paroco?'

He had already bet the two threes; he won; afterwards they both required the thirty-six to make the winning number.

It was noticed all round.

'Come on, let's see if the two of them can make the winning number together,' babbled Dona Maria of the Assumption, including them both in the same pettish look.

But the thirty-six didn't appear; there were other pictures on the other people's cards; Amelia feared that Dona Joaquina was going out, as she kept wriggling in her chair and asking for the forty-eight. Amaro, interested in spite of himself, laughed.

The canon drew the numbers with malicious slowness.

'Come on! Come on! hurry up there, senhor canon,' they called out to him.

Amelia, with shining eyes, leaned forward and murmured:

'I'd give anything for the thirty-six.'

'Good! Here you have it. Thirty-six,' said the canon.

'We're out!' Amelia shouted, very flushed; and triumphantly taking Amaro's card and her own she proudly held them up for confirmation.

'May God bless them,' said the canon jovially, as he turned the saucer full of ten reis coins upside down in front of them.

'It looks like a miracle!' considered Dona Maria of the Assumption, piously.

But it had struck eleven and after the last game the old people began to wrap themselves up. Amelia sat at the piano, lightly fingering out a polka. João Eduardo moved up to her and lowering his voice said:

'Congratulations on getting the winning number with the senhor paroco. How exciting!' And as she was going to reply, he called out a dry 'Good-night!' and furiously wrapping his cloak around him he left.

Ruça held the lamp to light up the stairs. The old ladies, muffled up in their warm clothes, went off yelping, 'Good-night!' Senhor Arthur hummed *The Infidel*, strumming the guitar.

Amaro went to his room and began to read his breviary, but he found it impossible to fix his mind on his prayers; visions of the faces of the old women, of Arthur's rotten teeth, above all of Amelia's profile, kept crossing his mind. Sitting on the edge of the bed, with his breviary opened in front of him and gazing at the light, he pictured her hair, her little brown fingers all pricked with the needle, the sweet soft down round her mouth.

His head felt heavy from the monotony of the game and from the dinner at the canon's. The sleeve-fish and the good port had left him with a terrible thirst. He wanted a drink but could find no water in the room. He then remembered that in the dining-room was an earthenware pot with pure fresh water from the Morenal spring. Putting on his carpet slippers, and taking the candlestick in his hand, he slowly ascended the stairs. There was a light in the parlour, the door curtain was drawn: he lifted it up and recoiled with an 'Ah!' He had caught a glimpse of Amelia standing in her white petticoat, undoing her bust bodice: she was near the lamp and the sleeveless low cut garment gave a vision of her white arms and her delicious breasts. She gave a little cry, and ran to her room.

Amaro stood transfixed, sweating to the roots of his hair. They might suspect him of being indecent: certainly indignant words were going to be flung at him from behind the curtain, which was still vibrating agitatedly!

But Amelia's voice, serene and calm, enquired from the other side: 'Do you want something, senhor paroco?'

'I came to look for water . . .' he muttered.

'Oh, that Ruça, she is so careless! Excuse us, senhor paroco, excuse us. Listen! there is the pot at the side of the table. Can you find it?'

'I see it! I see it!'

He slowly descended the stairs with the brimming glass—his hand trembling and the water dripping over his fingers.

He got into bed without saying his prayers. Far into the night Amelia heard in the room below nervous steps treading the floor: it was Amaro in carpet slippers and with his cloak thrown over his shoulders, excitedly walking up and down the room, smoking.

She, upstairs, didn't sleep either. On top of the chest of drawers, inside a basin, the nightlight burned itself out, permeating the room with a disagreeable smell of olive-oil fumes; the whiteness of fallen petticoats stood out on the floor; the restless eyes of the cat, made visible by the darkness of the room, shone with a green phosphorescent clearness.

In the neighbouring house a baby cried continuously. Amelia sensed the mother rocking the cradle, while she softly sang:

Sleep, my little one, sleep,
Your mother is gone to the well . . .

It was the poor ironing girl, Catharina, whom Lieutenant Sousa had left with a baby in the cradle, and expecting another—to marry in Extremoz! How pretty she had been, what lovely golden hair she had had—and now so worn, so used up!

Sleep, my little one, sleep,
Your mother is gone to the well . . .

How well she knew that song! When she was seven her mother, in the long winter nights, used to sing it to her little brother who died. She remembered it all so clearly. They then lived in another house, on the Lisbon Road; outside the window of her room was a lemon tree and on its bright branches her mother had hung little Joãozinho's napkins to dry in the sun. She had never known her father. He was a military man and had died young; her mother still sighed when she spoke of his beautiful figure when in his cavalry uniform.

Amelia was brought up amongst priests. Some she disliked: especially Father Valente, so fleshy, so sweaty, with his fat puffy hands, and their little nails! He liked to take her between his knees, and slowly twist her ear, and she felt his breath saturated with the smell of onions and cigarettes. Her little friend was Canon Cruz, thin, with a whole head of white hair, always spruce, his collar always clean, the buckles of his shoes brightly shining; he always entered slowly and with his hand on his chest greeted her mother in a soft lisping voice. She already knew her catechism and her doctrine; and by her teacher, and in the house, for the least trifle, she was threatened with the punishments of the heavens; so much so that God appeared to her as a Being who only knew how to deal out suffering and death, whom it was necessary to appease with prayers and fasting, reciting novenas and fawning on the priests. Because of this, if when she went to bed she forgot a Hail Mary, she did penance the next day, as she feared that God would send her malaria or cause her to fall down the stairs.

When Amelia was fifteen, she began to think of becoming a nun: she became still more devout, and now began to appear an exaggerated manifestation of the tendencies which, since childhood, the priests who visited her mother's house had slowly created in her impressionable mind. She read her prayer-books all day. She filled the walls of her room with coloured prints of the saints. She spent long hours in the church, piling up Hail Marys to Our Lady of the Incarnation. She attended Mass every day and went to communion every week—and her mother's friends described her as a model who would give faith to the unbeliever.

It was just then that Canon Dias and his sister, Dona Josepha, began to frequent Senhora Joanneira's house. In a short time the canon became a friend of the family. After lunch he was certain to turn up with his little dog.

'He is very friendly and so good to me,' Senhora Joanneira would say.

The canon's sister had just at this time organized, with the help of Senhora Joanneira, the Association of the Servants of Our Lady of Pity. Dona Maria of the Assumption and the Gansosos were enrolled as members, and Senhora Joanneira's house now became an ecclesiastical centre. This was the best time of Senhora Joanneira's life: the Cathedral, as Carlos the apothecary used to say in his drawling voice, was now in the Rua da Misericordia. Besides the canons, the precentor came every Friday. There were statues of the saints in the dining-room and the kitchen. To make sure of their piety, the servants, before being accepted, were examined in Christian doctrine. There, for a long time, reputations were made and lost; if they said of a man that he was wanting in fear of God it was one's duty to discredit him. The nominations of bell-ringers, grave-diggers and sacristans were arranged there by subtle intrigues and pious words. They adopted a dark purple habit, the whole house reeked of wax-candles and incense, and Senhora Joanneira was given the monopoly of the sale of the sacred wafers.

Amelia was twenty when she first became interested in João Eduardo, on the day of the Corpus Christi procession, in the house of the notary, Nunes Ferral, where he was a clerk. Amelia, her mother and Dona Josepha had gone to see the procession from the notary's beautiful balcony, all decorated with yellow damask bed-covers. João Eduardo was there, modest, serious, all dressed in black. Amelia had known him for some time; but that afternoon, noticing the whiteness of his skin, and the solemn way in which he knelt when the procession passed, she thought he seemed a very nice boy.

But, as she thought, it was just a passing flame—because later, when she knew João Eduardo better, when she spoke freely with him, she realized, as she herself put it, that she had no leaning towards the boy. She appreciated him, she thought he was a good kind fellow; he would make a good husband: but withal, she felt her heart unruffled.

The notary's clerk now began to visit the Rua da Misericordia almost every night. Senhora Joanneira looked on him with favour because of his nice manners and upright character. But Amelia continued to feel cold towards him; she watched for him at the window in the morning as he passed on the way to his office, and at night she made sweet eyes at him, but only to please him and to fill her otherwise empty life with an interesting little love affair.

One day João Eduardo spoke to her mother about marriage.

'It's just as Amelia wants,' she said; 'if she is satisfied I will be.'

When Amelia was consulted, she replied ambiguously:

'Later, I can't talk about it now. We'll see.'

In the end, he tacitly agreed to wait till he could get a position as clerk to the civil governor, a job which Dr Godinho had openly promised him—the daring Dr Godinho.

Thus lived Amelia till the arrival of Amaro: and during the night these memories came to her in fragments, like pieces of cloud broken and swept along by the wind. She didn't get to sleep till late and woke when the sun was already high in the sky. Stretching herself she heard Ruça, in the parlour, saying:

'The senhor paroco is going out with the senhor canon; they are going to the Cathedral!'

Amelia jumped from her bed and running to the window in her shift, lifted up the edge of the muslin curtain and looked out. The morning blazed forth: Father Amaro was in the middle of the road talking to the canon, blowing his nose with his white handkerchief and looking very graceful in his fine cloth cassock.

Chapter V

THUS, FROM the very beginning, softly wrapped in comforts, Amaro felt happy. Senhora Joanneira, always very maternal, took the greatest care of his white linen, prepared little dainties for him, and kept the senhor paroco's room so spick and span that she herself described it as shining like a mirror! The relationship between him and Amelia was one of teasing familiarity; he treated her as one treats one's pretty cousin: as Senhora Dona Maria of the Assumption said delightedly, 'they suit one another down to the ground'. Thus the days passed serenely for Amaro, with good food, a soft comfortable bed, and the soothing company of women. The season was so mild that even the limes in the garden of the Bishop's Palace were in full bloom. 'Almost a miracle!' the senhor precentor said, as every morning in his dressing-room he contemplated them from the window of his room, while he quoted verses from the *Eclogue*. And after his sad dreary life in his aunt's home in Estrela, the lack of comfort of the seminary, and the bitter winter in Gralheira, that time in Leiria for Amaro was like a house dry and sheltered—where the bright fire crackles and sparkles and the pleasant smell of the steaming soup rises to greet one's nostrils after a night's labour in the mountains under the thunder and rain.

Early in the morning he went to say Mass at the Cathedral, well wrapped in his long hooded cloak, his hands covered in cashmere gloves, and woollen socks inside his high-topped, light brown boots. The mornings were cold: and at that hour only a few devout parishioners, with black hoods over their heads, were scattered here and there at the foot of the shining white altar, praying.

He would immediately enter the sacristy and hurriedly put on his vestments, stamping his feet on the flagged floor, while the sacristan slowly recounted the latest news.

Then, with the chalice in his hand, and eyes cast down, he passed into the church; and rapidly bending his knee in front of the Blessed Sacrament, he slowly ascended the altar where the light from the wax candles was gradually fading into a pale glimmer in the brighter light of the morning; joining his hands and bowing he murmured:

'*Introibo ad altare Dei.*'

'*Ad Deum qui laetificat juventutem meam*', mumbled the sacristan, in his badly pronounced Latin.

Now Amaro didn't celebrate Mass moved by a tender devotion, as he had done in his first days as a priest. 'I'm used to it now,' he would say. And, as he hadn't breakfasted, the fresh, raw morning air increased his appetite, so that even before he began he felt hungry, and thoughtlessly, in a toneless voice, he gabbled the sacred readings from the Epistles and the Gospels. Behind him the sacristan, with his arms crossed, slowly passed his hand along his thick well-trimmed beard, as he looked behind him at Casimira Franca, wife of the Cathedral carpenter, a very devout person, on whom he had had his eye since Eastertime. Large sunbeams entered from the side windows. A lingering aroma of faded daffodils sweetened the air.

Amaro, after hurrying through the Offertory, cleaned out the chalice with the purificator; the sacristan, a little doubled up from weak kidneys, went to get the wine cruets, and bowing presented them; and Amaro got a whiff of the rank oil with which his hair shone. In that part of the Mass, because of an old feeling of mystical emotion, Amaro had a return of fervour: with arms wide open he turned towards the congregation and liberally called out the universal exhortation to prayer: '*Orate fratres!*' And the old women with slobbering mouths, leaning against the stone pillars, pressing their hands tighter over their breasts, from which hung large jet-black rosaries, presented a stupid, idiotic appearance. Then the sacristan went to kneel behind him and lightly raised up the hem of his vestment with one hand, while with the other he rang the bell. Amaro consecrated the wine, lifted up the Host and said: '*Hoc est enim corpus meum!*' as he raised his arms towards the figure of Christ on the cross of black wood, all full of bleeding wounds; the bell rang slowly; closed fists beat on breasts; and in the silence could be heard the bullock carts on their return from the market, rumbling over the flagstones of the Cathedral Square.

'*Ite, missa est!*' said Amaro finally.

'*Deo gratias!*' responded the sacristan, breathing a loud sigh of relief at the thought of a task accomplished.

And when, after kissing the altar, Amaro came down the steps to give the blessing, he was already thinking with joy of his breakfast, of the appetizing pieces of toast, in Senhora Joanneira's bright dining-room. He pictured Amelia, with her hair falling down over her dressing-gown and her fresh skin giving forth a pleasant smell of almond soap, sitting waiting for him.

About midday Amaro usually went up to the dining-room where Senhora Joanneira and Amelia were sewing. 'I was feeling so dull down stairs that I thought I would come and have a little chat,' he used to say. Senhora Joanneira, sitting on a small chair by the window, with the cat nestling on the edge of her merino skirt and her spectacles on the tip of her nose, sewed away. Amelia, seated near the table, worked with her sewing basket at her side: as her head bent over her work she showed her fine, neat parting, almost smothered in the abundance of her hair; her large gold earrings, formed like drops of wax, oscillated, brought into being and threw a trembling little shadow on her well-formed neck; the shadows under her bistre-tinted eyes showed up delicately over her beautiful brown skin, whose colour was heightened by her strong healthy blood, and her full bosom slowly rose and fell as she breathed. Sometimes, feeling tired, she dug the needle into the linen and slowly stretching herself smiled. Then Amaro would say jokingly:

'Ah, you lazybones, you lazybones! Now there's a nice woman of the house!'

She laughed; and then they began to talk. Senhora Joanneira knew all the interesting news of the day: the major had got rid of his servant, or someone had offered ten moedas for the pig owned by Carlos of the post office. From time to time Ruça came to get a plate or spoon from the cupboard: then the talk turned on the price of food, or what they were going to have for supper. Senhora Joanneira took off her spectacles, crossed her legs, and swinging her foot, covered in its list slipper, began to talk of the meal:

'Today we have chick-peas. I don't know if the senhor paroco will like them, I got them for a change.' But Amaro liked everything and during some meals he discovered that Amelia and he had similar tastes.

Afterwards, feeling lively, he rummaged in the sewing-basket. One day he found a letter and asked her who was her sweetheart; she replied, as she sewed quickly:

'Ah, me! indeed, senhor paroco, nobody loves me . . .'

'That is not quite the case,' he said without thinking. But pulling himself up and turning very red, he tried to cover his confusion with a cough.

Sometimes Amelia became pleasantly familiar with him. One day she even asked him to hold a skein of silk which she wanted to wind.

'Don't take any notice of her, senhor paroco!' exclaimed Senhora Joanneira. 'What nonsense! Really, she is very impertinent!'

But Amaro laughingly declared himself willing and feeling very happy said that he was there to oblige them in every way, even to serve them as a spindle! They just had to give him their orders, they just had to give him their orders. And the two women laughed heartily, charmed by the senhor paroco's pleasant manners, which went to one's heart!—as Senhora Joanneira said. Sometimes Amelia pushed away her sewing and put the cat on her lap; Amaro approached and ran his hand along Malteze's back, who curled up, purring with delight.

'You like it?' said she to the cat, as she blushed and looked tenderly at her.

And Amaro murmured, perturbed: 'Ah, the little cat! the good little cat!'

Later, Senhora Joanneira got up to give her idiot sister her medicine or to arrange something in the kitchen. They were alone together; they didn't talk, but their eyes held a long silent conversation. Then Amelia began to hum in a low voice *The Good-bye* or *The Infidel*. Amaro lit a cigarette and listened, swinging his leg to and fro, in time with the music.

'It is so lovely,' he would say.

Amelia sang it again, more clearly, quickly sewing; now and again raising her head she looked at the tacking or passed her hand, with its large shining nails, over the seam in order to adjust it.

Amaro thought those nails were wonderful, because all that was her or came from her appeared perfect to him: he loved the colour of her clothes, her manner of walking, her way of passing her fingers through her hair, and he even gazed with tenderness at the white skirts which she hung out of her window on a bamboo cane to dry. Never before had he been in such close intimacy with a woman's life. When he saw the door of her room ajar, his eyes wandered inside and feasted voraciously, as on a vision of a paradise seen from afar: a petticoat hanging on a nail, a stocking stretched out, a garter on top of the trunk, were revelations of her nakedness which made him pale and clench his teeth. He never tired of hearing her talk or laugh, of watching her stiffly starched skirts touching the sides of the narrow doors as she went through them. At her side, very helpless, very languorous, he forgot he was a priest: his Sacred Office, God, the Cathedral, Sin, all were at the back of his mind, very far away; he saw them on high, very much in relief as if he were viewing them in a trance, as from a mountain one sees the houses below disappear in the mists coming over the valley; and he only thought of the infinite sweetness of being able to plant a kiss on the whiteness of her neck, or the joy of biting her little ears.

He sometimes revolted against these fits of weakness and stamping his foot on the ground said to himself: 'To the devil with these thoughts, I must have sense! I must be firm with myself!'

When he went down to his room, he attempted to read his breviary; but the voice of Amelia came from above, the tic-tac of her little boots as she walked across the floor . . . Good-bye! his devotion fell like a sail without wind; his good resolutions took wings and his temptations returned in a band to take possession of his brain, quivering, rocking, rubbing against one another like a flock of pigeons rushing to their cote! He was completely vanquished, and suffered. It was then that he regretted his lost liberty: how he wished he had never met her; how he longed to be far away from Leiria in a lonely village amongst peaceful people, with a thrifty old servant full of wise saws; what a joy it would be to walk round his garden when lettuces were springing up fresh and green and the cocks were crowing to the sun! But Amelia called him from above—and the enchantment began again, always laying a firmer hold on him.

Suppertime, above all, was his happiest and most dangerous hour, the best hour of the day. Senhora Joanneira carved, while Amaro, as he chatted, spit out the olive stones into the palm of his hand and put them in a row on the tablecloth. Ruça, each day more wasted away, served badly, and was continually coughing: Amelia sometimes got up to get a knife or a plate from the cupboard. Amaro, very polite, would offer to help her:

'Don't you trouble, don't you trouble, senhor paroco,' she said. And as she put her hand on his shoulder, their eyes met.

Amaro, with his legs stretched out and his napkin over his stomach, felt very satisfied, enjoying the warm air of the dining-room; after the second glass of Bairrada he expanded, began to joke; sometimes, with a tender look in his eye, he even touched Amelia's foot under the table, lightly, as if by mistake; or at other times, with a meaning air, he would say that he regretted he hadn't a little sister like her.

He was always excited when he went down to his room at night. He set himself to read *The Canticles of Jesus*, a translation from the French, published by the Society of the Slaves of Jesus. It was a pious little work written in an ambiguous lyrical style, almost obscene, which gave to the prayer the language of lust. Jesus is invoked in the terms of the avid, eager desires of sexual appetite: 'Oh! come, beloved of my heart, adorable body, my impatient soul desires Thee! I love Thee passionately, madly! Embrace me! Inflame me! Come! Crush me!' Thus was divine love intentionally made grotesque and obscene in its meaning. It whined, it roared, it declaimed in a hundred flaming pages in which the words 'enjoy', 'delicious', 'delirious', 'ecstasy', were repeated every minute, with hysterical persistency. And after passionate monologues which exhaled a puff of the ecstasy of copulation, there followed imbecilities of the sacristy, pious notes resolving difficulties in cases of fasting, and prayers for the woman in child-labour! A bishop recommended this small well-bound book; the pupils in schools conducted by priests and nuns were given it to read. It was both fanatical and exciting; it had all the eloquence of erotic, amorous delirium, all the ticklish points of devotion; it was bound in morocco and given to penitents in the confessional. It was the canonical sex drug.

Amaro read till quite late, very disturbed by these sonorous discourses which left him teeming with desire; sometimes in the silence he heard Amelia's bed creaking overhead: then the book slipped from his hands, he propped his head on the back of the armchair, shut his eyes and had a vision of her in front of the dressing-table in her bust bodice, undoing her plaits, or leaning over, taking off her garters, the half-opened neck of her shift disclosing her two white breasts. He got up grinding his teeth, with a brutal determination to possess her.

At this time he began to recommend her to read *The Canticles of Jesus*.

'You will see, it is very nice and very holy,' he said one night as he left the book in her work-basket.

The next day at breakfast Amelia was very pale, with deep furrows under her eyes. She complained of insomnia, of palpitations.

'Did you like *The Canticles*?'

'Very much. What lovely prayers!' she replied.

During the whole of that day her eyes refused to meet Amaro's. She appeared sad and sometimes, for no apparent reason, her cheeks flamed up.

The worst moments for Amaro were on Mondays and Wednesdays, when João Eduardo came to pass the evenings with the family. Not till nine o'clock did the paroco come out of his room; and when he went up for tea he felt annoyed at seeing the clerk, wrapped in his cloak, sitting at Amelia's side.

'Ah, how these two have been chatting together, senhor paroco,' said Senhora Joanneira.

Amaro, with a livid smile, slowly broke his toast, his eyes fixed on his cup.

Amelia, now that João Eduardo was there, wasn't as pleasantly familiar with the paroco and hardly ever lifted her eyes from her sewing; the clerk silently puffed his cigarette; and in the long pauses came the sound of the wind howling through the street.

'God help all those poor people who are on the sea tonight!' said Senhora Joanneira, as she slowly knitted her stocking.

'God preserve us all!' said João Eduardo.

His words, his mannerisms, irritated Father Amaro: he detested him for his want of devotion and for his beautiful black moustache. In his presence he felt bound tighter in his ecclesiastical chains.

'Play something, child,' said Senhora Joanneira to Amelia.

'Oh, I'm so tired!' replied Amelia, leaning back in her chair with a little sigh of fatigue.

Then her mother, who didn't like to see people dissatisfied, proposed a game of cards for three, and Father Amaro, taking his tin lamp, went down to his room feeling very unhappy.

Those nights he almost hated Amelia: he thought her sulky and obstinate. The intimacy of the clerk in the house appeared to him scandalous: he even decided to talk to Senhora Joanneira about it. He would say to her: 'The fact that her sweetheart is allowed to enter the house cannot be pleasing to God.' Afterwards, when he came to his senses, he made up his mind to forget it: he thought of leaving the house and even the parish. He then pictured Amelia with her crown of orange blossoms, and João Eduardo in his morning coat, blushing all over his face as they returned from the Cathedral after being married . . . He saw the bridal bed with its lace-edged sheets . . . And all the proofs, the certainties of her love for that idiot of a clerk dug themselves like daggers into his heart. 'Well, let them marry, and then to the devil with them.'

He really detested Amelia then. He violently turned the key in the lock to prevent the sound of her voice or the frou-frou of her skirts penetrating the room. But after a while, as on every other night, he listened, still and anxious and with beating heart, to the noise she made upstairs talking to her mother and getting ready to go to her room.

One evening Amaro went to take supper in the house of Dona Maria of the Assumption, and afterwards went for a walk along the Marrazes Road. On approaching the house on his return at the end of the evening, he found the street door open: on the straw mat in the passage were Ruça's felt slippers.

'Silly girl!' thought Amaro, 'she went to the fountain for water and forgot to shut the door.'

He remembered that Amelia had gone to pass the evening with Senhora Joaquina Gansoso, in her farmhouse at the foot of the Piedade, and that Senhora Joanneira had spoken of going to see the canon's sister. He slowly closed the door, and went up to the kitchen to light his lamp; as the streets were wet he still had on his goloshes, so his steps made no sound on the floor; as he passed the dining-room he heard a loud cough come from behind the chintz curtain of Senhora Joanneira's bedroom door. Surprised, he dexterously stepped to one side of the curtain and peeped through the half-open door. 'Oh, God of Heaven!' Senhora Joanneira in a white petticoat doing up her stays; and the canon sitting on the side of the bed in his shirt sleeves, puffing heavily!

Amaro descended the stairs keeping close to the banisters and went out very carefully closing the door. He walked in a daze round the Cathedral. The sky was cloudy and light drops of rain began to fall.

'So that's how it is! so that's how it is!' he said amazed.

He had never suspected anything so scandalous. Senhora Joanneira, the easy-going Senhora Joanneira! The canon, his master of moral! And he was old and without the impetus of young blood, a man who had already reached the time of life when his passions should have cooled down and he should be giving his thoughts to preserving his health and his dignity as an ecclesiastic! What then was to be expected of a young strong man, full of life, with his hot blood clamouring and burning in his veins! It was the truth, then—what was whispered in the seminary, and what old Father Sequeira, who had been parish priest of Gralheira for fifty years, used to say: 'They all play the same game!' Yes, all played the same game. They occupied high positions, they entered the Chapter, reigned in the seminaries, directed the conscience of man, cloaking themselves in God as a permanent remission of their sins and, at the same time, had a fat easy-going woman behind the scenes, in whose house they could rest from the austerity of their priestly office, smoking cigarettes and patting rounded arms!

Then came other reflections: what kind of people were this Senhora Joanneira and her daughter, who were maintained by the lingering lust of an old canon? Senhora Joanneira had certainly been a pretty woman, well-made, desirable—but in other days! Through how many arms had she passed till she arrived in her declining years to this senile and ill-recompensed love? The two women—what the devil, they weren't honest! They received lodgers, and they lived on the proceeds of immoral earnings. Amelia went alone to church, to do the shopping, to the farm; and with those big black eyes, perhaps she had already had a lover! Following his train of thought, certain things, unnoticed at the time, came to his mind. One day when they were alone, she stood at the window showing him a vase of buttercups, and blushing a great deal, she put her hand on his shoulder and her eyes were alight and pleading; on another occasion she rubbed her bosom against his arm!

The night fell, with fine rain. Amaro didn't feel it, walking quickly, full of one single delicious idea which sent a thrill through his whole body: to be the girl's lover, as the canon was the lover of her mother! He already pictured the good shameful life, full of enjoyment; while the fat Senhora Joanneira in the room above kissed her canon, breathing with difficulty on account of his asthma, Amelia would come down to his room, placing one foot carefully in front of the other, holding up her white petticoats, a shawl thrown over her nude shoulders . . . With what frenzy he awaited her! And now he didn't feel for her the same sentimental, almost dolorous love. He had the knavish idea of the two priests and their two women, making a nice little clique. The mean intriguing gave him, chained as he was by his vows, a depraved satisfaction. He leapt along the street—what a handy house with its two easy women!

Heavy rain fell. When he entered there was already light in the dining-room. He mounted the stairs.

'Oh, how cold he is!' said Amelia as she shook his hand, which was wet from the rain.

She was sitting at the table sewing, with a cloak over her shoulders. João Eduardo, at her side, was playing a game of *bisca* with Senhora Joanneira.

Amaro felt a little embarrassed; the presence of the clerk suddenly gave him, without knowing why, the hard shock of unpleasant reality; and all his hopes, which had been dancing a saraband in his imagination, shrivelled up one by one and faded away, as he saw Amelia there by the side of her intended, bending over her honest sewing, sitting under the family lamp, and wearing a dark high-necked dress.

And all around him appeared more decent, the walls covered with green-branched wallpaper, the cupboard full of bright china made in Vista-Alegre, the kindly fat-paunched water pot, the old piano standing unsteadily on its three twisted legs; the bookcase which they all loved, the chubby Cupid with his open umbrella all bristling with toothpicks, and the peaceful game of *bisca* played with its time-worn jokes. All so decorous and respectable!

He then looked attentively at Senhora Joanneira's heaving bosom, as if he were searching for the marks of the canon's kisses: ah! you, there is no doubt you are a kept woman. But Amelia, with those long drooping eyelashes, and lovely fresh lips . . . ! She knew nothing of her mother's loose life; or, if she did know, she was determined to establish herself solidly in the security of a legal love! And Amaro, in the shadows, examined her closely for a long time, seeking to assure himself by the placidity of her countenance of the purity of her past.

'You're a little tired, senhor paroco, aren't you?' said Senhora Joanneira. And looking at João Eduardo: 'Please trump, your thoughts are not on the game tonight.'

The clerk, who was in love, was inattentive.

'It's your turn to play,' Senhora Joanneira had to say to him every minute.

Afterwards he forgot to buy cards.

'Ah, boy, boy!' said she in her good-natured voice, 'I'd like to pull those ears of yours.'

Amelia, with bowed head, continued her sewing; she wore a little short black jacket with glass buttons, which concealed the form of her breasts.

And Amaro became irritated by those eyes fixed on the sewing and by that loose jacket, which hid the most appetizing part of her beauty! And he had nothing to hope for. Nothing of her would ever belong to him, not the light from those eyes, not the whiteness of those breasts! She wanted to marry—to keep all for that other one, that idiot, with his silly smile, playing clubs! He hated him then, with a complicated envious hate, which included his black moustache and his right to love . . .

'Are you uncomfortable, senhor paroco?' asked Amelia, as she saw him turning and twisting in his chair.

'No,' he answered shortly.

'Ah!' she replied with a faint sigh as she rapidly stitched.

The clerk, as he shuffled the cards, began to talk of a house that he would like to rent; the conversation turned on domestic affairs.

'Bring me a light!' shouted Amaro to Ruça.

He went to his room feeling desperate. He put the candle on the chest of drawers; the mirror was in front of him and looking at his reflection, he thought himself ugly, ridiculous, with his clean-shaven face, his collar stiff as a dog's collar, and at the back that hideous tonsure. He instinctively compared himself with the other who had a moustache and all his hair and complete liberty! Why should I torment myself? he thought. The other could be a husband; he could give her his name, a home, a child; he, Amaro, could only give her criminal pleasures and afterwards terrors of sin! Perhaps she liked him, in spite of the fact that he was a priest; but before all, above all, she wanted to marry; there was nothing more natural! She could see herself, though beautiful, poor and alone; she desired a legitimate and lasting union, the respect of the neighbours, the consideration of the shopkeepers, all the advantages of an honourable connection.

But at these times he detested her, her high-necked dress, her chastity. She was stupid if she couldn't see that there lurked there at her side, under a black cassock, a devoted passion, pursuing her, trembling and dying with impatience for her! He wished then that she was like her mother—or worse, all free, with gaudy coloured clothes, her hair twisted in an impudent knot, crossing her legs and eyeing the men, an easy woman, an open door . . .

'That's fine! here I am longing for the girl to be a whore!' he thought, drawing back into himself a little ashamed. 'It's clear: we can't think of decent women, we only have the right to prostitutes! A nice dogma!'

He felt smothered. He opened the window. The sky was gloomy, the rain had stopped; the only sound which broke the silence was the puling of the owls in the Misericordia.

He softened then, with the darkness, the tranquillity of the sleeping town. And again he felt, rising from the depths of his being, that first love which he had felt for Amelia, very pure, sentimentally devoted: he saw her beautiful head, transfigured and luminous, stand out in the thickness of the black air; and all his soul went to her, weak with adoration, as in his veneration for Mary in her Immaculate Conception; he anxiously begged her pardon for having offended her and said aloud: 'You are a saint! pardon me!' For a moment he had a sweet feeling from having renounced all carnal thoughts.

Surprised at these delicate sentiments which he suddenly discovered in himself, he began to think with longing that if he were a free man he would be such a good husband! So loving, so attentive, so devoted, always on his knees full of adoration. How he would love his son, so tiny, playing with his beard! At the idea of these unattainable joys his eyes filled with tears. In his despair he cursed that chatterbox of a marqueza who had made him a priest and the bishop who had anointed him!

'They've been my ruin! They've been my ruin!' he called out distraught.

He then heard João Eduardo's steps as he descended the stairs and the swish of Amelia's skirts. He ran to peep through the keyhole, digging his teeth into his lips with jealousy. The gate swung to, Amelia came up humming softly. But the feeling of mystical love, which had taken possession of him for a moment as he looked at the night, had gone, leaving him with a furious desire for her and her kisses.

Some days later Father Amaro and Canon Dias went to dine with the Abbot of Cortegassa. He was a very charitable, jovial old man, who had lived in the district for the last thirty years. He had the name of being the best cook in the diocese and all the neighbouring clergy knew his famous *cabadella da casa*. It was the abbot's birthday, and there were two other guests, Father Natario and Father Brito. Father Natario was a dry, bilious little individual, with two very malignant sunken eyes and skin pitted all over from smallpox. He was extremely irritable and was nicknamed the Ferret. He was always on the alert and loved to argue; he had the name of being a great Latin scholar and of having a cast-iron logic—and a viper's tongue! He lived with two orphaned nieces, on whom he doted: he was eternally praising their virtues and usually spoke of them as 'the two roses of his garden'. Father Brito was the most stupid and the strongest priest of the diocese; he had the appearance and the manners of a robust shepherd of Beira, who managed his flock well with a liberal use of his stick. He drained to the last drop an *amude* of wine, he gaily took a hand at the plough, he worked with the trowel when the workmen were arranging the threshing floor, and during the siestas of the hot summer days he threw the young girls on the straw and brutally raped them. The senhor precentor, always correct in his mythological comparisons, called him the Lion of Nemea.

He had an enormous head, and a mop of woolly hair which hung down to his eyebrows; his weather-beaten skin had a blue tone from the vigorous use of the razor; and his bestial laugh revealed his very small teeth, whitened by his habitual diet of maize bread.

Just as they sat down to table Libaninho arrived, very flustered, waddling from side to side, sweat dropping from his bald head, exclaiming in his high-pitched voice:

'Ah, children! excuse me, I am a little late. I passed the Church of Our Lady of the Hermitage, and Father Nunes was saying a Mass for a special intention. Ah, children! I gobbled it up, and now I've arrived feeling so consoled.'

Gertrude, the abbot's tall, strongly-built old housekeeper, then entered with a deep tureen of chicken broth; and Libaninho, leaping round her, began making his little jokes:

'Ah, little Gertrude! I know someone whom you could make very happy!'

The old countrywoman laughed, with her deep hearty laugh, which shook her massive bosom: 'It seems to me I'm a bit too old now for you to think of these things.'

'But, my dear girl! I like women as I do pears—ripe and with plenty of flesh, it is thus that they are most appetizing!'

All the priests laughed loudly. Then they joyfully sat down at the table.

The whole lunch had been cooked by the abbot. Immediately they had tasted the soup the exclamations began:

'Yes, dear sir, it's splendid! There isn't the equal of this in the heavens. It is wonderful!'

The good abbot blushed scarlet with satisfaction. He was, as the senhor precentor put it, a divine artist. He studied *The Cook's Complete Guide* from cover to cover; he invented recipes and, as he asserted, knocking his skull: 'Many dainty dishes have come out of this clever noddle.' He lived entirely absorbed in his art, and so it befell that in his sermons on Sundays, when the faithful knelt to receive the word of God, he gave them advice on the cooking of *bacalau* or the seasoning of *sarrabulhos*. He lived happily there with his old Gertrude (who also had a good palate), and his garden full of lovely vegetables, having only one ambition in his life—to invite the bishop one day to dine with him.

'Oh, senhor paroco!' he said to Amaro, 'don't behave like that! One more little mouthful of giblets, do please! These little pieces of crust soaked in the gravy! That's it! That's it!' And with a modest air: 'I know it's not for me to say so, but the *casedella* turned out splendidly today!'

The lunch was, as Canon Dias said, delicious enough to tempt St Anthony in the desert. They had all taken off their cloaks and clad only in their cassocks, their collars loosened, they ate slowly, and talked very little. As the following day was the feast of Our Lady of Joy, the bells of the chapel at the side chimed; and the beautiful midday sun gave gay tones to the china, to the fat blue jugs full of Bairrada wine, to the saucers of bright red pimentos, to the dishes of shining black olives— while the good abbot, with eyes wide open and biting his lip, carefully cut white slices off the breast of a stuffed capon.

The abbot then proposed that they should take coffee on the vine-terrace.

It was three o'clock. As they got up they all staggered a little, belching loudly and laughing heavily; Amaro was the only one whose head was clear and whose feet were firm, though he felt very affectionately disposed.

'Now then, colleagues,' said the abbot, draining the last drop of coffee, 'the best thing now would be a walk to my farm.'

'To digest our dinner,' shouted the canon as he rose with difficulty from his chair. 'Come on, let's go to the abbot's farm!'

They went by the Barraco short cut, a narrow cart-road. The day was very blue, with a tepid sun. The path wound along through bristling bramble bushes; on the other side, the flat lands extended covered with stubble; here and there olive trees in their fine foliage stood out with great clearness; towards the horizon, small hills, covered with the dark green branches of the pine trees, spread all round; there was a vast silence broken only by the sound of a creaking waggon on a distant road. And in that serenity of landscape and light, the priests walked along slowly, stumbling a little, with eyes lit up, stomachs well satisfied, joking merrily and thinking that life was good.

In front of all walked Natario with legs wide apart, his cloak hanging from his arm and dragging along the ground; the collar of his cassock, unbuttoned at the back, revealed its filthy lining; and as he rolled from side to side he struck against the bramble bushes, showing his thin legs and black woollen stockings full of holes.

Suddenly they all stopped, as Natario in front cried out furiously:

'You donkey, can't you see? You beast!'

It was a turn in the road. They had collided against an old man leading a sheep; Natario stumbled forward in a drunken rage and threatened him with his closed fist.

'I hope your honour will pardon me,' said the old man humbly.

'You beast!' bellowed Natario with flaming eyes. 'I'd like to smash you with a hatchet!'

The old man stammered, he had taken off his hat, one saw his white hairs; he appeared to be an ancient farm hand, grown old in his work; he was probably a grandfather. Cringing down, red with shame, he shrunk into the hedge beside the narrow cart-track to let the reverend fathers, jovial and excited from the wine, pass on their way.

Amaro decided that he wouldn't accompany them to the farm. When they reached the crossroads at the end of the village, he took the Sobres Road to Leiria.

'Do you realize it is five kilometres to town?' said the abbot. 'I'll order them to harness the mare, colleague.'

'What nonsense, abbot, I have good strong legs!'

Gaily slinging his cloak over his shoulders he took his leave, humming the *Good-bye*.

At the foot of Cortegassa the road became wider, and near by was a farm wall all covered with moss, the top bristling with pieces of bottle which glistened in the sun. When Amaro arrived near a low, yellow painted gateway, he saw a big spotted cow standing in the middle of the road. Feeling lively, he diverted himself by poking it in the ribs with his umbrella; the cow trotted off shaking its udders—and Amaro turning round saw Amelia at the gate. She saluted him, and said, all smiles:

'Now then, senhor paroco, are you frightening my cow?'

'Ah, it's you! What miracle is this?'

She blushed a little:

'I came home with Dona Maria of the Assumption. Now I'm going to have a look round the farm.'

At Amelia's side a girl was collecting cabbage plants in a large basket.

'This then is Dona Maria's farm?' said Amaro, stepping to the other side of the gate.

A wide path lined with old cork trees, extending almost to the house, which could be seen in the distance shining white in the sun, gave a soft shade.

'Yes, it is. Our farm is at the other side, but one can also reach it from here. Go on, Joanna, hurry up!'

The girl put the basket on her head and with a 'good evening' she turned down the Sobros Road, swinging her hips as she walked.

'Yes, yes! it seems to me a good property,' said the paroco thoughtfully.

'Come and see our farm!' said Amelia. 'It is just a little patch of land, but you will get an idea of what it's like. We can go through here . . . Listen, let us go below and meet Dona Maria first, would you like to?'

'I'm willing. Yes, we'll go and meet Dona Maria,' said Amaro.

They walked silently up through the rows of cork trees. The ground was covered with dry leaves and between the trees shrubs of hydrangeas hung drooping, beaten down by the rain; at the end an old low-built, one-storeyed house stood heavily. All along the wall huge pumpkins ripened in the sun and on the tiles, blackened from the winter, pigeons circled. At the back the orange trees formed a mass of dark green foliage; a well wheel creaked monotonously.

A young boy passed with a pail of washing.

'Where did the senhora go, João?' asked Amelia.

'She went to the olive grove,' answered the boy in his little piping voice.

The olive groves were far away, at the other end of the farm. The way was still very muddy and they couldn't go there without wooden clogs.

'We'd get ourselves all dirty,' said Amelia. 'Don't let's trouble about Dona Maria. I'll show you our farm . . . This way, senhor paroco.'

They were in front of an old wall covered with clematis. Amelia opened a green gate and they descended by three displaced steps to a path roofed with great trellised vines. Against the wall grew perennial roses; at the other end, between the stone pillars which bore up the arbour and the twisted trunks of the vines, one caught a glimpse of a

66

large meadow on which the sun beat down giving it a yellow hue; the low thatched roofs of the cowsheds could be seen in the distance, and from this side a thin white line of smoke lost itself in the blue air.

Amelia stopped every minute to explain things about the farm. It was there that the oats were sown . . . farther on the onions which were sprouting up beautifully . . .

'Indeed, Dona Maria of the Assumption works her farm very well.'

Amaro listened to her talking, with his head bent, and as he looked sideways at her, her voice in the silence of these fields seemed richer and sweeter; the fresh air brought a lovelier colour to her cheeks and to her sparkling eyes. In order to jump over the mire, she caught up her skirts, and the whiteness of her stockings, of which he caught a glimpse, disturbed him as a beginning of her nudity.

At the end of the vine arbour they crossed a field along which ran a brook. Amelia laughed heartily at Amaro who was afraid of the frogs. He exaggerated his fears and pretending he saw a viper, he rubbed against her in avoiding the long grass.

'Do you see that ditch?' she asked: 'Well, at the other side of it is our farm, by that gate, can you see it? But one can see that you are tired! It seems to me that you, senhor, are not a very good walker . . . Ah, there's another frog!'

Amaro gave a jump and touched her shoulder. She pushed him away gently and said with a warm smile:

'Oh, you coward! you coward!'

She was very happy and full of life. She spoke of her little farm with a self-satisfied pride at being able to understand the work, and at being its proprietor.

'It looks as if the gate is locked,' said Amaro.

'Is it?' she answered, and picking up her skirts she ran round to see. 'Yes, it is locked. What a shame!' she added, impatiently shaking the narrow railings between the two strong wooden pillars, dug into the thickness of the brambles.

'It was the caretaker who took the key!'

She leaned forward and trailing out her voice she called round the field: 'Antonio! Antonio!' There was no reply.

'He's gone to the other end of the farm,' she said. 'How annoying! If you like, senhor paroco, we could go on here in front. There is an opening in the fence called the Goat's Leap. We could jump over to the other side.'

And walking along, keeping close to the bramble bushes, dabbling her feet in the mud, she was very merry:

'When I was little,' she said, 'I never entered by the gate, I always sprung across there. And when the ground was slippery from the rain I tumbled. I was a lively little devil then, nobody would think it to see me now. Ah, yes! I'm growing old!' And turning towards him with a little smile which lit up the enamel of her teeth: 'Isn't it true? I'm growing old, don't you think so?'

He laughed. He couldn't trust himself to answer. The sun beating down on his shoulders after the abbot's wine soothed him, and her face, her shoulders, her presence, gave him a continuous intense desire for her.

'Here is the Goat's Leap,' she said stopping.

It was a narrow opening in the hedge, and the lower ground at the other side was all muddy. Through the gap Senhora Joanneira's farm was visible; the flat fields, star-strewn with white daisies, extended to the olive-grove; farther on appeared the shining wet roofs of the dwelling houses over which flocks of sparrows circled.

'And now?' asked Amaro.

'Now jump,' said she laughing.

He caught up his cloak and jumped, but slipped in the wet ground: immediately Amelia, leaning over and laughing loudly and waving her arms, sang out:

'Now, good-bye, senhor paroco, as I'm going to run off to Senhora Maria. You will stay here a prisoner in the field. Over you can't jump, through the gate you can't pass. Oh-ho, the senhor paroco is caught!'

'Oh, Menina Amelia? Oh, Menina Amelia!'

She chanted mockingly:

> *'I am here alone on the veranda*
> *As my beloved is in prison.'*

Her playful ways excited the priest. With arms outstretched he called invitingly:

'Jump, jump!'

She lisped in a pettish, babyish tone:

'I'm afraid, I'm afraid . . .'

'Jump, girl.'

'Here I come!' she cried suddenly.

She jumped and fell on his chest with a little cry. Amaro slipped, but immediately recovered his balance; then feeling her body in his arms, he crushed her brutally to him and kissed her passionately on the neck.

Amelia worked herself free and stood in front of him gasping, her face ablaze. With trembling hands she arranged her woollen cloak over her head and bosom.

'My little Amelia,' he murmured.

She suddenly gathered up her skirts and ran along by the side of the hedge. Amaro, beside himself, followed her with long strides.

When they arrived at the gate, Amelia spoke to the caretaker, who was coming along with the key.

They walked together along by the brook, and afterwards to the vine-arbour. Amelia, in front, chatted with the caretaker and Amaro followed behind with head lowered, feeling very guilty. Amelia stopped just before they reached the house, and turning very red and all the time pulling her woollen cloak up round her neck, she said:

'Oh, Antonio, see the senhor paroco to the gate. Good-evening, senhor paroco.'

She ran through the wet earth to the end of the farm, at the side of the olive groves.

Dona Maria of the Assumption had returned and was sitting on a stone gossiping with Uncle Patricio; a band of women were beating the branches of the olive trees all round with long switches.

'What is the matter, you silly girl?' said Dona Maria. 'Where have you come running from? Heavens, what madness!'

'I've been running hard,' she said all flushed, suffocating.

She sat at the feet of the old lady and remained motionless, breathing heavily through her half-opened lips, with her hands hanging in her lap and her eyes looking abstractedly into space, all her being sunk in the abyss of only one thought:

'He loves me! He loves me!' she breathed to herself.

For a long time she had been in love with Father Amaro—and at times, alone in her room, she grew desperate with the thought that he couldn't read in her eyes the confession of her love. From the very first days, she no sooner heard him in the morning asking for his breakfast, than she felt, without any cause, a joy penetrate all her being, and began to sing with the volubility of a bird. Afterwards she became a little sad. Why? She didn't know his past, and thinking of the friar of Evora, she began to imagine that he had become a priest through some disappointment in love. Then she idealized him, pictured him as having a very tender nature; it appeared to her that his pale, graceful person radiated fascination. She longed to have him as her confessor. How good it would be to kneel at his feet in the confessional, to be close to his black eyes, to hear his soft voice speak of paradise! She loved the freshness of his mouth; she paled at the idea that she might one day embrace him in his long black cassock! When Amaro went out, she went into his room, kissed his pillows, and saved up the short hairs left in the teeth of his comb. Her cheeks burned when she heard him ring the door bell.

If Amaro dined out with the canon, she was in bad humour all day, she found fault with Ruça, and sometimes she even spoke badly of Amaro, saying that he was rude, that he was so young that one couldn't feel respect for him. When he spoke of a new woman penitent she pouted with childish jealousy. Her old devotion came back to her with an overflow of sentimental fervour: she felt a vague physical love for the church; she wanted to embrace, with little lingering kisses, the altar, the organ, the missal, the saints, the sky, as she couldn't distinguish them from Amaro and they all seemed subordinate to his person. She read her missal thinking of him as her particular God. And Amaro didn't know, as he walked agitatedly up and down his room, that she above was listening to him, regulating the beatings of her heart by the number of his steps, embracing the bolster, weak with desire, kissing the air where she imagined his lips!

Night had fallen when Dona Maria and Amelia returned to the town. Amelia rode in front, silent, beating her little donkey, while Dona Maria chatted with the farm boy who held the halter. As they passed the Cathedral the Angelus was ringing and Amelia, praying, could not take her eyes away from the stone masonry of the Cathedral standing so majestically, surely because he celebrated there! She called to mind the Sundays on which she had seen him, at the chiming of the bell, give Benediction from the steps of the High Altar, and all bowed down, even the senhoras of the Morgado of Carreiro, even Senhora Baroness of Via Clara and the proud wife of the civil governor with her hooked nose! Yes! they bowed down in front of his raised fingers, and surely they also thought his black eyes beautiful! But it was she whom he had clasped in his arms beside the hedge! She still felt the hot pressure of his kisses on her neck: a burning passion flamed through all her being: she let go her little donkey's reins, pressed her hands against her bosom, and closing her eyes, she threw her whole soul into a prayer:

'Oh, Our Lady Mother of Sorrows, my Protectress, make him continue loving me.'

Canons in conversation passed to and fro across the flagged Cathedral yard. The gas jets shone in the apothecary's across the way; and behind the counter the figure of Carlos, in his round skull cap, embroidered with beads, moved majestically up and down.

Chapter VI

FATHER AMARO returned home terrified.

'And now? And now?' he gasped as he stood with his back against the frame of the window, feeling his heart shrivelling up inside him.

He must leave Senhora Joanneira's house immediately. It would be impossible to continue living there in the same family intimacy, after having had that daring adventure with the little one.

She didn't seem to have been very indignant, hardly disturbed; due perhaps to her respect for him as a priest, or to her delicacy towards him as her mother's lodger, or perhaps to her consideration for him as the canon's friend. But she may have related the whole thing to her mother or to the clerk—what a scandal! He could already see the senhor precentor crossing his legs and glaring at him—which was the attitude he took when reprehending—and saying pompously: 'This is the sort of irregular conduct which brings dishonour on our Sacred Office. It is thus that a satyr on Mount Olympus would have comported himself!' They might banish him to another village in the mountains! What would the Condessa of Ribamar say?

And then if he did continue in that close family intimacy, he would have constantly in front of him those black eyes, that warm smile which made a little dimple in her chin, the curve of those breasts—and his passion, silently increasing and continually exciting him, would conquer his soul, make him so mad that he would be guilty of some indiscretion!

He then decided to talk with Canon Dias, his weak nature always needing to receive strength from reasonings, from the experience of others . . . Ordinarily he consulted the canon, whom from the habit of ecclesiastical discipline, he judged to be more intelligent, because he was his superior in the hierarchy, and, since his time in the seminary as his pupil, he had not altogether lost his dependence on him. Also, if he wanted to arrange a house and servant the canon's help was necessary. He knew Leiria as well as if he himself had built it.

He found him in the dining-room. The olive-oil lamp, as it died down, was giving out yellowish fumes. The fire-irons, lying at the side of the charcoal-stove, were covered with fine ashes and showed up vaguely red in the light of the fire. And the canon, seated in a deep arm-chair, with his cloak over his shoulders, his legs wrapped in a rug and his breviary on his knees, had become drowsy from the heat of the fire and was now sleeping. Tigueira, cuddled in the folds of the rug, also slept.

71

Hearing Amaro's footsteps the canon very slowly opened his eyes, and mumbled.

'I've been sleeping, eh!'

'It's early, the soldiers' tattoo hasn't yet sounded. What's the reason for the laziness?'

'Ah! it's you,' said the canon with an enormous yawn. 'I arrived late from the abbot's, took a drop of tea, now you've broken my sleep . . . What have you been doing?'

'I've come here . . .'

'The abbot gave us a grand meal. The *cabedella da casa* was delicious! I filled my stomach a bit too much,' said the canon, drumming on the cover of his breviary.

Amaro sat down at his side and began slowly to poke the fire.

'Do you know, master,' he said suddenly, then almost added, 'I am in trouble!'; but he retrieved himself and murmured: 'I feel a little strange today. The fact is I've been a little out of sorts lately . . .'

'Yes,' said the canon considering, 'I must say I've noticed you looking yellow. Purge yourself, man!'

Amaro remained silent a minute gazing at the flames:

'I have the idea of moving from my lodgings.'

The canon lifted up his head, and sleepily opened wide his little eyes:

'Move your lodgings! Now listen to that! Why?'

Father Amaro moved his chair nearer to him and speaking softly, answered: 'You must see . . . I've been thinking that it is a strange thing to be in the house with two women, one of whom is a young girl . . .'

'What a tale! Is that what you've come to tell me. You are a lodger . . . don't worry about that, man! It is just as if you were in a lodging house.'

'No, no, master, I know what I am about.' He sighed, hoping that that canon would question him, would make it easy for him to give his confidence.

'Then was it only today you thought of this, Amaro?'

'Yes, I've been thinking about it only today. I have my reasons.' He intended to say: 'I did something stupid,' but he grew shy and didn't continue.

The canon looked at him a minute:

'Be frank, man!'

'I am.'

'Do you think you are paying too much?'

'No!' said Amaro, shaking his head impatiently.

'Good, then it is something else . . .'

72

'It is. What do you think?' And then continuing in a waggish tone which he thought might please the canon: 'We all admire nice things . . .'

'Good, good,' said the canon laughing, 'I see. You, like myself, are treated as one of the family. Do you want to tell me nicely that you are disgusted with that?'

'Nonsense!' said Amaro, as he got up, feeling irritated at so much density.

'Oh, man!' said the canon, opening his arms. 'You would like to leave the house? I see there is something wrong! Now listen, it appears to me it would be better . . .'

'It's a fact, it's a fact,' said Amaro, who was now taking long strides up and down the room. 'Yes, I've fixed my mind on it! If you could arrange a cheap furnished house for me . . . You understand these things better than I do . . .'

The canon remained silent, deeply buried in his chair, and slowly scratching his chin.

'A cheap house . . .' he muttered in the end. 'I'll see, I'll see . . . Perhaps.'

'You understand,' Amaro interrupted in the end, going close to the canon. 'Senhora Joanneira's house . . .'

But the door creaked and Dona Josepha Dias entered, and after talking about the supper at the abbot's, poor Dona Maria of the Assumption's cold, and the jolly Canon Sanches' liver trouble, which was sapping away all his strength, Amaro left, now almost pleased that he hadn't opened his heart to his master.

The canon remained in front of the fire ruminating. Amaro's decision to leave Senhora Joanneira's house was a welcome one. When he had brought the lodger to the Rua da Misericordia, he had arranged with Senhora Joanneira to lessen the monthly allowance which he had been giving her for years, paid regularly on the last day of every month. But later he was sorry. When Senhora Joanneira had no lodger she slept alone on the first floor: the canon could then freely enjoy the caresses of his old friend, and Amelia in her little bed upstairs had no idea that her mother and the canon were indulging in their comforts below. When Father Amaro came, Senhora Joanneira gave up her room to him and slept in an iron bed at her daughter's side: and the canon then realized, as he said, that he was without consolation, and that the new arrangement had spoilt everything. In order to enjoy the pleasures of the siesta with his Senhora Joanneira, it was necessary for Amelia to dine with friends, for Ruça to go to the fountain, and other tiresome arrangements; and he, canon of the Chapter, in the egoism of age, when he wanted to have relations with his woman, saw himself

73

obliged to wait, to manoeuvre, to have in the obtaining of his regular, hygienic pleasures the difficulties encountered by a college boy who loves the lady professor. If Amaro left, Senhora Joanneira would come down to her own room on the first floor; all the old enjoyments of the tranquil siestas would return. It was true he would have to give her the same monthly allowance as formerly. Well, he'd give it to her . . .

'The devil take it all! at least I will be able to do as I want,' he muttered aloud.

'What is my brother talking to himself about?' said Dona Josepha, waking up from the doze into which she had been falling in front of the fire.

'I have nearly gone mad thinking how I am going to punish the flesh during Lent,' said the canon with a coarse laugh.

Just at this hour Ruça was calling Father Amaro to tea; and he went up slowly with a shrunken heart, fearing to meet Senhora Joanneira's angry frown, as he felt sure that she had already been informed of the insult. He found Amelia alone: having heard his steps on the stairs, she hurriedly took up her work, sewing swiftly with her head very low, her face as red as the handkerchief which she was hemming for the canon.

'A very good evening, Menina Amelia.'

'A very good evening, senhor paroco.'

Amelia had always greeted him very amiably, with a 'Hello', or 'How goes it?' This dryness terrified him; he said very perturbed:

'Menina Amelia, I humbly ask your pardon . . . I did something very daring . . . I didn't know what I was doing. But believe me . . . I've decided to leave here. I've already asked Senhor Canon Dias to arrange a house for me . . .'

He spoke with his head down, and didn't see Amelia lifting her eyes and looking at him, surprised and wretched.

At that moment Senora Joanneira entered, and immediately on arriving at the door she opened her arms and cried out:

'Hello! Now I know, I know! Senhor Father Natario told me: a splendid meal! Tell me all about it, tell me all about it!'

Amaro had to describe the different courses, Libaninho's jokes, the theological discussion they had had; afterwards they spoke of the farm; and Amaro went down to his room without having the courage to tell Senhora Joanneira that he was leaving—a loss of six tostões a day for her, God help the poor woman!

The following morning the canon, before going to divine service at the Cathedral, went to see Amaro, who was standing at the window shaving.

74

'Hello, master. What's the news?'

'I think I've arranged something! I came across it accidentally this morning. It is a little house here at my end of the town, a find. It belonged to Major Nunes, who moved to number 5.'

This precipitation displeased Amaro; and he asked as he wearily sharpened his razor:

'Is it furnished?'

'Yes, it's furnished, and has china, bedclothes and everything.'

'And now what's to be done?'

'Now there is nothing to do except enter and begin to enjoy it. And between ourselves, Amaro, you are right. I have been thinking . . . It's better for you to have a place of your own. So get yourself dressed and we'll go and see the little house.'

Amaro remained silent, passing the razor over his face, and feeling wretched.

The house was in Rua das Sousas, had only one storey, and was very old, with the wood all worm-eaten; the furniture, as the canon remarked, had served its time and should be pensioned off; some faded prints hung sadly from great black nails; and the filthy Major Nunes had left the windows broken, the floor covered with spit, the walls all scratched from striking matches on them; and on the windowsill lay two socks almost black with dirt.

Amaro decided to take the house. And the same morning the canon arranged a servant for him, a Senhora Maria Vicencia, a very devout person, thin and tall as a pine tree, formerly Dr Godinho's cook. And (as Canon Dias had taken into consideration) she was a sister of the famous Dionysia!

In her young days, Dionysia was the Lady of the Camelias, the Ninon de Lenclos and the Manon Lescaut of Leiria: she enjoyed the honour of having been the mistress of two civil governors and of the terrible Morgado of Sertejeira; and the mad passions which she had inspired had been a cause of tears and swoonings to nearly all the wives of Leiria. She now went out as an ironing-woman, she was entrusted with articles for the pawnshop, she knew a great deal about childbirth (according to a singular expression of old Dona Luiz de Barrosa, nick-named the Backbiter), she protected the rich adulterer; she procured young laundresses for officials of the public works, she knew all the amorous history of the district. She could be seen every day in the street in her checkered shawl tied across her chest, her heavy breasts shaking inside her dirty gown, walking with small discreet steps and wearing her smile of other days—but two front teeth were missing.

The canon then informed Senhora Joanneira of Amaro's resolution.

It was a great shock for the excellent senhora. She complained bitterly of the senhor paroco's ingratitude.

The canon coughed deeply and said:

'Listen, senhora, it was I who arranged this. And I'm going to tell you why: it was because this idea of you sleeping on the top floor is ruining my health.'

Passing his fingers in a sweeping gesture along his chest: 'It is he who is going to lose all his comforts, you are not going to suffer: I will give you the housekeeping money as before; and as the harvest was good I'll give you half a moeda more for pin-money for the little one. Come along, Agostinha, you rascal, what about a little kiss! And listen, I'll have supper here tonight with you.'

Downstairs, Amaro was packing his clothes. But he stopped every minute and sighing wearily, gazed all round the room, fixing his eyes on the soft bed, the table with its white cloth, the large chintz-covered chair, where he used to sit and read his breviary, listening to Amelia humming upstairs.

Never again! he thought. Never again! Good-bye to the pleasant mornings spent at her side, looking at her sewing! Good-bye to the happy mealtimes, prolonged till the lamp died out. Good-bye to the teas in front of the charcoal stove, while the wind outside howled and whistled through the cold eaves! All was finished!

Senhora Joanneira and the canon appeared at the door of the room. The canon was beaming, and Senhora Joanneira looking very pained, said: 'I know, I know, you ungrateful one!'

'It's true, my dear senhora', said Amaro, sadly shrugging his shoulders. 'But there are reasons—I feel——'

'Listen, senhor paroco,' said Senhora Joanneira, 'don't be offended with what I am going to say to you, but I loved you as if you were my own son . . .' She then put her handkerchief up to her eyes.

'Nonsense!' exclaimed the canon. 'Isn't he still a friend, and can't he come here any night for a chat and a cup of coffee? . . . The man isn't going to Brazil, senhora!'

'That's true, that's true,' said the poor senhora in a disconsolate tone, 'but it's not like having him here in the house.'

In the end she stated that she knew well that people were better off in her house than anywhere else. She then advised him to tell the washerwoman to be careful with his linen, and added that if he wanted to borrow anything, such as china or tablecloths, he could send the washerwoman to fetch them.

'And see that she returns all your clean linen safely, senhor paroco.'

'Thank you very much, senhora, thank you very much,' he said as he continued to arrange his things, full of despair because of the resolution he had taken. The little one had evidently not opened her mouth about what had happened. Why should he leave this house where life was so cheap, so comfortable, so friendly? He hated the canon for his zeal in rushing the matter.

Supper time passed sadly; Amelia, in order to explain her lividness, complained of pains in her head. During the coffee the canon asked for his nightly dose of music; and Amelia, thoughtlessly or intentionally, sang her favourite song:

> *Ah! good-bye! the days are ended*
> *When I lived so happily by your side!*
> *This is the hour, the fatal moment*
> *In which we must part!*

That mournful melody, added to the pain of separation, upset Amaro so much that he got up abruptly and rushing to the window put his face against the glass, to hide the tears which rushed to his eyes. Amelia's fingers became confused among the keys; and her mother said:

'Oh, heavens, child, play something else!'

The canon, rising with difficulty from his chair, said:

'Well, senhores, it's getting late. Let us go, Amaro. I'll accompany you to Rua das Sousas.'

Amaro then wanted to say good-bye to the idiot sister; but after a violent fit of coughing, she had become very weak and was now sleeping soundly.

'Let her rest,' said Amaro. And squeezing Senhora Joanneira's hand: 'Thank you for all, my dear senhora, believe me . . .'

He remained silent, repressing a sob.

Senhora Joanneira put the edge of her white apron up to her eyes.

'Oh, senhora!' said the canon laughing, 'didn't I say only a short time ago that the man isn't sailing for the Indies!'

'But I had become so fond of him . . .' she answered, on the point of tears.

Amaro tried to treat it lightly. Amelia, very white, bit her little lips.

In the end Amaro descended the stairs: and João Ruco, who on his arrival in Leiria had carried his trunk to the Rua da Misericordia, very drunk, singing *Praise be to God*, now carried his trunk to the Rua das Sousas, again drunk, but this time singing *The King Has Come*.

When night came and Amaro found himself alone in that sad house, he felt a melancholy so poignant and a weariness of life so black, that with his listless nature, he had a longing to put his shoulder against a corner of the wall and stay there till he died.

He stopped in the middle of the room, and cast his eye all round: the bed was a small iron one, with a hard mattress and a red bedspread; the mirror, with its tarnished glass, shone on the table; as there was no washstand, the basin and jug, with a piece of soap, were set on the windowsill; everything there smelt musty; and outside, in the black street, the dreary rain fell incessantly. What an existence! And it would be always thus.

He then got furious with Amelia: he accused her, as he waved his clenched fist, of being the cause of his lost comforts, the scarcity of furniture, the extra expenses he would have to incur, the loneliness to which he was condemned! If she had the heart of a true woman she would have come to his room and said to him: 'Senhor Father Amaro, why are you leaving the house? I am not angry with you!' Finally, why did she stimulate his desire? She with her gentle ways, her sweet little eyes! But no, she let him pack his things and descend the stairs, without a friendly word, while she noisily played *The Kiss Waltz*.

He then swore that he would never again return to Senhora Joanneira's house. And, as he took long strides up and down the room, he thought of what he could do to humiliate Amelia. Yes, he had it. He would condemn her as a loose woman! He would gain influence with the devout society of Leiria, he would become an intimate friend of the senhor precentor; he would manoeuvre and cause an estrangement between them and the canon and the Gansosos, so that they too would cease their visits to the Rua da Misericordia; he would intrigue with the better-class women so that they would cut her at Mass on Sunday, he would give people to understand that the mother was a prostitute. He would put terror into her heart! cover her with mud! And in the Cathedral, as the people came out from Mass, he would gloat as he saw her pass, wrapped in her little black shawl, shrinking with shame, shunned by all, while he, deliberately taking up his position at the door, would stand conversing with the wife of the civil governor and joking with the Baroness of Via Clara! During Lent he would preach a grand sermon, and she would hear people in the shops and in the Arcade saying: 'What a great man is Father Amaro!' He would become ambitious, he would plot and plan and, because of his influence with the Senhora Condessa of Ribamar, he would rise to the highest dignities of the Church: and what would she think when one day she saw him as Bishop of Leiria, looking pale and interesting in his gold-adorned mitre, walking down the Cathedral nave, followed by the altar boys waving incense, passing between a kneeling penitent congregation, under the deep sounds of the organ? And she, what would she be then? A thin, dried-up creature, wrapped in a cheap shawl! And Senhor João Eduardo, the man of her choice, her husband? He would be just a poor, badly-paid copyist, in his short shabby coat, with his fingers all stained from cigarettes, leaning over his thick pile of papers, a nobody, fawning on those above him and envying those below him! And he, a bishop, a dignitary on that vast hierarchical ladder which reached even to the sky, he would be far above men, in that zone of light which surrounded the throne of God Our Father! And he would be a dignitary of both Church and State, and the priests of his diocese would tremble at his frown!

In the church, at the side, the clock slowly struck ten.

What would she be doing at this hour? Surely she was sitting sewing in the dining-room: the clerk was at her side: they were playing *bisca* and laughing, and perhaps in the darkness she was touching his foot under the table! He remembered her foot, the little bit of stocking of which he had caught a glimpse when she jumped over the mire in the field; his curiosity was kindled and rose from the back of her thigh to her breasts, running over suspected beauties . . . Oh, how he loved that cursed one! And it was impossible for him to have her! And any man, no matter how ugly or stupid, could go to the Rua da Misericordia and ask her mother for her, they could come to the Cathedral and say to him: 'Senhor paroco, marry me to this woman'; they could, under the protection of the Church and the State, kiss those arms and those breasts! But he, no. He was a priest! All through the fault of that infernal magpie of a Marqueza d'Alegros!

He then abominated all the secular world because he had lost those privileges for ever: and, as his sacred office excluded him from participation in those human, social pleasures, in compensation he took refuge in the idea of the spiritual superiority which his priesthood gave him over men. That miserable clerk could marry and possess the girl—but what was he in comparison with a priest to whom God had given supreme power? And feeding on this sentiment, his soul swelled up with pride at his sacred calling. But very quickly the desolate idea came to him that this domination was valid only in the abstract region of the soul; never could he manifest it in triumphal acts to society at large. It was a God inside the Church: but He no sooner appeared in the open than He was just an obscure plebeian. The world without religion reduced all sacerdotal action to a paltry influence over fanatical church-goers. . . . And it was this that he lamented, this lessening of the influence of the Church in social life, this mutilation of ecclesiastical power, limiting it to the spiritual only, without any right over the body, the

79

life and the wealth of man. What was missing was the authority of the times in which the Church was the nation and the priest the temporal owner of his flock. Of what importance to him was the mystical right to open or shut the gates of heaven, in this case? What he would like would be the ancient right to open or shut the gates of the dungeon! He wanted the clerks and the Amelias to tremble at the shadow of his cassock. He longed to be a priest of the ancient Church, to enjoy the advantages of the power of denouncing and of the terrors at the thought of the hangman, and there in this same town, under the jurisdiction of the Church, cause to tremble, at the idea of tortures and cruel punishments, those two who aspired to happiness—then he and she would be interdicted: and meditating on João Eduardo and Amelia, he lamented that he couldn't light again the fires of the Inquisition!

Thus that inoffensive young man, for several hours, under the choleric excitement of a thwarted passion, had grand ambitions for the return to the world of Catholic tyranny: because all priests, even the most stupid, have moments in which they are pierced by the spirit of the Church in her imposition of spiritual renunciation or by her ambitions of universal domination. Every sub-deacon has an hour in which he judges himself capable of being a saint or a pope: there has never yet been a seminarist who, for at least an instant, has not tenderly aspired to the cavern in the desert in which St Jerome, gazing at the starry sky, felt descending on his bosom as an abundant river of milk, the grace of God: and even the pot-bellied abbot, who in the evening sits on his veranda with a paternal air, enjoying his coffee and picking the holes in his teeth, has in his innermost soul the makings of a Torquemada.

Amaro's life became dreary. March continued very wet and cold; and after service at the Cathedral, he entered his house, pulled off his muddy boots, put on his carpet slippers and settled down to boredom. He dined at three; and he never lifted the chipped lid of the soup tureen without remembering, with pungent longing, dinner-time in the Rua da Misericordia, when Amelia, in her pure white neckerchief, passed the chick-pea soup, all tenderness and smiles. At his side the lean, angular Vicencia, with her soldier's body dressed in skirts, served him, with a continual cold in her head; and from time to time she turned aside and noisily blew her nose in her apron. She was very dirty: the knives she put on the table were still wet from the greasy water in which she had washed them. Amaro, disgusted and indifferent, never complained; he ate badly and hurriedly. After ordering his coffee, he spent hours at the table, sunk in oblivion, squashing his cigarette ends on the edge of his plate, lost in a mute tediousness, feeling his knees and feet cold from the wind which entered through the chinks of the badly-constructed doors.

The canon never came to the Rua das Sousas, because, as he said: 'The very thought of entering that house gives one an agonizing pain in the stomach.' And Amaro, growing every day more sullen, didn't return to Senhora Joanneira's house. He was disgusted that she didn't send for him to join the party on the Friday evenings; he attributed this neglect to the hostility of Amelia; and, so that he wouldn't meet her, he changed his Mass time with Father Silverio and so avoided the midday Mass which she was in the habit of attending, and said the nine o'clock Mass instead, furious with his new sacrifice!

Every night Amelia, when she heard the bell ring, had such a strong palpitation of the heart that for a minute she almost seemed to suffocate. Then João Eduardo's boots creaked on the stairs, or she recognized the flip-flap of the Gansoso' goloshes: she would lean back in her chair and close her eyes with pain at the repeated disappointment. She expected Father Amaro; and sometimes, when ten o'clock struck and there was no possibility of him arriving, her melancholy was so poignant that her throat swelled with repressed sobs, and she pushed away her sewing, and said:

'I must go to bed, I have such a headache. I get no relief from it!'

She threw herself down on the bed, and murmured in agony:

'Oh, Our Lady of Sorrows, my protectress! why doesn't he come, why doesn't he come?'

After he left she hardly ever went out of doors. Now the whole house seemed empty and dreary. When she looked in his room and saw the coat-hangers without his clothes, the chest of drawers without his books on top, she burst out crying. She rushed to kiss the pillow on which he had slept, she deliriously pressed to her bosom the last towel on which he had dried his hands. His face was constantly before her eyes, he was always present in her dreams. And with absence the flame of her love burnt stronger and higher, like a piece of lighted wood which one draws apart from the others.

One afternoon she went out to visit a cousin who was a nurse in the hospital. When she arrived at the bridge she saw a crowd gazing amazedly at a girl with her hair done in a chignon and wearing a short scarlet coat. Waving her fist in the air, she was cursing and shouting hoarsely at a soldier. The lad, a Beirian with a round stupid face covered with the fair down of his first beard, turned his back on her, and with his hands deeply buried in his pockets, shrugged his shoulders, muttering:

'I did nothing to her, I did nothing to her . . .'

Senhor Vasques, who had a cloth shop in the Arcade, stopped to look, disapproving of such a lack of public order.

'What is the noise about?' asked Amelia.

'Listen, Menina Amelia! It was just a soldier's joke. He threw a dead rat in her face, and the woman caused all this commotion. They are both drunk, of course!'

The girl with the scarlet coat turned round—and Amelia, terrified, recognized her school friend, Joanninha Gomes, who had been Father Abilio's mistress! The priest was suspended; he deserted her; she went to Pombal, afterwards to Oporto, and after passing from one misery to another she returned to Leiria, and there she lived in a laneway beside the barracks, consumptive, used by the whole regiment! What an example, Holy God, what an example!

And she also loved a priest! She also, just like Joanninha in other times, cried over her sewing when the priest didn't come to visit her. Where would that passion lead her? To the same fate as Joanninha. She could already see herself abandoned by the senhor paroco; and people pointing their fingers at her as she walked along the street, with a baby in her womb, and not a crust of bread to eat. And like a blast of wind which in a moment clears a cloudy sky, the sharp terror that the encounter with Joanninha gave her swept from her mind the morbid feelings of love in which she had been losing herself. She decided to take advantage of the separation to forget Amaro: she reminded herself that she must hurry on her marriage with João Eduardo in order to seek refuge in a dominating moral duty: for some days she forced herself to take an interest in him, she even began to embroider him some bedroom slippers.

The idea of the wickedness of loving a priest, when it attacked her love, made it shrivel up and feign death; but little by little the love which she had thought dead began slowly to uncoil itself, to rise up to invade her whole being. During the day, at night, whether sewing or praying, the vision of Father Amaro, of his eyes, of his voice, persistently appeared, with increasing enchantment, to tempt her. What was he doing? Why didn't he come? Perhaps he loved somebody else? She had more burning fits of jealousy. And this passion continued enveloping her in an atmosphere from which she could not escape. If she ran away from it, it followed her, coiled itself round her and forced her to dwell within it. Her good resolutions withered, died as tender flowers, in that fire which ran through all her being. If at times the thought of Joanninha returned, she repelled it irritably, and voraciously clutched at all the insensate reasons that came to her for loving Father Amaro!

Now she had only one idea, to draw him into her arms and kiss him--oh! kiss him! Afterwards, if it was necessary, to die!

She then began to get impatient with João Eduardo's love. She thought him a ninny.

'Oh, what a nuisance!' she muttered to herself at night when she heard his footsteps on the stairs.

She couldn't stand his eyes continually gazing at her, his short black jacket, his boring talks about the civil governor.

She idealized Amaro. At night in bed she tossed and turned in dreams of lust; during the day feelings of jealousy and hopelessness disturbed her, turned her, as her mother said, into a sulky mad-woman.

'Heavens, girl! what is the matter with you?' exclaimed her mother.

'I don't feel well! I feel some sickness coming on me!'

In fact, she became yellow and lost her appetite. Finally one morning she was feverish and remained in bed. Her mother got frightened and called Dr Gouvea. The old practitioner, after seeing Amelia, entered the dining-room contentedly taking his pinch of snuff.

'Well, doctor, what is it?' said Senhora Joanneira.

'Marry the girl, Senhora Joanneira, marry the girl. I've told you this so many times, woman!'

'But, doctor . . .'

'Marry the girl. Senhora Joanneira, that is all, marry the girl!' he repeated, as he went down the stairs slightly dragging his right foot in which his rheumatism had centred.

At last Amelia got better—to the great joy of João Eduardo, who, while she was sick, lived in desolation, bemoaning the fact that he couldn't be her nurse, and sometimes, when in the office, dropping a sad tear on the stamped documents of the severe Nunes Ferral.

The following Sunday, at the nine o'clock Mass at the Cathedral, Amaro, as he ascended the altar, caught a glimpse of Amelia among the congregation, in her black silk dress with the large flounces, kneeling beside her mother. He closed his eyes for a minute and found difficulty in holding the chalice in his trembling hands.

When, after having mumbled the Gospel, Amaro made the Sign of the Cross on the missal and afterwards on himself, then turned towards the people and said: '*Dominus vobiscum*', the wife of Carlos the apothecary whispered to Amelia that the senhor paroco was so yellow, he must have a pain. Amelia, leaning over her prayer book with the blood rushing to her face, didn't reply. And during the Mass, sitting back on her heels, absorbed in a sentimental, childish ecstasy, she delighted in his presence, his thin, delicate hands holding up the Host, his well-made

83

head bent in adoration, according to the ritual; a sweet thrill ran through her when his voice, as he hastily pronounced some Latin phrase, rose a little louder; and when the priest with his left hand on his heart and his right extended in the air, turned to the congregation and said the *Benedicat Vos*, with wide open eyes she cast all her soul on the altar, as if he were her particular God who blessed the bowed heads which extended along the Cathedral, to the very end, where the countrymen, with their stout sticks grasped in their hands, gazed in stupid wonder at the golden tabernacle.

As the congregation filed out it began to rain; and Amelia and her mother sheltered in the doorway, waiting for the shower to pass.

'Hello, you here?' said Amaro appearing suddenly, looking very white.

'We're waiting till the rain passes, senhor paroco,' said Senhora Joanneira turning towards him. And immediately she rebuked him: 'And why have you never come round, senhor paroco? Really! What have we done to you? Heavens, people are even talking about it . . .'

'I've been so busy, so busy . . .' muttered the paroco.

'But a little while at night. Listen, you may not believe it, but I've been so upset—and everybody has remarked on it. Senhor paroco, you have been so unkind!'

Amaro said, colouring:

'Very well then, it's fixed. Tonight I'll come round, I hope that will make peace.'

Amelia, who was blushing furiously, in order to cover her confusion looked all over the heavily clouded sky as if she feared a storm.

Amaro then offered Senhora Joanneira his umbrella. And while she opened it, carefully catching up her silk dress, Amelia whispered to him:

'Till tonight, yes?' And lowering her voice still more and looking nervously all round: 'Oh, dear! I've been so sad! I've nearly gone mad! Go now, I beg of you!'

On the way home, Amaro had to restrain himself from the indignity of running through the streets in his cassock. He entered his room, sat on the end of the bed, and remained there saturated with happiness, like a contented sparrow enjoying a ray of very warm sunshine: he saw again Amelia's face, her shapely shoulders, the beauty of her brows. The words which she had said: 'I've nearly gone mad!' echoed through his brain. The certainty that the girl loved him now entered his soul with the violence of a blast of wind, and remained purling, humming through every nook and cranny of his being, with a melodious murmur of awakening happiness. He paced with long strides up and down his room, stretching out his arms, longing to possess her body immediately: he felt an exquisite pride: he stopped in front of the mirror and stuck

84

out his chest, as if the world was a pedestal which supported him alone! He was too excited to eat well. With what impatience he longed for the night to arrive! The evening had cleared up; he was restless; every minute he pulled out his old silver watch, and went to look out of the window to watch the light of day creep slowly away from the horizon. He polished his shoes himself, rubbed lard into his hair to make it shine. And before going out he carefully read some prayers from his breviary, because in the presence of that newly acquired love he felt a superstitious fear that God or the saints would be scandalized at seeing him so moved; and he did not want, on account of his laxity of devotion, to give them reason to complain.

When he entered the Rua da Misericordia his heart was beating so vigorously that he felt suffocated, and had to stop; and the puling of the owls in the old Misericordia now appeared melodious to him, as he hadn't heard their sound for so many weeks.

What cries of welcome when he appeared in the dining-room!

'What a cure for sore eyes! We thought you were dead! What a miracle . . . !'

Senhora Dona Maria of the Assumption and the Gansosos were there. They enthusiastically drew back their chairs to make room for him. They all made a great fuss of him.

'Now what have you been doing, what have you been doing? Look at him, he is much thinner!' came the voices all round.

Libaninho, in the middle of the room, imitated rockets going up into the air. Senhor Arthur Couceiro, accompanying himself on the guitar, improvised and sang a little *fado*:

> *Here we have again our senhor paroco*
> *At Senhora Joanneira's tea-parties*
> *Which have once more become merry!*
> *Long live our pleasant chatter!*

All clapped delightedly. And Senhora Joanneira, wrapped in smiles, said:

'Ah, he has been an ungrateful one!'

'The senhora says an ungrateful one, a rude one I say!' muttered the canon.

Amelia remained silent, her cheeks burning, her moist eyes gazing towards Father Amaro, who had been given the canon's armchair, and who was feeling so puffed up with joy that he leaned back in it and stretching out his legs made the senhoras roar with laughter as he recounted tales of Vicencia's absent-mindedness.

João Eduardo, alone in a corner, turned over the leaves of an old album.

Chapter VII

THUS BEGAN again Amaro's intimate connection with the Rua da Misericordia. He dined early, afterwards read his breviary; and hardly waiting till the Cathedral clock had finished striking seven, he wrapped his cloak round him and made for the Square, passing close to the apothecary's, where the passers by, with their damp hands placed lightly on the knobs of their umbrellas, discussed the trivial events of the town. He no sooner saw the light in the dining-room window than all his desires surged through his body; but when he heard the sharp sound of the door-bell he sometimes felt a vague fear at the thought that he might find the mother suspicious or Amelia cold towards him. In order to avoid bad luck, he always entered with the right foot first.

The Gansosos and Dona Josepha would already have arrived; and the canon, who now dined very frequently with Senhora Joanneira, was always to be found, at that hour, stretched out in his chair finishing his little sleep. He would say, yawning loudly:

'Long live this handsome young man!'

Amelia sat at the table sewing, and Amaro took his place at her side; the penetrating look which they exchanged every day was a mutual silent affirmation that each one's love had grown since the previous evening; and often underneath the table they rubbed their knees together excitedly. Then the gossip began. The topics of interest were always the same: the question that had arisen in the Misericordia, what the precentor had said, how Canon Campos had dismissed his servant, what was being whispered about Novaes' wife . . .

'More love of one's neighbour!' muttered the canon, stirring in his chair; then letting out a short belch he turned round and again began to doze off.

Then João Eduardo's boots creaked on the stairs, and Amelia immediately opened up the little table for a game of quadrille: the Gansosos, Dona Josepha and the paroco made the set; and as Amaro played badly, Amelia, who was an expert at the game, sat behind him in order to guide him. After the first tricks the arguments began. Then Amaro turned his face so near Amelia's that their breaths mingled:

'This one?' he asked, turning a languid eye on a card.

'No! no! wait, let us see,' she answered blushing.

Her arm rubbed against the priest's shoulder: Amaro got a smell of the eau-de-cologne with which she had liberally sprinkled herself.

Opposite, beside Joaquina Gansoso, João Eduardo, chewing his moustache, painfully contemplated them; Amelia, to rid herself of those two pining eyes that were fixed on her, said to him in the end that it was almost indecent in front of the priest, who was so formal, for him to sit staring suspiciously at her all evening.

At other times she would say, laughing:

'Oh, João Eduardo, go over there and talk with mamma, if not we will have her falling asleep down here.'

And João Eduardo went to sit beside Senhora Joanneira, who, with her spectacles on the tip of her nose, was dozing over her knitting.

Amaro always left Senhora Joanneira's house more deeply in love with Amelia. He walked slowly through the street, ruminating with joy on the delicious sensations which that love gave him—the way she looked at certain times, the appetizing palpitating of her lovely breasts, the sensuous contact of her knees and her hands. When he arrived home he hurriedly undressed himself, as he liked to think of her in the dark, wrapped up in the bedclothes; and he ran over, one by one, in his mind's eye, the successive proofs she had given him of her love, as if each proof were a flower whose perfume he inhaled until at last he became drunk with pride: she was the prettiest girl in the town! And she had chosen him, and he a priest, a being eternally excluded from the dreams of her sex, the melancholy and neutral being who went through the world a suspect dangling on the brink of sentiment! His passion was then mixed with gratitude to her; and with closed eyelids he murmured: 'She is so good, the dear little girl, she is so good!'

But sometimes his passion caused him great fits of impatience. When he had been bewitched by her presence for three hours of the night, absorbing the voluptuousness which she exhaled with all her movements, he became weighed down with desires which made it necessary for him to curb himself, or else he might have been guilty of a rash act there in the parlour, in front of her mother. But afterwards, when he arrived home and was alone, he twisted his arms in despair: he wanted her there at once in order to offer her his desires: then he thought he would intrigue—he would write to her, he would arrange a discreet little house where they could make love, he would plan a walk to some farm. But all these means appeared incomplete and dangerous, when he thought of the searching eye of the canon's sister, of those busybodies the Gansosos! And in face of those difficulties, which rose like the several walls of a citadel, the old complaints returned: he could never be free! he could never openly enter the house and ask her mother for her, he could never possess her in comfort, without committing sin! Why had they made him a priest? It was all the doing of that old chatterbox, the Marqueza d'Alegros! He hadn't voluntarily surrendered his virility! They had driven him to the priesthood as an ox was driven to the stable!

Then, excitedly walking up and down the room, he brought many more accusations against celibacy and the Church: why did they forbid their priests, men living amongst men, the most natural satisfaction, which even the very animals had? Who could imagine that from the minute an old bishop said '*seras casto*', the hot blood of a strong young man would suddenly become cold?—and that one Latin word *accedo*, quakingly uttered by a frightened seminarist, would be sufficient to restrain forever the formidable rebellion of the flesh? And who had invented this? A council of decrepit bishops, coming from the depths of their cloisters, or from the peace of their schools, all as dry as parchment and as impotent as eunuchs! What did they know of the body and its temptations? If they would only come here, for two or three hours, to the side of Ameliazinha, they would see that in spite of his cloak of sanctity his desires arose storming him! All could be dodged or cheated except love. And if it was inescapable, why did they try to hinder a priest from feeling it, from satisfying his desires with dignity and purity? Perhaps it was better that he should procure it in the obscene alleyways! Because the flesh is weak!

The flesh! He then set himself to think on the three enemies of the soul—the world, the devil and the flesh. He pictured them as three living figures: a very beautiful woman; a black form with a brass eye and a goat's foot; and the world, something vague and marvellous (riches, horses, palaces)—that appeared to him sufficiently personified in the Senhor Conde of Ribamar. But what harm had they done to his soul? The devil he had never seen; the beautiful woman loved him and was the only consolation in his existence; and as for the world, the senhor conde, from that he only received protection, good-will, a squeeze of the hand . . . And how could he prevent the influence of the flesh and the world? Only by running away, as did the saints of old, to the sands of the desert, or to the company of the wild beasts! But hadn't the professors in the seminary told him that he belonged to the Church Militant? And hadn't they taught him that asceticism was wrong, as it was a desertion from sacred duties?

'I can't understand, I can't understand.'

He then tried to justify his love with examples from divine books. The Bible was full of nuptials. Amorous queens advanced in garments studded with precious stones; their future husbands came to meet them

88

with their heads covered in bands of pure linen, and dragging a white lamb by the ears; while the Levites beat on silver discs, crying out the name of God; the great iron gates of the city opened to allow the caravan with the newly-wed couple to pass through; and the chests of sandal-wood containing the treasures of the woman's dowry, tied with purple cords, on top of the camels' backs, creaked along. The martyrs in the circus married one another with a kiss, under the very breath of the lions and the acclamations of the multitude! Even Jesus Himself didn't always live in His inhuman saintliness. He was cold and contemplative in the streets of Jerusalem and in the market places of the City of David; but over in Bethany He had His haven of tenderness and abandon under the sycamores of the Garden of Lazarus; there, while His friends the lean Nazarenes drank their milk and conspired aside in whispers, He looked in front of the gilded roofs of the Temple, at the Roman soldiers throwing the discus at the foot of the Golden Door, at the loving couples who passed under the trees in the Garden of Gethsemane —while He put His hand over the fair golden hair of Martha, whom He loved, and who now sat at His feet spinning.

His love then was just an infraction of a canonical law, not a sin of the soul: it would displease the senhor precentor, but not God: it would be legitimate in a priesthood which had more human laws. He then thought of making a protest: but where, to whom? It appeared to him more impossible than to transport the old Cathedral to the top of the castle hill.

He shrugged his shoulders, flouting all those vague, intricate arguments—just philosophy and phantoms! He was mad about the girl. That was positive. He wanted her love, he wanted her kisses, he wanted her soul . . . And the senhor bishop, if he wasn't so old, would want the same, likewise the Pope!

He walked up and down his room till three o'clock in the morning, talking to himself.

How many times had João Eduardo, passing late at night through the Rua das Sousas, seen a faint light in the paroco's window! Because lately João Eduardo, like many men whose love affairs are not running smoothly, had the sad habit of walking the streets till late at night.

The clerk, from the very first, noticed Amelia's sympathy for the priest. But knowing her education and the devout ways of the house, he attributed those almost humble attentions to the pious respect which she had for his cassock, for his privileges as a confessor.

Nevertheless, he began instinctively to hate Amaro. He had always been an enemy of priests. He thought them a danger to civilization and to liberty; he always looked on them as intriguers, with luxurious habits, eternally conspiring to bring back the world to the darkness ot the Middle Ages; he hated the confessional, which he judged to be a terrible weapon against the peace of the hearth. He had a vague religion—hostile towards divine worship, prayers and fasting, but full of admiration for Jesus as a poet, a revolutionary, a friend of the poor, and for the sublime spirit of God which filled the Universe. It was only since he had fallen in love with Amelia that he had begun going to Mass, in order to please her and Senhora Joanneira.

He wished above all to hurry on his marriage with Amelia, so that he could take her away from that atmosphere of *beatas* and priests; fearing to have later a woman who trembled with the fear of hell, spent hours praying in front of the Stations of the Cross in the Cathedral, and confessed to the priests, who dragged from the penitents the very secrets of the marriage bed. When Amaro again began to frequent the Rua da Misericordia he was annoyed. Now, he thought, here is that scoundrel back again! But what disgust he felt when he noticed that Amelia was now treating the priest with more affectionate kindness. There was in fact some kind of love there. How she blushed when he entered! How she listened to him with childish admiration! How she manoeuvred always to sit by his side at the games of lotto!

One morning, feeling worried about the matter, he went to the Rua da Misericordia, and while Senhora Joanneira was talking in the kitchen, he said brusquely to Amelia:

'Do you know, Menina Amelia, I feel very disgusted at the friendly way in which you treat Senhor Father Amaro.'

She lifted up her eyes very surprised:

'What way? Now listen to that! Then how do you want me to treat him? He is a friend of the family, he was here as a lodger . . .'

'Yes, yes.'

'Ah, rest easy. If you are angry about it, you'll see. I won't go near him again.'

João Eduardo calmed down, and reasoned with himself that he had been mistaken. Her behaviour was just an excess of fanaticism, of ardent zeal for the clerical clique!

Amelia then decided to disguise what was in her heart. She had always considered the clerk a little slow-witted, and if he had noticed something, what about the Gansosos, so shrewd, and the canon's sister, so steeped in malice! On account of this, no sooner did she hear Amaro's footsteps on the stairs than she took up a very artificial, inattentive attitude: but behold! immediately he began to speak in his suave voice, or turned those black eyes towards her, she thrilled in every vein, her cold attitude melting away like a light layer of snow in the hot sun, her whole person becoming a continuous expression of her passion. Sometimes, absorbed in her rapture, forgetting that João Eduardo was there, she became surprised when she heard his melancholy voice coming from a corner of the room.

In addition, she felt that her mother's friends looked on her leaning for the priest with silent, kindly approval. He was, as the canon used to say, the handsome young man, and the manners and looks of the old ladies expressed an admiration for him which created a favourable atmosphere for the development of Amelia's passion. Dona Maria of the Assumption sometimes whispered in her ear:

'Now just to look at him is sufficient to inspire fervour! He is an honour to the clergy. There is no one like him!'

And they all summed up João Eduardo as a good-for-nothing! Thus Amelia didn't attempt to hide her indifference towards him: the bedroom slippers which she had been embroidering had long ago disappeared from her work-basket, and now she never went to the window to look at him going to the office.

The truth of his suspicion was then firmly established in João Eduardo's mind—his mind, which as he said, was now blacker than the night.

The girl loves a priest, was his conclusion. And the pain he felt for his lost happiness was mixed with sorrow for her threatened honour.

One evening, seeing her coming out of the Cathedral, he waited for her in front of the apothecary's, and said very resolutely:

'I would like to talk to you, Menina Amelia. Things can't continue like this . . . I can't . . . You are in love with the senhor paroco!'

She became deadly white, and biting her lips said indignantly, as she attempted to run away:

'Senhor, you are insulting me.'

He pulled her back by the sleeve of her coat:

'Listen, Menina Amelia. I have no wish to insult you, it is just that I am in doubt . . . I've suffered till my heart is almost broken!' He was so moved that his voice failed him.

'There is no reason for you to worry, no reason,' she muttered.

'Swear to me that there is nothing between you and the priest!'

'I swear by my eternal salvation that there is nothing! I'd also like to tell you, that if you ever bring up this subject again, or try to insult me, I will tell mamma all, and you, senhor, will never again be allowed to enter our house.'

'Oh, Amelia . . .'

'We can't stay here talking any longer. Dona Michaela is already watching us.'

She was an old woman who, lifting up the muslin curtain of a low window, was spying with her little eyes all lit up with greed for gossip, and her withered cheek voraciously pasted against the pane of glass. They then separated, and the old woman, disappointed, dropped the curtain.

That same night Amelia, while the old ladies, making much ado, discussed the missionaries who were then preaching in Barrosa, said to to Amaro in an undertone:

'We must be careful. Don't look at me so often or come so near me . . . Someone has already noticed.'

Amaro then drew out a chair in order to sit near Dona Maria of the Assumption; but in spite of Amelia's warning, his eyes were glued to her in mute anxious interrogation. He was frightened that her mother had become suspicious or that the malicious old ladies would raise a scandal. After tea, he took advantage of the noise of the chairs as they were being arranged for lotto to ask anxiously:

'Who noticed?'

'Nobody, it's just that I'm afraid. We must be more careful.'

From then on the sweet little looks, the contacts at the table, the secrets, ceased; and they felt an exciting pleasure in affecting cold manners towards one another, being vaingloriously sure of the passion which inflamed them. It was delicious for Amelia—while Father Amaro sat far away from her chatting with the senhoras—to adore his presence, his voice, his pleasantries, with her eyes chastely applied to João Eduardo's bedroom-slippers, which now, very cunningly, she had again begun to embroider.

The clerk was still uneasy: it made him bitter to see the priest installed there every night sitting with his legs crossed, and a self-satisfied look on his face, enjoying the veneration of the old ladies. Little Amelia now behaved very well, and was loyal to him, yes, she was loyal to him: but he knew well that the priest desired her, had his eye on her; and in spite of Amelia's oath on her eternal salvation, and her affirmation that there was nothing between them, he feared that she would be slowly penetrated by the stupid, obstinate admiration of the old people for whom the senhor paroco was an angel. He would only be content when he could drag Amelia away (as soon as he got employment with the civil governor) from that house of religious fanaticism: but this happiness was slow in arriving, and every night he left the Rua da Misericordia more passionately in love, eaten up with jealousy, detesting the priests more and more but lacking the courage to leave it all. It was then that he began to walk the streets late at night, sometimes returning to look up at the closed windows of her house. He afterwards went to the poplar avenue beside the river, but the cold, spreading branches leaning over the black water made him sadder still; he then went to the billiard-saloon, and looked for a minute at the players knocking the balls, at the marker, with his pronounced squint, yawning as he leant on his billiard cue. A smell of bad paraffin-oil suffocated him. He left, slowly directing his footsteps to the office of *The Voice of the District*.

Chapter VIII

THE EDITOR of *The Voice of the District*, Agostinho Pinheiro, was João Eduardo's cousin. He was generally known as the Humpetyback, as he had a large hump on his back and a body infected with tuberculosis. He was extremely dirty; and his little yellow, effeminate face, with its depraved eyes, revealed past indulgence in shameful vices. He had taken part (so it was stated in Leiria) in all kinds of roguery. And often one could hear shouted at him: 'If you weren't deformed, I'd break every bone in your body.' Realizing that his hump was sufficient protection, he had serenely achieved a state of unscrupulous villainy. He had come from Lisbon, a fact which made him an object of greater suspicion to the more serious members of the community: his hoarse rasping voice was attributed to the want of a glottis; and his tobacco-stained fingers terminated in very long nails, seen as he played the guitar.

The Voice of the District had been founded by a group of men called in Leiria the Group of Maia. It was particularly hostile to the senhor civil governor. Dr Godinho, who was the chief and the candidate of the group, had, as he said, found in Agostinho the very man he required: what the group wanted was a rogue with orthography, without scruples, who could write up pointedly, in high-sounding phrases, the insults, the allusions, and the calumnies, rough notes for which he himself brought to the office. Agostinho was a master stylist of indecency. They gave him fifteen mil reis a month and quarters in the office, which was on the third floor of an old broken-down building in an alleyway off the Square.

Agostinho wrote the leading article, the local news, and the *Lisbon Correspondence*; and Bachelor Prudencio was responsible for the literary page entitled *Leiria Chats*: he was a very decent, honourable young fellow, to whom Senhor Agostinho was repulsive; but he had such a craving for publicity that he forced himself to sit down fraternally on the same bench with him every Saturday to revise the proofs of his prose, a prose so fantastically florid in its imagery that when read in the town there were murmurs of: 'How rich! How rich, Jesus!'

João Eduardo also recognized that Agostinho was a rogue; he didn't dare to be seen walking in the street with him during the day: but he liked to go to the office late at night to smoke cigarettes, and to hear Agostinho talking of Lisbon, of the time when he was employed in the office of two papers, in the theatre in the Rua dos Condes, in a pawn-shop, and other businesses. These visits were secret.

At that hour of the night the printing-room on the first floor was closed (the paper was printed on Saturdays); and João Eduardo would find Agostinho sitting upstairs in a dark, cave-like room, dressed in an old fur jacket whose silver clasps had been pawned. Bowed down, ruminating over long galleys in the light of a miserable paraffin lamp, he was preparing the newspaper. João Eduardo would stretch himself out on the cane-bottomed sofa, or going to look in a corner for Agostinho's old guitar, he would strum the latest *fado*. The journalist meanwhile, leaning with his forehead on his closed fist, laboriously produced an article with which he was not satisfied: and as not even the *fado* inspired him, he went to a cupboard to procure himself a glass of gin which he rolled wearily round in his foul mouth before swallow-ing; then, yawning loudly and stretching himself, he lit a cigarette, and taking advantage of the accompaniment sang hoarsely:

> *It was my tyrannical destiny*
> *Which brought me to this pass*

And the guitar went: dir-lin, din, din, dir-lin, din, don.

> *It was through black fate*
> *That my life was thus lost . . .*

This always seemed to bring memories of Lisbon to his mind, as he invariably said with venom:

'What a pigsty of a place this is!'

He could never be reconciled to living in Leiria; not to be able to drink his three pints of wine in Uncle João's Tavern, at Mouraria, with Anna Alfaiata or with Bigodinha, while he listened to João das Biscas, with his cigar in the corner of his mouth, his half-closed eye full of tears from tobacco smoke, making the guitar cry as it told of the death of Sophia!

Afterwards, to console himself with an assurance of the certainty of his talent, he read his articles in a very loud voice to João Eduardo. And João was interested, as ultimately these productions, full of insults to the clergy, corresponded with his preoccupations.

It was just at this time that, on account of the famous question of the Misericordia, Dr Godinho became very hostile to the Chapter and the clergy in general. He had always hated priests; he had a bad disease of the liver, and because the Church made him think of the cemetery, he detested the cassock, as it appeared to him a threat of death. And as Agostinho had a profound deposit of spleen to spill, and was instigated by Dr Godinho, he exaggerated his calumnies: but, as his literary ability was weak, he covered his vituperations with such frequent eruptions of rhetoric that, as the canon said, it was just barking, not biting!

One night João Eduardo found Agostinho very enthusiastic about an article that he had composed that evening, and which he had filled with jibes in the style of Victor Hugo.

'You will see!' he said, 'it will cause a sensation.'

As always, it was a declamation against the clergy and a eulogy of Dr Godinho. After recounting the virtues of the doctor, 'that very respectable head of a family', commenting on his eloquence in the court, 'where he tore so many unfortunates from the cruel arms of the law', the article, taking a tone of bravado, brusquely dragged in the figure of Christ: 'Who could have said to Thee', (bawled Agostinho) 'O Immortal Crucified One! who could have said to Thee, when on the heights of Golgotha Thou wert expiring from loss of blood, who could have said to Thee that one day, in Thy name under Thy very shadow, Dr Godinho would be expelled from a house of charity—the purest soul, the most active brain . . .' And Dr Godinho's virtues passed as in a procession, solemn and sublime, dragging in their train copious noble adjectives.

After leaving the contemplation of Dr Godinho for a moment, Agostinho led his reader directly to Rome: 'And in this the nineteenth century, who dares to throw in the face of liberal Leiria the dictates of the Syllabus? Good. Do you want a war? Well, you have one!'

'Eh, João?' he said. 'Isn't it strong? Isn't it philosophical?'

And again taking up the article: 'Do you want a war? Well, you have one! We will lift on high our noble standard, which is not the standard of the demagogue, mark it well! and raising it aloft with a firm arm, to the highest bulwarks of public liberties, we shout in the face of Leiria, in the face of Europe: sons of the nineteenth century to arms! To arms in the name of progress!'

'Eh? This is going to finish them!'

João Eduardo, who had remained silent for a minute, then said, lifting up his expression in harmony with Agostinho's high-sounding prose:

'The clergy would like to drag us back to the baleful days of the dark middle ages!'

That literary outburst surprised the journalist: gazing at João Eduardo, he said:

'Why don't you write something too?'

The clerk replied, smiling:

'Me, Agostinho, I am just the one to write an article against the clergy. I can touch on all their rottenness. I'm the one who knows them!'

Agostinho thereupon insisted that he should write the article: 'It will be just what we want, boy!'

The evening before Dr Godinho had advised him:

'All that smells of the priesthood is vile! If there is a scandal, recount it! If there isn't one, invent it!'

And Agostinho added benevolently:

'And don't bother about your style, I will make it flowery for you!'

'We'll see, we'll see,' said João Eduardo.

From then on Agostinho was always saying to him:

'And the article, man? Bring me the article.'

He was avid for it; knowing that João Eduardo lived in the intriguing canonical clique which visited Senhora Joanneira, he supposed that he was privy to some specially infamous secrets.

João Eduardo, however, hesitated, saying:

'If it were found out?'

'It couldn't be!' affirmed Agostinho. 'The thing would be published as mine. It would be an article by the office. Who the devil could know?'

It happened that the following night João Eduardo surprised Father Amaro slyly slipping something to Amelia; and the next day he appeared in the office with the pale face that follows a sleepless night, carrying five large sheets of paper carefully written in block letters. It was the article, and was entitled: *Modern Pharisees!* After a few thoughts, full of embellishments, on Jesus and Golgotha, João Eduardo's article, with allusions as transparent as a spider's web, vindictively attacked Canon Dias, Father Brito, Father Amaro and Father Natario.

'Each one has his dose!' Agostinho exclaimed jubilantly.

'And when will it be published!' asked João Eduardo.

Agostinho rubbed his hands, reflected, and said:

'It's very strong, you devil! It's just as if you had put their very names! But rest easy, I will arrange it.'

He cautiously went to show the article to Dr Godinho, who declared it 'an atrociously vehement satire'. Between Dr Godinho and the Church there was just a little pique: he recognized, in general, the necessity for religion among the masses; besides, his wife, the beautiful Dona Candida, was religiously inclined, and had begun to say that the war between the paper and the clergy was causing her many scruples: and Dr Godinho stated that he didn't want to provoke unnecessary odium between himself and the priests, and that he foresaw that his love of domestic peace, the interests of order and his duty as a Christian, would very soon force him to a reconciliation, much against his opinions, but . . .

For these reasons he said curtly to Agostinho:

'This can't go as an article by the office, it must appear as a communication. Comply with these orders.'

And Agostinho informed the clerk that his work would be published under the heading of *Communication* and signed: *A Liberal*. Only João Eduardo had terminated the article with the exclamation: 'Be on the alert, mothers of families!' Agostinho suggested that this ending could give rise to the jocose reply: 'Alert we are!'

After trying several combinations of words they decided to wind up the article with: 'Take care, black cassocks!'

On Sunday the communication signed *A Liberal* appeared.

The whole of that Sunday morning, Father Amaro, after returning from the Cathedral, was busy laboriously composing a letter to Amelia. 'Impatient', as he said to himself, 'with those relations which went neither backwards nor forwards, which passed no further than a look or a squeeze of the hand.' One night at the lotto table he had given her a note in which he had carefully written in blue ink: 'I want to meet you alone, as I have much to talk to you about. Where can you suggest as a safe place? May God protect our love.' She didn't reply. And Amaro, vexed, and also unhappy because he hadn't seen her at the nine o'clock Mass that morning, resolved to write her a love-letter, making all clear: he prepared tender sentimental sentences which made his heart jump inside his body, and walking up and down the room, he strewed the floor with his cigarette butts, while each moment he leaned over the *Dictionary of Synonyms*.

'Ameliazinha of my heart,' (he wrote) 'I can't guess the serious reasons why you haven't replied to the little note which I gave you in the house of senhora, your mamma; I pointed out to you that it was necessary that I should talk to you alone; and that my intentions were pure, and that in the innocence of this soul which loves you so much there is no thought of sin.

'You must understand that I vow and declare a fervent affection for you, and it appears to me (if those eyes which are the beacon-light of my existence, and whose brightness guides me as the stars guide the navigator, have not deceived me) that you also, my Ameliazinha, are favourably disposed to him who adores you so much; also when the other day Libaninho went out with the first six numbers, and you, taking advantage of the hubbub, squeezed my hand under the table with so much tenderness, it appeared as if the sky had opened in front of me and that I could hear the angels raising their voices in Hosannas! Why then haven't you replied? If you think that our love would be disapproved of by our guardian angels, then I can tell you that you are committing a greater sin in dragging me through this uncertainty and torture, so that even when I am celebrating Mass I am unable to raise up my mind to the Divine Sacrifice. If I could see that this our mutual affection was the work of the Tempter, I myself would say, "Oh my well-beloved child, let us sacrifice our love to Jesus, in order to repay Him for a little of the blood He spilt for us!" But I have questioned my soul and see in it the whiteness of lilies. And your love too is as pure as your soul, that one day will unite with mine, amongst the celestial choirs in the glorious life to come. If you only knew how much I love you, my dear Ameliazinha, so much that at times I feel I could eat you up in little mouthfuls!

'Reply to this, and tell me if you think it possible that we could meet in Morenal one afternoon. I am longing to tell you of the flame which is burning me up, also to talk to you of some important things, and to feel in my hand that little hand of yours, which I desire to guide me along the road of love, even to the ecstasies of heavenly bliss.

'Good-bye, my bewitching angel, receive the offer of his heart from your lover and spiritual father, Amaro.'

After supper he copied this letter in blue ink, and doubling it well into the pocket of his cassock he went to the Rua da Misericordia. Immediately he arrived at the bottom of the stairs he heard Natario's sharp voice arguing.

'Who's there?' he asked Ruça, as she appeared with the light, wrapped up tightly in her shawl.

'All the senhoras, and also Father Brito and Father Natario.'

'Good! A great gathering!' He leaped up the stairs two steps at a time, and as he reached the door of the parlour, with his cloak still over his shoulders, he lifted his hat well off his head and said:

'A very good-evening to all, beginning with the senhoras.'

Natario immediately planted himself in front of him and exclaimed:

'Well, and what do you think of it?'

'Of what?' asked Amaro. Then noticing the silence, and all the eyes nailed on him: 'What is it? Has something new happened?'

'Then you haven't read it, senhor paroco?' they exclaimed. 'You haven't read *The District*?'

'It's a paper on which I never lay my eyes,' he said.

Then the senhoras burst out indignantly:

'Ah! it is shameless!'

'Ah! it's a scandal, senhor paroco!'

Natario, with his hands buried in his pockets, and contemplating the paroco with a sarcastic little smile, hissed out from between his teeth:

'You haven't read it! you haven't read it! What have you been doing?'

Amaro, now terrified, noticed the whiteness of Amelia's face, and her very red eyes. In the end the canon, lifting himself heavily out of his chair, said:

'Friend Amaro, we have had a great slap in the face!'

'Good heavens!' exclaimed Amaro.

'Yes, a violent one!'

'The senhor canon has a copy of the paper and must read the article aloud,' the old ladies suggested

'Read it, Dias, read it,' said Natario, supporting them. 'Read it to regale us!'

Senhora Joanneira turned up the wick of the lamp; Canon Dias, making himself comfortable at the table, unfolded the newspaper, carefully put on his glasses, and with his snuff handkerchief on his knees, began in his sleepy voice to read the article in the communications column.

The beginning didn't interest them: there were moving paragraphs in which *A Liberal* upbraided the Pharisees for the crucifixion of Jesus: 'Why did you kill Him?' (he exclaimed). 'Reply!' and the Pharisees replied: 'We killed Him because He was the figure of Liberty, of emancipation, the dawn of a new era, etc.' Then *A Liberal* drew, with large strokes, a picture of the night of Calvary: 'There He is hanging from the cross, pierced with swords, for His garments the soldiers cast lots while the unruly crowd jostled and pressed, etc.'; and again returning to point the finger at the unhappy Pharisees, *A Liberal* cried out ironically: 'Contemplate your good work!'; afterwards, cleverly descending, step by step, from Jerusalem to Leiria: 'Perhaps our readers think that the Pharisees are dead? How they deceive themselves! They live! We know them; Leiria is full of them, and now we are going to present them to you . . .'

'Now it is that they begin,' said the canon, looking over his glasses all round the company.

As a matter of fact they did begin; in a brutal form they presented a gallery of ecclesiastical photographs: the first being Father Brito: 'Look at him,' exclaimed *A Liberal*, 'fat as a bull, mounted on his brown mare . . .'

'Even to the colour of the mare!' murmured Dona Maria of the Assumption with pious indignation.

'. . . Stupid as a melon, and doesn't even know Latin . . .'

Father Amaro, thunderstruck, ejaculated: 'Oh! Oh!' and Father Brito, with his cheeks blazing, moved in his chair, and slowly rubbed his knees.

'One might call it a blow from a club,' remarked the canon, as he continued reading these cruel phrases with a sugared tranquillity: '. . . rough in his manners, but is not, as we are well informed, reluctant, on occasions, in displaying tenderness, choosing as his Dulcinea the true and legitimate wife of his regedor . . .'

Father Brito couldn't contain himself:

'I'll slash him from head to toe!' he exclaimed rising up in his chair, and again falling back heavily with the force of his fury.

'Listen, man!' said Natario.

'Who is going to listen! What I will do is, I'll slash him!'

'But if you don't know who *A Liberal* is?' said Natario.

'What liberal!' he bawled. 'The man I'm going to smash is Dr Godinho. Dr Godinho is the proprietor of the paper. It's Dr Godinho I'll smash!' His voice was hoarse, and as he spoke he furiously smacked his thighs.

'Remember that the duty of a Christian is to pardon injuries,' said Senhora Joanneira soothingly, citing the blows that Christ so meekly bore. 'We must imitate Christ.'

'That Christ, that pumpkin-head!' bawled Brito apoplectically.

That blasphemy created terror.

'Heavens, Senhor Father Brito, heavens!' exclaimed the canon's sister, falling back in her chair.

Libaninho, with his head in his hands, crushed by the disaster, murmured:

'Oh, Holy Mother of Sorrows, it is sufficient to bring a ray of lightning from heaven to strike you dead!'

Seeing Amelia's shocked face, Father Amaro said gravely:

'Really, Brito, you exceeded yourself.'

'But why are you all attacking me!'

'Man, nobody is attacking you!' said Amaro severely. Then continuing in a pedagogic tone: 'I have just remembered, that in such cases, as a duty when one is guilty of a great blasphemy the Reverend Father Scomelli recommended a general confession, two days of retirement from the world and a fast on bread and water.'

Father Brito moaned.

'Good, good,' resumed Natario. 'Brito committed a great sin, but he knows how to beg pardon of God, and the mercy of God is infinite!'

There was a troubled pause, and Senhora Dona Maria of the Assumption was heard to murmur that every drop of blood had left her body;

and the canon, who during the catastrophe had laid his glasses on the table, took them up again, and serenely continued the reading:

'. . . Do you know another with the face of a ferret? . . .'

Eyes all round were fixed on Father Natario.

'. . . Don't trust him: he wouldn't hesitate to play the traitor; he would wrong you if he could; pause! look out! His intrigues have caused confusion in the Chapter, because he is the most damnable viper in the diocese, but withal he is much given to horticulture, as he carefully cultivates "the two roses of his garden".'

'Heavens, that!' exclaimed Amaro.

'And now you see what it is,' said Natario as he rose from his chair livid. 'What do you think of it? You know that when I speak of my nieces, I usually call them the two roses of my garden. It is a little joke of mine. And, my dear people, they even had to bring that in!' And with a smile, weak with venom: 'But tomorrow I must know who it is! Mark it! I must know who it is!'

'Treat it with contempt, Senhor Father Natario, treat it with contempt . . .' said Senhora Joanneira trying to pacify him.

'Thank you, senhora,' answered Natario bowing ironically, 'thank you! That's gone home!'

But the imperturbable voice of the canon again took up the reading. Now it was a picture of himself drawn with much odium:

'. . . A canon swollen and gluttonous (in his youth whipper to King Dom Miguel), who was expelled from the district of Ourem, formerly master of moral in a seminary and today Master of Immorality in Leiria . . .'

'It is infamous!' exclaimed Amaro excitedly.

The canon put down the newspaper, and in his slow, heavy voice stated:

'Do you people think I'm going to take any notice of this? Am I? I have enough to eat and drink, thanks be to God! Anyone who wants to growl about me, let them growl!'

'That's all right, brother,' interrupted his sister, 'but at the same time one has one's little bit of pride!'

'Now look here, sister!' replied the canon, with the bitterness of concentrated rage. 'Look here, sister! no one asked you for your opinion!'

'Nor is it necessary to bite me!' she shouted, throwing herself into a fighting attitude. 'I'll give my opinion when I like and how I like. If you have no shame, well I have!'

'Now! now!' came the voices all round, endeavouring to calm her.

'Less lip, sister, less lip!' said the canon shutting his glasses. 'If not your false teeth will drop out!'

'You ill-mannered fellow!'

She wanted to say more but her breath failed her, and she suddenly began to ejaculate, 'Ah, ah!'

Fearing that she would have hysterics, Senhora Joanneira and Dona Joaquina Gansoso, supporting her by the arms, led her to the room below, calming her with soothing words:

'You are both ridiculous! What is it all about, dear woman? What a scandal! Our Lady will help you!'

Amelia sent out for orange blossoms to make her some tea.

'Leave her alone,' muttered the canon. 'Leave her alone! It will pass. It's just temper!'

Amelia, turning a sad eye towards Father Amaro, descended to the room below accompanied by Dona Maria of the Assumption and the deaf Gansoso who also wanted to soothe Dona Josepha, 'the poor thing!' The priests were now alone; and the canon turning towards Amaro said, as he again took up the paper: 'Now you, it is your turn.'

'And you'll see what a dose you get!' said Natario.

The canon cleared his throat, and getting nearer to the lamp, declaimed:

'. . . But the real danger is in a certain priest, young and puppyish, priest of a parish because of the influence of a conde of the capital, living in the intimacy of a good family where there is an inexperienced young maiden, and taking advantage of the influence of his sacred mission to sow in the soul of the innocent the seeds of a criminal passion!'

'How shameful!' murmured Amaro, livid.

'We ask you, priest of Christ, whither would you like to decoy this undefiled virgin? Would you like to drag her through the sink of vice? What have you come to do here in the bosom of this respectable family? You hover round your prey like the kite round the innocent dove! Get behind, it is a sacrilege! You murmur seductive phrases to her in order to divert her from the path of honour, to condemn her to disgrace; and any honourable man who wishes to offer her his hand and the fruits of his work, you doom to disappointment; you are preparing for her a dreadful future of tears. And all for what? To satiate the vile impulses of your criminal lust!'

'How infamous!' muttered Father Amaro from between his clenched teeth.

'. . . But we warn you, perverse priest!'—and the canon's voice took on deep hollow tones as he poured out those foul accusations. 'Already the archangel has lifted up the sword of justice. And on you and your accomplices, the opinion of illustrious Leiria has already fixed its impartial eye. And we are here, we the sons of Labour, to mark on your foreheads the stigma of infamy. Tremble, sectarians of the Syllabus! Take care, black cassocks!'

'What a crushing blow!' said the canon, sweating, and folding *The Voice of the District*.

Father Amaro, whose eyes were clouded with tears of rage, slowly passed his handkerchief over his forehead, and said with trembling lips:

'I, colleagues, do not know what I have to say to this. But by the God who now hears me, this is the calumny of calumnies.'

'An infamous calumny . . .' they all murmured.

'It appears to me,' continued Amaro, 'that we must appeal to the authorities!'

'It's just what I said,' agreed Natario.

'A whipping is what is wanted!' roared Father Brito. 'The authorities! What will happen is that I'll slash him! I'll drink his blood!'

The canon, who had been gravely scratching his jaw as he meditated, then said:

'It is you, Natario, it is you who must go to the authorities. You speak well and are logical . . .'

'If my colleagues decide,' said Natario bowing, 'I'll go. I'll have a nice tale to tell them.'

Amaro remained near the table with his head between his hands, beaten. And Libaninho murmured:

'Ah, children, this is nothing to do with me, but only to hear this list of accusations almost takes away the power from my legs. Ah, children, such a misfortune . . .'

But they heard the voice of Dona Joaquina Gansoso as she came up the stairs; and the canon immediately in a cautious voice advised:

'Colleagues, it's better not to talk any more about this in front of the senhoras. Enough is enough.'

A few moments after Amelia entered, and Amaro, rising, declared that he had a bad headache, and would say good-night to the company.

'And without a cup of tea?' said Senhora Joanneira.

'Yes, my dear senhora,' he said, putting on his cloak, 'I'm not feeling very well. Good-night . . . And you, Natario, will be at the Cathedral tomorrow at one.'

When he shook Amelia's hand he felt it passive and soft between his fingers. With bent shoulders he took his leave.

Senhora Joanneira noted his grief, and remarked feelingly:

'The senhor paroco turned very pale.'

The canon got up and said in an impatient, angry tone:

'If he's pale today, he'll be red tomorrow. And now I'd like to say something: this accusation against us in the paper is the calumny of calumnies! I don't know who wrote it, nor why they wrote it. But it is stupid and infamous. We know what we must do now, and as we've already talked enough over the case, the senhora can order the tea. What's done is done, there is no need to speak any more about the question.'

As the faces around him still remained distressed, he added: 'Ah! I want to say something else: as no one has died, there is no necessity for you all to sit around with funereal faces. And you, little one, sit down at the piano and play me that *Chiquita*!'

Chapter IX

JOÃO EDUARDO immensely enjoyed all the talk which was going on round the town.

He reread the article with paternal delight; and if he hadn't been frightened of offending Senhora Joanneira, he would have liked to run past the shops shouting out: 'It was I, I, it was I who wrote it!' And he was already ruminating on another, more terrible still, which he would call *The Devil Turned Hermit or The Priesthood of Leiria in the Nineteenth Century.*

Dr Godhinho met him in the Square, and condescendingly stopped to say:

'The affair has caused a lot of noise. You are a devil. That joke against Brito was well played—I didn't know that before. They say the regedor's wife is pretty . . .'

'Your excellency didn't know?'

'No, I didn't know, and I enjoyed it. You are a devil! I advised Agostinho to publish the article as a communication. You understand . . . It wouldn't suit me to have more disputes with the clergy—and also my wife has her scruples . . . In fine, she is a woman, and it is necessary for the women to have religion. But in my heart I enjoyed it. Above all that joke on Brito. At the last election the rogue fought me like the devil . . . Ah! something else, your affair is settled. Next month you begin work with the civil governor.'

'Oh, senhor doctor—your excellency . . .'

'Now, there is nothing to say! you well deserve it!'

João Eduardo went to the office, trembling with joy. Senhor Nunes Ferral was out: the clerk slowly pared a pen and began to copy a procuration—but suddenly he snatched his hat, and ran to the Rua da Misericordia.

Senhora Joanneira was sitting alone sewing at the window; Amelia had gone to Morenal, and João Eduardo, immediately he arrived at the door, said:

'Do you know, Senhora Joanneira, I was with Dr Godinho just now. He said that next month I will have my new position . . .'

Senhora Joanneira took off her spectacles and dropped her hands in her lap: 'What's that you said?'

'It's true, it's true . . .' said the clerk rubbing his hands and chuckling nervously with glee. 'What a gift from the blue!' he exclaimed. 'So that now if Amelia agrees——'

'Ah, João Eduardo!' said Senhora Joanneira with a big sigh, 'this takes a heavy weight from my heart. What a state I've been in ... You know, I haven't slept!'

João Eduardo felt that she was going to talk of the *Communication*. He went to put his hat on a chair in the corner; then turning towards the window, with his hands in his pockets, said: 'Why then, why?'

'That shameless thing in *The District*! What did you think about it? That calumny! Ah! it's put years on me!'

João Eduardo had written the article under the impulse of jealousy, with the sole idea of plunging a dagger in Amaro's heart: he hadn't foreseen the sorrow of the two senhoras; and now, looking at Senhora Joanneira with tears in her eyes, he almost repented. He said ambiguously:

'I read it, it's the devil ...'

But taking advantage of Senhora Joanneira's emotion to serve his own grievance, he added, as he drew a chair close to hers and sat down:

'I never wanted to talk about this, Senhora Joanneira, but—I can see that Ameliazinha treats the paroco with great familiarity. And through the Gansosos, through Libaninho, without any evil intention on their part, people are beginning to know and to talk about it ... I know well that she, poor little girl, sees no evil in it, but—you know what Leiria is. What tongues, heavens!'

Senhora Joanneira then declared that she was going to talk to him as to her son. The article upset her, above all on account of him, João Eduardo. Because in the end he might believe it and break off the engagement, and then what a sorrow! And she could tell him, as a good woman, as a mother, that between the little one and the senhor paroco there was nothing, nothing, nothing! It was just that the girl had those friendly ways with her! And the paroco had a nice way of speaking, always very delicate ... As she had so often said, Senhor Father Amaro *had* little ways that went to one's heart.

'Certainly,' said João Eduardo, his head down, nibbling at his moustache.

Senhora Joanneira then put her hand lightly on the clerk's knee, and looked directly at him:

'Listen, I don't know if I really ought to tell you, but the girl is honestly very fond of you, João Eduardo.'

His heart beat violently.

'And as for me!' he said, 'you know the great love that I have for her ... As for the article, it will make no difference to me.'

Then Senhora Joanneira wiped her eyes in her white apron. Ah! it was a great joy for her! She had always said that there wasn't a better fellow than he in the whole of Leiria!

'You know I love you as a son!'

The clerk was very touched: 'Well, let us have the wedding soon, and shut people's mouths . . .'

And getting up, he said in mock solemnity:

'Senhora Joanneira! I have the honour to ask the hand . . .'

She laughed—and in his joy João Eduardo kissed her filially on the forehead.

'You speak to Ameliazinha tonight,' he requested, as he prepared to leave, 'I'll come tomorrow. I'm sure we are going to be very happy.'

'Praise be to God!' added Senhora Joanneira with a great sigh of relief, again taking up her sewing.

That same evening, when Amelia returned from Morenal, her mother, as she laid the table, said to her:

'João Eduardo was here tonight.'

'Oh!'

'Yes, he came to talk to me, the poor fellow.'

Amelia remained silent as she folded her woollen cloak.

'Ah yes, he came to complain,' continued her mother.

'But of what?' she asked, very red.

'Of what? Of the fact that there is much talk in the town about the article in *The District*; that people are asking to whom the paper is alluding when it speaks of the "inexperienced young maiden": who must it be? and that the answer is: Senhora Joanneira's Amelia, in the Rua da Misericordia! Poor João said that he has been so upset! but, on account of the delicacy of the question, he didn't dare to speak to you. At last . . .'

'But what can I do, mamma?' exclaimed Amelia with her eyes suddenly full of tears at those words, which fell on her tormented soul like drops of vinegar on an open wound.

'I am telling you this so that you can decide on your line of procedure. Do what you like, daughter. I know well they are calumnies! But you know what people's tongues are. What I can tell you is that the boy doesn't believe what the paper says. It was of that that I was afraid! Heavens! it robbed me of my sleep . . . But no, he says the article doesn't matter, that he loves you just the same, and he is longing for the wedding. If I were you what I should do would be to marry at once, in order to silence the gossip. I well know that you aren't dying of love for him, I know it. That isn't important! It will come later. It is a fact that João is a good boy, and he is going to take up his new position.'

'He has secured the position?'

'Yes, it was that which he also came to tell me. He saw Dr Godinho, who told him that next month he can begin his new work. In fine, you do as you think fit. But remember that I am growing old, daughter, and may be leaving you any day . . .'

Amelia remained silent, gazing at the roof in front where the sparrows circled—at that instant, less turbulent than her thoughts.

Since Sunday she had gone about distracted. She knew well who was the 'inexperienced young maiden' to whom the *Communication* alluded. It was she, Amelia, and she was tortured with the humiliation of seeing her love thus published in the paper. Now (she thought, as she bit her lip with silent rage, while her eyes clouded with tears) that had arrived to destroy all. In the Square, in the arcade, they were already saying with ugly sneers: 'Then Senhora Joanneira's little Amelia is having an affair with the paroco, eh?' Surely the senhor precentor, so strict with regard to affairs with women, had already reprehended Father Amaro . . . And just for a few looks, a few little pressures of the hand, her reputation was ruined, her love destroyed!

On Monday on the way to Morenal she seemed to feel mocking jeers when her back was turned, and in the nod which the respectable Carlos gave her at the door of his shop she imagined she saw a curt rebuke; on her return she met Marques, the ironmonger, who didn't lift his hat to her, and when she got home she decided that people no longer had any respect for her—forgetting that the good Marques was so short-sighted that in the shop he had to use two pairs of spectacles, one on the top of the other.

'What can I do? what can I do?' she murmured, squeezing her head between her hands. Her devout brain could only furnish devout solutions—enter a convent, make a Promise to Our Lady of Sorrows asking her to free her from her anguish, go and confess all to Father Silverio . . . And she ended by finding herself sitting resignedly at her mother's feet with her sewing, feeling, very pathetically, that from the time she had been a little child she had always been very unhappy!

Her mother hadn't spoken clearly to her about the *Communication*; she had just referred to it in a few ambiguous words:

'It's a disgrace . . . It is sufficient for everyone to slight us. The more clear one's conscience, the more talk there is about one . . .'

But Amelia could well see how deeply she was afflicted—in her face, now grown older, in her sad silences, in the sudden sighs which she gave when, with her spectacles on the tip of her nose, she was knitting her stocking at the window; and then she would rather that there should be all that talk round the town, than that her mother, poor darling, be kept informed by the Gansosos and by Dona Josepha Dias—whose mouths produced scandal more naturally than saliva. How shameful, Jesus!

And her love for the paroco, which up to then, in those reunions of cassocks and skirts in the Rua da Misericordia, had seemed so natural, now, seeing that it was disapproved of by the people whose judgment, from infancy, she had been accustomed to respect—the Guedes, the Marqueses, the Vazes—already appeared to her monstrous: as the colours of a picture painted in the light of an olive-oil lamp, in the light of that lamp appear right, but take on false and deformed tones when they fall under the light of the sun. And she almost wished that Father Amaro wouldn't return to the Rua da Misericordia.

Nevertheless, with what anxiety she waited every night for his ring at the bell! But he didn't come; and that absence, which her reason judged prudent, gave her heart a feeling of having been betrayed and abandoned. When Wednesday evening came she couldn't contain herself, and said, as she blushed over her sewing:

'Whatever has happened to the senhor paroco?'

The canon, who appeared to be asleep in his armchair, gave a big cough, then turned and muttered:

'That's nothing. It is useless to expect him so soon . . .'

And Amelia, who had become white as chalk, immediately felt certain that the paroco, terrified because of the scandal in the paper, and warned of the dangers by the timorous priests, zealous for the good name of the clergy, had decided to cut off all connection with her! But in front of her mother's friends, she cautiously hid her despair: she even sat at the piano and banged out mazurkas so loudly that the canon, turning over in his armchair, growled:

'Less noise and more feeling, my girl!'

She passed a tearless agonizing night. Her passion for the priest flamed up more excitedly, though she still detested him for his cowardice. Just an allusion in the paper had stung him, made him tremble with terror under his cassock, so that he didn't even dare to come and see her—not thinking that her reputation too had been impaired, though she had had no satisfaction in her love! And it was he who had tempted her with his sweet little words, his coy, affected manners! Disgraceful! She had a violent desire to squeeze him to her heart—and to slap his face. She had the insensate idea to go next day to the Rua das Sousas, clasp him in her arms, install herself in his room, make such a scandal that they would be obliged to fly from the diocese . . . Why not? They were young, they were strong, they could live far away in another town—and her imagination began to feed hysterically on the delicious prospect of such an existence, in which she figured herself eternally giving him kisses! Because of her state of intense excitement such a plan appeared very practical to her, very easy: they would run away to Algrave; once there, he would let his hair grow (how much handsomer he would be then!) and nobody would know that he was a priest; he could teach Latin, she could go out as a sewing-maid; they could live in a little house, where the most attractive thing would be the bed with its two little pillows close together . . . And the only difficult thing she could see in this radiant plan was how she could leave the house without her mother seeing the trunk containing her clothes! But when she awoke from her dreams and viewed these morbid resolutions in the clear light of day, they faded away like shadows: now it all appeared so impractical, and he so separated from her, that between the Rua da Misericordia and the Rua das Sousas all the inaccessible mountains of the earth seemed to arise. Ah, the senhor paroco had abandoned her, that was certain! He didn't want to lose the proceeds of his parish or the esteem of his superiors . . . Poor her! She believed that she was going to be unhappy forever and lose all interest in life. She still had a very intense desire to revenge herself on Father Amaro.

It was then that she reflected, for the first time, that since the publication of the *Communication* João Eduardo hadn't appeared at the Rua da Misericordia. He also is turning his back on me, she thought bitterly. But it doesn't matter! In the midst of the affliction which Father Amaro's desertion caused her, the loss of the clerk's ridiculous and tiresome love, which brought her neither gain nor pleasure, was just an imperceptible hurt: a misfortune had arrived which brusquely snatched all affection from her, both the love which filled all her soul and the love which just flattered her vanity; and it irritated her, yes, not still to feel the clerk's love as he hung on to her skirts with the docility of a dog—but all her tears were for the senhor paroco, who now didn't even want to hear about her! She only lamented the desertion of João Eduardo because he was always a ready means which she could use to torment Father Amaro . . .

Therefore, that evening at the window, silently watching the sparrows in front circling round the roof—after she knew that João Eduardo, sure of his employment, had eventually come to talk to her mother—she thought with satisfaction of the despair of the paroco when he heard the banns of her marriage called out in the Cathedral. Afterwards her mother's very practical words had worked silently in her mind: his employment with the Civil Government would mean twenty-five mil reis monthly; as a married woman she would again enter the respectable life of a senhora; and if her mother died, with her husband's salary and the rent from Morenal, she could live with decency, even go to the seaside in the summer . . . And she already saw herself in Vieira, very much admired by the *cavalheiros* and perhaps claiming acquaintance with the civil governor.

'What do you think, mamma dear?' she asked brusquely. Because of the advantages which she pictured, she had quite made up her mind; but, on account of the lassitude of her nature, she wished to be persuaded and forced.

'I would take the safe course, daughter,' was Senhora Joanneira's reply.

'It's always better,' murmured Amelia as she went into her room. And she sat down sadly at the foot of the bed, because the melancholy which took possession of her in the twilight made more poignant her longings for the happy times with the senhor paroco.

That night it rained heavily, and the two senhoras passed the evening alone. Senhora Joanneira, now recovered from her disquietude, was very sleepy, and every minute her stocking fell on her lap as she nodded her head. Amelia pushed away her sewing and with her elbow on the table, and twisting the green lamp-shade with her finger, she thought of her approaching marriage. João Eduardo, God bless him, was a good boy, he was exactly the type of husband who was so esteemed in a small town—he wasn't ugly, and would have a good job; certainly the offer of his hand, in spite of the defamations in the newspaper, didn't appear to her, as her mother said, the ideal thing, but after Amaro's cowardly desertion, his devotion touched her, and poor João Eduardo had loved her for two years . . . She then began laboriously to call to mind all in him that pleased her—his serious air, his lovely white teeth, his spruce attire.

Outside a strong wind was blowing, and the rain, coldly beating against the windowpanes, gave her a more intense desire for home comforts, a bright fire, her husband at her side, her baby sleeping in his cradle near them—it would be a boy, and they would call him Carlos, and he would have Father Amaro's black eyes. Oh, Father Amaro . . . And then an idea crossed her mind which made her get up abruptly, and instinctively seek the darkness of the window recess to hide her blushes. Oh! not that, not that! It was horrible . . . ! But the idea seized her implacably like a very strong arm, suffocated her and gave her a delicious agony. And then the old love, which disgust and exigency had thrust down to the bottom of her mind, broke loose, inundated her: she murmured repeatedly and passionately, as she wrung her hands, the name of Amaro; she avidly desired his kisses—oh! she adored him! And all was finished, all was finished! And she must marry, how unfortunate she was! There at the window, with her face against the darkness of the night, she softly sobbed.

During the tea her mother said to her suddenly:

'The thing to do, daughter, is to start at once. It's best to begin making things for your bottom drawer, and, if possible, marry at the end of the month.'

She didn't reply—but these words pleasantly stirred her imagination. Married within the month, she! In spite of the fact that she was indifferent to João Eduardo, the idea of that man, young and passionately in love with her, who was going to live with her, sleep with her, disturbed all her being.

And when her mother was about to go down to her room, she said:

'What do you think, mamma? It is going to be a lot of trouble entering into explanations with João Eduardo, telling him that I am going to accept him. It appears to me my best plan would be to write him a letter . . .'

'Yes, I think the same, daughter, write it. Ruça will deliver it tomorrow. A nice letter that will please the boy.'

Amelia remained all morning in the dining-room planning the letter, and in the end wrote:

'Senhor João Eduardo,

Mamma informed me of the conversation which she had with you. And if you truly care for me, which I believe you do, as you have given me so many proofs, I am very willing to marry you, so now you know my feelings. With regard to the preparations for the marriage and the necessary papers, as we expect you for tea tomorrow we will then be able to talk about those matters. Mamma is very happy about us and I wish that all will be for our future happiness, as with God's help I'm sure it will be. Mamma sends her kind regards and
I remain,
One who loves you very much,
Amelia Caminha.'

She had hardly sealed the letter, when the white sheets of paper spread in front of her gave her the desire to write to Father Amaro. But of what? To confess her love to him with the same pen, wet with the same ink with which she had accepted the other as a husband . . . To accuse him of cowardice, show her disgust—would just be to humiliate herself! But, in spite of the fact that she could find no reason for writing to him, her hand involuntarily traced with delight the first words: 'My adored Amaro . . .' She stopped herself, considering that she had no one by whom she could send the letter. Ah! she would have to be separated from him thus, in silence, forever . . . Separated from him, but why? After her marriage she could easily see Senhor Father Amaro. And the same idea returned, subtly, but now in a form so honest that she didn't repel it: to be sure, he could be her confessor; in all the Christian world he was the one person who best knew how to guide her soul, her will, her conscience; there would be between them a delicious and constant exchange of confidences, of sweet admonitions. Every Saturday she would go to confession to him, and in the light of his eyes, in the sound of his words, would be a wealth of happiness for her; and it would all be so chaste, so thrilling, and all for the glory of God.

She felt almost satisfied with the impression, which she couldn't well define, of an existence in which the flesh would be legitimately content, and her soul would enjoy the transports of an amorous devotion. All would turn out well in the end . . . A little while afterwards she slept serenely, dreaming that she was in her own house with her husband, and that they were playing quadrille with all the old friends, with the approbation of the whole parish, as she sat on the senhor paroco's knees.

The next day Ruça took the letter to João Eduardo, and the whole morning the two senhoras talked about the wedding. Amelia didn't want to leave her mother, and, as the house was big enough, the newly-wed couple could live on the first floor; Senhora Joanneira could sleep in the room above; it was certain that the senhor canon would help her to furnish her bottom drawer; and they could spend their honeymoon in Dona Maria's farmhouse. Her prospective happiness, which her mother, with her spectacles on the point of her nose, pictured to her, as she gazed at her with fond admiration, made Amelia turn scarlet.

That evening when the Angelus bell rang, Senhora Joanneira shut herself up in her room in order to say her rosary, and also to leave Amelia and João Eduardo alone together so that they would begin to understand one another better. A little while later the clerk rang the door-bell. He arrived in black gloves and soaked in eau-de-cologne, feeling very nervous. When he reached the dining-room door the lamp hadn't yet been lit, but he picked out the beautiful form of Amelia as she stood near the window. He put his cloak in a corner, as was his custom, and approaching her, as she stood there motionless, he said, nervously rubbing his hands together:

'I got your little note, Menina Amelia . . .'

'I sent Ruça with it early this morning, in order to catch you at home,' she said immediately, with burning cheeks.

'I was just going to the office, I was already on the stairs—it must have been nine o'clock . . .'

'It must have been . . .' she said.

They both remained silent, very agitated. He then very delicately took hold of both her wrists, and whispered:

'Then you love me?'

'I love you,' murmured Amelia.

'And as soon as possible, eh?'

'Yes . . .'

He gave a sigh of great happiness.

'We will be very happy together, we will be very happy together!' he said. And very tenderly he took possession of her arms from her wrists to her elbows.

'Mamma says that we can live with her,' she said, forcing herself to speak calmly.

'That's all right, and I'll arrange the linen,' he added, all excited.

He then suddenly drew her towards him, and kissed her on the lips; she gave a little sob, and surrendered herself to his embrace, all weak, all languid.

'Oh, my little girl!' he murmured.

But her mother's shoes creaked on the stairs, and Amelia excitedly rushed to the table to light the lamp.

Senhora Joanneira halted at the door; and in order to give the first signs of her maternal approbation, she said pleasantly:

'So you are both here in the dark, children?'

It was Canon Dias who, one morning in the Cathedral, first informed Amaro of Amelia's approaching marriage. He spoke of the advantages of the union, and added:

'I regard it favourably, as it is for the girl's happiness, and also it will ease her poor mother's mind.'

'That's true, that's true . . .' murmured Amaro turning very pale.

The canon loudly cleared his throat, and continued:

'Now that all is in order you can go round and visit them again. That villainy of the newspaper is now ancient history. What's past is past!'

'That's true, that's true . . .' muttered Amaro. And brusquely swinging his cloak over his shoulders, he left the Cathedral.

He felt indignant; and had to hold himself in so as not to curse out loud as he went along the street. At the corner of Sousa's lane-way he almost bumped into Natario, who immediately took him by the sleeve, to whisper into his ear:

'Up to now I know nothing!'

'Of what?'

'Of *A Liberal* of the *Communication*. But I'm working at it, I'm working at it!'

Amaro, who was anxious to relieve his feelings, then said:

'Now have you heard the news? Amelia's marriage . . . What do you think of it?'

'That animal Libaninho told me. He said the fellow had got the job. It was Dr Godinho—and some other scamp . . . Just look at that rabble: Dr Godinho, in his newspaper, is wrangling with the civil governor, and the civil governor finds jobs for Dr Godinho's protégés . . . They understand one another! This is a country of villains!'

'They say there is great rejoicing at Senhora Joanneira's house,' said the paroco, with black bitterness.

'Let them enjoy themselves! I have no time to go there—I have time for nothing! I live with one purpose, to know who is *A Liberal* and to cleave him! I can't understand those people who punish with a whipping or a beating, or pulling people by the ears. I don't do that, no! I save it up!' And with a contraction of rancour which curved his fingers like claws and shrunk his narrow chest, he said from between his closed teeth: 'And, when I hate, I hate well!'

He remained silent a moment, enjoying the taste of his spleen.

'You must go to the Rua da Misericordia to congratulate these people,' he then added as he fixed his little eyes on Amaro. 'That blockhead of a clerk has captured the prettiest girl in the town! He is a lucky fellow!'

'Good-bye for the present!' said Amaro, as he turned away abruptly, and swung furiously down the street.

After that terrible Sunday in which the *Communication* appeared, Father Amaro at the beginning only worried about the probable consequences to himself—ruinous consequences, Holy God!—which would bring a scandal in their trail. Heavens! if it spread around the town that he was the puppyish priest whom *A Liberal* had attacked! He lived two days of terror, trembling at the thought that Father Saldanha, with his little effeminate face, might appear and say in his mellifluous voice: 'His excellency, the senhor precentor, requires your presence!' He spent much time preparing explanations, clever answers, flatteries for his excellency. But when he saw that, in spite of the violence of the article, his excellency seemed disposed to give it the deaf ear, he then tranquilly occupied himself with the interests of his passion, which had been so violently disturbed. His fear made him cunning, and he decided not to return to the Rua da Misericordia for some time.

'Let the storm blow over,' he thought.

At the end of two or three weeks, when the article was forgotten, he would once more appear at Senhora Joanneira's, to see again the girl whom he would adore forever; but he would avoid the old familiarity, the little whispered conversations, the seats beside her at the lotto games; afterwards, he decided that, with the influence of Dona Maria of the Assumption and Dona Josepha Dias, he could arrange that Amelia would leave Father Silveiro and go to confession to him: they could come to an understanding in the secrecy of the confessional: they would arrange to act discreetly, to meet here and there in certain suitable places, to send little notes by the servant; and their love, thus prudently conducted, would not run them into danger through being announced in the newspaper! And he was rejoicing at the cleverness of these arrangements when the great shock arrived—the girl was going to get married!

After the first feeling of desperation, when he vented his anger by stamping his feet on the floor and blaspheming, for which he immediately asked pardon of Our Lord Jesus Christ, he wanted to calm himself, to fix the reason of things. Where would that love lead him? To disgrace. On the other hand, if she married, each one would enter upon his or her legitimate destiny—she in her family life, and he in his parish. Afterwards, when they met, they could salute one another amiably; and he could walk through the town with head well erect, without fear of whisperings in the arcade or insinuations in the paper, the censure of his excellency or the prickings of his conscience! And his life would be happy . . . No, for the love of God! he couldn't be happy without her! If she were removed from his existence the interest of those visits to the Rua da Misericordia, the squeezing of hands, the hope of better delights—what was left for him? To vegetate, like one of the mushrooms in a damp corner of the Cathedral yard! And she, she who drove him mad with her sweet little looks and manners, turned her back on him as soon as the other appeared with his offer of marriage, and his twenty-five mil reis per month! All those signs, all those changes of colour—only to make fun of him! The senhor paroco was just an object of derision!

Oh, how he hated her!—less than the other however, the other who triumphed because he was a man, and had his liberty and all his hair, his moustache, and his arm free to offer her in the street! He rancorously fed his imagination on visions of the happiness of the clerk: he could see him leading her triumphantly from the church; he saw him kissing her on the neck and on the breasts . . . These thoughts caused him to stamp so furiously on the ground that he frightened Vicencia in the kitchen.

Then he succeeded in quietening his feelings, again resuming the command of his faculties, and applying all of them in inventing a revenge, a great revenge! Then returned the old regret that they didn't all live in the time of the Inquisition, when by denouncing them for heresy or witchcraft he could send both to the dungeon. Ah! in those days a priest could enjoy life! But today, with the spread of liberalism, he was forced to see that miserable clerk with his six vintens a day take possession of the girl—and he, an ordained priest, who could be a bishop, who could even be Pope, had to bow his head and ruminate in silence on his passion! Ah! if the curses of God had any value— cursed be them both! He wished to see them with a large family, without a loaf of bread on the shelf, their last blanket pawned, shrunken with hunger, pocketing all classes of affronts—and he laughing at them, he enjoying it all!

When Monday arrived he couldn't control himself any longer, so he went to the Rua da Misericordia. Senhora Joanneira was downstairs in the little parlour with Canon Dias. As Amaro appeared she exclaimed:

'Oh, senhor paroco! you are welcome! We were just talking about you. We were surprised you hadn't been round to see us, now that we have such joy in the house.'

'I know, I know,' murmured Amaro, turning very pale.

'Well, it had to happen some time,' said the canon jovially. 'God grant that they may be happy and that they may have few children, as bread is dear.'

Amaro smiled—listening to the sounds of the piano upstairs.

It was Amelia playing, as in other days, the waltz of the *Two Worlds*; and João Eduardo, standing very close to her, turning over the leaves of the music.

'Who came in, Ruça?' she shouted, as she heard the girl's steps on the stairs.

'Senhor Father Amaro.'

The blood rushed to her cheeks—and her heart beat so violently that she remained a minute with her fingers motionless on the keys.

'We have no need of Senhor Father Amaro here,' muttered João Eduardo between his teeth.

Amelia bit her lip. She hated the clerk: in an instant, his voice, his

118

moustache, his whole figure standing there beside her, were repugnant to her: she thought with delight that after her marriage (she would have to marry him) she would confess all to Father Amaro and would continue loving him! Just then she felt no scruples; and almost wished that the clerk could read in her face the passion which was boiling up inside her.

'Heavens, man!' she said. 'Go a bit away from me, I can hardly move my arms sufficiently to play!'

She brusquely finished the waltz of the *Two Worlds*, and began to sing *The Good-bye*.

> *Ah! good-bye! the days are ended*
> *When I lived so happily by your side!*

Her voice, which rose melodiously ardent, was directed to the corner, across the floor, and intended to reach the heart of the priest below.

And the priest, sitting on the sofa with his walking-stick between his knees, devoured all the tones of her voice—while Senhora Joanneira chatted, describing the pieces of cotton which she had bought to make sheets, how she was going to arrange the room for the newly-wed couple, and the advantages of all living together . . .

'A great happiness for all,' interrupted the canon, painfully rising from his chair. 'And now let us go upstairs, as I don't like this idea of leaving sweethearts alone . . .'

'Ah, you needn't worry about that,' said Senhora Joanneira laughing, 'I have every confidence in him, he is a very honourable fellow.'

Amaro trembled as he mounted the stairs—and as he entered the room Amelia's cheeks, lit up by the candles of the piano, dazzled him. It seemed that the eve of marriage had beautified her face, and that separation had made her more desirable. He approached her, and gravely taking her hand and then that of the clerk, he muttered, without looking at them:

'My congratulations . . . My congratulations . . .'

He turned away and went to talk to the canon who, buried in his armchair, was complaining of feeling weary and calling for the tea.

Amelia's thoughts were far away as her fingers heedlessly ran up and down the keys. Amaro's behaviour confirmed her surmises: what he desired at all costs was to be free of her, the ungrateful fellow! He acted as if nothing had passed between them, the villain! In his cowardice as a priest, his terror of the senhor precentor, of the newspaper, of the arcade, of all—he shook her off from his mind, from his heart, as one shakes off a poisonous insect! Then, to annoy him, she began to whisper tenderly to the clerk; she rubbed against his shoulder, overcome with laughter; she had little secrets with him; she jovially wheedled him into playing a duet with her; afterwards she tickled him and he gave exaggerated little screams—and Senhora Joanneira pettishly contemplated them, while the canon slept, and Father Amaro, abandoned in a corner, like the clerk in other days, turned over the leaves of the old album.

But a sudden loud ring of the door-bell startled everyone: quick steps bounded up the stairs, and stopped in the little parlour. Ruça appeared saying that it was Senhor Father Natario, who didn't wish to come up, but would like to have a word with the senhor canon.

'Strange hours for a message,' muttered the canon dragging himself with difficulty out of the depths of his chair.

Amelia then shut the piano, and Senhora Joanneira, pushing away her stocking, went on tiptoe to listen at the top of the stairs: there was a strong wind blowing, and from the sides of the Square came the sound of the tattoo.

In the end the canon's voice called from the door of the parlour below:

'Amaro?'

'Yes, master?'

'Come here, man. And tell the senhora that she can come as well.'

Senhora Joanneira then went down, very frightened. Amaro thought that in the end Natario had discovered the identity of *A Liberal*.

The little parlour appeared cold and dreary with just the weak light from a candle flickering on the table: and on the wall, in a very dark frame, was an old picture which the canon had given to Senhora Joanneira a short time before, and from which stood out the livid face and prominent forehead of a monk, and the frontal bone of a skull.

Canon Dias was seated at one end of the sofa, thoughtfully taking his pinches of snuff; and Natario, who moved agitatedly round the room, immediately exclaimed:

'Good evening, senhora! Hello, Amaro! I've got some news! I didn't go up as I was sure the clerk would be there, and these things are better between ourselves. I was just telling colleague Dias—I was at Father Saldanha's house. Something new has happened!'

Father Saldanha was the senhor precentor's confidential friend. Father Amaro, now very uneasy, asked:

'Is it anything to do with us?'

Natario solemnly raised his arm on high, and began:

'First: Colleague Brito has been moved to the parish of Amor at the foot of Alcobaça, to the mountains, to the infernal regions.'

'You don't say so!' said Senhora Joanneira.

'The work of *A Liberal*, my dear senhora! Our worthy precentor took a little time to meditate on the *Communication* in *The District*, but in the end he made up his mind! Poor Brito is now cooling his heels up in the mountains.'

'There has always been talk about the wife of the regedor . . .' murmured the good senhora.

'Good God!' interrupted the canon severely. 'Now then, senhora, now then! This isn't a house of gossip! Go on with your story, colleague Natario.'

'Secondly,' continued Natario, 'as I have been saying to colleague Dias—the senhor precentor, in view of the *Communication* and other attacks in the press, is determined to reform the habits of the diocesan clergy (Father Saldanha's words). What he doesn't approve of chiefly are the friendships of senhoras and ecclesiastics . . . What he would like to know is who are these "puppyish priests tempting inexperienced young maidens" . . . In short, the exact words of his excellency were: "I have decided to clean up the carousals in the Augean stables!" What he would like to say, my dear senhora, putting it in plain Portuguese, is that he is going to get busy and change things.'

There was a frightened pause. And Natario, planted in the middle of the little parlour, with his hands deeply buried in his pockets, exclaimed:

'Now what do you think of the latest news, eh?'

The canon got up lazily, and said:

'Listen, friend, between killed and wounded some are bound to escape. And the senhora, instead of sitting there with the face of *Mater Dolorosa*, can order the tea, which is the important thing.'

'I said to Father Saldanha——' began Natario, anxious to prolong the scene.

But the canon interrupted him determinedly:

'Father Saldanha is a humbug! Let us go up to the toast, and remember: silence in front of the young people.'

All were very quiet at the tea. The canon, with brows wrinkled, puffed violently at each mouthful of toast, and Senhora Joanneira, after telling them what a heavy cold Dona Maria of the Assumption had, sat with her head in her hands, feeling in very low spirits. Natario, taking long strides up and down the room, made a little breeze with the flapping of his overcoat.

'And when is this wedding coming off?' he enquired, as he suddenly stopped in front of Amelia and the clerk, who were taking tea by the piano.

'One day soon,' she replied smiling.

Amaro got up slowly, and taking out his watch said in a weary tone:

'It's time I was going to the Rua das Sousas, senhoras.'

But Senhora Joanneira objected:

'Heavens, you are all so glum, one would think that someone had died! Stay and have a game of lotto to cheer yourselves up.'

The canon, however, waking out of his torpor, said severely:

'The senhora is making a mistake, no one is glum. There are no reasons for being unhappy, are there, Senhor Bridegroom-to-be?'

João Eduardo rose, and smiled.

'Oh me, senhor canon, I surely have every reason for being happy.'

'That's obvious,' answered the canon. 'And now may God give you all a good night, and I'm going to play lotto in the valley of the sheets. And Amaro also.'

Amaro approached Amelia and shook her hand, and the three priests silently descended the stairs.

The candle in the little parlour was still flickering and giving out fumes. The canon entered to get his umbrella; and then calling the others he slowly closed the door, and said in an undertone:

'Well, colleagues, I didn't want to frighten the poor senhora, but these affairs of the precentor, this talk . . . It's the devil!'

'We must be very careful, friends,' counselled Natario, holding his hand to the side of his mouth.

'It's serious, it's serious,' murmured Father Amaro sadly.

They were standing in the middle of the room. The wind outside howled; the light of the candle flickered and made the frontal bone of the skull come and go; and upstairs Amelia sang *Chiquita*.

Amaro thought of other happy nights on which he, triumphant and without a care, made the senhoras laugh, and Amelia warbled *Ay little girl*, yes, giving him sweet looks . . .

'I,' said the canon, 'as you know, colleagues, have enough to eat and drink, it doesn't matter so much to me . . . But it is necessary to uphold the honour of our cloth.'

'And without a doubt,' added Natario, 'if there is another article and more talk, the blow will fall.'

'Think of poor Brito,' murmured Amaro, 'cooling his heels up in the mountains!'

Some joke was going on upstairs, as they could hear the clerk's laugh.

Amaro growled with rancour:

'Great merrymaking there above!'

They descended the stairs. On opening the door a gust of wind and fine rain blew in Natario's face:

'Heavens, what a night!' he exclaimed with annoyance.

Only the canon had an umbrella; and opening it slowly he said:
'Well, friends, it's easy to see we are properly in the soup.'

From the lighted window above came the sounds of the accompaniment to *Chiquita*. The canon panted and puffed, firmly grasping his umbrella in the wind; at his side Natario, shrivelled up inside his cloak, ground his teeth, full of spleen; Amaro walked along with head down, shrunken and depressed with defeat; and while the three priests, sheltering under the canon's umbrella, went sploshing along in the pools through the dark streets, the rain, penetrating and sonorous, beat down on them ironically.

Chapter X

SOME DAYS later, those who frequented the apothecary's in the Square were astonished to see Father Natario and Dr Godinho harmoniously conversing together at the door of Guedes, the ironmonger. The tax-gatherer—who was listened to with deference on questions of foreign policy—regarded them attentively from the other side of the glass door of the apothecary's and then declared, in a profound tone, that he wouldn't be more surprised if he saw King Victor Emmanuel and Pius IX walking arm in arm!

On the other hand, the municipal doctor found nothing strange in what he called 'a business friendship'. According to him, the last article in *The Voice of the District*, evidently written by Dr Godinho (it was his incisive style, full of logic, and choked with learning!), plainly showed that the folks of Maia would like to approach the folks of the Misericordia with a view to an understanding. Dr Godinho (as the municipal doctor put it) was making fawning speeches to the civil governor and the diocesan clergy: the concluding phrase of the article was significant: 'We are not the kind of people who haggle with the clergy over the methods they employ in the profitable exercise of their divine mission.'

The truth was (as an obese individual, friend Pimenta, observed) that, if there wasn't yet peace, there were negotiations; for the day before he had seen with his very eyes (which would one day be eaten by worms) Father Natario leaving the office of *The Voice of the District* very early in the morning!

'Oh, friend Pimenta,' they cried, 'that's a fabrication.'

Friend Pimenta stood up majestically, gravely heaved up his breeches by the band, and prepared to reply indignantly, when the tax-gatherer came to his support:

'No, no, friend Pimenta is right. The truth is that the other day I saw that rascal Agostinho cringing like a cur before Father Natario. And Natario has some game up his sleeve, that's certain! I like to observe people . . . Then, senhores, Natario, who never appears here in the arcade, now comes every day to poke his nose into the shops. Then there is his great friendship with Father Silverio. Notice that they are both sure to be in the Square when the Angelus rings . . . It is something to do with Dr Godinho and Co. Father Silverio is Godinho's wife's confessor . . . One thing fits into another!'

As a matter of fact, the new friendship between Father Natario and Father Silverio was very much the cause of comment. Five years earlier a scandalous argument had taken place between the two clergymen in the Cathedral sacristy: Natario ran at Father Silverio with his umbrella raised, at which the good Canon Sarmento, bathed in tears, pulled him back by the cassock, crying out: 'Oh, brother, this could be the ruin of our religion!' Since then Natario and Silverio hadn't spoken —much to the disgust of Silverio, a good-natured individual of dropsical obesity, who, according to his women penitents, was all love and forgiveness. But Natario, small and dry, was tenacious in his rancour. When the senhor precentor, Valladares, began to administer the bishopric, he called them both, and after eloquently reminding them of the necessity of maintaining peace in the Church, and bidding them remember the touching example of Castor and Pollux, he pushed Natario with gentle severity into the arms of Father Silverio—who held him for a moment buried in the vastness of his bosom and stomach, agitatedly murmuring:

'We are all brothers, we are all brothers!'

But Natario, whose nature, as hard and coarse as doubled cardboard, never lost the marks of an injury, maintained a surly tone with Father Silverio: when he met him in the Cathedral or in the street, he edged close to him and brusquely turned his head, barely muttering: 'At your orders, Senhor Father Silverio.'

Two weeks later, on a rainy night, Natario paid an unexpected visit to Father Silverio under the pretext that he had got caught in a sudden shower of rain, and was coming in for a moment to shelter himself.

'And also,' he added, 'to ask you, brother, for a recipe for earache, from which one of my nieces, the poor little thing, is going mad!'

The good Silverio, no doubt forgetting that only that very morning he had seen Natario's two nieces safe and sound as two sparrows, hurried to write the recipe, delighted to be able to make use of his beloved study of home-made remedies, and said, bathed in smiles: 'What a joy, brother, to see you here in one's own house again!'

The reconciliation was so public that the son-in-law of the Baron of Via Clara, a Bachelor of Arts with great poetical gifts, dedicated to it one of his satires, which he entitled *Stings*, written by hand and passed from house to house, very much enjoyed and very much dreaded: he called this composition (having surely in mind the forms of the two clergymen) *Famous Reconciliation between the Monkey and the Whale!* In fact, one could now frequently see the small figure of Natario gesticulating and jumping at the side of the enormous, easy-going bulk of Silverio.

One morning, the employees of the Administration of Justice (which was then in the Cathedral Square) were very entertained to observe the two priests trotting up and down the terrace in the early May morning sun. The senhor administrator—who passed his office hours standing at the window of his room, wooing with his binoculars the wife of Telles the tailor—suddenly gave vent to loud chuckles of laughter; the clerk Borges ran immediately to the veranda with his pen in his hand to see what was amusing his chief, and very entertained, cackled loudly, and hurriedly called Arthur Couceiro, who was copying, in order to practise it on the guitar, a song from *Grinalda*. The manuscript-copyist Pires, severe and dignified, approached, pulling his little silk cap down over his ear with horror at the danger of a draught of air; and in a group, their eyes lit up with enjoyment, they observed the two priests, who had stopped at the corner of the Cathedral.

Natario, who appeared excited, was evidently trying to persuade Father Silverio to do something for him; planted on tiptoe in front of him, he was frantically waving his lean hands. Then, he suddenly took hold of Silverio's arm, pulled him along the whole length of the flagged terrace, stopped at the end, leaned back, and made a grand gesture of desolation, as if he were attesting the possible perdition of himself, of the Cathedral at his side, of the town, of the entire universe; the good Silverio, his eyes widely dilated, appeared terrified. They resumed their walk. But Natario began to provoke his companion, to pull him backwards brusquely; he thrust his long finger in Silverio's vast stomach, stamping furiously on the shining flagstones; and suddenly, dropping his hands helplessly by his side, he manifested despair. Then the good Silverio spoke a minute with his hand spread out on his chest; immediately Natario's bilious face lit up; he jumped, then jubilantly patted his colleague on the shoulder, and the two priests, very close together and laughing softly, entered the Cathedral.

'What a feast for sore eyes! What a pair of playboys!' said the clerk Borges, who hated the cassock.

'That's all to do with the newspaper,' said Arthur Couceiro, as he resumed his lyrical study: 'Natario will never rest until he has found out who wrote the *Communication*, he said so in Senhora Joanneira's house. And now this affair with Silverio proves that I'm right, as he is Godinho's wife's confessor.'

'What a dirty crowd!' muttered Borges with disgust. And he slowly continued his pitiful task, arranging the dispatch of a prisoner to Alcobaça. The unfortunate man was waiting at the end of the room, sitting on a bench between two soldiers, handcuffed, crushed by brutal treatment, his face plainly showing his hunger.

A few days afterwards the ceremony of the Office for the Dead, the body being present, was held in the Cathedral for the rich landowner Moraes, who had died of an aneurism. His wife (no doubt in penance for her disorderly attachments to lieutenants of infantry) was now giving him, as was said, 'royal funeral obsequies'. Amaro, after taking off his vestments in the sacristy, was writing up unpaid dues by the light of an old tin lamp, when the oaken door creaked, and the excited voice of Natario called out:

'Oh, Amaro, you here?'

'What's the matter?'

Father Natario shut the door, and throwing up his hands in the air, said:

'Great news, it is the clerk!'

'What clerk?'

'João Eduardo! It's he! He is *A Liberal*! It was he who wrote the *Communication*!'

'You don't say so!' said Amaro astonished.

'I have proofs, my friend! I saw the original, written in his handwriting. I saw it with my own eyes! Five sheets of paper!'

Amaro stared at Natario, his eyes dilated.

'It was a lot of trouble!' exclaimed Natario. 'But now I know all! Five sheets of paper! And he'd like to write another! Senhor João Eduardo! Our dear friend, Senhor João Eduardo!'

'Are you sure of this?'

'I'm certain. I told you what I saw, man!'

'And how did you find out, Natario?'

Natario leaned forwards, with his head buried in his shoulders, and dragged out his words:

'Ah, brother, that is asking me . . . the hows and the whys . . . you understand . . . *sigillus magnus*!'

He then added in a voice of triumph, as he took great strides up and down the sacristy:

'But that's nothing! Senhor Eduardo, whom we all saw there in Senhora Joanneira's house and thought such a good boy, is a practised villain. He is an intimate friend of Agostinho, that rascal of *The Voice of the District*. He is there in the office with him till all hours of the night —orgies, wine, women . . . And he boasts of being an atheist. He hasn't been to confession for six years—he calls us the canonical rabble—he is a republican . . . A wild beast, my dear senhor, a wild beast!'

Amaro, as he listened to Natario, fumbled with trembling hands amongst the papers in the drawer of the writing-desk.

'And now?' he asked.

'Now!' exclaimed Natario. 'Now is the time to smash him!'

Amaro shut the drawer, and very nervous, wiping his dry lips with his handkerchief, said:

'That type of fellow, that type of fellow! And the poor girl, God help her—she is going to marry a man like that—a hopeless scoundrel!'

The two priests now looked fixedly at one another. In the silence the old sacristy clock ticked sadly. Natario put his hand in his breeches pocket and drew out his snuff-box, then with a pinch between his fingers he fixed his eyes on Amaro, and said with a cold smile:

'Break up the marriage, eh?'

'My dear colleague, it is a question of conscience—for me it is a duty! One can't let the poor girl marry a scamp, a freemason, an atheist . . .'

'You're quite right, quite right!' said Amaro.

'Things are happening, eh?' said Natario, as he snuffed contentedly.

But the sacristan entered; it was time to shut the Cathedral; he came to ask his masters if they intended to remain long.

'An instant, Senhor Domigos.' While the sacristan drew the great iron bolts of the interior door of the yard, the two priests whispered close together.

'You can deal with Senhora Joanneira,' said Natario. 'No, listen, it is better for Dias to speak to her; yes, Dias is the one who must speak to Senhora Joanneira. Let us make things quite sure. You talk to the little one and tell her simply to put him out of the house!' Then in Amaro's ear: 'Tell the girl that he is living with a prostitute!'

'Man!' said Amaro recoiling: 'I don't know if that is true!'

'It must be true. He is capable of anything. And after all it is a means of saving the girl . . .'

They walked down the Cathedral behind the sacristan, who jingled his bunch of keys as he loudly cleared his throat.

In one of the chapels hung the black tapestry curtains, tied with silver cords; in the centre, between four big candlestands containing candles with great thick wicks, was the tomb set up in honour of the dead man, with a large velvet fringed cloth covering the coffin of Moraes, and falling down at the sides in folds; at the head was a big wreath of immortelles; and at the end, hanging from an enormous bow of scarlet ribbon, was his habit of the Knights of Christ.

Father Natario then stopped, and taking Amaro's arm, said with a satisfied air:

'And after that, my dear friend, I have something else prepared for that *cavalheiro*.'

'What is it?'

'Take away his means of livelihood!'

'Take away his means of livelihood?'

'The scamp was to be employed in the Governor's office, chief clerk, eh? Then I'm going to smash up that arrangement! And Nunes Ferral, who is my friend, a man with the right ideas, will throw him out of his office, now we know who wrote the *Communication*!'

Amaro was horrified at this spiteful intriguing:

'For the love of God, Natario, this will be the ruin of the boy . . .'

'Until I see him in these very streets begging for a crust of bread, I'll not stop, Father Amaro, no, I'll not stop!'

'Oh, Natario! oh, brother! that shows a want of charity—that would be unworthy of a Christian . . . You say that here where God is listening to us . . .'

'Don't worry about that, my dear friend. It is thus one serves God, not by muttering Our Fathers. For the impious there is no charity! The Inquisition attacked them with fire, it doesn't seem to me a bad idea to attack them with hunger. All is permitted to him who serves a holy cause. Now don't you interfere with me!'

They were on the way out when Natario noticed the coffin, and pointing to it with his umbrella enquired:

'Who is there?'

'Moraes,' said Amaro.

'That fat fellow all pitted with smallpox?'

'Yes.'

'A proper beast.'

And after a silence he added:

'The Office for the Dead was for Moraes. I didn't know that, I've been so occupied with my campaign. . . . He leaves a rich widow. She's generous and fond of giving presents. Silverio is her confessor, eh? He has all the most profitable penitents of Leiria, that elephant!'

They went out. Carlos the apothecary's was shut, the sky was very dark. Natario stopped in the Square:

'To sum up: Dias will speak to Senhora Joanneira, and you to the little one. I will come to an understanding with the civil governor and Nunes Ferral. You take charge of the wedding and I'll take charge of the employment!' And patting the paroco jovially on the shoulder: 'To put it nicely, we'll attack him through his heart and through his stomach! Good-bye now, the little ones are holding up supper for me. Rosa, the poor little thing, has a dreadful cold. She is so weak, that child, that I worry a great deal about her—I'm sometimes so discouraged about her that I can't sleep. But what can I do? That is the worst of having too much heart. Till tomorrow, Amaro.'

'Till tomorrow, Natario.'

The two priests separated, just as the Cathedral clock struck nine.

Amaro arrived home still trembling a little, but quite decided and very happy: he had a delightful task to perform! He walked gravely round the room, and in order to convince himself definitely of the justice of his undertaking, he cried aloud: 'It's my duty! It's my duty!'

As a Christian, as a priest, as a friend of Senhora Joanneira's, his duty was to get hold of Amelia and simply, dispassionately, without self-interest, tell her that it was João Eduardo, her sweetheart, who had written the *Communication*.

It was he! He defamed the intimates of the house, men of learning and of dignity; he discredited her; he passed whole nights in debauchery in that pigsty of Agostinho's; he whispered insults against the clergy; he prided himself on having no religion; he hadn't been to confession for six years! As Natario said, he was a wild beast! Poor little girl! No, no, she couldn't marry a man who would prevent her from leading the life of a good Catholic, who would mock and deride her beliefs! He would forbid her to pray, to fast, to take moral direction from her confessor, and, as the Holy Father St Chrysostom said, 'He would harden her soul for the fire of hell!' He, Amaro, wasn't her father, nor her teacher, but he was her priest, her spiritual director: if he didn't use his advice and the influence of her mother and her mother's friends to save her from that godless destiny, he would be like a man who had charge of his father's sheep and basely opened the gate to the wolf! No, Ameliazinha must not marry that atheist!

And his heart beat wildly as new thoughts and hopes flowed through his being. No, the other wouldn't have her! When he came to take legal possession of that waist, those breasts, those eyes, all of Ameliazinha—he, the priest, was there to call out to him in a loud voice: 'Get behind, you villain! What is here is for God!'

And then he would take great care to guide the girl to salvation! When the *Communication* was forgotten the senhor precentor would rest easy, and in a short time he could return without fear to the Rua da Misericordia, to begin anew those delicious evenings, to take possession of that soul again and form it for paradise. . . .

And that, Jesus! wasn't an intrigue to separate her from her sweetheart: his motives (he said this aloud, in order to convince himself better) were very honest, very pure: it was a holy work to save her from the devil: he didn't want her for himself, he wanted her for God! Incidentally, yes, his interests as a lover coincided with his duty as a priest. But if she were squint-eyed, ugly and a fool, he would go just the same to the Rua da Misericordia, in the service of heaven, to tear the mask from Senhor João Eduardo, that defamer and atheist!

And comforted by these arguments he lay tranquilly down to sleep.

That same night João Eduardo, as he reached the Square on his way to Senhora Joanneira's house, was astonished to see the Blessed Sacrament in procession appear in the street, alongside the Cathedral.

And it was making for the house of the senhoras! From among the old women with the hooded cloaks the great wax candles showed up the long tunics of scarlet cloth; from under the canopy shone the gold braid of the paroco's stole; a little bell was ringing in front, and lights appeared in the windows; and in the dark night the Cathedral bell clanged continuously.

João Eduardo ran along terrified; and eventually learned that it was the Extreme Unction for the paralytic.

On the stairs they had placed a paraffin-oil lamp on a chair. The servers leant the tall poles of the canopy against the street wall, and the paroco entered. João Eduardo, very nervous, also ascended the stairs: as he went up he began to think that the death of the paralytic and the mourning would retard his wedding; he was annoyed at the presence of the paroco and at the influence which he acquired at that moment; and it was almost with annoyance that he enquired of Ruça in the little parlour:

'Well, and how did this happen?'

'The poor thing got worse this afternoon, the senhor doctor saw her and said that the end was near, and the senhora sent for the sacraments.'

João Eduardo then decided that as an act of delicacy he would attend the ceremony.

The old lady's room was next to the kitchen, and at that moment it was filled with a mournful solemnity.

On top of the table, which was covered with a frilled cloth, was a plate with five little balls of cotton wool, placed between two wax candles. The head of the paralytic, all white, and her face, the colour of wax, could hardly be distinguished from the linen of the bolster-cover; her eyes were stupidly dilated; with a slow gesture she continuously fumbled with the folds of the embroidered sheet.

Senhora Joanneira and Amelia knelt in prayer at the foot of the bed; Dona Maria of the Assumption (who had entered accidentally, on her return from her farm) remained at the door of the room, terrified, crouching on her heels and murmuring Hail Marys. João Eduardo noiselessly knelt down at her side.

Father Amaro, leaning over till he almost touched the ear of the paralytic, exhorted her to abandon herself to the divine mercy; but seeing that she didn't understand him, he dropped on his knees and rapidly recited the *Misereatur*; and in the silence, his voice, raised louder as he pronounced the more piercing Latin syllables, gave a feeling of death and burial that drew pity and made the two senhoras weep. Then he got up, and dipping his finger in the holy oils, murmured the ritual expressions of the penitent as he anointed the eyes, the bosom, the mouth, the hands—which for the last ten years had only moved to reach the spittoon—and the soles of the feet which for the same period had only been used to seek the heat of the earthen water-bottle. And after burning the balls of cotton-wool, saturated with oil, he knelt down, and remained motionless with his eyes fixed on his breviary.

João Eduardo returned on tiptoe to the parlour, and sat on the piano stool: it was certain that Amelia would now not play the piano for four or five weeks to come . . . A great melancholy came over him as he saw this brusque interruption in the sweet progress of his love caused by death and its ceremonies.

Dona Maria then entered, very upset by the scene. She was followed by Amelia, whose eyes were red from crying. 'Oh! what a good thing João Eduardo is here,' said the old lady. 'If you would like to do me the favour of accompanying me to my house—I'm all trembling—I wasn't prepared for this, and may God pardon me, but I can't bear to see people in agony. She, poor thing, will pass out like a little bird . . . She has no sins. . . . Listen, we'll go by the Square as it's nearer. And excuse me— you, child, excuse me, but I can't remain . . . But it is better for her. Now listen, I feel I'm going to faint . . .'

It was necessary for Amelia to take her downstairs to her mother's room, to comfort her with a glass of the old *geropiga*.

'Ameliazinha,' João Eduardo then said, 'if I can do anything for you——'

'No, thank you. She will go any minute, the poor thing.'

'Don't forget, girl,' recommended Dona Maria of the Assumption, as she went down the stairs, 'to put the two blessed candles at the head of the bed. It gives much relief in the death agony. And if the death rattle continues put two others, unlit, in the form of a cross. Good-night . . . Ah, how bad I feel!'

At the door, they no sooner caught sight of the canopy and the man with the candlestands, than she grasped João Eduardo's arm, and leaned against him in terror—perhaps due a little to the tenderness with which the *geropiga* always filled her.

Amaro promised to return later in order to keep the women company as a friend in their trouble. And the canon, who arrived when the procession with the canopy turned the corner by the Cathedral, informed of the senhor paroco's delicate offer, declared that as he saw that colleague Amaro intended to pass the night th·re, he would go home and rest his poor body. God could bear him witness that these upsets had a bad effect on his health. 'And I'm sure the senhora wouldn't like to see me catching some disease, and dying from it, like the poor paralytic.'

'Good God, senhor canon!' exclaimed Senhora Joanneira, 'don't talk like that!' And she burst out crying, very shaken at the thought of such things happening.

'Well then, good-night,' said the canon, 'and don't fret too much. As the poor creature had no joy in life and as she has no sins she hasn't any fear of facing God. Considering all sides of the matter, senhora, it is all for the best! Well, good-bye now, I'm not feeling too well...'

Senhora Joanneira also didn't feel well. The shock, just after she had eaten, had given her a migraine, and when Amaro returned at eleven Amelia, who went to open the door, said as they went up to the dining-room:

'Oh, senhor paroco, excuse us... Mamma, poor thing, has a migraine. She was almost blind with it. She lay down after taking a sedative, and is sleeping.'

'Ah! let her sleep!'

They entered the paralytic's room. She had her head turned towards the wall: from her two open lips came a weak continuous moan. On the table there was now a very large blessed candle filling the room with unpleasant fumes and giving out a dreary light: in a corner Ruça, full of fear, following the instructions of Senhora Joanneira, recited the rosary.

'The senhor doctor,' said Amelia in a whisper, 'said she will die without knowing it. He said she will moan and moan, and then suddenly pass out like a little bird.'

'That all may come to pass exactly as God wills,' murmured Father Amaro gravely.

They returned to the dining-room. The whole house was silent: outside a strong wind was blowing. It was the first time for many weeks that they had found themselves alone together. Amaro, very embarrassed, went over near the window; Amelia stood against the cupboard.

'The night is going to be wet,' said the paroco.

'Yes, and it's cold,' said she, drawing her shawl more tightly round her. 'I have been so frightened.'

'Have you never seen anyone die before?'

133

'Never.'

They remained silent: he, motionless at the side of the window, she, with her back against the cupboard and her eyes cast down.

'Yes, it is cold,' said Amaro, his voice altered from the agitation that her presence at that hour of the night gave him.

'The brazier in the kitchen is alight,' said Amelia. 'It is better for us to go in there.'

'Yes, it's better.'

They entered the kitchen. Amelia carried the tin lamp, and Amaro as he poked the pieces of red charcoal, said:

'It is a long time since I've been here in the kitchen. You still have the vases with the shrubs outside the window?'

'Yes, and a pot of carnations.'

They sat down on low chairs beside the brazier. Amelia, leaning over the fire, felt the eyes of Father Amaro silently devouring her. He was surely going to speak! His hands were trembling; he didn't dare to move, to lift his eyelashes for fear that he would burst into tears. Be his words sweet or bitter, he must begin . . .

They came in the end and were very grave.

'Amelia, I didn't expect that I would be able to speak to you as we are, alone. But it happens so. It is certainly the will of God! And then, your manner completely changed towards me . . .'

She turned round suddenly, her face scarlet, her little lips trembling, and exclaimed almost crying:

'But you well know why!'

'Yes. If it wasn't for that infamous *Communication* and its calumnies, nothing would have happened, and our friendship would have gone on the same, and all would have been well. It is just with regard to this that I wish to talk to you.'

He drew his chair nearer to her, and very suavely, very calmly, he said:

'Do you remember that article, in which all the friends of the house were insulted?—in which I was bitterly dragged through the mud?—in which you and your honour were attacked? You remember it, don't you? Do you know who wrote it?'

'Who?' asked Amelia, very surprised.

'Senhor João Eduardo!' said the paroco very tranquilly, crossing his arms over his chest.

'It couldn't be!'

She had got up from her chair, and Amaro, laying his hand very gently on her skirt, forced her back. His voice continued patient and suave:

134

'Listen. Keep seated. It was he who wrote it. Yesterday I knew all. Father Natario saw the original in his writing. It was he who discovered it. Certainly by just means—because it was the will of God that the truth should come to light. Now listen. You don't know this man.' Then, speaking in a whisper, he recounted what Natario had said of João Eduardo: his nights with Agostinho, his insults against the clergy, his irreligion. . . .

'Ask him if he has been to confession for the last six years, and get him to show you his attendance tickets!'

She murmured, with her hands fallen in her lap:

'Jesus . . . Jesus . . .'

'I then decided that as a friend of the house, as a priest, as a Christian, as your friend, Menina Amelia—because believe me, I like you . . . In fine, I considered it my duty to warn you! If I were your brother, I would simply say: Amelia, order this man out of the house! Unhappily, I'm not. But I come, because of my devotion to your soul, to say to you: the man whom you would like to marry took advantage of your good faith and that of your mother; he came here, yes, child, with the appearance of a good, straight fellow, and at heart he is . . .'

He rose from his chair, and as if boiling with unrestrainable indignation:

'Menina Amelia, he is the man who wrote the *Communication*: who was the cause of poor Father Brito being sent to the mountains of Alcobaça! who called me a seducer! who called Senhor Canon Dias a debaucher! debaucher! who threw poisonous suspicion on the relations between him and your mamma! who, in plain Portuguese, accused you of being willing to let yourself be seduced! Tell me, do you still want to marry this man?'

She remained quiet, with her eyes glued to the fire, and two tears running silently down her cheeks.

Amaro walked excitedly up and down the kitchen; then turning round and standing in front of her, he said in a very soft voice and with very friendly gestures:

'But let us suppose that he wasn't the author of the *Communication*, that he didn't insult, in flaming colours, your mamma, the senhor canon, your friends, there still remains his impiety! Think of your future if you marry him! You will have to give in to the fellow on all sides, abandon your devotions, break off your relations with your mamma's friends, never put your foot in the church, give scandal to all honest people—or else put yourself in opposition to him, and then your home will be a hell on earth. There will be arguments about all questions! To fast on Friday, to go to the exposition of the Blessed Sacrament, Mass on

Sunday, all will bring difficulty. . . . And if you want to go to confession, what discord! A horror! Then you must subject yourself to listen to him mocking the mysteries of your faith! I still remember, on the first night I was here, with what disrespect he spoke of the saint of Arregassa. I remember still another night when Father Natario spoke here of the sufferings of our Holy Father Pope Pius IX, who would have been a prisoner if the Liberals had entered Rome. How mockingly he laughed, saying that these were exaggerations! As if it wasn't absolutely certain that if the Liberals had their way, we would see the head of the Church, the Vicar of Christ, sleeping in a dungeon on a heap of straw! These are his opinions, which he proclaims on all sides. Father Natario says that he and Agostinho were in the café at the foot of Terreiro stating that Baptism was just a superstition because each one must choose the religion which he likes, and not be forced from childhood to be a Christian! Eh, what do you think of it? I speak to you as your friend . . . Rather than see your soul lost by being joined to this man, I would see you dead! If you marry him, you lose forever the grace of God!'

Amelia lifted up her hands to her temples, and falling back in the chair, murmured, very distressed:

'Oh, my God, my God!'

Amaro then sat at her side, almost touching her dress with his knee, and putting a good-natured fatherly tone into his voice, he continued:

'And then, my child, you don't think that a man like that will have a good heart, will appreciate your virtue, love you as a Christian husband? "He who has no religion has no morality. He who doesn't believe doesn't love," said one of our Holy Fathers. After he has passed the first glow of passion, he will begin to be hard with you, ill-humoured, he will again seek the company of Agostinho and the street women, and probably ill-treat you . . . And what a constant fear for you. Those who do not respect religion have no scruples: they lie, they rob, they calumniate. Look at the *Communication*. He came here to take the senhor canon's hand in friendship, and then went to the newspaper to describe him as debaucher! What remorse you would have later at the hour of death! Everything's all right when one is healthy and young; but when your last hour comes, when you are in your last agony, as that poor creature is in the next room, when the death rattle is in your throat, what terror you will feel at the thought of appearing before Jesus Christ, after having lived in sin with this man! Who knows but that he will refuse to let you have Extreme Unction! To die without the sacraments, to die as an animal . . .'

'For the love of God! For the love of God, senhor paroco!' exclaimed Amelia, breaking into a nervous fit of crying.

'Don't cry,' he said, softly taking her hands between his two trembling ones. 'Listen, open your heart to me. Come, be calm, all will come right in the end. The banns are not published. Tell him that you don't want to marry him, that you know all, that you hate him . . .'

He caught Amelia's hand and slowly stroked and squeezed it. Then suddenly with a voice full of eagerness:

'You are not very fond of him, isn't that so?'

She replied very softly, with her head fallen on her chest:

'No.'

'Then that's all right!' he cried excitedly. 'Now tell me, do you love somebody else?'

She remained silent, with her bosom strongly palpitating, and eyes wide open staring at the fire.

'Do you love somebody? Tell me, tell me!'

He passed his hand round her shoulder, and gently drew her to him. Her hands lay listless in her lap; without moving her body she turned towards him, her eyes resplendent under a cloud of tears; then she slowly parted her lips, pale and weak. He stretched out his trembling lips to meet hers—and they remained motionless, their mouths joined in a kiss, very long, very deep, teeth against teeth.

'Senhora! Senhora!' suddenly came the terrified voice of Ruça from inside.

Amaro jumped up and ran to the paralytic's room. Amelia was trembling so much that she had to lean for a minute against the door of the kitchen, her legs sagging and her hand on her heart. She recovered herself, and went down to call her mother. When they entered the old woman's room, Amaro was on his knees, with his face over the bed, praying; the two senhoras rocked on their knees on the floor; a quickening respiration shook the chest and sides of the paralytic; in proportion as the breath became shorter the paroco precipitated his prayers. Suddenly the agonizing sound ceased; he got up; the old woman was motionless, her eyes protruding and dull. She had expired.

Father Amaro then led the senhoras to the parlour; and there Senhora Joanneira, cured of her migraine by the shock, gave vent to her grief in attacks of weeping, calling to mind the time when her poor sister was young, and how pretty she was! and what a good marriage she was going to make with the Morgado of Vigareira!

'And what a generous nature she had, senhor paroco! A saint! And when Amelia was born, and I was so ill, she never left my side, night or day! And for fun—there was no one like her . . . Ah, God of my soul, God of my soul!'

Amelia, leaning against the window, gazed dazedly at the black night.

The door bell rang. Amaro went down with a candle in his hand. It was João Eduardo, who on seeing the paroco in the house at that hour of the night became petrified there at the open door; in the end he muttered:

'I came to know if there is any news . . .'

'The poor senhora expired just now.'

'Ah!'

The two men looked fixedly at one another for a minute.

'If there is anything I can do——' said João Eduardo.

'No, thank you. The senhoras are going to bed.'

João Eduardo became pale with choler at Amaro's proprietary manner. He hesitated for a moment more, but seeing the paroco sheltering the light from the wind with his hand, he said:

'Well, good-night.'

'Good-night.'

Father Amaro went up the stairs; and then saw the two senhoras to Senhora Joanneira's room (since, full of terror, they were going to keep each other company there). He returned to the room with the corpse, trimmed the wick of the candle on the table, made himself comfortable in a chair, and began to read his breviary.

Later, when all the house was silent, the paroco, feeling that sleep was coming over him, went to the dining-room and comforted himself with a glass of port which he found in the cupboard; and he was enjoying the flavour of his cigarette, when he heard heavy steps comng and going under the window. As the night was dark he couldn't distinguish the promenader. It was João Eduardo walking round the house, furious.

Chapter XI

EARLY THE next morning Dona Josepha, who had just returned home from Mass, was very surprised when she heard the servant, who was washing the stairs, call up from below:

'Senhor Father Amaro is here, Senhora Dona Josepha!'

Lately the paroco very seldom came to the canon's house; and Dona Josepha, feeling honoured by the visit, and already curious, called out:

'Come on up, we don't stand on ceremony with you! You are like one of the family. Come on up!'

She was in the dining-room, arranging little blocks of jam on a tray. She was dressed in a black woollen dress slit at the sides and arched out by one sole crinoline round the ankles; this morning she had on blue glasses; she went to the head of the stairs, dragging her hideous felt slippers, while below the black kerchief falling down over her forehead, she prepared an agreeable air for the senhor paroco.

'What a sight for sore eyes,' she exclaimed. 'Just a few minutes ago I came in from the first Mass. Today I went to the chapel of Our Lady of the Rosary—Father Vincent said it. Ah! and what great grace I derived from the Mass today, senhor paroco. Sit down. No, not there as there is a draught from the door. And the poor paralytic has passed away . . . Tell me all about it, senhor paroco.'

The paroco had to describe the death agony of the paralytic; Senhora Joanneira's grief; how after death the old lady's face seemed to jeer; what the senhoras had decided to do with regard to the funeral . . .

'Between ourselves, Dona Josepha, it is a great relief for Senhora Joanneira.' And suddenly, leaning out on the edge of the chair and resting his hands on his knees: 'And what do you think of Senhor João Eduardo? Have you heard? It was he who wrote the article!'

'Ah! don't talk about that, senhor paroco!' the old lady cried as she put her hands up to her head. 'It has almost made me ill!'

'So you already know?'

'Yes, I know all, senhor paroco! Senhor Father Natario had the kindness to come here yesterday and tell me everything! Ah, what a scoundrel! Ah, he is a lost soul!'

'And do you know that he is an intimate friend of Agostinho, that they have drinking parties in the printing-office till the early hours of the morning, that they go into the Terreiro billiard saloon and scoff at religion . . .'

'For God's sake don't tell me that, senhor paroco, don't tell me, don't tell me! Yesterday when Senhor Father Natario was here I had scruples at listening to so much sin. I feel very much obliged to him, as immediately he knew he came to tell me—it was very delicate of him. And listen, senhor paroco, to me the clerk always appeared that type of man. I never said so! That's what I'm like, I never like to stick my nose into other people's business—but I had a feeling inside me. He went to Mass and kept the fasts; but I was always suspicious that that was to deceive Senhora Joanneira and the little one. Now you see I was right! As far as I was concerned he never appealed to me! Never, senhor paroco!' And suddenly, with her little eyes alight with perverse delight: 'And now, of course, the wedding won't take place?'

Father Amaro sat back in his chair and said very slowly:

'My dear senhora, it is very evident that a girl of good principles cannot marry a freemason, who hasn't been to confession for six years!'

'Heavens, senhor paroco! I'd rather see her dead! It is necessary to tell the girl all.'

Father Amaro interrupted her, quickly pulling his chair up beside hers: 'It was just for that that I came to see you, my dear senhora. I spoke to the little one yesterday evening. But you understand, it was in the middle of all that trouble, with the poor senhora expiring at our side, so I couldn't insist. But I said what I had to say, I counselled her in the best way I could and pointed out that she would lose her soul, have a life of misery, etc. I did what I could, my dear senhora, as a friend of the family and as her priest. And as it was my duty (though it was very hard for me to do it, really hard) I reminded her that as a Christian and as a woman it was a moral obligation on her part to break off her engagement with the clerk.'

'And she?'

Father Amaro's face expressed dissatisfaction.

'She said neither yes nor no. She pouted and sobbed. It is true that she was very upset on account of the death in the house. That the girl is not dying of love for him is clear; but she wants to marry, she is afraid that her mother will die and that she will be left alone. You know what girls are! I could see that my words had an effect on her. But after all, I thought it was better that you should talk to her. You, senhora, are a friend of the family, and her godmother. You have known her since she was a child—I'm sure that you have remembered her well in your will—all these are considerations.'

'Ah, leave that to me, senhor paroco!' exclaimed the excellent senhora, 'I'll show her the line she must take.'

'What the girl wants is someone to direct her. Between ourselves, she wants a different confessor. Father Silverio is her confessor, but without wishing to say anything bad about him, the poor man, I must say he is not of much use. He is very charitable, very virtuous; but he hasn't what one might call ability. For him confession is just a dry impersonal affair. He puts questions in doctrine, and afterwards makes the examination of conscience by the Commandments of God. Now just think of that, senhora! It's obvious that the girl doesn't steal, nor kill, nor covet her neighbour's wife! She doesn't get the best out of that type of confession; what she requires is a confessor who is firm with her, who will say to her: 'This way, girl!'—and will allow no arguments. She is weak of spirit; and like the majority of women, she doesn't know how to manage her life; for that reason she requires a confessor who will govern her with a rod of iron, whom she will obey, to whom she will tell all, of whom she will be afraid . . . This is what her confessor must be like.

'You, senhor paroco, are just that person.'

Amaro smiled modestly:

'I won't say that I'm not. I am a friend of her mother. I think she is a good girl and worthy of the grace of God. I always give her all the best advice that I can, on all her conduct. But you, senhora, will understand, there are things which one cannot talk about in the parlour, with so many people about. One can only speak at one's ease in the confessional. That is just what I am wanting, the opportunity to speak with her alone. But I can't go and say to her: "You must now come to confession to me!" I am very scrupulous in these matters.'

'But I must tell her, senhor paroco. Ah, I must tell her!'

'Now that would be a great favour. You would be conferring a great benefit on her soul! Because if the girl gives me the direction of her mind we can be sure that all her difficulties will end, and she will walk in the path of grace . . . And when do you intend to talk to her, Dona Josepha?'

Dona Josepha (who thought it would be a sin to delay the matter) decided to speak that same night.

'I don't think that's possible, Dona Josepha. There will be a wake tonight. Naturally the clerk will be there——'

'Heavens, senhor paroco! Then my friends and I will have to pass the night under the same roof as a heretic?'

'It must be so. After all the boy is still considered a friend of the family. We know, Dona Josepha, that you, Dona Maria, and the Gansosos are people of the highest virtue—but we mustn't be proud of our virtues. If we are, we run the risk of losing all their fruits. It is an act of humility which is pleasing to God, to mix sometimes with evil-doers; as when a great landowner stands side by side with a tiller of the soil. . . . And as we might say: I am your superior in virtue, but in comparison with what I should be in order to enter into glory, who knows if I am not as great a sinner as you. . . . And this humiliation of our spirit is the greatest gift we can offer to Jesus . . .'

Dona Josepha listened to him with childish attention, and then said admiringly: 'Ah, senhor paroco, one gains virtue just by listening to you!'

Amaro bowed:

'God, in His bounty, sometimes inspires me with the right words. Well, my dear senhora, I don't wish to trouble you any further. We understand one another. You, senhora, will speak to the little one tomorrow; and if, as I believe possible, she consents to listen to my counsels, bring her to the Cathedral at eight o'clock on Saturday. And speak firmly to her, Dona Josepha!'

'Leave that to me, senhor paroco. Now wouldn't you like to try my jam?'

'Yes, I will try it,' said Amaro, digging his teeth with dignity into a block.

'This was made with Dona Maria's quinces. It always turns out better than the Gansosos'.'

'Well, good-bye, Dona Josepha. Ah, I forgot, what does our canon think of this affair of the clerk?'

'My brother——?'

At this instant there was a furious ring at the door-bell below.

'This must be he,' said Dona Josepha. 'And he is in a temper!'

He came, as a matter of fact, from his farm, furious with the care-taker, the regedor, the governor, and the perversity of mankind in general. He had been robbed of some onions; and suffocating with rage, he relieved himself by repeating with enjoyment the name of the Evil One.

'Heavens, brother, some calamity will befall you!' said Dona Josepha, shocked.

'Listen, sister, leave these scruples for Lent! I say to the devil with them, and I repeat it, to the devil with them! I told the caretaker that if he sees anyone in the farm he is to load his gun and fire on them!'

'There is a great want of respect for property,' said Amaro.

'There is a want of respect for all things,' exclaimed the canon. 'They were young onions which would do one good just to look at them! Then, senhores, there you are! This is what I call a sacrilege—a daring sacrilege!' he added with conviction; as the robbery of an onion, the onion of a canon, appeared to him a grave act of impiety, and as serious as the robbery of the sacred vessels of the Cathedral.

'There is a want of the fear of God, a lack of religion!' observed Dona Josepha.

'What are you talking about with your lack of religion!' he replied exasperated. 'A lack of police, that's what it is!' Then turning towards Amaro: 'Today is the funeral of the old lady, eh? One calamity on top of another. Go inside, sister, and arrange me a clean collar and my buckled shoes!'

Father Amaro then returned to his preoccupation:

'We were just talking about the case of João Eduardo: the *Communication*.'

'Ah, that is another type of villainy!' said the canon. 'Just think of that too. What a band of rascals there are in this world, what a band of rascals.' He stood with his arms crossed, his eyes lit up, as if he were contemplating a legion of monsters let loose on the world, devouring with shameless impudence the reputations of honest people, the principles of the Church, the honour of family life and the onions of the clergy.

On taking his leave, Father Amaro renewed his recommendations to Dona Josepha, who accompanied him to the top of the stairs.

'Then tonight, as there is the wake, you will do nothing. Tomorrow you will speak to the girl, and at the end of the week you'll bring her to the Cathedral. Good, you must convince the girl, Dona Josepha: plan to save her soul! Remember that God has his eyes on you. Speak firmly to her, speak firmly to her! And our canon will speak to Senhora Joanneira.'

'You can go away with an easy mind, senhor paroco. I am her godmother, and whether she likes it or not I have to put her on the road to salvation.'

'Amen,' said Father Amaro.

That night, indeed, Dona Josepha did nothing. It was the night of the wake in the Rua da Misericordia. All were downstairs in the little parlour, dismally lit with one solitary candle covered with a dark-green shade. Senhora Joanneira and Amelia, in mourning crêpe, sadly occupied the sofa in the centre of the room; and all around, on the rows of chairs placed against the walls, the friends, heavily clothed in black, remained in a silent torpor, their faces drawn with grief: sometimes two voices lisped a phrase, or from a corner, in the shadows, came a sigh: then Libaninho or Arthur Couceiro went on tiptoe to trim the wick of the candle, or Dona Maria of the Assumption coughed up her catarrh with a mournful sound. In the silence could be heard the clatter

143

of wooden shoes on the flagged street, or the Misericordia clock striking the quarter hours.

At intervals Ruça, all in black, entered with a tray of sweetmeats and cups of weak tea, lifting up the shade of the candle; and the old ladies, who had been dozing, becoming sensible of the clearer light, raised their handkerchiefs to their eyes with sighs of 'Ah!' and served themselves with pastries from the Incarnation.

João Eduardo was there in a corner, ignored, at the side of the deaf Gansoso, who slept with her mouth open: all evening he tried to catch Amelia's eye, but she never looked at him, as, with her head down on her chest and her hands in her lap, she twisted and untwisted her cotton handkerchief.

Father Amaro and Canon Dias arrived at nine o'clock: the paroco with grave steps went to speak to Senhora Joanneira: 'My dear senhora, the blow is heavy. But we must console ourselves with the thought that your very esteemed sister is now enjoying the company of Our Lord Jesus Christ.'

There was a murmur of sobs all round; and as there were no more chairs, the two priests sat one at each corner of the sofa, having Senhora Joanneira and Amelia in the middle, weeping copiously. They were thus recognized as members of the family; and Dona Maria of the Assumption remarked in a whisper to Dona Joaquina Gansoso:

'Ah, it does one's eyes good to see the four of them there together!'

Till ten o'clock at night the wake continued silent and dreary, disturbed only by the constant cough of João Eduardo, who had a cold; and it was the opinion of Dona Josepha, as she afterwards informed the company, that 'he coughed purposely to interrupt, and to scoff at the respect shown to the dead.'

Two days later, at eight o'clock in the morning, Dona Josepha and Amelia entered the Cathedral together, after they had talked in the terrace to Amparo, wife of the apothecary, who had one of her children down with measles, and who in spite of the fact that the case was not serious, decided as a precaution to offer up a Promise.

The day was cloudy, the Cathedral was sombre and dreary. Amelia, very pale beneath her black lace mantilla, stopped in front of the altar of Our Lady of Sorrows, fell on her knees, and remained motionless, with her eyes on her prayer book. Dona Josepha, after having prostrated herself in front of the chapel of the Blessed Sacrament and the High Altar, went, treading very softly, to the door of the sacristy and slowly pushed it open: Father Amaro was walking up and down there with shoulders bent and hands behind his back.

'How has it gone?' he enquired immediately, lifting up his very clean-shaven face, in which the eyes shone apprehensively.

'She is here,' said the old lady in a whisper, with an air of triumph. 'I went myself to fetch her! Ah! speak firmly to her, senhor paroco, don't spare her. I'll leave her in your charge.'

'Thank you, thank you, Dona Josepha!' said the priest, warmly squeezing both her hands. 'God will reward you for this.'

He looked all round very nervously; then patting his cassock to feel his handkerchief and his case of papers, he gently closed the sacristy door. He went down the Cathedral. Amelia was still kneeling, making a black mass against the white pillar.

'Come,' said Dona Josepha.

She got up slowly, her face scarlet, tremblingly arranging the folds of her mantilla over her bosom.

'I'll leave her here, senhor paroco,' said the old lady. 'I'm going to the apothecary's to speak to Amparo and afterwards I'll come back for her. Go, child, go. May God give light to your soul!'

She left, after bowing in front of all the altars.

Carlos, the apothecary, who was a tenant of the canon's and a bit behind with his rent, immediately Dona Josepha appeared at his door ostentatiously lifted his cap to her, and conducted her upstairs to the parlour with the muslin curtains, where Amparo sat sewing at the window.

'Ah, don't wait, Senhor Carlos,' said the old lady. 'Don't leave your business. I left my godchild in the Cathedral, and came in here to rest a little.'

'Very well then, if you will excuse me . . . And how is our canon?'

'He has had one of his attacks—and a little dizziness.'

'It's the beginning of spring,' said Carlos, again taking up his majestic air, standing in the middle of the parlour, with his fingers in the arm-holes of his waistcoat. 'I also feel something wrong with me. We full-blooded people always suffer with what one might call the re-birth of the sap. There is an abundance of humours in the blood, which, when not eliminated through the proper channels, make their way, as we might describe it, here and there to the other parts of the body under the form of pimples, or boils, often appearing in very inconvenient places, and though in themselves insignificant, they are always accom-panied, let us say, by a train . . . But, pardon me, it is the doctor in me talking! . . . Tell him to use James's Magnesia!'

Dona Josepha then asked to see the child with the measles. But she went no further than the door of the room; she recommended the little one, who was muffled up in the bedclothes, with eyes alight with fever, not to forget to say her morning and evening prayers. She advised Amparo to try some remedies, which were miraculously effective in cases of measles; but if the Promise was made with faith she could consider the child cured . . . Ah, every day she thanked God she wasn't married! Children only gave work and affliction; and with the trouble they brought and the time they took up looking after them, they could be the cause of a woman neglecting her religion and sending her soul to hell . . .

'You are right, Dona Josepha,' said Amparo, 'they are a punishment from God. And me with five! Sometimes they drive me so mad, that I sit down here on this little chair and cry to myself.'

They had gone near the window, and they enjoyed themselves watching the senhor administrator of the Council of Justice, who, from the office window, was gazing amorously through his binoculars at the wife of Telles the tailor. Ah, what a scandal! Never before in Leiria had they had authorities like that! Look at the General Secretary carrying on shamelessly with Novaes' wife . . . But what could one expect of men without religion, educated in Lisbon—who according to Dona Josepha were predestined to perish like Gomorrah under fire from heaven? Amparo sewed with her head down, ashamed perhaps, in front of that pious indignation, of the culpable longings, which persistently gnawed her, to go to Lisbon and see the Passeio Publico and hear the singers in St Carlos' Theatre.

Soon after, Dona Josepha began to speak of the clerk. Amparo knew nothing of the story; and the old lady had the satisfaction of giving her a longwinded account, taking it point by point, of the history of the *Communication*, of the disgust in the Rua da Misericordia, and Natario's campaign to discover *A Liberal*. She dwelt principally on the character of João Eduardo, his impiety, his orgies . . . And she considered it a Christian duty to annihilate the atheist; she even gave it to be understood that some robberies, lately committed in Leiria, were the work of João Eduardo.

The Cathedral clock slowly struck eleven; and Dona Josepha hurriedly wrapped herself in her mantle in order to go and look for the little one, poor child, she must be so tired of waiting.

Carlos accompanied her, raising his hat and saying (as a little advance which he was remitting to his landlord):

'You must tell the canon that with regard to the *Communication* and the attacks on the clergy, I am heart and soul with the priesthood. Your servant, my dear senhora . . . The sky looks dark and threatening.'

When Dona Josepha entered the Cathedral, Amelia was still in the confessional. The old lady coughed loudly, fell on her knees, and with her hands over her face sank into a devotion to Our Lady of the Rosary. The Cathedral remained silent and deserted. Afterwards Dona Josepha again went over to the confessional and peeped between her fingers: Amelia was kneeling quite still, with her mantilla almost covering her face, and her black dress spread out all round her; Dona Josepha again fell into prayer. A fine rain now beat against one of the side windows. At last the boards of the confessional creaked and there was a rustle of skirts on the flagstones—and Dona Josepha, turning round, saw in front of her Amelia with her face scarlet and her eyes very bright.

'Have you been waiting long, godmother?'

'Quite a little while. Are you ready, eh?'

She got up and made the Sign of the Cross, and the two senhoras left the Cathedral. The fine rain was still falling; but Senhor Arthur Couceiro, who was passing through the Square on some business for the civil governor, conducted them under his umbrella to the Rua da Misericordia.

Chapter XII

EARLY THE following evening, João Eduardo was leaving his house to go to the Rua da Misericordia, carrying under his arm a roll of wall-paper patterns for Amelia to choose from. As he opened the door to go out he met Ruça, who was on the point of ringing his bell:

'What is it, Ruça?'

'The senhoras went to pass the evening with some friends, and here is a letter Menina Amelia left for you.'

João Eduardo felt his heart contract, and gave a look of amazement at Ruça, who went down the street clacking her wooden clogs. He walked to the lantern in front, opened the letter and read:

'Senhor João Eduardo,

'What was decided on with regard to our marriage was under the conviction that you were an upright, honourable person who would make me happy; but as we now know all, and are aware that it was you who wrote the article in *The District* calumniating the friends of our house and insulting me, and as your way of life is not likely to guarantee me happiness in the married state, from today on you must consider all at an end between us, there being no banns pub-lished and no expenses incurred. And I, as well as mamma, hope that you will have sufficient delicacy not to visit our house again nor to follow us in the street. All that I have communicated to you I have done under mamma's orders.

I am,
Yours truly,
Amelia Caminha.'

João Eduardo remained motionless as a stone, staring stupidly at the wall in front on which the light from the street-lantern was shining, with his roll of coloured wallpaper patterns under his arm. He returned mechanically to his house. His hands trembled so much that he could hardly light the lamp. Standing near the table, he reread the letter. Afterwards he remained there, tiring his eyes gazing at the wick of the lamp, with a hopeless frozen sensation of immobility and silence, as if suddenly the whole life of the universe had stopped. Then he thought of where 'they' had gone to pass the night. Memories of happy evenings in the Rua da Misericordia slowly crossed his mind: Amelia at her work with her head bent, and between her jet-black hair and her snow-white collar her neck with a pallor softened by the light. . . . Then the idea of losing her forever stabbed his heart with a cold despair. He squeezed his temples between his hands, mad with grief. What could he do? what could he do? Sudden resolutions flashed through his mind, made him dizzy. Write to her! drag her to the courts! go to Brazil! find out who discovered that he was the author of the article! And as that was the most practical at that hour, he ran to the office of *The Voice of the District*.

Agostinho, stretched on the sofa, with a candle on a chair at his side, was enjoying the Lisbon papers. João Eduardo's agitated face frightened him.

'What is it?'

'You've ruined me, you villain!'

In one breath he furiously accused the hunchback of having betrayed him.

Agostinho slowly raised himself on the sofa, and after calmly looking in his jacket pocket for his tobacco pouch:

'Man, there is no need for such a row. I give you my word of honour I told no one of the *Communication*. Though it's true that nobody asked me.'

'But who was it then?' bawled the clerk.

Agostinho buried his head in his shoulders:

'What I do know is that the priests have been going round like lunatics trying to find out who it was. Natario was here one morning to enquire about an advertisement from a widow who was applying for public charity, but he said nothing about the *Communication*, not one word. Dr Godinho is the one who will know, get an explanation from him! Anyway, what have they done to you?'

'Ruined me!' said João Eduardo mournfully.

He remained a minute with his eyes fixed on the ground, completely crushed, and then rushed headlong out the door. He crossed the Square; then wandered haphazardly through the streets; afterwards, he was drawn by the darkness to the Marrazes Road. He suffocated, and felt an intolerable deafening throbbing against his temples; in spite of the strong wind sweeping through the fields it appeared to him that he existed in a universal silence; at times the idea of his sorrow tore his heart, then he imagined he could see the whole landscape oscillate, and the surface of the road seemed soft as a quagmire. He returned to the Cathedral just as eleven o'clock was striking, and then found himself in the Rua da Misericordia, with his eyes nailed to the window of the dining-room, where a light was still shining; the window of Amelia's room was also lighted up—surely she was going to bed ... Then came a furious desire for her beauty, for her body, for her kisses. He ran home, and prostrated himself on the bed in an intolerable fatigue; afterwards a deep undefined longing softened him, and he cried for a long time, his own sobs soothing him, till in the end he slept flat on his face, an inert mass.

Early the next day, Amelia was walking from the Rua da Misericordia to the Square; when she arrived at the foot of the archway João Eduardo appeared from his hiding place where he had been lying in wait for her:

'I would like to speak to you, Menina Amelia.'

She drew back frightened, and said tremblingly:

'You can have nothing to say to me.'

He planted himself in front of her very determinedly, with his eyes like two burning coals:

'I'd like to say ... As to the article, it's true, it was I who wrote it, it was a shameful thing for me to do; but you had driven me mad with jealousy. . . . But what you say of my evil way of life is a calumny. I was always a well-conducted fellow!'

'The Senhor Father Amaro is the one who knows about you! Have the goodness to let me pass.'

At the name of the priest, João Eduardo became livid with rage:

'Ah! it is the Senhor Father Amaro! It is the villain of a priest! Then we'll see! Listen——'

'Kindly let me pass!' said she irritatedly, and so loudly that a fat individual in a *chale manta* stopped to look.

João Eduardo stepped aside, lifting his hat; and she immediately sought refuge in Fernandos' shop.

Then, in despair, he ran to Dr Godinho's house. Already the evening before, between his fits of crying, when he felt so abandoned, he had thought of Dr Godinho. He was formerly his clerk; and it was on his recommendation that he had entered Nunes Ferral's office, and because of his influence that he was going to be employed by the civil governor, so he looked on him as a prodigal, inexhaustible providence. Besides, since writing the *Communication*, he considered himself on the staff of *The Voice of the District* and of the Group of Maia: now that he was attacked by the clergy, it was clear that he must go and shelter under the strong protection of his chief, Dr Godinho, the enemy of reaction, the 'Cavour of Leiria', as Bachelor Azevedo, author of *Stings,* used to say with a grin. And João Eduardo, making for the big yellow house at the foot of Terreiro, where the doctor lived, went in a transport of hope, happy as a dog which had been turned out into the street, to find a refuge between the legs of that colossus.

Dr Godinho was already at his writing-desk, lying back in his luxurious abbatial armchair with its yellow nails, with his eyes on the dark oak ceiling, blissfully finishing his after-breakfast cigar. He received João Eduardo's 'Good-day' very majestically.

'Well, how are things going with you, my friend?'

The high stands of grave folios, the reams of deeds, the showy panel representing the Marquis of Pombal standing on a terrace overlooking the Tagus, expelling the British squadron with his finger, always overawed João Eduardo and made him bashful; and it was with a very embarrassed voice that he said that he came there to see if his excellency could help him in some trouble into which he had fallen.

'Disorderly conduct, fighting?'

'No, senhor, private affairs.'

He then gave a detailed account of all that had befallen him since the publication of the *Communication*: he read, very agitatedly, Amelia's letter; described the scene at the foot of the archway . . . There he was now, thrown out of the Rua da Misericordia through the underhand work of the senhor paroco. And it seemed to him, in spite of the fact that he hadn't taken his law degree at Coimbra, that against a priest who gained admittance into a family, importuned a simple young girl, and worked intrigues to separate her from her sweetheart and become master of her, there must be laws!

'I don't know, senhor doctor, but there must be laws!'

Dr Godinho appeared to disagree.

'Laws?' he exclaimed, vigorously crossing his legs. 'What laws do you think there should be? Would you like to take an action against the senhor paroco? Why? Did he beat you? rob your watch? insult you in the newspaper? No. Well . . . ?'

'Oh, senhor doctor! but he intrigued against me with the senhoras! I was never a man of evil habits, senhor doctor! He calumniated me!'

'Have you witnesses?'

'No, senhor.'

'Then?'

And Dr Godinho, leaning his elbows on the desk, declared that as an advocate he could do nothing. The law-courts didn't recognize these questions, these moral dramas, as one might call them, which took place in the privacy of the home. As a man, as an individual, as Alipio de Vasconcellos Godinho he also couldn't interfere, as he didn't happen to know Senhor Father Amaro nor these senhoras in the Rua da Misericordia. He sympathized with him, because he had once been young and felt the poetry of youth, and knew (unhappily he knew) the pain and anguish of love . . . And there it was, all that he could do—sympathize. In any case, why had he given his affections to a *beata*?

João Eduardo interrupted him:

'She is not to blame, senhor doctor! All the fault lies with the priest who has led her astray! Those villains of the Chapter are to blame for all!'

Dr Godinho raised his hand with severity, and counselled Senhor João Eduardo to be careful about making these assertions! There was nothing to prove that the senhor paroco possessed in that house any other influence than that of a wise spiritual director. And he recommended Senhor João Eduardo, with all the authority which his age and his position in the country gave him, not to spread, just for spite, accusations which would only serve to destroy the prestige of the clergy, a prestige which was indispensable in a well-constituted society! Without that all would be anarchy and orgies!

He lay back in his chair, satisfied that this morning he had the gift of words.

But the dismayed face of the clerk, who stood motionless at the side of the desk, irritated him; and he said curtly as he pushed a bundle of deeds in front of him:

'Well, let us finish, what do you want now? You can see I can offer no remedy.'

João Eduardo replied with the courage of desperation:

'I imagined that you, senhor doctor, could do something for me—because, you know, I was a victim. All this has come about because they found out that I wrote the *Communication*. And we had agreed that it was to be kept a secret. Agostinho didn't disclose it, and only you, senhor doctor, knew . . .'

The doctor jumped with indignation in his abbatial chair:

'What are you trying to insinuate? Do you want to suggest that it was I who told? I didn't tell. What I mean to say is I told it, but only to my wife, as in a well-constituted family there should be no secrets between husband and wife. She asked me and I told her. But even suppose it was I who spread it through the streets? With you it must be either of these two things: the *Communication* was a calumny, and then it is I who must accuse you of having polluted an honourable newspaper with a pile of defamations; or it was the truth, and in that case senhor, it appears that you are ashamed of the truth which you pronounced, and that you don't dare to maintain in the light of day the opinions which you had printed in the obscurity of the night!'

Tears clouded the eyes of João Eduardo. Then in the face of his dismayed expression, and satisfied that he had smashed him with his arguments, so powerful and so logical, Dr Godinho added more blandly:

'Good, don't let us get angry over the matter. Don't speak any more of points of honour. What you can believe is that I am sincerely sorry for your trouble.'

With paternal solicitude he gave him advice. That he mustn't give in; that there were other girls in Leiria, girls who had good principles and didn't live under the direction of the cassock. That he was strong, and he could console himself thinking that he, Dr Godinho—yes, he!— in his youth also had disappointments in love. That he mustn't neglect to dominate his angry passions as they would be prejudicial to him in his public career, And if he wouldn't consider these counsels in his own interests, he would at least give attention to them in consideration for him, Dr Godinho!

João Eduardo left the office indignant, considering that he had been betrayed by the doctor.

'This happens to me,' he muttered to himself, 'because I am a poor devil, with no votes in the elections, no invitations to the soirées of Novaes, no subscription to the club. Ah, what a world! If I only had a few thousand mil reis!'

He was then possessed with a furious desire to revenge himself on the priests, the rich, and the religion which justified them. He returned very determined to Dr Godinho's office, and partly opening the door, said:

'Your excellency will now at least give me permission to expose them in the newspaper? I wish to relate this, their latest villainy, to lash the scoundrels . . .'

The audacity of the clerk filled the doctor with indignation. He sat up severely in his chair, and crossed his arms in a terrible attitude:

'Senhor João Eduardo, this is really an affront! So you, senhor, come here to ask me if you can change a newspaper of ideas into a newspaper of defamation!? Go, you needn't wait! You ask me to allow you to express views that insult the principles of religion, that mock the Redeemer, that repeat the inanities of Renan, that attack the fundamental laws of the State, that injure the King, that pour vituperations on the sacredness of family life! You have lost all control of yourself!'

'Oh, senhor doctor!'

'You have lost all control of yourself! Take care, my dear friend, take care, look before you go downhill! Before you go down the road which will bring you to loss of respect for authority, for law and order, for the holy things of the hearth. That road which leads to crime! There is no need for you to stare. To crime, I say! I have twenty years' experience as a magistrate. Man, control yourself! Curb these passions of yours! Away with them! How old are you?'

'Twenty-six!'

'Well then, there is no excuse for a man of twenty-six years having these subversive ideas. Good-bye, shut the door. And listen: there is no use in your thinking of sending another communication to any other paper. I will not consent to it, and remember I have always protected you! You must be making a noise and a bother . . . Don't deny it, I can read it in your eyes. Mark it well, I will not consent! And for your good, to save you from an evil social action!'

He took a grand attitude in the chair, and repeated with greater force:

'An evil social action! Where would you senhores land us with your materialism and your atheism? When you have done away with the religion of our fathers, what have you to substitute for it? What have you? Show it to me!'

The embarrassed expression of João Eduardo (who hadn't a religion there to substitute for that of our fathers) caused the doctor to add triumphantly:

'You have nothing! When you've finished with high-sounding phrases, you have mud! But as long as I live, at least in Leiria, the Faith and the principles of order must be respected. These materialists can plunge Europe into blood and fire, but in Leiria they will never be allowed to raise their heads. I am alert here in Leiria, and swear that I will bring disaster on them!'

João Eduardo received these threats with bent head, without understanding them. How could his *Communication* and the intrigues of the Rua da Misericordia produce such social catastrophes and religious revolutions? So much severity reduced him to nothing. He was surely going to lose the doctor's friendship and the employment with the civil governor, so he attempted to soften him:

'Oh, senhor doctor, but surely your excellency can see——'

The doctor interrupted him with a pompous gesture. 'I see perfectly. I see that your spirit of vengeance, your passions, are leading you on the road to disaster. I only hope that my good advice will deter you. Well, good-bye. Shut the door, man!'

João Eduardo left absolutely overwhelmed. What was he to do now? Dr Godinho, that powerful giant, had repelled him with thundering words! And what could he, a poor office clerk, do against Father Amaro who had on his side the clergy, the precentor, the chapter, the bishops, the Pope, a solid and compact class that seemed to him a hideous citadel of bronze rising right up to the sky! It was they who had formed Amelia's resolution, her letter, her hard words. It was an intrigue of priests, canons and *beatas*. he could only uproot her from that influence she would again become his Ameliazinha who embroidered bedroom slippers for him, and who came, all blushing, to watch him pass the window! The suspicions which he had held had disappeared during those happy evenings after the marriage had been decided, when she, as she sat near the lamp sewing, talked of the furniture they would have to buy and of the arrangements of their little home. She loved him, surely she did . . . But who had told her that he was the author of the *Communication*, that he was a heretic, that he led a loose life? The paroco, in his pedantic voice, had threatened her with hell; the canon, who must be furious, and who was certainly all-powerful in the Rua da Misericordia, as he kept the pot boiling, had spoken firmly with her— and the poor little girl, frightened, dominated by that gloomy band of priests and *beatas* whispering in her ear, the poor little girl had to give in to them! Perhaps she was now of the opinion that he was a beast! And at that very hour, while he wandered the streets rejected and disgraced, Father Amaro, in the little parlour of the Rua da Misericordia, was sitting back comfortably in the armchair with his legs crossed, master of the house and master of the girl, talking out loud! Ruffians! And there were no laws by which he could wreak vengeance on them! And now he couldn't even make a scandal against them, as *The Voice of the District* was closed to him!

He then became possessed of a fierce desire to demolish the parish to its very foundations with the force of Father Brito. But what would satisfy him more would be terrifying articles in the newspaper, which would reveal the intrigues in the Rua da Misericordia, alarm public opinion, fall on the priest like a catastrophe, and force him, the canon, and others to disappear, running, from the house of Senhora Joanneira! Ah! he was certain that Ameliazinha, free from these gourmandizers, would immediately fall into his arms with tears of reconciliation . . .

It was thus that he forced on himself the conviction that she had no blame in the matter; he recalled the months of happiness before the paroco arrived; he found natural explanations for those tender ways which she had for Father Amaro, and which had given him desperate fits of jealousy: it was the desire, poor little girl, to be agreeable to the lodger, to the canon's friend, and to retain him for her mother's advantage and the advantage of the house. And besides this, how happy she had been after she had consented to marry him. Her indignation against the *Communication* he was sure was not genuine—it had been produced by the insinuations of the priest and the religious fanatics. And he found consolation in the idea that he hadn't been repelled as a lover or as a husband, but that he was just a victim of the intrigues of that lascivious Father Amaro, who desired his sweetheart, and detested him because he was a liberal. A violent rancour against the priest grew in his mind; he walked down the street anxiously thinking how he could find a means of revenge, casting his mind from one thing to another—but the same idea always returned, the article in the newspaper, the violent attack, the printed word! The certainty of his unprotected, weak position infuriated him. Ah, if he only had a man of distinction on his side!

A country man, yellow as a lemon, who was walking along slowly with his arm in a sling, stopped him to ask where Dr Gouvea lived.

'In the first street on the left, the green gate in front of the streetlantern,' said João Eduardo.

A great hope suddenly lit up his mind: Dr Gouvea was the one who could save him! The doctor was his friend! He had addressed him with the familiar 'tu' since the time two years before, when he had cured his pneumonia; he looked with great approval on his proposed marriage with Amelia; a few weeks ago he had asked him in the Square: 'Now when are you going to make this young girl happy?' And what respect, what fear they had for him in the Rua da Misericordia! He was a doctor to all the friends of the house who, in spite of the fact that he scandalized them with his irreligion, humbly depended on his science for purgatives, remedies for fainting fits, and cough syrups. Apart from that, Dr Gouvea, a definite enemy of the clergy, would certainly be indignant with the intrigues of those religious bigots: and João Eduardo could already see himself entering the Rua da Misericordia behind Dr Gouvea, who would reprehend Senhora Joanneira, humiliate Father Amaro, and convince the old ladies—and his happiness would begin again, but now unassailable!

'Is the senhor doctor in?' he asked, almost happy, addressing the servant, who was hanging out the clothes to dry.

'He is in his consulting room, Senhor Joãozinho, kindly enter.'

On market days the sick people from the country usually flocked in. But at that hour—when neighbours from the different districts met in the taverns—there was only one old man, a woman with a baby in her lap, and the man with his arm in a sling, waiting in a low-ceilinged room with benches ranged round the walls; there were two sweet-basil plants in the window, and a large engraving of *The Coronation of Queen Victoria* hung on the wall. In spite of the bright sun which entered from the patio and of the fresh foliage of the limes which touched the window-bars, the room was dull and dreary, as if the walls and benches and even the sweet-basil plants had imbibed the melancholy of the sick people who had waited there. João Eduardo entered and sat down in a corner.

Twelve o'clock had just finished striking, and the woman was complaining of having to wait so long: she had come from a long distance, she had left her sister in the market place, and the senhor doctor had been an hour with two senhoras! Every few minutes the child whined and the mother rocked her in her arms till she became calm; the old man pulled up his trouser-leg and took pleasure in contemplating a wound on his shin, wrapped in rags; and the other man gave great discouraging yawns which made his long dreary face look more yellow. This long wait unnerved the clerk, weakened his purpose; he felt himself gradually losing the courage to take up Dr Gouvea's time; he laboriously prepared his story, but it now appeared too trivial to be of any interest. He was then filled with a despair which the dull uninteresting faces of the sick people made still more intense. Life was definitely a sad affair, full of misery, betrayed feelings, and sickness! He got up, and with his hands behind his back went disconsolately to look at *The Coronation of Queen Victoria*.

From time to time the woman half-opened the door, and peeped to see if the two senhoras were still there. They were there; and from the other side of the green baize folding door, which shut off the doctor's consulting room, came voices, calmly chatting.

'I've lost a whole day coming here!' muttered the old man.

Also he had left his beast at the door of the bacon factory and his daughter in the Square—and afterwards he'd have to wait at the apothecary's! And then he had to journey home nine miles! It was good to be ill, but only for those who were rich and had plenty of leisure!

The thought of illness, and the responsibility it brought, made the loss of Amelia more bitter. If he were ill he now would have to go to the hospital. That cursed priest had taken all from him—woman, happiness, family comforts, all the sweet balms of life!

At last he heard the two senhoras walking through the corridor. The woman with the child picked up her basket, and hurried in to the doctor. And the old man, taking possession of the seat near the door, said with satisfaction:

'Now this belongs to me!'

'Have you much to see the doctor about?' asked João Eduardo.

'No, senhor, I have only to receive a prescription.'

He immediately began to recount the history of his wound: it was caused by a beam of wood falling on top of it; he took no notice of it; afterwards it became septic and now here he was, crippled, and worn out with pain.

'And you, senhor, have you anything serious?' he asked.

'I'm not ill,' replied the clerk. 'I have some business with the senhor doctor.'

The two men looked enviously at him. It was the old man's turn next, and then the yellow-faced man with his arm in a sling. João Eduardo, now alone, walked nervously up and down the room. It seemed to him very difficult to enter thus, without ceremony, to ask help from the doctor. With what right? He then thought of first complaining of pains in his chest or stomach trouble and afterwards, incidentally, recounting his troubles . . .

But the door opened. The doctor was in front of him, with his long grizzly beard falling down over his black velvet jacket, his large wide-brimmed hat pulled well down on his head, and his hands immersed in Scotch wool gloves.

'Hello! so it's you, boy! Anything new in the Rua da Misericordia?'

João Eduardo coloured:

'No, senhor, but, senhor doctor, I'd like to talk to you on a private matter.'

'Come into my surgery,'—the well-known surgery of Dr Gouvea, which with its chaos of books, its dusty atmosphere, its collection of savage arrows adorning the walls, and its two storks, packed in straw, had the name of the Alchemist's Cave in the town.

The doctor pulled out his old silver watch:

'A quarter to two. Be brief.'

The face of the clerk expressed his embarrassment at having to condense such a complicated narrative.

'It's all right,' said the doctor, 'explain it how you will. There is nothing more difficult than being brief and clear; for that it's necessary to be a genius. What is it?'

João Eduardo then stammered out his story, insisting, above all, on the perfidy of the priest, and exaggerating the innocence of Amelia.

The doctor listened to him, stroking his beard.

'I see what it is,' he said. 'You and the priest, you both want the girl. As he is the more wide-awake and the more decided, he has taken her. It is the law of nature: the strongest one robs, and eliminates the weaker; and the woman, the prey, belongs to him.'

This appeared ridiculous to João Eduardo, and he said excitedly:

'Your excellency is joking, to you it is funny, but it is breaking my heart!'

'Man,' added the doctor graciously, 'I am philosophizing, not joking. But, look here, what would you like me to do?'

It was exactly what Dr Godinho had said to him, though more pompously!

'I am certain that if your excellency spoke——'

The doctor smiled:

'I could prescribe for the girl this or that medicine, but I can't prescribe this or that man! Would you like me to go and say to her: 'Menina, you must take João Eduardo.' Would you like me to go and say to the priest, a rogue that I've never even seen: "Senhor, would you be kind enough not to seduce this girl?"'

'But they calumniated me, senhor doctor, they gave out that I was a man of bad habits, a villain.'

'No, no, they didn't calumniate you. From the point of view of the priests and those senhoras who play lotto at night in the Rua da Misericordia you are a villain. A Christian who—in the newspapers—pours vituperations on abbots, canons, and priests, people so important that they hold communication with God and save souls, is a villain. They didn't calumniate you, my friend!'

'But senhor doctor . . .'

'Listen. And the girl getting rid of you in obedience to such and such a priest, comports herself as a good Catholic should. It is as I say: all the life of a good Catholic, his thoughts, his ideas, his feelings, his conversations, the employment of his days and his nights, his relations towards his family and his neighbours, the food he eats, the clothes he wears, his diversions—all is regulated by the ecclesiastical authority (abbot, bishop, or canon), approved or censured by his confessor, counselled and ordered by him as the director of his conscience. The good Catholic, such as your little girl, doesn't belong to herself; she has no judgment, no wishes, no free will, nor individual feeling; her priest thinks, wishes, determines, feels for her. Her only work in this world, which is at the same time her only right and her only task, is to accept this direction; accept it without discussion; obey it, no matter what its demands; if it is against her ideas, she must think that her ideas are false; if her love is wounded she must think that it is her love which is at fault. This being the case, if the priest says to the girl that she mustn't marry you, that she mustn't even talk to you, she proves by her obedience that she is a good Catholic, a devout adherent, and logically lives her life according to the moral rule which she has chosen. Here is the explanation, and excuse the sermon . . .'

João Eduardo listened with astonishment and respect to these phrases, to which the doctor's placid face and beautiful grey beard gave an added authority. It now seemed to him to be an impossibility to regain Amelia, if she belonged absolutely, body and soul, to the priest who confessed her. But anyway, why was he considered such an undesirable husband?

'I could understand,' he said, 'if I were a man who lived an evil life, senhor doctor. But I behave well; I only do my work; I don't frequent taverns or take part in brawls; I don't drink, I don't gamble; I pass my evenings in the Rua da Misericordia or sometimes I take home office work to do in the evening . . .'

'My boy, socially you could possess all the virtues; but according to the religion of our fathers, all the virtues which are not Catholic are useless and pernicious. To be a good worker, chaste, honourable, just, truthful, are great virtues, but for the priests and the Church they don't count. If you were a model of goodness but didn't go to Mass, didn't fast, nor go to confession, didn't take your hat off to the senhor paroco, you would be simply a scoundrel. Other people more important than you, whose souls were perfect and whose rule of life was impeccable, have been judged real rogues because they hadn't been baptized before they became perfect. You must have heard of Socrates, of another man called Plato, of Cato and others. They were individuals famous for their virtues. Well, a certain Bossuet, who was a great authority on doctrine, said that hell was full of the virtues of such men. This proves that Catholic morality is different from natural morality or social morality. But these are things you don't understand very well . . . Would you like an example: I, according to the Catholic doctrine, am one of the most shameless scoundrels walking the streets of the town; and my neighbour Peixoto, who beat his wife to death and who is slowly killing, by the same process, his little daughter of ten, is considered amongst the clergy an excellent man, because he performs his religious duties and plays the ophicleide at High Mass. To conclude, friend, these things stand like that. And it appears to me they are good, since there are millions of respectable people who think them good; the State maintains them, and spends a large amount of money maintaining them, and also obliges us to respect them—and I, who am here talking, pay a quartinho every year so that they will continue as they are. You naturally pay less . . .'

'I pay seven vintens, senhor doctor.'

'But then you attend the church feasts, hear music, listen to sermons, and get the worth of your seven vintens. And I lose my quartinho; I can't even console myself with the idea that it helps to maintain the splendour of the Church—the Church which during my life considers me a villain, and for my death has prepared a first-class hell. In fine, it appears to me we have talked enough. Is there anything else you'd like?'

João Eduardo was crushed. Now that he had listened to the doctor, he appeared to him, more than ever, a man so wise of speech, with so many ideas, that if he would only interest himself in him, all the intrigues would be easily broken up, his happiness would return and his place in the Rua da Misericordia recovered for all time.

'Then your excellency can't do anything for me?' he said very sadly.

'Perhaps I could cure you of another attack of pneumonia. Have you pneumonia? No? Well . . .'

João Eduardo sighed.

'I am a victim, senhor doctor.'

'You shouldn't make yourself a victim. Remember that if there were no victims, there would be no tyrants,' said the doctor putting on his big broad-brimmed hat.

'Because one fact remains sure,' exclaimed João Eduardo, who hung on to the doctor with the grip of a drowning man, 'in the end what that rogue of a priest wants, in spite of all his pretexts, is the girl! If she had an ugly face, the scoundrel wouldn't care whether I was impious or not! What he wants is the girl!'

The doctor shrugged his shoulders.

'It's natural, the poor fellow,' he said with his hand on the doorknob. 'What else do you expect? As a man he has passions and organs which make him want a woman; and as her confessor he has the importance of a God in her eyes. It is evident that he must utilize this importance in order to satisfy these passions; and he has to cover these natural satisfactions with the appearance and under the pretext of a divine service. . . . It is natural.'

João Eduardo, then, watching him opening the door, seeing all the hopes which he had brought with him disappear, shouted, slashing the air with his hat:

'That pack of priestly rabble! They were always a race which I detested! I'd like to see them swept off the face of the earth, senhor doctor!'

'This is more nonsense,' said the doctor, stopping at the door, and resigning himself to listen again. 'Look here. You believe in God? in the God of the heavens, in the God who is up there in the sky, and who is, there on high, the source of all truth and all justice?'

João Eduardo surprised, answered:

'Yes, senhor, I believe.'

'And in original sin?'

'Also.'

'And in the life to come, and the Redemption and the rest?'

'I was brought up in those beliefs.'

'Well then, why do you want to sweep the priests from the face of the earth? On the contrary, you must think that there are not really too many. You declare yourself a liberal rationalist, and yet you believe in these things. You believe there is a God in the heavens, who directs us from above, in original sin, and in the life to come. Then you must believe that a religious body is necessary to explain the doctrine and the moral revealed by God, who will aid you to purify your soul from original sin, and prepare your place in paradise! You require the priests. And it even appears to me a terrible lack of logic on your part to discredit them in the press.'

João Eduardo, astonished, muttered:

'But your excellency, senhor doctor—excuse me, your excellency, but . . .'

'Say it, man. What?'

'Your excellency doesn't require the priests in this world . . .'

'Nor in any other. I don't require the priests in the world because I don't require God in the sky. This is what I want to say, boy, that I have my God inside me, that is, the principle which directs my actions and my judgments. Commonly called conscience. Perhaps you don't understand very well. The fact is I am here expounding subversive doctrines . . . It is actually three o'clock.' He showed him his watch.

At the patio gate, João Eduardo said:

'I hope your excellency will excuse me——'

'There is nothing to excuse. Send the Rua da Misericordia to the devil!'

João Eduardo heatedly interrupted him:

'It is all very well to talk like that, senhor doctor, but when love is devouring one!'

'Ah!' said the doctor, 'what a beautiful and wonderful thing is love! Love is one of the greatest forces of civilization. Well directed it could lift up the whole world and be sufficient to cause a moral revolution.' Then changing his tone: 'But listen. Be well aware that sometimes this is not love, this is not in the heart. The heart is a term which usually serves us, for decency's sake, to designate another organ. It is precisely this other organ which is the only one interested, in the majority of cases, in affairs of sentiment. In those cases the grief doesn't last. Goodbye, I hope it is so with you!'

Chapter XIII

JoÃo EDUARDO walked down the street rolling a cigarette. He felt unnerved and tired out from the night of despair which he had passed, and from the morning full of useless journeys and fruitless conversations with Dr Godinho and Dr Gouvea.

'It's finished,' he thought. 'I can't do anything more. I must put up with it.'

His soul was weak after so much violent grief, so many lost hopes and so much anger. He would have liked to stretch himself out at full length in an isolated place, far away from lawyers, from women and priests, and sleep for months. But as it was already past three, he hurried to the office. Perhaps to hear a sermon from Nunes because he had arrived so late. What a sad life was his!

He turned the corner of Terreiro, and when he arrived at Osorio's tavern he ran into a young man in a long bright jacket, bordered with wide black ribbon, and with a little beard so black that against his extremely pale face it appeared false.

'Hello! what are you up to, João Eduardo?'

It was one Gustavo, printer of *The Voice of the District*, who had just returned from a two months' stay in Lisbon. He was, according to Agostinho, 'a boy with a good head and well informed, but with devilish ideas'. He sometimes wrote articles on foreign policy, into which he introduced poetical and high-sounding phrases, cursing Napoleon III, the Czar of Russia and all oppressors of the people, crying over the slavery of Poland and the misery of the proletariat. He and João Eduardo had the same ideas on religion, resulting in conversations between them in which both expressed their hatred of the clergy and their admiration for Jesus Christ. The revolution in Spain inspired Gustavo with so much enthusiasm that he wished to join the International; and the desire to live in a working-class centre, where there were associations, discourses and brotherhood, took him to Lisbon. He found good work and good comrades there. But as he had to support his mother, who was old and ill, he found it more economical to live with her, and therefore he returned to Leiria. Besides this, as it was the eve of the elections, *The District* was prospering so well that the proprietors were able to increase the salaries of their three printers.

On account of all this he was there again with the hunchback.

He was on his way to dinner, and immediately invited João Eduardo to come and keep him company. The devil take it, the sky wouldn't fall down if he missed one day in the office!

João Eduardo suddenly remembered that he hadn't eaten anything since the previous day. It was the weakness of hunger which made him feel so stupid and so easily discouraged. He accepted immediately, content, after the emotions and fatigues of the morning, to sit at his ease on a bench in the tavern, with a full plate in front of him, and talk familiarly with a comrade with the same hatreds as himself. Besides, the rebuffs which he had suffered gave him a desire, an avidity for sympathy; so that it was with great warmth that he said:

'Man, I'll certainly come! You're like a gift from heaven. This world is a pigsty. If it wasn't for the few hours that we pass with our friends, hell, life wouldn't be worth living!'

This way of talking from João Eduardo, whom the boys nicknamed the Peaceful One, surprised Gustavo.

'Why? Aren't things going well? Trouble with the beast of a Nunes, eh?' he enquired.

'No, just a little spleen.'

'But spleen is English and has nothing to do with us! Oh, friend, you should have seen Taborda in *London Love*! Leave the spleen. Eat and drink, fill up your belly, that will do away with your spleen.'

He took him by the arm, and led him into the tavern, shouting:

'Long live Uncle Osorio! Health and brotherhood to you!'

The owner of the tavern, Uncle Osorio, was a very fat individual, satisfied with life, with his shirt-sleeves tucked up to his shoulders, his bare white arms leaning on the counter, his sly face all swollen and puffy. He immediately welcomed Gustavo back to Leiria. He thought he looked thinner, which must be on account of the bad water of Lisbon and the amount of long-wood dye which they put in the wine. And what could he serve for the *cavalheiros*?

Gustavo, planting himself in front of the counter, with his hat on the nape of his neck, hurried to get out his joke, which had met with so much applause in Lisbon.

'Uncle Osorio, serve us with the King's liver and two priests' kidneys, roasted.'

Uncle Osorio, who always had a ready answer, replied at once, as he swished the dish-cloth lightly over the zinc counter:

'We have nothing like that here, Senhor Gustavo. These are dainties of the capital.'

'Well then, you people here are very behind the times. I had them for lunch every day in Lisbon. Good, never mind, give us two sandwiches with potatoes—and well-salted, mind!'

They sat themselves down at a table made of two planks of pine, shut off from the rest of the shop by a chintz curtain. Uncle Osorio, who appreciated Gustavo as a well-educated lad who respected others, came himself to bring the bottle of red wine and the olives; and as he wiped the glasses with his filthy apron, said:

'Well, and what's the news from the capital, Senhor Gustavo? How are things going there?'

The printer immediately drew a serious face, passed his hand through his hair, and let fall a few enigmatical phrases:

'All is doubtful. Very dirty work in politics—the working-class are moving, but as yet they lack unity—they are waiting to see how things will go in Spain. They are sure to go well! All depends on Spain . . .'

But Uncle Osorio, who had saved up his coppers and bought a farm, had a horror of disturbances. The only thing he wanted in the country was peace. What he disliked above all was to depend on Spaniards. The *cavalheiros* must know the proverb: 'From Spain never comes either a good wind or a good marriage.'

'The people are all brothers!' exclaimed Gustavo. 'When one talks of dragging down Bourbons and emperors, members of parliament and aristocrats, there are no Portuguese and no Spaniards, all are brothers! All is fraternity, Uncle Osorio!'

'Well then, the best thing is to drink their health, and drink it heartily, that's what makes business go,' said Uncle Osorio calmly, as he rolled his huge bulk out of the cubicle.

'Elephant!' growled the printer, shocked by such indifference to the Brotherhood of Man. Anyway, what could one expect of a property owner and an election agent?

He hummed the *Marseillaise*, as he filled their glasses to the brim, and wished to know what friend João Eduardo had been doing with himself these days, now that he never went to *The District*? The hunchback had said that nothing could drag him away from the Rua da Misericordia.

'And when is this marriage going to be, definitely?'

João Eduardo coloured, and said vaguely:

'There is nothing decided. Some difficulties have arisen.' He then added with a sad smile: 'We've quarrelled.'

'Silly nonsense!' let fly the printer with a shrug of his shoulders, which expressed the disdain of a revolutionary for the frivolities of sentiment.

'Silly nonsense—I don't know if it is nonsense,' said João Eduardo. 'All I do know is that it has brought me a great deal of suffering. They have destroyed me, Gustavo.'

He stopped talking, and bit his lip in order to press down the emotion which ran through all his body.

But the printer found all these tales of women ridiculous. It wasn't the time for love-making. The man of the people, the worker who hung on to a woman's skirts and wouldn't let go, was good for nothing—he had sold himself! What one should occupy one's mind with was not love, but trying to bring liberty to the people, freeing the worker from the claws of the capitalist, finishing with monopolies, working for a republic! We didn't want moans, what we wanted was action, what we wanted was force! And furiously hanging on to the 'r' he repeated 'forrrce!' as he agitatedly waved his wrists, wasted with tuberculosis, over the pile of sandwiches which the boy had just brought.

João Eduardo, as he listened to him, thought of the time when the printer, madly in love with Julia, the baker's assistant, appeared at the office with eyes like burning coals, and thundered at the type with horrible sighs. And at each 'Ah!' his comrades, mocking him, gave little coughs. One day Gustavo and Medeiros had come to blows over it in the patio.

'Listen to who's talking!' he said in the end. 'You are just like everybody else. You are here blathering, but when love strikes you, you are just like the others.'

The printer—who since he had been to Lisbon, had frequented the democratic club of Alcantara and had helped to print a manifesto for his fellow cigarette-makers on strike, considered himself exclusively vowed to the service of the Proletariat and the Republic—was annoyed. He? He like the others? He to lose his time chasing skirts?

'You, senhor, are making a big mistake!' he replied. And he fell into a brooding silence, furiously tearing his sandwich with his teeth.

João Eduardo, fearing he had offended him, said in a changed voice:

'Oh Gustavo, we must be reasonable: a man could have his principles, work for a cause, but at the same time he could marry, have a home, rear a family.'

'Never!' exclaimed the printer excitedly. 'The man who marries is lost! From then on he can only think of providing food for his children, he can never leave the nest, he can't get a moment to mix with his friends, he must pass the night walking up and down the room with his brats, while they are bawling with their teething. He is good for nothing. He has sold himself. Women understand nothing of politics. They are always in terror that their man will get mixed up in rows, have trouble with the police . . . He is a patriot tied hand and foot! And when there is a secret to be kept? A married man can't keep it! Then a revolution is often betrayed. To hell with family life! Some more olives, Uncle Osorio!'

Uncle Osorio's paunch appeared between the planks.

'Now what are the senhores discussing here, does it appear that the Group of Maia will enter the district council?'

Gustavo moved to the end of the bench, and stretching out his legs, interrupted loudly:

'It is Uncle Osorio who is going to settle the question. Now tell me, my friend. Are you a man who changes your political opinions according to the will of your mistress?'

Uncle Osorio scratched the nape of his neck and said in a shrewd tone:

'I can reply to that, Senhor Gustavo. Women are more wide-awake than we are, and in politics, as in business, those who act on their advice are sure to do right. I always consult mine, and I would like to tell you that I've followed her counsel for twenty years and haven't regretted it.'

Gustavo sprang up from the bench and shouted:

'You have sold yourself!'

Uncle Osorio, who was used to that expression, beloved of the printer, took no offence; but with his love of ready answers he replied jokingly:

'Sold, I wouldn't say that, but if you'd like to call me a salesman you would be nearer the mark. Now what I advise, Senhor Gustavo, is that you marry first and afterwards talk about it.'

'What I have to talk about is, that when the revolution comes I'll come in here with my rifle on my shoulder, and drag you before the council of war—you capitalist!'

'Well, until that time comes, there is nothing to do but drink and drink heartily,' said Uncle Osorio quietly retiring.

'Hippopotamus!' muttered the printer.

As he loved discussions, he began again, affirming that the man who was under the influence of a skirt could never be depended on in politics.

João Eduardo smiled sadly, mutely disagreeing, thinking that, in spite of his love for Amelia, he hadn't been to confession for the last two years!

'I can prove what I say!' roared Gustavo.

He cited the case of a freethinker of his acquaintance who, in order to maintain his domestic peace, was induced by his wife to fast on Friday, and on Sundays footed it to Mass with his prayer-book under his arm.

'That is what's bound to happen! Now your ideas on religion are not bad, but I expect I'll see you one day in a long red tunic and with a wax candle in your hand, following in the procession of Our Lord of the Cross. Philosophy and atheism don't cost anything when boys just talk in the tavern among themselves. But to practise in family life when one has a pretty, loving wife, is the devil! And what is bound to happen to you, if it hasn't already happened, is that you will have to give up your liberal ideas and make cringing bows to the family confessor!'

João Eduardo turned scarlet with indignation. Even during the time of his happiness, when he was sure of Amelia, such an accusation (which the printer made just for the sake of argument) would have annoyed him. But now! Just as he had lost Amelia for saying openly in a newspaper what he thought of the clergy. Today, when he found himself here with his heart broken in two, robbed of all his joy in life, precisely for his liberal opinions . . .

'It is particularly funny that you should say that to me!' he said with bitterness.

The printer scoffed:

'Man, don't tell me that you are a martyr in the cause of liberty!'

'Why do you torment me, Gustavo?' said the clerk very vexed. 'You don't know what has happened. If you knew, you wouldn't talk to me like that.'

He then recounted the history of the *Communication*—not mentioning that he had written it when burning with jealousy, but presenting it as a pure affirmation of principles. And he must note this circumstance well: that he was then on the point of marrying a pious girl, who came from a house which was more frequented by priests than the Cathedral sacristy . . .

'Did you sign your name to it?' asked Gustavo, surprised at the revelation.

'Doctor Godinho wouldn't let me,' said the clerk, colouring a little.

'And so you insulted each one, eh?'

'I tore them all to shreds!'

The printer, very excited, bawled for another bottle of red wine.

He filled the glasses in a transport of joy, and drank much health to João Eduardo.

'Heavens, I'd like to see that article. I want to send it to the boys in Lisbon! What effect did it have?'

'A first-class scandal.'

'And those vermin, the clergy?'

'All up in arms!'

'But how did they know it was you?'

João Eduardo shrugged his shoulders. Agostinho hadn't told. He was suspicious of Dr Godinho's wife, who knew all about it from her husband, and who probably ran to put the information in her confessor's snout, Father Silverio of Rua das Therezas.

'A very fat man, who appears dropsical?'

'Yes.'

'The beast!' roared the printer, rancorously.

He now looked with respect on João Eduardo, that João Eduardo who had unexpectedly revealed himself as a knight of free thought.

'Drink, friend, drink!' he said affectionately filling up his friend's glass, as if that heroic effort of liberalism still required special strengthening.

'And what happened afterwards? What did the people of the Rua da Misericordia say?'

So much interest touched João Eduardo: and in one breath he gave all his confidence, even showing Amelia's letter, which she had surely written, poor little girl, under the terror of hell and the pressure of the angry clergy. . . .

'And here you have me, the victim of it all, Gustavo!'

He was in effect the victim; and the printer considered him with growing admiration. He was now no longer the Peaceful One, Nunes' clerk, the beau of the Rua da Misericordia: he was the victim of religious persecution. He was the first one the printer had seen; and in spite of the fact that he didn't appear in the traditional attitude of the propaganda prints, tied to a burning post, or flying with his affrighted family from the galloping soldiers, he thought him interesting. He secretly envied him that social honour. What prestige that would give him amongst the boys of Lisbon! It would be a great advantage to him to be a victim of reaction without losing the comforts of Uncle Osorio's sandwiches and his full salary on Saturday. But the conduct of the clergy made him furious! How dare they wreak vengeance on a Liberal, intrigue against him, take away his sweetheart! Oh, what villains . . . And forgetting his sarcasms against marriage and family life, he thundered aloud against the priests, who were the people who sought to destroy these perfect social institutions of divine origin.

'This requires a terrible vengeance, boy! They must be destroyed!'

João Eduardo avidly wished to revenge himself. But what revenge could he take?

'What revenge! Write up the whole thing in *The District* in a startling article!'

João Eduardo quoted Dr Godinho's words: from now on *The District* was closed to all free-thinkers.

'What a lot of swine!' roared the printer.

But heavens, he had a grand idea! Why not publish a lampoon of about twenty pages, what they called in Brazil a *mofina*, but in a flowery style (he himself would see to that) showering deadly blows on the clergy!

João Eduardo became enthusiastic. And because of this active sympathy of Gustavo's, he saw a friend and a brother in him, and so gave him his ultimate confidence, the saddest of all. The object of all the intrigue was Father Amaro's passion for the little girl, and it was in order to take her that he had him thrown out of the house. The enemy, the cursed one, the hangman, was—the paroco!

The printer squeezed his head between his hands: that such a thing (though the case appeared to him trivial compared to some of those he had written up in offices where he had been working) should happen to a friend of his, who was there drinking with him, to a democrat, appeared to him monstrous, something similar to the vile passions of Tiberius, who in his old age violated the bodies of young patricians in perfumed baths.

He could hardly believe it. João Eduardo gave him all the proofs which he had. And then Gustavo, who by this time had spilt plenty of red wine over the liver sandwiches, stood up and waving his closed fists, with his face all puffed out, and grinding his teeth, shouted hoarsely:

'Down with religion!'

From the other side of the curtain a mocking voice responded:

'Long live Pius IX!'

Gustavo got up in a rage and wished to go and punch the interrupter. But João Eduardo quietened him. And the printer sat down and tranquilly drained his glass to the bottom.

Then, with their elbows on the table, their faces close together and the bottle between them, they conversed in a low tone over the plan of the pamphlet. The thing was easy: they would both write it. João Eduardo wanted it in romantic form, with black intrigues, and proposed giving to the character which represented the paroco the vice and perversities of Caligula and Heliogabalus. The printer, on the other hand, would prefer a pamphlet which was philosophical in style and principle, which would demolish once and for all the power of the Pope on earth. He himself would take on the job of printing it, in the evenings, gratis of course. But he suddenly saw a difficulty.

The paper! How were they going to manage about paper?

It would be an expenditure of about nine or ten mil reis; neither of them had that much. They had not even a friend who, sympathizing with their principles, might lend them the money.

'Ask Nunes to advance it and you can pay it back from your salary,' suggested the printer excitedly.

João Eduardo scratched his head disconsolately. He had just been thinking of Nunes and of his indignation, as a devout member of the parish council and friend of the precentor, when he read the pamphlet. And if he knew that it was his clerk who had written it with the office pens and on the thick office paper? He could picture him purple with rage, balancing his fat body on the toes of his white shoes, and shouting in his cricket's voice: 'Out of here, you freemason, out of here!'

'I'd be in a nice fix then,' said João Eduardo very seriously, 'without a girl and without bread!'

This made Gustavo think of the probable indignation of Dr Godinho, proprietor of the printing press. Dr Godinho, who since his reconciliation with the people of the Misericordia had again taken up his high position as pillar of the Church and prop of the Faith.

'It's the devil, it might turn out expensive for us,' he said.

'It's impossible!' said the clerk.

They then swore with rage at the thought of losing such a glorious opportunity of uncovering the villainy of the clergy. Their plan of the pamphlet, like a column which, when it has tumbled and is lying on the ground, seems larger than it actually is, appeared to them of colossal importance and profundity. It was not just the demolition of a profligate local priest, it was the ruin throughout the length and breadth of the world of all the clergy, including the Jesuits, of their temporal power and other deadly things . . . Hell! if it wasn't for Nunes, if it wasn't for Godinho, if it wasn't for the nine mil reis of paper.

Those perpetual obstacles of the poor, lack of money and dependence on the employer, so that just for a few packets of paper their design was frustrated, turned them against society.

'A revolution is absolutely necessary!' affirmed the printer. 'It is imperative that all should be rooted up, all, all!' And the wide gesture which he made over the table indicated a formidable social levelling, a demolition of churches, palaces, banks, barracks and properties of Godinhos. 'Another bottle of red wine, Uncle Osorio!'

But Uncle Osorio didn't appear. Gustavo banged the table with all his force with the handle of the knife. And in the end, furious, he went out to the counter to punch the belly of that villain who dared to keep a citizen waiting.

He found him radiant, making servile bows, conversing with the Baron of Via Clara, who on the eve of elections came to the taverns to squeeze the hands of his compatriots. And there in the tavern the baron did appear magnificent, with his gold-rimmed spectacles, and his patent-leather boots shining on the earthen floor, while he coughed from the acrid smell of the frying oil and the fumes of the wine dregs.

Gustavo, on seeing him, discreetly drew back into the cubicle.

'He is with the baron,' he said in a voice of secret respect.

But seeing João Eduardo with his head between his hands, looking beaten, the printer exhorted him not to despair. What the devil! After all, he'd escaped marriage with a *beata*.

'But I can never revenge myself on that rogue!' interrupted João Eduardo pushing back his plate.

'Don't fret about that, vengeance isn't very far away,' promised the printer solemnly.

He then whispered to him, in confidence, of the things which were preparing in Lisbon. He had heard that there was a republican club to which many important people belonged—a fact which was for him the best guarantee of triumph. Besides this, the workers were moving! He himself—and he murmured this almost touching the face of João Eduardo, who was leaning over the table—it was suggested that he himself should join a section of the International, which a Spaniard from Madrid was going to organize; he had never seen the Spaniard, who went about disguised as he was hiding from the police; and the thing fell through as the Committee lacked funds. But it was certain there was a man, who had a meat stall, who had promised a hundred mil reis. And another thing, the army was also in it: at a reunion he had seen an individual with a protruding stomach, whom they said was a major, and who had the face of a major. All this being the case, with all those elements, his opinion, Gustavo's, was that within a few months, government, King, aristocracy, capitalists, bishops, and all such monsters would be blown up in the air!

'And then we'll be the kings, my boy! Godinho, Nunes, and all that rabble we will shut up in the dungeons of San Francisco. The one I'm going to drag off is Godinho. We'll break the backs of the priests! And at last the people will be able to breathe freely!'

'But from now till then!' sighed João Eduardo, thinking with bitterness that when the revolution came it would already be too late to recover his Ameliazinha.

Uncle Osorio then appeared with the bottle of wine.

'So you've arrived at last, you aristocrat!' said the printer sarcastically, trying to upset his good humour.

'I don't belong to his class, but the baron treats me with consideration,' replied Uncle Osorio, whose contentment made him appear fatter.

'On account of half a dozen votes!'

'Eighteen in the district, and hopes of nineteen. Is there anything else that you *cavalheiros* would like? Nothing more? What a shame! Well then, drink and drink heartily.'

He left, closing the curtain and leaving the two friends in front of a full bottle of wine, one hoping for a revolution which would allow him to have his Amelia again, and the other to smash his employer Godinho.

It was almost five o'clock when they left the cubicle. Uncle Osorio, who took an interest in them because they were educated boys, remarked immediately as he examined them from the corner of the counter where he was enjoying his *Popular*, that both were tipsy. Especially João Eduardo, with his hat hanging off the back of his head and a sulky look on his lips; he is a fellow who can't hold his wine, thought Uncle Osorio, who knew him only slightly. But Senhor Gustavo, as always, was jubilantly resplendent after his third litre. A great boy that! It was he who paid the bill, and staggering forward he beat loudly on the counter with his two placas:

'Tie those up in your old stocking, barrel-belly Osorio!'

'What a pity there are only two, Senhor Gustavo.'

'Ah, you thief! do you think the sweat of the people, the wages of work, are only to serve to swell the paunches of the Philistines? But the day of reckoning is not far ahead, and the one who will have the honour of boring this paunch must be Bibi. And I am that Bibi . . . It's I who am Bibi! Isn't it true, João Eduardo, who is Bibi?'

João Eduardo wasn't listening to him: with an ugly frown on his forehead, he looked suspiciously at a drunkard, who at the end table, in front of his empty litre bottle, holding his chin in the palm of his hand and his pipe between his teeth, gazed amazedly at the two friends.

The printer leaned over the counter:

'Tell me here now, Uncle Osorio, who is Bibi? Listen to this, Uncle Osorio! I am a good chap and talented. Mind this. With two strokes of my pen I can destroy all the power of the Pope on earth. That's what I'd like to do. And, between ourselves, it will be for life or death. Give me the account, Fatty Osorio, and listen to what I say. This is a good boy. And if he returns and wants two litres on credit you give them to him—Bibi will be responsible for all.'

'We have besides,' began Uncle Osorio, 'sandwiches for two, salad for two——'

But the drunkard dragged himself forcibly from his bench, with his pipe stuck in his mouth, and belching loudly came and planted himself in front of the printer, his knees trembling, and holding out his hand. Gustavo looked down on it with disgust:

'What do you want? I bet it was you who a short time ago called out "Long live Pius IX!" You rogue—take away that paw!'

The drunkard, repelled, growled; and staggering against João Eduardo offered him his open palm.

'Get away from here, you animal!' said the clerk roughly.

'All meant in friendship—all meant in friendship—' muttered the drunkard.

But he didn't go away, he stood there holding out his hand, with the five fingers stretched out, poisoning the air with his fetid breath.

João Eduardo, furious, pushed him roughly against the counter.

'Rough conduct, no!' said Uncle Osorio severely. 'Brutality, no!'

'Don't interfere with me,' roared the clerk 'or I'll do the same to you!'

'Whoever can't behave themselves had better go outside,' said Uncle Osorio very gravely.

'Who is going outside, who is going outside?' bawled the clerk, threatening him with his closed fist. 'You repeat that if you dare. Who do you think you are talking to?'

Uncle Osorio didn't reply, but leaning his hands on the counter he exposed his enormous arms by which he kept his establishment respectable.

But Gustavo authoritatively put himself between the two, and declared that it was necessary to be *cavalheiros*! Fighting and ugly words, no! They could joke and argue as friends, as *cavalheiros*! Here there must only be *cavalheiros*!'

He dragged the clerk, who was muttering with resentment, into a corner.

'Oh, João! Oh, João!' he said making elaborate gestures, 'this is not fit conduct for an illustrious man. What the devil! It is necessary to have decent manners. Sudden brawls and drunken, disorderly behaviour bring no enjoyment, nor sociability, nor brotherhood!'

He went back to Uncle Osorio, and said excitedly over his shoulder:

'I'll answer for him, Osorio. He is a *cavalheiro*. But he has had a lot of trouble, and is not accustomed to so much wine. That's what it is! But he is one of the best. Excuse him, Uncle Osorio. I will be responsible for him . . .'

He went to get the clerk, and persuaded him to take Uncle Osorio's hand. The tavern-keeper emphatically declared that he didn't wish to insult the *cavalheiro*. A hearty handshake followed. To consolidate the reconciliation, the printer paid for three glasses of *aguardente*. João Eduardo, to prove his generosity, offered another round. And with their glasses in a row on the counter they exchanged pleasant words, and treated one another as *cavalheiros*—while the drunkard, forgotten in his corner, fallen over the table, with his head on his closed fists and his nose on the bottle, silently dribbled over his pipe.

'Now this is what I like!' said the printer, as the *aguardente* increased his tenderness. 'Harmony! My weak point is harmony. Harmony amongst youth and amongst mankind in general. What I'd like to see is a big table, and all humanity seated round at a great banquet, guns and bullets put away, and amidst pleasant jest and laughter all social questions would be decided. And the day is not far off when you will see this happen, Uncle Osorio! In Lisbon things are preparing for this. And it is Uncle Osorio who will have to furnish the wine. Eh, what a good little bit of business! Now you can never say that I'm not your friend.'

'Thank you, Senhor Gustavo, thank you.'

'This is all between ourselves, yes, as we are all *cavalheiros*. And that's how it is.' (Here he embraced João Eduardo.) 'You are just like a brother to me! Come life or come death we are still friends. Send your sorrow to the devil, boy! One day we'll write the pamphlet. Godinho and Nunes——'

'I'll smash Nunes!' shouted the clerk with force. Since they had drunk one another's health with *aguardente* he appeared moodier and more resentful. Two soldiers then entered the tavern, and Gustavo decided that it was time to go to the printing office. If they had to separate for a whole day, well it wasn't a parting for life. But work is a duty, work is a virtue!

They left in the end, after more handshaking with Uncle Osorio. At the door Gustavo again swore brotherly loyalty to the clerk, and insisted on him accepting his pouch of tobacco; he disappeared round the corner with his hat on the back of his head, humming the *Hymn of Work*.

Chapter XIV

JOÃO EDUARDO, now alone, immediately wandered to the Rua da Misericordia. On arriving at Senhora Joanneira's house, he carefully squashed out his cigarette on the sole of his shoe, and then pulled the door-bell cord violently.

Ruça came running down.

'I'd like to speak to Ameliazinha.'

'The senhoras have gone out,' said Ruça, astonished at Senhor Joãozinho's strange behaviour.

'You're lying, you're drunk!' bawled the clerk.

The girl, terrified, banged the door in his face.

João Eduardo went and leant against the wall in front, and remained there, with arms crossed, observing the house: the windows were shut, the muslin curtains drawn; two of the canon's snuff handkerchiefs were hanging out to dry on the veranda below.

He again approached the door and rapped slowly. Next he gave a tremendous pull at the bell-cord. Nobody appeared: he became indignant and left, walking towards the Cathedral.

When he arrived in the Square, in front of the Cathedral, he stopped and looked all round, his brows drawn; but the Square appeared deserted; at the door of Carlos the apothecary's a boy was sitting on the step holding the reins of his donkey, which was laden with grass; here and there chickens voraciously pecked; the large front door of the Cathedral was shut, and there was a faint sound of hammers in a house at the side which was being repaired.

João Eduardo decided to walk on towards the old poplar avenue, when Father Silverio and Father Amaro appeared on the terrace, at the side of the sacristy. They walked along slowly, conversing.

The tower clock was just striking the quarter, and Father Silverio stopped to put his watch right. Then the two priests maliciously observed the window of the Administration of Justice, which was open: in the shadow could be seen the form of the senhor administrator, with his binoculars focused on the house of Telles, the tailor. They descended the Cathedral steps, shoulder to shoulder, laughing, diverted by that passion which was scandalizing the whole of Leiria.

It was then that the paroco saw João Eduardo posted in the middle of the Square. He stopped with the idea of returning to the Cathedral in order to avoid the encounter; but seeing that the door was shut, he continued, with his eyes fixed on the ground, beside the good Silverio, who was tranquilly taking out his box of snuff; when João Eduardo, without a word, jumped forward and gave Amaro a vigorous punch on the shoulder.

The paroco, terrified, weakly raised his umbrella.

'Help!' bawled Father Silverio, stepping back and waving his arms in the air, 'Help!'

From the door of the Administration a man came running, and hastily grabbed the clerk by the coat collar:

'You are a prisoner!' he cried. 'You are a prisoner!'

'Help, help!' roared Silverio from a distance.

The windows in the Square opened quickly. The apothecary's Amparo, scared, appeared on the veranda in a white petticoat; Carlos hurried from the laboratory in his carpet-slippers; and the senhor administrator leaned over the balcony railings, frantically waving his binoculars.

In the end one of the clerks of the Administration, Domingos, came out looking very grave in his threadbare lustre sleeves: with the help of the police he arrested the clerk, who was livid and offered no resistance.

Carlos himself hurried to conduct the senhor paroco to the pharmacy; then, with much fuss and noise, he ordered a preparation of orange-flower tea and shouted for his wife to come and arrange a bed. He proposed examining his reverence's shoulder, there might be intumescence.

'Thank you, it is nothing,' said the priest, who was very pale. 'It is nothing. Just a scratch. All I want is a drop of water.' But Amparo thought that a glass of port wine would be better for him; and she ran upstairs to get it, tripping over the children, who hung on to her skirts, giving out 'Ahs', and explaining, while still on the stairs, to the servant above, that they had tried to kill the senhor paroco.

A crowd had gathered round the door of the pharmacy, gazing stupidly inside; one of the carpenters who was working in the Cathedral declared that it was a case of stabbing; and an old woman at the back agitatedly pushed forward to get a sight of the blood. In the end, at the request of the paroco, who feared a scandal, Carlos came majestically to declare that he didn't want a disturbance at his door. The senhor paroco was better. It was just a blow, a scratch of the hand. He would be responsible for the safety of his reverence.

And as the donkey at the side began to bray, the apothecary turned indignantly towards the boy who was still holding him by the reins: 'Aren't you ashamed, in the middle of a misfortune like this, a misfortune for the whole town, to remain here with this animal which does nothing but bawl? Get away, you insolent fellow, get away!'

He then advised the priests to come upstairs to the parlour, in order to avoid the curiosity of the rabble. And the good Amparo appeared immediately with two glasses of port wine, one for the senhor paroco and the other for Senhor Father Silverio, who had fallen into the corner of the sofa, still terrified and prostrate with emotion.

'I'm fifty-five years old,' he said, after he had finished his last drop of port, 'and it's the first time I have been in a row!'

Father Amaro, now calmed down and affecting a courage which he was far from feeling, ridiculed Father Silverio:

'You are taking the case very seriously, colleague. And as for being the first time, there is no use your pretending that. Everybody knows about your fight with Natario.'

'Ah, yes,' exclaimed Silverio, 'but that was between clergymen, my friend!'

But Amparo, still trembling violently as she filled another glass for the senhor paroco, wished to know the particulars, all the particulars . . .

'There are no particulars, my dear senhora. I was walking along with my colleague here—we were chatting. The fellow came up to me, and as I was unprepared, he gave me a punch on the shoulder.'

'But what for? Why?' said the good senhora, wringing her hands in amazement.

Carlos then gave his opinion. A few days ago he had said in the presence of Amparozinha and Dona Josepha, the sister of our esteemed Canon Dias, that these ideas of materialism and atheism were leading the youth of Leiria to the most pernicious excesses. And little did he then think what he was prophesying!

'Look, senhores, at this young man! He begins by neglecting all his religious duties (so Dona Josepha informed me), associating with undesirables, frequenting taverns, where he ridicules the Church dogmas. Afterwards (notice the gradual downfall), not content with perversions, he publishes low attacks against religion in the papers. And in the end, blinded by his atheism, he assaults, in front of that sacred edifice, the Cathedral, an exemplary priest (I'm not saying this just because your reverence is present) and tries to assassinate him! Now, I ask, what is at the bottom of all this? Hatred, pure hatred of the religion of our fathers!'

'Unhappily it is the truth,' sighed Father Silverio.

But Amparo, indifferent as to the philosophical causes of the delinquency, was burning with curiosity to know what was happening at the Administration, what the clerk was saying, if they had put him in chains. Carlos got ready immediately to go and testify.

Besides, he said, it was his duty as a man of science to enlighten the representatives of justice over the consequences which could follow from a blow on the shoulder, with the full force of an arm, in the delicate region of the clavicle. (As yet, praise be to God, there wasn't a fracture, nor even a swelling.) And most important of all, he would like to reveal to the authorities, so that they could make a better judgment, that this attempt against the priest's life didn't arise from any personal grievance. What could the senhor paroco of the Cathedral have to do with Nunes' clerk? He would warn them of a vast conspiracy of atheists and republicans against the clergy of Christ!

'We agree, we agree,' said the two priests gravely.

'And all this I will prove to the very hilt to the senhor administrator of the council!'

Such was his zealous speed as an indignant conservative, that he was leaving in his laboratory jacket and carpet slippers; but Amparo rushed down the corridor after him:

'Oh, man! your overcoat, at least put on your overcoat, the administrator is very ceremonious!'

She herself helped him to get into it, while Carlos, with his imagination working vigorously (that unfortunate imagination which, as he said, sometimes brought him pains in his head), continued preparing his deposition, which would make a great noise in the town. He would stand up to speak. In the room of the Administration of Justice all would surely be carried out in official state: the senhor administrator, grave and the very personification of Order, would be sitting at his table; and all round him the clerks working on the stamped paper; and in front of him the prisoner, in the traditional attitude of all political criminals, his arms crossed over his chest, and his head held high, defying death. He, Carlos, would then enter and say: 'Senhor administrator, I've come here spontaneously, to put myself at the service of justice, to vindicate its rights.'

'I'll have to show them with an iron logic that all this is the result of a rationalist conspiracy. You can be certain, Amparozinha, that it is a rationalist conspiracy!' he said, groaning as he forced together the studs of his high boots.

'And notice whether they speak of Senhora Joanneira's little girl.'

'I must of course take notice of all. But Senhora Joanneira won't be mentioned. This is a political case!'

He majestically crossed the Cathedral Square, sure that the neighbours, standing at their doors, were murmuring: 'There goes Carlos to make his deposition . . .' Yes, he was going to make his deposition, but not over the punch on the paroco's shoulder. Of what importance was the punch? The serious thing was that which was behind that punch—

a conspiracy against the Law, the Church, the Constitution and property! And this he would thoroughly prove to the senhor administrator: this punch, most excellent senhor, is a signal of a great social revolution!

Pushing open the green baize folding door which gave access to the Administration of Justice of Leiria, he remained a minute with his hand on the knob, filling the frame of the door with the pomp of his person. No, no, there was not the judicial state that he had expected. The prisoner was there, yes, poor João Eduardo, but just sitting on the edge of a bench, with ears burning, and eyes gazing stupidly at the ground. Arthur Couceiro, embarrassed by the presence of his former intimate friend of the evenings at Senhora Joanneira's, now there on the prisoners' bench, in order not to look at him fixed his nose over an immense register, on top of which he had arranged *The Popular* of the previous evening. The clerk Pires, with his eyebrows raised high and looking very serious, carefully studied the point of the duck's quill pen which he was sharpening over his nail. The clerk Domingos, yes, he was bursting with activity. He furiously pared his pencil; the trial was certainly coming off soon; it was time to expound his idea. Carlos now moved forward:

'My dear sirs! The senhor administrator?'

At that moment the voice of his excellency called from within his cabinet:

'Senhor Domingos?'

The clerk lifted up his head, and pushed his glasses up to his forehead.

'Senhor administrator!'

'Have you any matches?'

Domingos anxiously searched his pockets, the drawers, amongst the papers . . .

'Have any of you senhores got any matches?'

All now searched. No, nobody had any matches.

'Perhaps Senhor Carlos has some matches?'

'I haven't, Senhor Domingos, I'm sorry.'

The senhor administrator then appeared, waving his tortoise-shell spectacles:

'Nobody has matches, eh? It is an extraordinary thing that there is never a match to be found here! An office like this without a match. Whatever do you senhores do with the matches? Send at once for a half dozen boxes!'

The employees looked with consternation on this flagrant want of equipment in the administrative service. And Carlos, wishing to take advantage of the presence and attention of his excellency, began:

'Senhor administrator, I came here, voluntarily and spontaneously, in order to say——'

'Tell me one thing, Senhor Carlos,' interrupted the authority, 'are the paroco and the other priest still in the pharmacy?'

'The senhor paroco and Senhor Father Silverio remained with my spouse in order to rest from the commotion that——'

'Have the kindness to tell them that their presence is required here.'

'I am at the service of the law.'

'Tell them to come as soon as possible. It is now half-past five, we want to get away. Look what trouble there has been today! The office shuts at three!'

His excellency turned on his heels and went to lean over the balcony of his office—that balcony from which every day, from eleven till three, twisting his fair moustache and pulling at his large blue cravat, he dishonoured the wife of Telles.

Carlos had already opened the green baize door when a 'pssst!' from Domingos stopped him.

'Oh, friend Carlos,' and the smile of the clerk was one of touching supplication, 'excuse me, eh? But—bring me a small box of matches?'

At that moment Father Amaro appeared at the door, followed by the enormous bulk of Father Silverio.

'I would like to speak privately with the senhor administrator,' said Amaro.

All the employees stood up; so did João Eduardo, white as the paint on the wall. The paroco, with his subtle ecclesiastical walk, crossed the office, followed by the good Silverio who, as he passed in front of the prisoner, obliquely described a semicircle, through terror of the criminal; the senhor administrator rushed to receive the clergymen, and the door of his office was discreetly shut.

'They are going to come to some arrangement,' muttered the experienced Domingos, winking at his colleagues.

Carlos sat down, dissatisfied. He had come there to enlighten the authorities about the social dangers which were threatening Leiria, the District, and Society in general, in order to play his part in that trial which, according to him, was purely political: and here he was, silent, forgotten, and seated on the same bench as the prisoner! They hadn't even offered him a chair! It would really be intolerable if the paroco and the administrator arranged the whole affair without consulting him. He, the only one who could see that that blow given to the shoulder of the priest was not really from the fist of the clerk but the deadly hand of Rationalism. Such disdain for his inspirations appeared to him a fatal error on the part of the administration of the state. Frankly speaking, the administrator hadn't the capabilities necessary to save Leiria from the dangers of the threatened revolution. They were right in the arcade—he was a slacker!

The door of the office was half opened, and the administrator's spectacles shone:

'Senhor Domingos, have the kindness to come in here and talk to us,' said his excellency.

The clerk hurried in importantly; and the door was again closed confidentially. Ah! that door shut in front of him, leaving him outside, filled Carlos with indignation. There he was, stuck with Pires, with Arthur, with all the people of inferior intellect, he who had promised Amparozinha to talk strongly to the administrator! And who were they listening to, and whom had they called? Domingos, a notorious animal, who began the word 'satisfaction' with a 'c'! What could one expect of an authority who spent all his mornings gazing through his binoculars, dishonouring a family? Poor Telles, his neighbour, his friend . . . Yes, he really must speak to Telles.

But his indignation increased when he saw Arthur Couceiro, an employee of the administration, in the absence of his chief, get up from his desk, walk in a friendly manner towards the prisoner, and say sympathetically: 'Ah, João, what a silly lad, what a silly lad! But things will be arranged all right, you'll see!'

João had sadly shrugged his shoulders. He had now been sitting there for half an hour on the edge of the bench, without moving, without taking his eyes from the ground, feeling his mind so empty of ideas that it seemed as if his brains had been removed. All the wine, which in Uncle Osorio's tavern and in the Cathedral Square had lit up his mind with burning anger and filled his pulse with a desire to fight, seemed to have been suddenly eliminated from his system. He now felt as inoffensive as when in the office he carefully sharpened his duck's quill pen. A terrible weariness numbed him; and he waited there on the bench, inert in all his being, thinking stupidly that he would now be sent to a dungeon in the San Francisco prison, that he would sleep on a heap of straw, and feed from the Misericordia. He wouldn't be able to walk in the old poplar avenue; he wouldn't see Amelia. His little house would be let to someone else. Who would take care of his canary? Poor little animal, it would surely die of hunger. But perhaps his neighbour, Eugenia, would look after him . . .

Domingos suddenly came out of his excellency's office, and excitedly closing the door after him, said triumphantly:

'What did I tell you? All is arranged!'

And turning towards João Eduardo:

'Be happy! Congratulations! Congratulations!'

Carlos thought it was the greatest administrative scandal since the time of the Cabraes! He was preparing to leave disgusted (as in the classical picture the Stoic is seen retiring from a Patrician orgy) when the senhor administrator opened the door of his office. Everybody stood up.

His excellency advanced two paces into the office, and again clothed in gravity, he said, distilling his words and fixing his spectacles on the prisoner:

'Senhor Father Amaro, who is a priest full of charity and goodness, came to make a deposition to me. In fact, he came to plead with me not to let this case go any further. Surely you too would not like your name to be dragged through the courts. Besides this, as his reverence so truly said, the religion of which he is—of which he is, as one might say, an emblem and a model—imposes forgiveness for injuries received. His reverence realizes that the attack was brutal, but frustrated—also it appears that you were drunk.'

All eyes were fixed on João Eduardo, who was scarlet. This moment seemed worse to him than prison.

'To conclude,' continued the administrator, 'for serious reasons which I have carefully weighed, I take the responsibility of letting you go. See that you behave yourself now. The authorities will have their eyes on you. Good, go with God!'

His excellency returned to his office. João Eduardo remained standing there stupidly.

'I can go, eh?' he muttered.

'To China, to wherever you like! *Liberus, libera, liberum!*' exclaimed Domingos, who in his heart detested the clergy, and felt jubilant at the verdict.

João Eduardo looked round him for a minute at the clerks and at the sulky-looking Carlos; tears glittering on his eyelashes; he suddenly grabbed his hat and hurried away.

'He was saved a lot of trouble!' said Domingos, excitedly rubbing his hands.

Immediately everybody's papers were quickly tidied and shoved away. It was late. Pires gathered up his lustre sleeves and his little cap, which he used to keep the draught from his ears. Arthur rolled up his music papers. And in the recess of the window, still waiting, silent and angry, Carlos looked drearily out on the Square.

In the end the two priests left, accompanied to the door by the senhor administrator, who now that he had finished his public duties reappeared as a man of society. Why then hadn't friend Silverio come to the house of the Baroness of Via Clara? They had had an exciting game of quadrille; Peixoto had got two *codillos*. He had sworn like a trooper! 'Always at your service, senhores. I'm delighted that all has been settled so harmoniously. Mind the step. At your service, senhores . . .'

As he returned to his cabinet he deigned to stand in front of Domingos' desk, and again resuming some of his solemn air, he said:

'It's all gone off very well. It was a bit irregular, but the wisest thing to do. There have been quite enough attacks on the clergy in the papers. This could have given rise to a scandal. The fellow was quite capable of saying that he was jealous of the priest who wanted to seduce the girl, etc. It was better to smother the whole thing. And also, according to the paroco who, I believe, is right, all the influence which he has exercised in the Rua da Misericordia, or wherever the devil it is, was directed towards saving the girl from a marriage with the fellow, who, as one can see, is a drunkard and a beast!'

Carlos was in a rage. All these explanations were given to Domingos! To him, nothing! There he was, stuck in the recess of the window, forgotten.

But no! His excellency, from inside his cabinet, beckoned him mysteriously with his finger.

At last! He hurried, radiant, suddenly reconciled to authority.

'I was intending to pass by the pharmacy,' said the administrator in a whisper, giving him a folded paper, 'to ask you to send this to my house today. It is a prescription from Dr Gouvea. But now that you are here, my friend——'

'I came here to make a deposition on the vindictive——'

'That's finished!' his excellency interrupted brusquely. 'Don't forget, send me this before six. It's to be taken tonight. Good-bye. Don't forget!'

'I won't fail,' said Carlos dryly.

As he entered the pharmacy his anger flamed up. As sure as his name was Carlos he'd start a vigorous correspondence against them in *The Popular*!

But Amparo, who had been watching out for him on the veranda, ran down to meet him, and began to fire questions at him:

'What happened? Was the boy let off? What did he say? How was it all?'

Carlos looked at her with his eyes blazing:

'It wasn't my fault, but materialism has triumphed! They'll pay well for this!'

'But you? What did you say?'

Then, seeing the eyes of Amparo and those of his assistant open to devour the account of his deposition, Carlos, in order to preserve his dignity as a husband and his superiority as an employer, said laconically:

'I gave my opinion, with firmness!'

'And what did the administrator say?'

It was then that Carlos, remembering it, read the prescription which he held securely in his hand. His indignation choked him as he looked at this thing which was the whole result of his important interview with the authorities.

'What is it?' asked Amparo avidly.

What was it? In his fury, disdaining his professional secrecy and the good name of the authority, Carlos exclaimed:

'It is a flask of Gilbert's syrup for the senhor administrator! Here, take the prescription, Senhor Augusto.'

Amparo, who had some practical experience of chemistry and knew the benefits of mercury, became as scarlet as the flaming ribbon tied round her bun of hair.

All that same evening there was much excited talk in the town about the attempted assassination of which the senhor paroco was to have been the victim. Some people censured the administrator for not having proceeded with the case; above all the *cavalheiros* of the opposition, who saw in the weakness of the functionary an incontestable proof of where the government was going. With its waste and its corruption it was certainly leading the country to ruin!

But Father Amaro was admired as a saint. What piety! What meekness! The senhor precentor had sent for him early in the evening, received him paternally with a 'Long live my Paschal Lamb!' and after listening to the history of the insult and the generous intervention, he exclaimed:

'My son, this is joining the youthfulness of Telemachus to the prudence of Mentor. Father Amaro, you are worthy of being a priest of Minerva in the town of Salento.'

When Amaro went that evening to Senhora Joanneira's house, he was received like the apparition of a saint escaped from the wild beasts of the circus, or from the mob of Diocletian. Amelia, not attempting to hide her delight, pressed both his hands for a long time, her whole body trembling and her eyes damp. They gave him, as on all great nights, the canon's green armchair. Dona Maria of the Assumption insisted on placing a cushion for him to lean his wounded shoulder on. Then he had to recount the whole scene point by point, from the moment in which, talking with colleague Silverio (who had comported himself very well) he had seen the clerk in the middle of the Square, with his thick stick lifted in the air, ready to deal him deadly blows.

These details made the senhoras indignant. The clerk appeared to them worse than Longinus or Pilate. What wickedness! The senhor paroco should have knocked him down and jumped on him! Ah! he was a saint, he had pardoned him!

'I did what my conscience told me to do,' he said, lowering his eyes. 'I remembered the words of Our Lord Jesus Christ: "If a man strikes thee on the right cheek turn to him also the left."'

At this the canon noisily cleared his throat and spat:

'What I say is, that if anyone struck me on the right cheek—well, as they are the orders of Our Lord Jesus Christ, I'd also offer him the left cheek. These are orders from above. But after having done my duty as a Christian, oh, senhoras, I'd break the thief's back!'

'Does it hurt much, senhor paroco?' came a faint unknown voice from a corner of the room.

An extraordinary happening! It was Dona Anna Gansoso, who had spoken after ten long years of somnolent taciturnity! That torpor which nothing could shake, neither feasts nor funerals, had in the end, under an impulse of sympathy for the senhor paroco, humanly vibrated! All the senhoras laughed with delight, and Amaro, flattered, graciously replied:

'Very little, Dona Anna. Almost nothing, my dear senhora. He gave a strong blow, but my flesh is tough.'

'Ah, what a monster!' exclaimed Dona Josepha, furious at the idea of the clerk's fist touching that saintly shoulder. 'What a monster! I would like to see him in convict chains working on the roads. I know him well. He never deceived me . . . I always thought he had the face of an assassin.'

'He was drunk, and men when in wine——' Senhora Joanneira timidly hazarded.

There was a clamour. Ah, there was no excuse for him. It seemed almost a sacrilege! He was a beast, he was a beast!

And the exultation was great when Arthur Couceiro appeared and, while still at the door, gave the latest news: Nunes had sent for João Eduardo and said to him (these were the actual words): 'I'll not have villains and ruffians in my office. Get out of here!'

Senhora Joanneira was affected at this, and said:

'Poor boy, now he'll have nothing to eat!'

'Well then, let him drink! Let him drink!' cried Dona Maria of the Assumption.

They all laughed except Amelia, who leaning down over her sewing became very pale, terrified at the idea that João Eduardo would perhaps go hungry.

'Now listen, I don't find it a laughing matter!' said Senhora Joan-neira. 'It is enough to make me lose my sleep. To think that the boy may want a bit of bread and not be able to get it. Heavens! No, not that! And I hope Senhor Father Amaro will excuse me.'

But Amaro too had no wish that the boy should fall into misery. He wasn't a man of rancour; and if the clerk was in want and came to his door, two or three placas (he wasn't rich, he couldn't give more), but two or three placas he'd give. He'd give them with all his heart.

So much holiness made the old ladies fanatic. What an angel! They looked tenderly on him, with their hands held out vaguely. His presence, like that of St Vincent de Paul, exhaled charity, gave to the parlour the suavity of a chapel: Dona Maria of the Assumption sighed with pious pleasure.

But Natario arrived, radiant. He warmly pressed both hands of the company all round, and then broke out triumphantly:

'Then you've all heard? The villain, the blackguard is thrown out everywhere, like a dog! Nunes expelled him from the office. Dr Godinho told me just now that he'll never put his foot in the civil governor's office again. He is flattened out, demolished! It is a relief to all well-minded people!'

'And it is to Senhor Father Natario that we owe it all!' exclaimed Dona Josepha.

They all recognized it. It was he who with his ability, his clever tongue, had opened people's eyes to the perfidy of João Eduardo, thus saving Ameliazinha, Leiria, and Society.

'And in everything that he attempts to do the villain will find me there in front of him. As long as he remains in Leiria I'll not let go my hold of him. What did I tell you, my dear senhoras? That I'd smash him. Here I have him smashed!'

His bilious face shone. He moved with enjoyment in his armchair, taking his well-deserved rest after a hard-won victory. And turning towards Amelia:

'And now, what's done is done. There is one thing I can say, and that is that I've saved you from marrying a beast.'

Then the praises—which had already been so profusely repeated since she had broken with the beast—began again, but now louder:

'It is the most virtuous act of your life.'

'The grace of God will fall on you for this.'

'You are full of grace, child.'

'In fact she is St Amelia,' said the canon getting up from his chair, feeling annoyed at so much glorification. 'It seems to me that we've talked enough about that scamp. The senhora could now send for the tea, eh?'

Amelia had remained silent, sewing rapidly, sometimes raising her head and giving Amaro a quick disturbed look; she thought of João Eduardo, of Natario's threats; and she had a vision of the clerk with his cheeks hollow with hunger, a scared fugitive, sleeping on doorsteps ... And when the senhoras had settled themselves down comfortably at the tea table, and were busy chatting, she whispered to Amaro:

'I can't stop thinking that the boy will suffer from want. I know well that he is a wicked fellow, but—to think of him like that is like a thorn in my heart. It takes away all my joy.'

Father Amaro then said very bounteously, in an elevated spirit of Christian charity, presenting himself as superior to the injury he had suffered:

'My dear child, that is nonsense. The man won't die of hunger. Nobody dies of hunger in Portugal. He is young and healthy; he is not a fool; he will find something. Don't think of that. Father Natario is just talking. The fellow will naturally leave Leiria, we will never hear of him again. In all parts of the country there are ways of gaining a living. As for myself, I forgive him, and God will surely take that into consideration.'

These very generous words, spoken in a whisper, with the tender eye of a lover, calmed her mind. The clemency, the charity of the senhor paroco seemed to her better than all she had heard or read of the saints and holy monks.

After tea, at the game of lotto, she remained beside him. A sweet joy filled her whole being. All that up to then had seemed to her of importance or had frightened her—João Eduardo, her marriage, her duties—disappeared from her life: the boy would go far away and get work; and the senhor paroco was still there, belonging to her, in love with her! Sometimes under the table their trembling knees touched; at the moment when all made a hullabaloo against Arthur Couceiro who had won three times and triumphantly brandished his card, it was their hands which met and caressed; a simultaneous little sigh, lost in the croaking of the old ladies, came from the heart of both; and till the end of the evening they marked their cards, very silent, their faces radiant with the same overpowering desire.

When the senhoras were putting on their cloaks Amelia approached the piano in order to play a tune. Amaro took the opportunity of murmuring in her ear: 'Oh my little one, whom I love so much! But can we never be alone?'

She was going to reply when Natario, who was standing by the sideboard, wrapping himself up in his cloak, exclaimed very severely: 'The senhoras leave such a book lying about here?'

All turned round surprised at his indignation, and beheld Natario pointing with his umbrella at a large, bound volume, as if it were something abominable. Dona Maria of the Assumption came over immediately, with her eyes shining, thinking it might be one of those novels, now so famous, in which immoral scenes are described. And Amelia also approached the sideboard and said, surprised at the reprobation:

'But it is only *Panorama*—a volume of *Panorama*.'

'I can see it is *Panorama*,' said Natario dryly. 'But this I also see.' He opened the volume at the first blank page and read aloud: ' "This book belongs to me, João Eduardo Barbosa, and serves to entertain me in my moments of leisure." You don't understand, eh? Well, it's very simple. It seems incredible that the senhoras don't know that this man, from the time he put his hands on a priest, is *ipso facto* excommunicated, as are all things belonging to him!'

All the senhoras instinctively drew away from the sideboard where lay the open volume of the fatal *Panorama*. They banded themselves together, curled up with fear at the idea of this excommunication which presented itself to them as a downpour of catastrophes, a shower of thunderbolts sent from the hands of God the Avenger. They remained there silent, in a frightened semicircle around Natario who, with his cloak thrown over his shoulders and his arms crossed, was enjoying the effect of his revelation.

Then Senhora Joanneira, in her astonishment, ventured:

'Oh, Senhor Father Natario, are you speaking seriously?'

Natario was indignant:

'Am I speaking seriously? That is a bit strong! So, my dear senhora, you think I'm joking about a case of excommunication? Ask the senhor canon here if I'm joking!'

All eyes turned towards the canon, that inexhaustible fountain of ecclesiastical knowledge. He immediately took the pedagogic air which he had assumed in the seminary, and to which he always returned when explaining a point of doctrine, and declared that his colleague Natario was right. He who attacked a priest, knowing he was a priest, was *ipso facto* excommunicated. It was an established doctrine. It was what was called latent excommunication, not requiring the declaration of a pontiff or a bishop, nor a ceremony, in order to be valid; and all the faithful must consider the offender excommunicated. And they must treat him as such, avoid him and all that belonged to him. 'And this case of putting sacrilegious hands on a priest is so special,' continued the canon in a profound tone, 'that a bull of Pope Martin V, limiting the tacit cases of excommunication, conserved the one with regard to the ill-treatment of a priest.' He then cited more bulls, the Constitution of Innocent IX and of Alexander VII, the Apostolic Constitution and other terrible laws; he muttered Latin and terrified the senhoras.

'That is the doctrine,' he concluded: 'But it appears to me better not to make a commotion about it.'

Dona Josepha interrupted:

'But we can't risk our souls by leaving excommunicated things on the table in front of us.'

'It must be destroyed,' exclaimed Dona Maria of the Assumption. 'Burn it! burn it!'

Dona Joaquina Gansoso drew Amelia into the recess of the window, to ask her if she had any other objects belonging to the man. Amelia, confused, confessed that she had somewhere, she couldn't think where, a handkerchief, an old glove, and a straw cigarette-holder.

'For the fire, for the fire!' shouted the Gansoso excited.

The parlour now vibrated with the cackling of the old ladies, possessed of a holy fury. Dona Josepha and Dona Maria of the Assumption spoke with a vicious delight of the Fire, savouring the word in an inquisitorial enjoyment of devout extermination. Amelia and the Gansoso, in the bedroom, searched in the cupboard amongst the white underclothing, the ribbons and the little drawers, hunting for the excommunicated objects. And Senhora Joanneira assisted, astonished and scared at the display of the *auto da fé* which had brusquely entered her peaceful parlour. She then took refuge beside the canon, who after murmuring some words on 'the Inquisition in private cases' comfortably dug himself into his armchair.

'It is so that they will not lose with impunity their respect for the cassock,' Natario whispered to Amaro.

The paroco assented with a silent nod of the head, content at this display of fury, which was a noisy affirmation of the senhoras' love for him.

But Dona Josepha, becoming impatient, caught up the *Panorama* with the points of her shawl, to avoid contagion, and shouted into the room where the heated search in the drawers continued:

'Have you found them?'

'Yes, they're here, they're here!'

It was the Gansoso who entered triumphantly with the cigarette-holder, the glove and the cotton handkerchief.

And the senhoras, with great noise and fuss, carried them into the kitchen. Senhora Joanneira, as a good woman of the house, followed them in order to supervise the bonfire.

The three priests, now alone, looked at one another and laughed.

'The women have the devil in their bodies,' said the canon philosophically.

'No senhor, no senhor,' answered Natario putting on a serious face. 'I laughed, because the thing viewed thus seems funny. But the sentiment is good. It proves the true devotion to the priesthood and a horror of impiety—in fact, the sentiment is excellent.'

'The sentiment is excellent,' confirmed Amaro, also serious.

The canon said as he got up from his chair:

'If they could get hold of the man, they are capable of doing the same to him. I'm not saying it in fun, my sister has the guts for it. She is a Torquemada in petticoats.'

'That's true, that's true,' agreed Natario.

'I can't resist the temptation of going to see the execution,' exclaimed the canon. 'I want to see it with my own eyes.'

The three priests went to the kitchen door. The senhoras were there, standing in front of the stove, the violent light of the fire beating on them, making their black mantles, which they had already put on, stand out weirdly. Ruça, on her knees, had exhausted her breath blowing the fire. They had cut the cover of *Panorama* with a large knife; and the leaves twisted and blackened, flashed and sparkled as they flew up the chimney in bright tongues of fire. All was consumed except the sheepskin glove. It was in vain that they pushed it into the flame with the tongs: it gave out fumes and became a black devilish-looking mass, but refused to burn. And its resistance terrified the senhoras.

'It is because it was with his right hand that he committed the attack!' said Dona Maria of the Assumption full of fury.

'Blow it, girl, blow it!' advised the canon from the door, very entertained.

'Oh, brother, have the goodness not to joke about serious things!' shouted Dona Josepha.

'Oh, sister! I suppose you think you know better than a priest how to burn an impious article? Your pretensions aren't bad! Blow it, blow it!'

Then, with confidence in the senhor canon's science, the Gansoso and Dona Maria of the Assumption got down on their knees and joined in the blowing. The others looked on, mutely smiling, eyes brilliant and cruel, enjoying that extermination, pleasing to Our Lord. The fire crackled, leaping and springing into a sprightly dance, in the glory of its ancient function as a purifier of sin. In the end over the burning log nothing remained of *Panorama*, the handkerchief or the glove of the excommunicated clerk.

At that same hour João Eduardo, the excommunicated one, sat in his room on the end of his bed sobbing, his face bathed in tears, thinking of Amelia, of the grand evenings in the Rua da Misericordia, of the town to which he was going, of the clothes he must pawn, and asking himself in vain why people had treated him like this, he who was such a good worker and who wished nobody ill, and who loved *her* so much.

Chapter XV

THE FOLLOWING Sunday there was a sung Mass at the Cathedral, and Senhora Joanneira and Amelia crossed the Square on their way to fetch Dona Maria of the Assumption, who on market days or days on which the town was crowded, never went out alone, afraid that her jewellery might be robbed or her chastity assailed.

That morning, in fact, the flow of people filled the Square: the men were in groups, obstructing the pavements, very serious, very well shaved; with their jackets thrown over their shoulders; the women were in pairs, with a wealth of gold chains and gold hearts on their over-developed bosoms; in the shops, the assistants behind their counters strewn with chintzes and linens loudly proclaimed their goods; in the crowded taverns men talked noisily; along the market place, among the sacks of flour, the piles of china and the baskets of maize bread, continuous haggling and bargaining went on. There was a throng of feet around the stalls where the little round looking-glasses shone, and the rosaries hung outside in bundles; the old cake women, standing behind their plank counters, made much hubbub, and the professional beggars of the town whined Our Fathers from their corners.

Senhoras, all in silk and with serious faces, were already passing on their way to Mass; and the arcade was full of *cavalheiros*, in their suits of stiff new cashmere, smoking expensive cigars, and enjoying Sunday.

Amelia attracted a good deal of attention: the tax-gatherer's son, a daring fellow, said loudly to a group of boys: 'Ah, how she makes my heart beat!'; and hurrying along, the two senhoras turned into Rua do Correio, as Libaninho appeared in black gloves, a carnation in his buttonhole. They hadn't seen him since the 'desecration' in the Cathedral Square. He immediately broke into exclamations: 'Ah, children, what a disgusting thing that was! The cursed clerk!' He had had so much to do, that it was only that morning that he had been able to go to the senhor paroco to express his sympathy and admiration; the holy man, the saint, who was just dressing, received him so well; he saw his arm, and happily, praise be to God, there wasn't a trace of the blow left—and if they could only see his flesh, so delicate, and his lovely white skin—the skin of an archangel!

'But would you believe it, children? He is in great trouble.'

The two senhoras said, frightened: 'What's happened, Libaninho?'

The servant, Vicencia, who had been complaining for days, had been taken to hospital early that morning with fever.

'And here is the poor saint without a servant, without anyone! Can you imagine it? It's all right today, he is going to dine with our canon (I have just been there also, ah, what a saint!), but tomorrow and after? He already has Vicencia's sister Dionysia in the house. But, oh children, Dionysia! I said to him that Dionysia could be a perfect servant, but what a reputation! There is no worse in Leiria. A lost soul who never darkens the church door. I am certain that the senhor precentor himself will have to reprove her!'

The two senhoras agreed immediately that Dionysia (a woman who didn't perform her religious duties, and had been an actress in theatres of doubtful reputation) wasn't a suitable person for the senhor paroco.

'Listen, Senhora Joanneira,' said Libaninho, 'do you know what would suit him? Well, I'll tell you, I've already made the proposition to him. It is that you take him again into your house. That is where he would be best, with people who would be kind to him, who would look after his clothes, who know his tastes, and where all are virtuous. He didn't say either yes or no. But look, I could read in his face that he is dying for it. It is you who must speak to him, Senhora Joanneira.'

Amelia turned as red as her bow of Indian silk. And Senhora Joanneira answered ambiguously:

'No, I won't speak to him. I am very delicate with regard to those things. You understand——'

'It would be as if you had a saint inside your house, my friend!' said Libaninho heatedly. 'Remember that! And it would be a joy for all. I feel sure that even our Heavenly Father would rejoice. And now goodbye, little ones, as I must run. Don't you delay, as Mass will soon begin.'

The two senhoras remained silent till they reached Dona Maria of the Assumption's house. Neither one wanted to risk the first word about that very serious, unhoped-for possibility of the senhor paroco returning to the Rua da Misericordia! It was only when they stopped that Senhora Joanneira said, as she pushed the door-bell:

'Ah, it's right, the senhor paroco can't really keep Dionysia inside his house.'

'Heavens, it would be horrible!'

That was also Dona Maria of the Assumption's expression when they recounted the story of Vicencia's illness, and the installation of Dionysia: 'It would be horrible!'

'I don't know her personally,' said the excellent senhora. 'But I'm curious to meet her. They tell me that from top to toe she is a hardened sinner!'

Senhora Joanneira then spoke of Libaninho's proposition. Dona Maria of the Assumption ardently declared that it was an inspiration of Our Lord. The senhor paroco should never have left the Rua da Misericordia. Look at the evils which had befallen them since then, God had withdrawn His grace from the house. There had been nothing but misfortunes—the *Communication*, the canon's pain in the stomach, the death of the paralytic, that disgraceful marriage arrangement (what a horror! what an escape!), the scandal in the Cathedral Square . . . The house seemed to be under a spell of bad luck. And it was almost a sin to let that saintly man live in that state, with that dirty Vicencia, who didn't even know how to darn a hole in a sock!

'In fact, no one could be better off than in your house. They have everything they want there. And for you it would be an honour, you would be in a perpetual state of grace. Listen, friend, if I wasn't alone I would take him myself as a lodger; I've always said so. Here he would be well off. What a little parlour for him, eh?'

Her eyes were alight with glee as she looked all round and contemplated her treasures.

The parlour was an immense warehouse of images of saints, and devout bric-à-brac: over the two chests of drawers of black wood with copper locks were crowded, under glass domes placed on pedestals, statues of Our Blessed Lady dressed in blue silk, of baby Jesuses with frizzed hair and little fat stomachs, with their hands held out in benediction, of St Antonys in their habits of coarse woollen material, St Sebastians stuck with many arrows, and bearded St Josephs. There were exotic saints of which she was very proud, made in Alcobaça: St Didacio, St Chrisolo and many others. Then there were the scapulars, the rosaries of metal, olive stones, and coloured beads, lace now yellow with age, old albs, hearts of red glass, small cushions with the initials J. & M. interlaced and worked with beads, blessed branches, martyrs' palms, paper bags of incense. The walls had disappeared under prints of the Virgin in various devout attitudes—poised over the orb, kneeling at the foot of the Cross, penetrated with swords. There were hearts from which gushed blood, hearts from which came fire, hearts from which rays sparkled; prayers in little frames for all the most beloved private feasts, *The Marriage of Our Lady*, *The Discovery of the True Cross*, *The Stigmata of St Francis*, and most important of all *The Delivery of the Holy Virgin*, reserved for her devotions on the Ember Days. Little lamps were alight on the tables, all ready to be arranged without delay in front of special saints when the good senhora had her sciatica, or when her catarrh was troublesome, or her joints were stiff. She herself, only she, arranged and dusted them with a feather broom; it was she who polished that holy celestial mob, that blessed arsenal, which was only just sufficient for the salvation of her soul and the relief of her aches and pains. Her greatest concern was the placing of her saints; she continually altered their positions, as sometimes, for example, she felt that St Eleuterio wouldn't like to remain at the foot of St Justain and she took him to hang him at a distance amongst a company which was more sympathetic to the saint. She classed them according to the precepts of the ritual (which her confessor explained to her), giving them a graduated devotion, and not having for St Joseph of the second class the same respect which she had for St Joseph of the first class. Such a wealth was the envy of her friends and the edification of the curious. Libaninho, when he came to visit her, always said, as he cast a languorous eye round the room: 'Ah, friend, this is indeed the kingdom of heaven!'

'Now isn't it true,' continued the excellent senhora radiant, 'that here our sainted paroco would feel at home? Here he would have the heavens under his hand!'

The two senhoras agreed; and remarked that she could have her house full of devotion because she was rich . . .

'I won't deny it, I have spent some hundreds of mil reis on what is here, without counting the reliquary . . .'

Ah, the famous reliquary of sandalwood, lined with satin! It contained a splinter of the True Cross, a broken thorn from The Crown of Thorns, a rag from the swaddling clothes of the Infant Jesus. It was murmured with bitterness amongst the devout that such precious things, of divine origin, should be in the shrine for relics in the Cathedral. Dona Maria of the Assumption, fearing that the senhor preceptor would get to know of this seraphic treasure, only showed it in secret to her most intimate friends. And the holy priest who obtained it for her made her swear on the Gospels that she would never reveal how she got it, as otherwise there might be a lot of babbling.

Senhora Joanneira, as always, admired most the rag from the swaddling clothes.

And Dona Maria of the Assumption said in a very low voice:

'There is no better. It cost me twenty mil reis . . . But I'd give sixty, I'd give a hundred! I'd give all I have!' And slobbering with admiration in front of the precious rag, she whined, almost crying: 'Oh, little rag! My precious little Jesus, oh your little rag!'

She kissed it noisily and then locked it in the drawer of the reliquary.

As it was nearing midday, the three senhoras hurried to the Cathedral to secure a place at the High Altar.

They met Dona Josepha in the Square. She too was hurrying to the

Cathedral, avid for the Mass, with her mantle falling off her shoulders and a feather falling from her hat. She had been driven distracted that morning with the servant! She'd had to leave everything prepared for the meal . . . She was even afraid she wouldn't derive all the benefits from the Mass, she was so nervous.

'The senhor paroco will be there today. Do you know that his servant is ill? Ah, I nearly forgot, my brother would like you too to come and dine with us, Amelia. He says he wants to have two senhoras and two *cavalheiros*.'

Amelia laughed with pleasure.

'And can you come later to fetch her, Senhora Joanneira? Heavens, I dressed myself so quickly that I have the feeling my petticoat is falling down!'

When the three senhoras entered, the church was already full. It was a sung Mass to the Blessed Sacrament. And, according to a custom of the diocese and in spite of its being contrary to the ritual (the good Silverio, who was very strict about the liturgy, always looked on this procedure with disapproval), there was, the Eucharist being present, music from the double-bass, the violincello and the flute. The altar, highly adorned, with the relics exposed, stood out in a festive whiteness; the canopy, frontal and decorations of the missals were white relieved by tarnished gold. In the vases were pyramid-shaped bunches of white flowers and foliage; the decorative velvet hangings, arranged as awnings, were placed at both sides of the tabernacle in the form of two vast white spreading wings, representing the Holy Spirit as a Dove; and the twenty branched candlesticks, placed in tiers, threw their yellow flames up to the open tabernacle, a blaze of gold, set with jewels containing the dull-coloured Host. Through all the crowded church ran a slow murmur; here and there a cough was heard, a child whined; the air was already heavy from the many breaths and the smell of incense; and in the choir, where the forms of the musicians moved at the back of the double-basses and the music-stands, came every moment the groaning sound of the double-bass or the puling of a flute.

The four friends had only just sat down near the High Altar when the two acolytes, one firm and tall as a pine and the other fat and dirty-looking, entered from the side of the sacristy, very steadily holding aloft the two consecrated candlesticks; at the back Pimenta, nicknamed Squint Eye, in a surplice which was much too big for him, advanced in long pompous steps with the silver thurible; afterwards, during the noise made by the congregation as they knelt down, and the turning over of the pages, the two deacons appeared one after the other; and at the end, attired in pure white with hands joined and eyes cast down in that thoughtful attitude of humiliation which the ritual lays down and which personifies the meekness of Christ on his way to Calvary, entered Father Amaro, still flaming from a furious argument he had just had in the sacristy, before he put on his vestments, about the washing of the white tunics.

The choir immediately attacked the *Introit*.

Amelia spent her time during the Mass lost in admiration for the paroco, who was, as the canon said, a great artist for the sung Masses; all the chapter, all the senhoras recognized it. What dignity, what refinement in his ceremonial salutations to the deacons! How well he prostrated himself before the altar, in complete humiliation and renunciation, feeling himself ashes, feeling himself dust in front of God, who was there present surrounded by His court and His celestial family! But he was most wonderful in the benedictions: slowly passing his hand over the altar as if he wanted to gather, to take hold of the grace which fell there from Christ, who was standing near; afterwards dispensing it with a bountiful gesture of love through the whole nave, over the array of white kerchiefs which covered the women's heads; even to the very end where the countrymen, packed close together, with the long poles with which they travelled over the mountains in their hands, gazed with wonder at the shining tabernacle. Amelia loved him best when she thought that those hands, with which he blessed the people, were the same which passionately squeezed hers under the table; that voice with which he called her 'my little girl' now recited those wonderful prayers and seemed to her better than the groan of the double-bass, more moving than the deep tones of the organ. She proudly imagined that all the senhoras admired him as well; but the only jealousy she had was the jealousy of the devout as she felt the enchantments of the heavens, when he stood in front of the altar in the ecstatic position which the ritual ordered, so still that it seemed as if his soul had fled far away, to the heights, to the eternal, to the unperceivable. But she preferred him when she felt him more human, more accessible, during the *Kyrie* or the reading of the Gospels, or when he sat with the deacons on the red damask bench; then she would have liked to draw his attention with a look, but the senhor paroco remained with eyes cast down, in a modest attitude.

Amelia, sitting back on her heels, with her face bathed in smiles, admired his profile, his well-made head, his gold embroidered robes, and called to mind the first time she had seen him descending the stairs in the Rua da Misericordia, cigarette in hand. What romance had taken place since that night! She thought of Morenal, of the jump over the ditch, of the scene on the night of her aunt's wake, and that kiss beside the fire . . . Ah, how was it all going to end? She then tried to fix her attention on her prayer-book, but the idea of what Libaninho had said to her that morning came to her mind: 'his lovely white skin—the skin of an archangel!' It was surely very delicate and tender . . . An intense desire burned her: she imagined that it was the devil tempting her; and in order to repel him she fixed her eyes on the tabernacle and on the altar where Father Amaro, surrounded by the deacons in a semicircle, waved the incense signifying the Eternal Glorification of God, while the choir burst forth with the *Offertory*. Afterwards he himself, standing on the second step of the altar, with his arms crossed over his chest, was incensed; Squint Eye Pimenta gaily waved the thurible; a perfume of incense was wafted as a message to heaven; the tabernacle and the priest were enveloped in its coiling white fumes; the priest appeared to Amelia transfigured, almost divine . . . Oh, how she adored him then!

The church trembled to the sound of the organ in full blast; the choristers, with wide-open mouths, sol-fahed with all their might; while above, pompously perched between the necks of the double-basses, the master of the chapel, in the ardour of his performance, desperately waved his baton made from a roll of plain-chant.

Amelia left the church looking very tired and pale.

At the dinner in the canon's house Dona Josepha repeatedly censured her for not talking.

She didn't talk, but under the table her little feet never ceased seeking those of Father Amaro, rubbing against them, treading on them. It became dark early and the candles were lit; the canon opened a bottle of duque, not his famous 1815 vintage but the 1847, to accompany the dish of vermicelli in the centre of the table with the paroco's initials in cinnamon on the top (which was, as the canon explained, a little joke of his sister's to amuse the guests). Amaro raised his glass and proposed a drink to 'the gracious lady of the house'. She beamed, looking frightful in her ugly green wool dress. She was so sorry that the dinner was so bad—Gertrude had been on the point of doing something so careless. She almost burnt the duck and the vermicelli!

'Oh, my dear senhora, it was delicious!' protested the paroco.

'It is very nice of you to say so. Luckily I saved it in time . . . Another little spoonful of vermicelli, senhor paroco?'

'No more, my dear senhora, I've had sufficient.'

'Well then, in order not to waste it, take another little glass of the '47,' said the canon.

He himself took a long draught, gave a sigh of satisfaction, and said, as he sank back in his chair:

'A grand drop! This is the life.'

He was already flushed and appeared more obese, with his thick flannel jacket, and his napkin fixed on his chest.

'A grand drop!' he repeated: 'You didn't drink anything like this from the wine cruets today.'

'Heavens, brother!' exclaimed Dona Josepha, with her mouth full of strings of vermicelli, very shocked at such an irreverence.

The canon shrugged his shoulders contemptuously.

'Keep these exclamations of yours for your prayers! It is great presumption on your part to give your opinions on things you know nothing about! Now I'd like to inform you that the quality of the wine at the Mass is a question of great importance. It is essential that the wine should be good. . . .'

'In accordance with the dignity of the holy sacrifice,' said the paroco very seriously, as he squeezed Amelia's knee between his.

'And it is not only that,' said the canon, taking up a pedagogic tone. 'It is that the wine, when it is not good, being mixed with other ingredients, leaves a deposit in the wine cruets; and if the sacristan is not careful in cleaning them, the smell of the cruets becomes horrible. And does the senhora know with what results? The results are that the priest, when he goes to drink the blood of Our Lord Jesus Christ, is not expecting it, and makes a face. Now senhora, you have the explanation!'

He noisily sucked up his wine. But he was in a mood for talking that night, and after belching slowly, again attacked Dona Josepha, who was amazed at so much science.

'Now tell me one thing, senhora, as you know so much doctrine: should the wine in the divine sacrifice be white or red?'

Dona Josepha thought it must be red, in order to appear more like Our Saviour's blood.

'You have a lot to learn,' muttered the canon pointing at Amelia.

She drew back with a little laugh: as she wasn't a sacristan, she didn't know . . .

'Your turn now, senhor paroco!'

Amaro laughed at the easy question. If the wrong answer was red wine, then the right answer must be white wine.

'And why?'

Amaro had heard it said that it was the custom in Rome.

'And why?' continued the canon, pedantic and hoarse.

He didn't know.

'Because Our Lord Jesus Christ, when he consecrated for the first time, did so with white wine. And the reason is very simple: in Judea at that time, as is well known, they didn't make red wine. Another plate of vermicelli, please, sister.'

Then, as they talked of wine and the cleanliness of the wine cruets, Amaro was reminded of his complaint against Bento the sacristan. That morning, before he put on his vestments—just when the senhor canon entered the sacristy—he'd finished giving him a reprimand about the white tunics. In the first place he had given the things to be washed to a woman named Antonia who lived in sin with a carpenter, a great scandal; she was unworthy to touch the holy things. That was the first thing. Then the woman had brought them so badly done that it was a profanity to use them in the divine sacrifice.

'Ah, send them to me, senhor paroco, send them to me,' interrupted Dona Josepha. 'I'll give them to my washerwoman, who is a very virtuous woman, and returns the clothes as white as snow. Ah, it would be an honour for me! I myself would iron them. It would even bless our iron——'

But the canon (who that night was positively in a loquacious mood) broke in upon her speech and turning towards Father Amaro fixed him with a profound look:

'Now apropos of my entry into the sacristy, I wanted to say that today you, my friend and colleague, you committed an error in your behaviour at one of the ceremonies.'

'What error, master?' said Amaro, disturbed.

'After putting on your vestments again,' continued the canon very slowly, 'while the deacons were still at the side, when you genuflected to the cross in the sacristy, instead of making a low genuflection, you only made a half one.'

'Oh no, master!' exclaimed Father Amaro. 'The text of the rubrics is: *Facta reverentia cruci*, make a bow to the cross: that is a simple bow, a light lowering of the head . . .'

And, to illustrate his point, he bowed to Dona Josepha, who wriggled and smiled at him.

'I disagree!' exclaimed the canon formidably; in his house, at his table, he loudly upheld his opinions. 'I have my writers to support me. Here they are!' And as his authority he let fall, like a cluster of rocks, the venerable names of Laboranti, Baldeschi, Merati, Torrino and Pavonio.

Amaro leaned forward in his chair, put himself in a controversial attitude, happy that he could, in front of Amelia, confound the canon, master of moral theology and a colossus on practical liturgy.

'I affirm my statement,' he exclaimed. 'I affirm it with Castaldus!'

'Stop, you thief,' bawled the canon. 'Castaldus is mine.'

'Castaldus is mine, master!'

They became heated, each one claiming the venerable Castaldus and the authority of his eloquence for himself. Dona Josepha puled with delight in the chair, murmuring to Amelia with her face wrinkled in smiles:

'Ah, what a pleasure to look at them! Ah, what saints!'

Amaro continued, waving his arms aloft:

'And besides this, to me it seems only common sense, master! Firstly it is so according to the rubrics. Secondly, the priest, having, while in the sacristy, his biretta on his head, mustn't make a full genuflection, because his biretta might fall off, and this would constitute a major irreverence. Thirdly, if done as you say an absurdity would follow, because then the genuflection before the Mass to the sacristy cross would be greater than that which was made after the Mass to the cross on the altar!'

'But the genuflection in front of the altar cross——' vociferated the canon.

'It is a half genuflection. Read the rubrics: *Caput inclinat*. Read Gavantus, read Garrifaldi. And so it must be! Do you know why? Because after the Mass the priest is in the apogee of his dignity, having the body and blood of Our Lord Jesus Christ inside him. To conclude, the point is mine!'

And standing up, he vivaciously rubbed his hands, triumphant.

The canon patted the folds of his neck, sagging down on his napkin, with the air of a tormented bull. After a moment he answered: 'You are right. I just said it to see what you would say. . . . I feel proud of my pupil,' he added, winking his eye at Amelia. 'Now drink, man, drink! And afterwards bring the coffee, sister, and see that it is hot enough.'

But a violent ring at the door made them all jump.

'It must be Senhora Joanneira,' said Dona Josepha.

Gertrude entered with a shawl and a woollen mantle: 'These just came from Menina Amelia's house. The senhora sends kind regards to all, and says she couldn't come as she didn't feel very well.'

'Then how am I to get home?' said Amelia worried.

The canon stretched his arm over the table, and giving her hand a few soft pats, said:

'If there is no one else to go, I am at your service. Your virtue is quite safe with me.'

'You do say some terrible things, brother,' shouted the old lady.

'Keep quiet, sister. No matter what passes the mouth of a saint, a saint remains a saint.'

The paroco approved noisily:

'You are quite right, Senhor Canon Dias. No matter what passes the mouth of a saint, a saint remains a saint. Therefore I drink to your long life and health!'

'And yours!'

They clinked their glasses boyishly, reconciled after the controversy.

But Amelia was frightened, exclaiming: 'Jesus, what can be the matter with mamma? What can it be?'

'What can it be but laziness,' said the paroco, laughing.

'Don't fret, daughter,' said Dona Josepha. 'I'll take you home myself. We'll all take you.'

'We'll take the little girl in the *charola*,' chuckled the canon, as he peeled his pear.

But suddenly he put down his knife, his eyes wandered all round, and passing his hand over his stomach he moaned:

'Listen, I'm not feeling well either.'

'What is it? what is it?'

'Just a slight spasm of pain. It'll pass, it's nothing.'

Dona Josepha, now alarmed, didn't want him to eat the pear, as his last attack was caused by eating fruit.

But he obstinately dug his teeth into it.

'It's gone, it's gone,' he cried.

'It was sympathy with your mamma,' whispered Amaro to Amelia.

Suddenly the canon turned in his chair, and twisting himself round to the side shouted:

'I'm ill, I'm ill! oh Jesus! oh Satan! oh hell! ah! ah! I'm dying!'

All rushed agitatedly in a band round him. Dona Josepha led him by the arm into his room, shouting to the servant to go and fetch the doctor. Amelia ran to the kitchen to heat a flannel to put to his stomach. But nobody could find the flannel. Gertrude nervously knocked against chairs, looking for her shawl to go out.

'Go without a shawl, you stupid girl!' shouted Amaro.

The girl ran off. Inside in his room the canon roared.

Amaro, now really frightened, entered the room. Dona Josepha, on her knees before a big picture of Our Lady of Sorrows over the chest of drawers, groaned out prayers; and the poor master, stretched on his stomach on the bed, bit the pillow.

'But, my dear senhora,' said the paroco severely, 'now is not the time to pray. You must do something. What do you usually give him?'

'Oh, senhor paroco, we have nothing, we have nothing,' moaned the old lady. 'It is a pain which comes suddenly and may be gone in a minute. It doesn't leave time to do anything! Sometimes lime-leaf tea relieves it. But unfortunately we have no lime-leaves! Ah, Jesus!'

Amaro ran to his house to look for the lime-leaves, and after a little time returned breathless, with Dionysia, who came to offer her service and experience.

But happily the senhor canon suddenly felt better.

'I'm very much obliged, senhor paroco,' said Dona Josepha. 'Beautiful lime-leaves! You are very kind. He will now fall asleep quite naturally. He always does after his pain. If you'll excuse me I'll return to his side . . . This is the worst attack he has had. It was that fruit, curse—' She took back the blasphemy, terrified. 'They are the fruits of Our Lord. And it is His divine will . . . You will excuse me?'

Amelia and the priest remained alone in the room. Their eyes were alight with a mutual desire to touch one another, to kiss; but the doors were open, and in the room at the side they heard the tread of the old lady's carpet slippers.

'Poor master!' said Amaro loudly. 'The pain must have been terrible.'

'It comes every three months,' said Amelia. 'Mamma had the feeling that it was due. The day before yesterday she mentioned it to me saying: "It's time for the canon's pain to reappear, I am taking the greatest care . . ."'

The paroco sighed, and said in a whisper:

'Poor me, I have no one to worry about my pains . . .'

Amelia very earnestly turned on him her beautiful eyes full of tenderness:

'Don't say that . . .'

They passionately squeezed one another's hands over the table; but Dona Josepha appeared, wrapped up in her shawl. Her brother had gone to sleep. As for herself, she was so exhausted that she could hardly stand on her feet. Ah, those upsets were killing! She had lit two candles to St Joaquim and had made a Promise to Our Lady of Health. It was the second she had made that year for her brother's pain. And Our Blessed Lady had never failed her . . .

'She never fails those who approach her with faith, my dear senhora,' said Father Amaro unctuously.

The tall clock over the cupboard struck eight. Amelia again spoke of her worry about her mother. Besides, it was getting so late . . .

'When I went out it was drizzling,' said Amaro.

Amelia ran nervously to the window. The flags under the street-lantern were very wet and shining. The sky was dark.

'Jesus,' she said, 'the night will be wet!'

Dona Josepha was very grieved, but Amelia could now understand that it was impossible for her to leave the house, especially as Gertrude hadn't returned with the doctor: she surely couldn't find him, she was probably running around from one house to another. Who knew when she'd return?

The paroco then remembered that Dionysia (who was waiting for him in the kitchen) could accompany Menina Amelia. It was just a few steps, there was nobody on the streets. He himself would go with them as far as the corner of the Square. But they must hurry, it would soon be raining harder.

Dona Josepha went immediately to get an umbrella for Amelia. She advised her to tell her mamma all that had happened. But she must tell her not to worry, that her brother was now better . . .

'And listen!' she called down from the top of the stairs, 'Tell her we did all we could, but that the pain came and went so suddenly that there was no time for anything!'

'Yes, I'll tell her. Good-night.'

As they opened the door they saw that it was raining heavily. Amelia wanted to wait. The paroco, catching her arm, hurried her along, saying: 'It's no use, it's no use!'

They went down the deserted street, close together under the umbrella, Dionysia at their side, with her shawl over her head, very silent. All the windows were shut; in the silence the rain fell in torrents.

'Jesus, what a night!' said Amelia, 'my dress will be ruined.'

They were then in Rua das Sousas.

'Now it is falling in bucketfuls,' said Amaro. 'It really seems to me better that you should come into the patio of my house and wait a little.'

'No, no,' interrupted Amelia.

'Nonsense!' he exclaimed impatiently. 'Do you want to destroy your dress? It is just a sudden shower. You can see that it is clearing up over there. It will soon pass. It is nonsense—if your mamma knew that you were out in such terrible rain, she would be angry with you, and she would be right!'

'No, no!'

But Amaro stopped, quickly opened the gate and said, as he gently pushed Amelia inside: 'Come in, it will only be for an instant.'

They remained silently there in the dark patio, looking out at the shining streaks of water falling down in front of the street-lantern. Amelia was very disturbed. The darkness of the patio and the silence frightened her; but it seemed to her delicious to be there, at his side, unknown to all. Urged on by her desire, she instinctively went closer to him and rubbed against his shoulder; she then drew back, uneasy at hearing his panting breath as her skirts touched his side. She noticed at the back, without appearing to look, the stairs which led up to his room; and she had an intense desire to go up to see his furniture and how it was placed. The presence of Dionysia, shrinking against the door and very quiet, embarrassed her; she kept turning her eyes towards her, dreading that she would disappear, sucked up in the darkness of the patio or the night . . .

Amaro then began to stamp his feet on the ground and rub his hands, shivering.

'We will catch our death here,' he said. 'The stones are freezing. It's better to wait upstairs in the dining-room.'

'No, no!' she said.

'Ridiculous! Your mamma will be angry with you. Go up and put on the light, Dionysia.'

The matron immediately bounded up the stairs. He then whispered as he took Amelia's arm:

'Why not? What are you thinking of? It is nonsense. Come up just for a minute till the rain stops. Tell me——'

She remained silent, breathing loudly. Amaro put his hand on her shoulder and then on her breasts, pressing them, caressing the silk. Her whole body trembled. In the end she followed him up the stairs, dizzy, treading on her dress at every step, her ears burning.

'Come in here, this is the room,' he whispered in her ear.

He then ran down to the kitchen. Dionysia was lighting the candle.

'My dear Dionysia, you see—I want to confess Menina Amelia here. It is something very serious. Go out and return here in half an hour. Take this.' He put three placas in her hand.

Dionysia took off her shoes, went downstairs on tiptoe and shut herself into the coal-cellar.

He returned to the room with the light. Amelia was there pale and still. The paroco shut the door—and went to her silently, with his teeth closed, breathing like a bull.

Half an hour later Dionysia coughed on the stairs. Amelia came down, closely wrapped up in her shawl; as they opened the gate of the patio two drunkards passed talking; Amelia drew back quickly into the darkness. But Dionysia, after looking up and down a minute and seeing the street deserted, said:

'The road is clear, my dear senhora.'

Amelia pulled her cloak up round her face and they hurried to the Rua da Misericordia. The rain had stopped; the stars shone out; and a dry cold air announced the north wind and good weather.

Chapter XVI

THE FOLLOWING morning, Amaro, looking at his watch which hung over the bed, and seeing that the hour of Mass was drawing near, jumped joyfully out of bed. As he slipped his arms into the old coat which served him as a dressing-gown, he thought of the other morning in Feirão, when he had awakened terrified because the evening before, for the first time since he had been a priest, he had brutally sinned on the stable straw with Joanna Vaqueira. And he hadn't dared to say Mass with that sin weighing like a rock on his soul. He had considered himself, according to the Holy Fathers and The Holy Council of Trent, contaminated, unclean, ripe for the infernal pit. Three times he had arrived at the door of the church and each time he had drawn back frightened, sure that if he dared to touch the Eucharist with those hands which had dragged off Joanna Vaqueira's skirts, the chapel would fall on him and crush him, or he would stand paralysed as he saw standing before the tabernacle, with lifted sword, the blazing form of St Michael the Avenger! He had got on his horse and travelled for two hours through the fields of Dona João to Gralheira, to confess to the good Abbot Sequeira. Ah! that was in the days of his innocence, his pious scruples, his novice's terrors. Now he had opened his eyes to the human reality all round. Abbots, canons, cardinals and monsignori didn't sin on the stable straw, no—they had their comfortable alcoves, with their supper at the side. And the churches didn't fall on them, and St Michael the Avenger didn't leave the comforts of the sky to deal with such insignificant things!

It wasn't that which was disturbing him, but Dionysia, whom he heard bustling and coughing in the kitchen. He didn't dare to ask her for his shaving-water. He found it disagreeable to have that woman admitted, installed in his secret. He had no doubt about her discretion, it was her job; and a few half sovereigns would secure her fidelity. But it was repugnant to his pride as a priest to know that that former concubine of so many civil and military authorities, who rolled her great fat body into all the obscene secular affairs of the town, knew his weaknesses, the sensual desires which burnt under his priest's cloak. He would rather that it had been Silverio or Natario who had seen him so inflamed the evening before, it would at least have been amongst the clergy! And what made him feel uncomfortable was the idea of being observed by those cynical little eyes which were not impressed either with the austerity of the priestly robe or with the respectability of uniforms, knowing that beneath all was the same miserable, bestial call of the flesh . . .

I'll finish with her, he thought, I'll give her a sovereign and turn her out.

Her knuckles tapped discreetly on the door of his room.

'Come in!' said Amaro, immediately sitting down and quickly leaning over the table, as if absorbed in his pile of papers.

Dionysia entered, put the jug of water on the wash-stand, coughed and said over Amaro's shoulders:

'Senhor paroco, your handling of this affair shows no sense. Yesterday some people saw the little girl going out of here. It is very serious, young man. The greatest secrecy is essential for both your sakes!'

No, he couldn't send her away. The woman had forcibly established herself in his confidence. These words, murmured as if the walls had ears, revealed an officious prudence, and demonstrated to him the advantage of someone so experienced in complicity.

He turned towards her with a very red face:

'Somebody saw her, eh?'

'Yes, two drunkards. But it might have been two *cavalheiros*.'

'That's true.'

'And in your position, senhor paroco, and for the young girl's sake— all must be done so quietly—not even the ground must know! In the things in which I deal, I exercise as much caution as if the dead had ears.'

Amaro then suddenly decided to accept the protection of Dionysia.

He looked in the corner of the table drawer, drew out a half sovereign and put it in her hand.

'May the blessing of God fall on you, my son,' she murmured.

'Good; and now Dionysia, what do you propose?' he asked, sitting back in his chair, waiting for the matron's counsels.

She said very naturally, without any affectation of mystery or malice:

'It seems to me that for you to see the girl, there is nowhere as suitable as the sexton's house!'

'The sexton's house?'

She very calmly called to his mind its excellent position. One of the rooms at the side of the sacristy, as he was aware, opened on to a yard where, at the time when they had been repairing the Cathedral, they had put up a shed. Well then, just at the other side were the back walls of the sexton's house. Uncle Esguelhas' kitchen door opened on to the yard; all the senhor paroco would have to do would be to go out of the sacristy door, cross the yard and there he was in his little nest!

'And she?'

She could enter by the sexton's front door, which opened on to the Cathedral Square. Not a soul passed there; it was a regular hermitage. And if anyone did see there was a most natural explanation: Menina Amelia was going with a message to the sexton. This was just an outline, a beginning which he could improve on.

'Yes, I understand, it's an idea,' said Amaro walking up and down the room reflecting.

'I know the place very well, senhor paroco, and believe what I say, that for a clergyman who wants to arrange his little affair, there is no better.'

Amaro asked as he stood in front of her, laughing familiarly:

'Now Aunt Dionysia, tell me frankly; am I right in thinking that this isn't the first time that you have recommended the sexton's house, eh?'

She very decisively denied the truth of his suggestion. Uncle Esguelhas was a man she didn't know! The idea had come to her at night in bed as she lay thinking. She had gone early in the morning to examine the position, and realized it was excellent.

She coughed and edged towards the door; then turned to give a last counsel:

'This all depends on how you arrange things with the sexton.'

It was with this that Amaro was now preoccupied. Uncle Esguelhas, among the servers and other Cathedral sacristans, was known as Sour Face. He had only one leg and used a crutch; some of the clergy, who wanted the job for their own protégés, affirmed that this infirmity, according to the Rule, rendered him unfit for service in the Church. But the former paroco, José Migueis, in obedience to the senhor bishop, kept him on in the Cathedral, arguing that the disastrous fall which necessitated the amputation took place from the tower during a feast-day celebration, while he was on duty: *ergo*, it was clearly indicated that it was not the intention of Our Blessed Lord to dispense with the services of Uncle Esguelhas. And when Amaro took over the parish, the cripple made use of Senhora Joanneira's and Amelia's influence in order, as he put it, to hang on to the bell rope. Besides this (such was the opinion in the Rua da Misericordia) it was an act of charity. Uncle Esguelhas, who was a widower, had a daughter of fifteen, who from her infancy had been paralysed in both legs. As her father used to say: 'The devil has a spite against the family legs.' It was certainly this mismisfortune which made him so taciturn and sad. It was said that the girl (whose name was Antonia but whom the father called Toto) tormented him with her peevishness, her rages and other ugly whims. Dr Gouvea declared it hysteria: but it was certain, according to all people of right thinking, that Toto was possessed by the devil. It had even been planned that she should be exorcised; but the senhor bishop, who was always afraid of the press, hesitated about giving the ritual permission, so she was given, without result, the simple sprinklings of Holy Water. In addition to this the nature of her affliction was not known. Dona Maria of the Assumption was heard to say that it consisted in howling like a wolf; the Gansosinho, in another version, authoritatively stated that the unfortunate girl tore her flesh with her nails . . . When anyone asked Uncle Esguelhas how his daughter was, he replied curtly: 'She's there.'

He passed all his free time in the house with the girl; only crossing the Cathedral Square to the apothecary's to buy medicine, or calling at Theresa's for confectionery for her. The whole day that corner of the Cathedral, the yard, the shed, the high wall at the side covered with wallwort, and the house at the bottom with its mean entrance, half door and half window, in one of its miserable old walls, stood tranquilly in the shade; and the choir boys, who sometimes daringly stole on tiptoe along the yard to spy on Uncle Esguelhas, invariably saw him sadly leaning over the hearth, with his pipe in his hand, spitting into the fire.

It was his custom as a sign of respect to attend the senhor paroco's Mass every day. And Amaro that morning, as he put on his vestments, no sooner heard the sound of the crutch on the flags of the yard than he began preparing his story; because he couldn't ask Uncle Esguelhas for the use of his house without explaining in some way that he wanted to use it in the service of religion: and what better than to prepare in secret, far away from the intrusions of the world, a tender soul for the convent and for a life of saintliness?

When he saw him enter the sacristy, he gave him a cheery good-day. He complimented him on looking so well. Though he wasn't surprised —because, according to all the Holy Fathers, the association with the bells, on account of the particular grace communicated to them at their consecration, bestowed a special happiness and feeling of well-being. He then good-naturedly recounted to Uncle Esguelhas and to the two sacristans that when he was young, and living in the house of the Senhora Marqueza d'Alegros, his greatest ambition was one day to be a bell-ringer.

They all laughed, delighted with their master's joke.

'Don't laugh, it's true. And it wasn't a bad idea of mine. In former times it was the minor orders of the clergy who rang the bells. Our

Holy Fathers considering this the most efficacious means of obtaining grace.' He quoted, sounding the words as if coming from the mouth of the bell-ringer: '*Laudo deum, populum voco, congrego clerum, defunctum ploro, pestum fugo, festa decoro.* Which means, as you know: I praise God, I summon the people, I assemble the clergy, I mourn the dead, I put plagues to flight, I give joy on feast days.'

He recited the verse with reverence, standing in the middle of the sacristy, already attired in amice and alb; and Uncle Esguelhas, on hearing these words, which gave him an unexpected authority and importance, stood up straighter on his crutch.

The sacristan had approached with the purple chasuble. But Amaro hadn't finished his glorification of the bells: he now explained their great power in dispelling tempests (in spite of what some presumptuous scholars said to the contrary), not only because they communicated to the air the grace which they received from being blessed, but because they dispersed the demons which wandered amongst the storm and the thunder. The Holy Council of Milan recommended that whenever there was a storm the bells should be rung.

'In any case, Uncle Esguelhas,' he added smiling with solicitude at the bell-ringer: 'I advise you that in these cases it is wiser not to take any risks, because you are always there high in the belfry and near the tempest . . . Give me that, Uncle Mathias.'

He received the chasuble over his shoulders, and murmured very composedly: '*Domini, quis dixisti jugum meum . . .* Tighten the cords a little more behind, Uncle Mathias. *Suave est, et onus meum leve . . .*'

He genuflected before the image of Christ on the cross and then entered the church, in the attitude recommended by the rubrics, with eyes cast down and body erect; while Mathias, who had also just bobbed a curtsey to the vestry crucifix, hurried with the wine cruets, noisily clearing his throat.

During the whole Mass, as he turned towards the nave and at the *Offertory* and the *Orate fratres*, Father Amaro directed his words to the bell-ringer (a benevolence which the ritual permitted) as if the sacrifice was for his particular intention; and Uncle Esguelhas, with his crutch resting at his side, was sunk in a deeper devotion. But at the *Benedicat*, after he had begun the benediction, he turned towards the altar to gather from the living God His store of mercy; and then finished by turning slowly towards Uncle Esguelhas and gazing particularly at him, as if giving him alone the Graces and Gifts of Our Lord Jesus Christ!

'And now, Uncle Esguelhas,' he said in a whisper as he entered the sacristy, 'wait for me in the yard, as I wish to speak to you privately.'

He hurried to join him with a very solemn face which impressed the bell-ringer.

'Put on your hat, put on your hat, Uncle Esguelhas. I've come to talk to you about a very serious case—I really want to beg a favour of you.'

'Oh, senhor paroco!'

'No, it is not a favour . . . Because when one deals with the service of God it is the duty of all to contribute according to their ability. I want to make arrangements for a girl who wishes to become a nun.' Then to prove the confidence which he had in him he hurried to give the name: 'It is Senhor Joanneira's little Amelia.'

'You don't tell me so, senhor paroco!'

'A vocation, Uncle Esguelhas! You can see the finger of God in this! It is extraordinary . . .'

He then told a complex story, which he laboriously invented as he went along, according to the amount of surprise which he saw on the bell-ringer's face. The girl, after the disappointments she had had with her intended husband, had become disgusted with life and desired to enter a religious order. But the mother, who was old, supposing that it was just a passing fancy, and also requiring her services in the house, refused to give her consent . . . But, no, it was a true vocation, he knew it. Unfortunately, when there was opposition the position of the priest became a very delicate one. . . . Every day the ungodly newspapers (which were unhappily the majority!) cried out against the influences of the clergy. The authorities, still more ungodly, put obstacles in their way. There were some terrible laws . . . If it were known that he was instructing a girl for the convent he would be locked up in prison! What did Uncle Esguelhas think of that? It was due to the impiety and the atheism of the times! It was necessary that he should have many, many conferences with the girl: to find out, to examine her inclinations thoroughly, to make certain whether her vocation was for an enclosed order, a penitential order, a nursing order, for Perpetual Adoration, or for teaching. To sum up, he must study her inside out.

'But where?' he exclaimed, opening his arms in desolation at the idea of a holy task thwarted. 'Where? In her mother's house it couldn't be, as she is already suspicious. In the Cathedral it is impossible, as one might just as well be in the middle of the street. In my house I can't take a young girl——'

'That's obvious.'

'So Uncle Esguelhas—I'm sure you will oblige me in this—I thought of your house——'

'Oh, senhor paroco,' the sexton hastened to say. 'I, my house and all my furniture are at your disposal.'

'You can well see that it is in the interest of her soul, and that Our Lord will rejoice at your action . . .'

'It will be a great joy for me, senhor paroco, it will also be a great joy for me.'

What Uncle Esguelhas feared was that the house wasn't good enough, and hadn't sufficient conveniences . . .

'Now!' said the priest smiling, in a renouncement of all possible human comforts. 'All I want are two chairs and a table on which to put the prayer-book.'

Otherwise, the bell-ringer explained, the position of the house was so solitary and retired that it was exactly the thing. He and the girl would be as far away from the world as the monks in the desert. On the days when the senhor paroco came, he would go out for his little stroll. He couldn't offer them the kitchen, because poor Toto's little alcove was to one side of it. But there was his room upstairs.

Father Amaro tapped his forehead. He hadn't thought of the paralytic!

'That will destroy all our little arrangement, Uncle Esguelhas!' he exclaimed.

But the sexton quickly put his mind at rest. He was now absorbed in this conquest of a bride for Christ; with all his might he wished that his roof should shelter the holy preparation of the girl's soul: perhaps it would draw God's pity towards him! He heatedly put forth the advantages, the conveniences of the house. Toto wouldn't interfere with them. She never moved from her bed. The senhor paroco could enter by the kitchen door at the side of the sacristy, the girl could come in by the street door: they could go upstairs and shut themselves into the room.

'And how does Toto pass her time?' said Father Amaro still hesitating.

God help her, the poor little thing was just there . . . She had manias; sometimes she made rag dolls and loved them so passionately that she worked herself into a fever; other days she passed in a horrible silence with her eyes glued to the walls. But occasionally she was bright and talked and laughed. . . . It was a terrible calamity!

'She must entertain herself, she must read,' said Amaro, to show interest.

The sexton sighed. The child didn't know how to read, she had never wanted to learn. It was what he had always said, if she could only read life wouldn't be so dreary for her. But then she had a horror of applying herself. If the senhor paroco when he came would have the charity to persuade her . . .

213

But the paroco wasn't listening, being deeply sunk in an idea which lit up his whole face in a smile. He suddenly thought of a most natural explanation to give Senhora Joanneira and the friends who visited her house, of Amelia's visits to the bell-ringer's: it was to teach the paralytic to read! To educate her! To open her soul to the beauties of the lives of the saints, of the history of the martyrs and to prayer . . .

'It's fixed, Uncle Esguelhas,' he exclaimed, jubilantly rubbing his hands. 'And it is in your house that we must make the girl a saint.' Then he added in a grave tone: 'This must be a dead secret.'

'Oh, senhor paroco!' said the bell-ringer, almost offended.

'I trust you!' said Amaro.

He immediately went to the sacristy to write a letter, to be given secretly to Amelia, in which he explained in detail the arrangement by which, as he wrote, 'they could enjoy many new and divine delights.' He warned her that the pretext on which she was to visit the bell-ringer's house, every week, was the education of the paralytic; he himself would propose it one night in her mamma's house. 'In this,' he said 'there is some truth, as it will be pleasing to God that you should light up the darkness of that soul with suitable religious instruction. And so, my beloved angel, we will kill two birds with the one stone!'

He then returned to his house. How happy and self-satisfied he felt as he sat down at the breakfast table, full of contentment with life and the sweet facilities which he encountered in it. Jealousy, doubt, the tortures of unsatisfied desires, the loneliness of the flesh, all that had been consuming him for months and months in the Rua da Misericordia and in the Rua das Sousas had passed away. In the end he was completely installed in happiness. He called to mind, as he sat deep in thought, with the fork forgotten in his hand, all that half-hour of the evening before, pleasure by pleasure, mentally enjoying each one again, saturated with the delicious certainty of possession: like a labourer who runs over the piece of land which he had just acquired and on which he had been looking enviously for years. Ah, no, now he would not look bitterly on the *cavalheiros* who passed in the poplar avenue with their sweethearts on their arms! He now also had one, all his, soul and body, pretty, who adored him, who wore lovely white underclothing, and sprinkled her bosom with eau-de-cologne. He was a priest, it was true. But for that he had his great argument; it was that the conduct of a priest, as long as it didn't cause scandal amongst the faithful, in no way prejudiced the utility, the efficacy, the dignity of religion. All the theologians taught that the order of the priesthood was instituted to administer the sacraments, and that the essential thing is that the people receive the interior supernatural holiness which the sacraments contain;

and provided the sacraments are dispensed according to the sacred formulas, what does it matter whether the priest is a sinner or a saint? In both cases the sacrament gives the same grace. It is not through the merits of the priest that they operate, but through the merits of Jesus Christ. He who is baptized or anointed, be it with pure or impure hands, is equally well cleansed from original sin or prepared for the life to come. This is laid down by all the Holy Fathers, and established by the Holy Council of Trent. The faithful lose nothing, neither with regard to their souls nor their eternal salvation, because of the unworthiness of the priest. And if the priest repents on the death bed the gates of heaven will not be shut against him. All would certainly end well and for the good of all. And Father Amaro reasoning thus, sipped his coffee with enjoyment.

When breakfast was over Dionysia came in, all smiles, to know if the senhor paroco had spoken with Uncle Esguelhas.

'I made some suggestions,' he answered vaguely. 'There is nothing decided—Rome wasn't built in a day.'

'Ah!' she said.

She took herself off to the kitchen, thinking that the senhor paroco lied like a heretic. But it didn't matter. She never liked to arrange affairs for clergymen, they paid badly and were always suspicious . . .

But even so, as she heard Amaro going out she ran to the stairs to tell him that she had her own house to look after, and that she would like to know when the senhor paroco could arrange a servant.

'Dona Josepha is seeing to that for me, Dionysia. I hope to have some news from her tomorrow. But you will come—now that we are friends . . .'

'When you require me, senhor paroco, call across through the window,' she cried out from the top of the stairs. 'I am ready to do anything at all that you want. I know a little of everything, and can bring on abortions and act as a midwife——'

But the priest refused to listen to any more: he banged the door suddenly, escaping indignantly from that obscene service so crudely offered.

It was a few days later that he went to Senhora Joanneira's house with the intention of speaking about the sexton's daughter.

The evening before he had given the note to Amelia; and that night when the company were noisily prattling in the parlour, he went over to the piano, where Amelia was lazily running through her scales, and as he bent down to light his cigarette at the candle, said: 'Did you read it?'

'It's a splendid idea.'

Amaro then joined the group of senhoras, where the Gansoso was recounting a catastrophe which had occurred in England and of which she had read in the newspaper: a coal mine had fallen in and buried one hundred and twenty miners. The old ladies shivered with horror. The Gansoso, enjoying the effect she had produced, loquaciously accumulated the details: the people who were outside worked hard to dig out the victims: the moans and groans of the poor fellows could be plainly heard: it was in the dusk, and the snow was falling heavily . . .

'Very disagreeable!' muttered the canon, digging himself further into the armchair, with a keener enjoyment of the warmth of the parlour and the security of the roof.

Dona Maria of the Assumption declared that all these mines, these foreign machines, filled her with dread. She had seen a factory at the foot of Alcobaça and it seemed to her like an image of hell. It was certain that God did not look with approval on such things.

'Just like the railways,' said Dona Josepha. She was sure that they were inspired by the devil. She wasn't saying it as a joke. It was what she thought when she heard that roar and saw that glare and flare and bluster! Ah, how she shivered!

Father Amaro mocked such an idea, assuring Dona Josepha that they were very convenient when one wanted to travel quickly. Then, suddenly becoming very serious, he added:

'In any case it it indisputable that in these inventions of modern science there is much of the devil. And it is for this that our Holy Mother the Church blesses them, first with prayers and after with Holy Water. One must know why it is the custom. The Holy Water is to exorcise them, to expel the evil spirit; and the prayers are to redeem them from Original Sin, which not only exists in man but in the things which he constructs. And it is for this that locomotives are blessed and purified, so that the devil cannot employ them in his machinations.'

Dona Maria of the Assumption wanted an explanation there and then. What was the Enemy's usual mode of availing himself of this invention of railways?

Father Amaro graciously made the point clear. The Enemy had many ways of working, but the usual one was this: he caused a train to run off the rails and several passengers to be killed, and as these souls were not prepared by Extreme Unction, the devil waiting there, clap, twack, seized them!

'What a knave!' muttered the canon, with a secret admiration for the Enemy's clever trick.

Dona Maria of the Assumption, languidly waving her fan, and with her face bathed in a smile of beatitude, remarked: 'Ah, friends! (here she slowly looked all round) a thing like that could never happen to us—he could never seize us with our souls unprepared!'

It was true: and all enjoyed for a minute that delicious certainty of being prepared, and so being able to frustrate the malicious designs of the Tempter.

Father Amaro then coughed as if to prepare the way, and leaning forward with his hands on the table, said in a preaching tone: 'A great deal of vigilance is necessary to keep the devil at a distance. It was only today that I was thinking on this (it was the subject of my morning meditation), there having come to my knowledge a very sad case, there at the side of the Cathedral: the sexton's little girl.'

The senhoras had drawn up their chairs, drinking in his words with sudden excited curiosity, hoping to hear of another piquant feat of Satan. The paroco continued with a voice to which the silence all round gave solemnity:

'There is the girl, all God's blessed day, nailed to the bed. She can't read, she practises no daily devotions, she hasn't learnt the habit of meditation; and as a consequence she is, as St Clement describes it, a soul without defence. What results? The devil, who is constantly prowling round to see on what he can fix his claws, establishes himself there as if he were in his own house! On account of which, as poor Uncle Esguelhas informed me today, she is hysterical, gets despondent, suffers from uncontrollable fits of rage . . . To sum up, the poor man's life is spoilt.'

'And at two steps from the church of God!' said Dona Maria of the Assumption, feeling indignant at the impudence of Satan, installing himself in a body, in a bed which was separated from the walls of the Cathedral by just the width of the yard.

Amaro hurried to agree:

'Dona Maria is right. It is a terrible tragedy. But what's to be done? If the girl doesn't know a prayer, if she has no one to instruct her, to bring her the word of God, to fortify her, to teach her the secret with which to frustrate the Enemy . . .'

In his excitement he got up and walked a few steps along the parlour, with head bent, with the grief of a pastor from whom a strong cruel hand had snatched a beloved sheep. And, exalted by his own words, he actually felt a great pity invading him, a true compassion for that poor creature, in whom the want of consolation must intensify the agony of not being able to move.

The senhoras listened to him, pained by the thought of that

abandoned soul, and above all by the sorrow that it appeared to cause the senhor paroco.

Dona Maria of the Assumption, whose mind ran through her abundant devout arsenal, suggested that if she put some saints at the head of the bed, such as St Vincent, Our Lady of the Seven Wounds . . . But her friends' silence expressed very well their opinion of the insufficiency of that holy gallery.

'Perhaps the senhoras would like to tell me that we are only dealing with the sexton's child. But it is a soul! It is a soul the same as ours!' said Amaro again sitting down.

'All have the same right to the grace of God,' said the canon gravely, with a feeling of impartiality, admitting the equality of the classes when not dealing with material goods, but only with the comforts of the skies.

'For God there is neither rich nor poor,' sighed Senhora Joanneira. 'The poor come first. "Of the poor is the kingdom of heaven." '

'No, the rich come first,' interrupted the canon, stretching out his hand to stop that false interpretation of the divine law. 'The heavens are also for the rich. The senhora doesn't understand the precept. *Beati pauperes*, blessed are the poor, which means to say that the poor are blessed in their poverty, when they do not covet the goods of the rich; when they want no more than the crust of bread which they have; when they don't aspire to participate in the riches of others, under the pain of not being blessed. And because of this the senhora knows that those villains who tell the workers and the lower classes that they should live better than they are living, do so against the will of the Church and of Our Lord Jesus Christ, and deserve nothing but the whip. Excommunicated as they are! Ouf!'

He stretched himself in his chair, exhausted at having talked so much. Father Amaro remained silent, with his elbow on the table, slowly rubbing his forehead. He was about to spring his idea, as coming from a divine inspiration, his proposal that Amelia should give religious instruction to the unfortunate paralytic. He hesitated for a moment at the thought of his motive, all carnal, all concupiscence. Then came to his mind an exaggerated picture of the miserable state of the sexton's child, who now appeared sunk in a dark abyss of ignorance and agony. He thought of the great act of charity it would be to console her, to make her life less bitter . . . This action would surely redeem many sins and please God if it was done in a spirit of pure Christian love! He felt the sentimental compassion of a healthy man for that miserable body glued to the bed, never being able to see the sun nor the streets. He sat there puzzled by that pity which had invaded him, scratching the back of his neck, undecided, almost sorry that he had mentioned Toto to the senhoras.

But Dona Joaquina Gansoso had an idea:

'Would Senhor Father Amaro like to send her that book with pictures from the lives of the saints? They are edifying pictures. They are pictures which touch the heart. Isn't it you who have it, Amelia?'

'No,' she answered, without raising her eyes from her sewing.

Amaro then looked at her. He had almost forgotten her. She was now at the other side of the table, hemming a cloth: the very fine parting had disappeared in the abundance of her thick hair, on which the light from the lamp at the side threw a shining streak; her eyelashes appeared longer and blacker over her fresh brown skin, warmed by her rosy cheeks; her tight-fitting dress with a pleat over the shoulder showed up her ample breasts, the sight of which, moving rhythmically up and down as she breathed, excited him as he watched them. That was the most appetizing part of her beauty: he imagined them white as snow, round and full; he had touched them, yes, but covered with her clothes, and his greedy, avid hands had found only the cold silk. But in the sexton's house they would be his, without hindrance, without clothes, at the disposition of his lips. By God! and at the same time they could bring consolation to Toto's soul! Nothing would hinder that. He hesitated no longer. Raising his voice above the clatter of the old ladies, who were discussing the disappearance of the *Lives of the Saints*, he said:

'No, my dear senhoras, it is not books which will benefit the girl. Do you know the idea that has just come to my mind? It is that one of us, the one who is the least occupied, should convey the word of God to that soul.' And smiling he added: 'To speak the truth, the one amongst us with the most time on her hands is Menina Amelia.'

Then what a surprise! It appeared the will of Our Lord himself coming in a revelation. All their eyes lit up in devout exaltation at the thought of that charitable mission, which would begin from them, from the Rua da Misericordia. They went into ecstasies at the gluttonous thought of the eulogies of the senhor precentor and the chapter. Each one gave her advice, in eagerness to participate in the holy work so that she would share in the recompenses which the Lord would certainly rain on them. Dona Joaquina Gansoso warmly declared that she envied Amelia, and was very shocked when the latter suddenly laughed:

'I imagine that now you will not do it with sufficient devotion? You are already full of pride at the thought of your good action. It is not in this way that you will get the greatest grace from it!' she said reprovingly.

But Amelia continued laughing nervously, leaning back in her chair, stuffing her handkerchief into her mouth in her efforts to control herself.

Dona Joaquina's little eyes flamed.

'It's indecent, it's indecent!' she cried.

They calmed her down and Amelia had to swear on the Holy Gospels that it was just a funny idea which had struck her, and that she was nervous.

'Ah,' said Dona Maria of the Assumption, 'there is reason in her pride. It is an honour for the house! In knowing——'

The paroco interrupted her, and said severely: 'But no one must know, Dona Maria of the Assumption. A work for which one feels vainglory had no value in the eyes of God.'

Dona Maria bowed her head in humiliation at the rebuke. And Amaro gravely continued: 'The news of this must not leave this house. It is between God and us. We wish to save a soul, to console an afflicted person, and not eulogies in the papers. Don't you agree with me, master?'

The canon sat up with difficulty in his chair:

'Tonight you have spoken with the golden tongue of St Chrisostom. I am edified; and now I wouldn't mind seeing the toast.'

It was then, while they were waiting for Ruça to bring in the tea, that it was decided that Amelia, according to her feeling of devotion, should go once or twice a week in secret, as this would be most valued in the eyes of God; she would pass an hour at the paralytic's bedside, read to her the *Lives of the Saints*, teach her her prayers, and instil into her a sense of virtue.

'In fact,' resumed Dona Maria of the Assumption, turning towards Amelia, 'I must say this to you: you are shameless, the way you have grabbed this for yourself!'

Ruça entered with the tray in the middle of the laugh caused by Dona Maria's nonsensical remark, as Amelia, who had become scarlet, called it. It was thus that she and Father Amaro could freely meet for the glory of God and the humiliation of the Enemy.

They met sometimes once and sometimes twice a week, so that at the end of the month the charitable visits to the paralytic amounted to seven, symbolizing, according to the devout old ladies, the seven lessons of Mary. The evening before each rendezvous Amaro warned Uncle Esguelhas that after he had swept the house and prepared the room for the senhor paroco's religious task, he should leave the street door on the latch. Amelia got up early on those days; she always had some white skirts or petticoats to iron or some ribbons or laces to arrange; her mother was surprised at all these preparations, and at the amount of eau-de-cologne in which she drowned herself: Amelia explained that it was to inspire in Toto ideas of cleanliness and freshness. After she had dressed herself she sat down waiting for eleven o'clock to strike, very serious, responding heedlessly to her mother's questions, with cheeks ablaze and eyes glued to the hands of the old wall-wagger, which in the end deeply groaned out eleven; after a last look in the glass she left, kissing her mother good-bye.

She always went in fear of being watched. Every day she begged Our Lady of Safe Journeys to preserve her from evil encounters; and if she met a beggar she invariably gave him alms in order to please Our Blessed Lord who was a friend of all beggars and vagabonds. What frightened her most was the Cathedral Square, over which the apothecary's Amparo, as she sat sewing at the window, exercised an incessant vigilance. As she passed she crouched down, and held her sunshade over her face. She always entered the Cathedral with the right foot first.

The silence in the church, sleeping, deserted and in semi-darkness, filled her with dread: in the taciturnity of the saints and of the crosses she felt a reproof for her sin: she imagined that the glass eyes of the statues and the painted pupils of the saints' eyes in the pictures were fixed on her with a cruel insistence, as they watched the heaving of her bosom at the thought of the pleasure which awaited her. Sometimes, overpowered by superstition, in order to dissipate the disapproval of the saints, she promised to devote all her morning to Toto, charitably to give her all her attention and not to let Senhor Father Amaro even touch her dress. But when she entered the sexton's house and he wasn't there, she didn't delay for even a minute at the side of Toto's bed, but rushed to the kitchen window to watch for him, gazing at the massive door of the sacristy, whose strong black-plated panels she knew one by one.

He appeared in the end. It was then the beginning of March; the swallows had already arrived, and in that melancholy silence one could hear them fluttering and chirping in the Cathedral walls. Here and there, plants which grew only in humid places covered the corners of the walls with their dark green foliage. Sometimes Amaro very gallantly went to pick a flower. But Amelia, becoming impatient, tapped on the kitchen window. He hurried to her; and they remained for a minute at the door pressing hands and devouring one another with their eyes alight with passion; in the end they called to see Toto and give her the cakes which the paroco had brought her in his cassock pocket.

Toto's bed was in an alcove, at the side of the kitchen; her wasted consumptive body, buried in the straw-mattress, made only a faint bulge in the filthy frayed bedcover, from which, to pass the time, she tore the threads. For these days she wore a white nightgown, and her hair shone with oil; for latterly, since Amaro's visits began, as Uncle Esguelhas said with delight, she had a mania to appear somebody, to the point of keeping a comb and a looking-glass hidden under her pillow and ordering her father to push under the bed amongst the dirty linen the dolls which she now despised.

Amelia sat for an instant on the side of the iron bed, asking her if she had studied her ABC, making her name a letter here and there. Afterwards she asked her to repeat correctly the prayer which she had taught her; while the priest waited at the door, with his hands in his pockets, annoyed, embarrassed by the bright eyes of the paralytic, which never left him, penetrating him, running over his body with passionate wonder, and which every day appeared bigger and brighter in her brown face, so sunken that the cheek-bones seemed as if they would push through the skin. He now felt neither compassion nor pity for Toto; he detested the delay, and thought the girl savage and hateful. Amelia also thought these moments dreary in which, in order not to give too much offence to Our Blessed Lord, she resigned herself to speak to the paralytic. Toto appeared to hate her, and replied very sulkily to her questions; at other times she persisted in a rancorous silence, turning her face to the wall; one day she viciously tore the alphabet in shreds; and if Amelia attempted to arrange her shawl over her shoulders or pull up the bedclothes round her, her whole body stiffened and she shrank away.

In the end, Amaro made an impatient signal to Amelia; she immediately put the *Lives of the Saints* with the pictures in front of Toto: 'You look at the pictures—look, this is St Matthew, this the Holy Virgin . . . Good-bye, I'm going upstairs with the senhor paroco to pray that God will give you health and that you will be able to walk. Don't spoil the book, it would be a sin.'

They ascended the stairs, while the paralytic, stretching her head out, gazed greedily after them, listening to the creaking of the steps, her flashing eyes clouded with tears of rage. The room above was very low, and without a ceiling. It had a roof of black beams on which the tiles were placed. At the side of the bed hung a lamp, the fumes from which had left a feathery, fan-shaped mark on the wall. Amaro always laughed at the preparations which Uncle Esguelhas had made for them: the table in the corner with the New Testament laid on it, a jug of water, and two chairs placed at the side . . .

'It is for our conference, to teach you the duties of a nun,' said he, laughing mockingly.

'Well teach me then!' she murmured, placing herself in front of the priest with arms wide open and lips parted in a warm smile, showing her beautiful shining teeth; offering herself in total abandon.

He voraciously kissed her bosom, her neck and her hair, sometimes biting her ear, at which she gave a little cry. Then they both remained still, listening, in terror of the paralytic underneath. The priest afterwards closed the window shutters and the very obstinate door, which he had to push with his knee. Amelia slowly undressed herself, and with her skirts fallen at her feet she remained a minute motionless, a white figure standing out in the darkness of the room. At her side the priest, also undressing, breathed loudly. She then quickly made the Sign of the Cross, and as she got into the bed she gave a sad little sigh.

Amelia could only remain till midday. On account of this Father Amaro hung his old silver watch on the nail of the lamp. But when they didn't hear the loud strokes of the tower clock, Amelia knew the time by the crowing of a neighbouring cock, and murmured very wearily: 'I must go, my love.'

'Stay where you are . . . You are always in a hurry.'

They then remained silent for a minute in a sweet lassitude, very close together. Here and there through the chinks of the badly joined tiles of the roof little rays of light penetrated to the room; sometimes they heard the soft pad of a cat's foot as it wandered across the roof and shook the loose tiles; or a bird perching and chirping, while they listened to the quivering of its wings.

'It's late,' said Amelia.

The priest tried to detain her; he never tired of kissing her little ears.

'You glutton!' she murmured. 'Leave me alone!'

She dressed herself quickly in the darkness of the room; afterwards she opened the window, then turned to embrace Amaro's neck, which lay listless over the bed. They then moved the table and chairs to let the paralytic below know that the conference had ended.

Amaro continued kissing her; and in order to finish, she opened the door; Father Amaro went down the stairs, quickly crossed the kitchen without looking at Toto, and entered the sacristy.

Before she left Amelia went to see the paralytic, to ask her if she liked the pictures. She sometimes found her with her head under the bedclothes which she had dragged tightly up around her and held firmly with her hands, in order to hide herself. At other times she was sitting up in bed, and examined Amelia with eyes alight with vicious curiosity, pushing her face close to hers, with nostrils dilated as if smelling her; Amelia recoiled, disturbed and blushing furiously; she complained about being late, quickly picked up *The Lives of the Saints*, and left cursing that creature so malicious in her muteness.

As she passed the Square, Amparo was always at the window. In the end she had considered it wise to let her into the secret of her charitable visits to Toto. Amparo no sooner saw her than she leaned right over the veranda, and called out:

'Well, and how goes Toto?'

'She is doing well.'

'Can she read?'

'Yes, and also spell.'

'And the prayer to Our Lady?'

'She knows it now.'

'What a good work you are doing, child!'

Amelia modestly lowered her eyes. And Carlos, who was also in the secret, came from behind the counter to express his admiration of Amelia.

'You have just come from your great mission of charity, eh?' he said with eyes shining, balancing himself on the heels of his carpet slippers.

'I spent a little time with the poor child, to keep her company . . .'

'Wonderful!' murmured Carlos, 'You are an apostle. Well, go home, you saintly child, and give my kind regards to your mamma.'

He then went inside and said to the assistant:

'Now look at that, Senhor Augusto. Instead of passing her time in love-making like other girls, she makes herself a guardian angel. Passing the flower of her life with a paralytic! You can see, senhor, that philosophy, materialism, and all these other vile ideas are incapable of inspiring such actions. Only religion can do so, my dear senhor. I wish that those Renans and the rest of that rabble of philosophers could see this! Mark you, senhor, I am an admirer of philosophy, but only when it goes hand in hand with religion. I am a man of science and I admire Newton and Guizot—but (I speak very seriously, senhor)—if philosophy separates itself from religion (again I speak seriously), in ten years time, Senhor Augusto, philosophy is dead and buried.'

He continued walking slowly up and down the pharmacy, with his hands behind his back, ruminating on the end of philosophy.

Chapter XVII

THIS WAS the happiest time of Amaro's life.

I walk in the grace of God, he sometimes thought at night when he undressed, and when according to his priestly habit he had made an examination of his daily actions and saw that they continued so pleasant, so comfortable, so uniformly enjoyed. During the last two months he had had neither friction nor difficulty in his parochial duties; as Father Saldanha said, the whole world lived in a saintly humour. Dona Josepha had got him a very cheap and excellent servant: her name was Escolastica. In the Rua da Misericordia he had his devoted admiring court; once or twice every week came that delicious heavenly hour in Uncle Esguelhas' house; and to complete the harmony, the season was so beautiful that in Morenal the roses were already beginning to open.

But what delighted him most was that neither the old ladies, nor the priests, nor any of the sacristans suspected his rendezvous with Amelia. Those visits to Toto had become a custom of the house; they referred to them as 'the little one's devotions'; and they didn't ask any searching questions on the pious principle that it was a secret which they had with Our Lord. Sometimes, however, one of the senhoras would ask Amelia how the invalid was getting on; she would assure them that there was a great change in her, that she had begun to open her eyes to the law of God; then, very discreetly, she would change the subject. There was a vague plan for them all to go in pilgrimage, one day later on, when Toto knew her catechism and when, by the efficacy of their prayers, she had turned good, to admire the holy work of Amelia and to rejoice in the humiliation of the Enemy.

Amelia, on the strength of this great confidence in her virtue, proposed one day to Amaro, as a very clever idea, that she would inform the friends that the senhor paroco sometimes helped her in her pious instruction of Toto.

'So that if anyone did chance to see you entering Uncle Esguelhas' house it wouldn't arouse suspicion.'

'It doesn't seem to me necessary,' he answered. 'It is clear that God is with us, my child. It is better that we shouldn't interfere with His plans. He sees further than we do . . .'

She immediately agreed with him in this, as in all that came from his lips. From the first morning in Uncle Esguelhas' house, she had surrendered herself to him absolutely, body and soul, will and feeling: there wasn't a single little hair on her skin, nor the smallest idea in her head that didn't belong to the senhor paroco. This total possession of her being didn't invade her gradually; it was complete from the very moment that his strong arms had closed around her. It seemed as if his kisses had sucked her up, drained her very soul: she was now like an inert appendage of his person. And she didn't attempt to hide it from him: she loved to humiliate herself, to offer herself continually, completely enslaved; she wished that he should think for her and that her only life should be in him; she contentedly loaded him with that burden of responsibility which had always weighed down her soul; her judgments now came already formed from the priest's brain, as naturally as if the blood which came from his heart had flowed into her veins. 'The senhor paroco would like' or 'the senhor paroco said', was a sufficiently powerful reason for her. She lived with her eyes on him, in animal obedience; all she had to do was bow her head when he spoke and when the moment came, let down her skirts.

Amaro enjoyed this domination to the full: it compensated him for all his years of dependence—in his uncle's house, in the seminary, in the Conde of Ribamar's white salon. His existence as a priest was a series of humble cringings that wearied his soul: he lived in a state of obedience to the senhor bishop, the ecclesiastical council, the canonical laws, the Rule, which didn't even permit him to exercise his will with the sacristans. And now, at last, he had there at his feet that body, that soul, that living being over whom he reigned despotically. He had passed his life according to his profession, praising, adoring and offering incense to God; now he was the God of a creature who feared him and gave him punctual devotion. To her at least, he was beautiful, superior to the counts and the dukes, as worthy of the mitre as the most learned. She herself said to him one day after a minute's thought: 'You could one day be Pope!'

'I'm the stuff of which they are made,' he answered seriously.

She believed him; and dreaded that one day the Church authorities would take him from her, and send him far away from Leiria. That passion, in which she was saturated and immersed, made her stupid and dense with regard to all which did not refer to her senhor paroco and her love. Also, Amaro would not allow her any interest or any curiosity outside of his person. He even forbade her to read romances or poetry. What had she to do with these things? What did it matter to her what went on in the world? One day when she spoke rather enthusiastically of a ball which the Via Claras were giving, he became as offended as if she had betrayed him, and when they were in Uncle Esguelhas' house he made terrible accusations against her, calling her a silly vain girl, a lost soul, a child of Satan. . . .

'I'll kill you! Do you hear me? I'll kill you!' he exclaimed, seizing her wrists tightly, and fuming at her with eyes alight.

He had a fear, which galled him, that she would free herself of his dominion, lose the mute absolute adoration which she had for him. He sometimes thought that she might, in time, tire of him, a man who couldn't satisfy the vanities and tastes of a woman and who was always dressed in a black cassock, with his face clean-shaven and his head tonsured. He knew that coloured ties, a well-twisted moustache, a trotting horse, and a military uniform exercised a decided fascination on a woman. And if he heard her talk of an officer of the detachment, or one of the youths of the town, there were tempestuous explosions of jealousy:

'You like him! Is it for his trappings or his moustache?'

'I like him! Oh, I've never seen the man!'

'Well then, don't talk about the fellow. You are just curious. You mustn't give even a thought to another man. This lack of vigilance over your soul and your will is the kind of thing of which the devil takes advantage . . .'

He thus began to have a hatred of the whole secular world which might attract her, drag her by force from the gloom of his cassock. He forbade her, under various complicated pretexts, all communication with the town. He even tried to persuade her mother not to let her go alone to the arcade or the shops. And he never ceased representing the men as monsters of impiety, covered with a crust of sin, stupid and false, doomed to eternal damnation. He told her dreadful things about all the young men of Leiria. She asked, terrified, but curious:

'How do you know?'

'I can't tell you,' he replied with reticence, indicating that his lips were shut with the seal of confession.

And at the same time he hammered into her ears praise of the priestly office. He unrolled with pomp the learning of its ancient compendiums, eulogizing the function, the superiority of the ecclesiastic. In Egypt, the great nation of antiquity, a man could only be king if he were a priest. In Persia, in Ethiopia, a simple priest had the power to dethrone a king and dispose of his crown. Where was there another authority equal to his? Not even in the courts of heaven. The priest was superior to the angels and seraphim; because to them was not given as to the priest, the marvellous power of forgiving sin. And even the Virgin Mary, had She a power greater than this, Father Amaro's? No: with all the respect due to the majesty of Our Blessed Lady, he

227

could say with St Bernard of Siena: 'The priest is greater than You, Beloved Mother!' If the Virgin had conceived Christ in Her chaste womb, it was only once, and he, the priest, in the holy sacrifice of the Mass, changed the bread and wine into Christ's body and blood, every day. And that was not just a subtle argument of his, all the Holy Fathers admitted it.

'Eh, what do you think of it?'

'Oh, my love!' she murmured in admiration, swooning with passion.

He then dazzled her with the time-honoured quotations: St Clement, who called the priest 'the God of the earth', the eloquent St Chrysostom, who said that the priest is the ambassador who comes to give the orders of God, and St Ambrose, who wrote: 'Between the dignity of a king and the dignity of a priest there is more difference than between lead and gold.'

'And the gold is here, my child,' said Amaro patting his chest. 'What do you think of it?'

She drew him into her arms and covered him with voracious kisses, as if to touch, to possess in him the gold of St Ambrose, the ambassador of Jesus, all the highest and noblest things of the earth, the being who exceeded the archangels in grace.

This divine power of the priest, his familiarity with God, influenced her as much as or even more than his voice, which made her believe in the promise which he so often repeated to her: that being loved by a priest called down on her the interest, the friendship of God; that after her death two angels would come to accompany her and would take her by the hand to St Peter, the Gate Keeper of Heaven, and there clear up any doubts which might bar her entrance; and that on her tomb, as happened with a French girl who was loved by a priest, white roses would spring up spontaneously as a celestial proof that a girl's virginity was not damaged in a priest's saintly arms.

That idea delighted her. At the thought of her tomb being perfumed with white roses she became pensive, with a foretaste of such mystical delights. She gave little sighs of pleasure, and affirmed, as she pursed up her mouth, that she wanted to die.

Amaro laughed at her: 'How can you speak of dying with that lovely flesh . . .'

She had in fact become fatter. She was now in the fullness of her beauty. She had lost that uneasy expression which made her mouth look cold and dry and her nose sharp. Her lips were a warm moist red; her laughing eyes were serene and clear; her whole person had the ripe appearance of fecundity. She had become lazy: when at home, at every moment she stopped her work and fixed her gaze far away with a mute set smile, and all appeared to sleep for a minute, the needle, the cloth that she was sewing, her whole person. She was seeing again the bell-ringer's room, the iron bed, the senhor paroco in his shirt sleeves.

She spent the whole day waiting for eight o'clock, the hour at which he appeared regularly with the canon. But she now found the evenings heavy. He advised her to be very distant with him; in an excess of obedience she exaggerated her reserve to the point of never sitting at his side during tea and never offering him the cakes. She detested the presence of the old ladies, the squeaking of their voices, the weary game of lotto: everything in the world seemed intolerable except being alone with him. But then when they were in the bell-ringer's house, what compensations! What a different face, what stifled cries of delirium, what agonizing sighs. Afterwards her deathly stillness sometimes frightened the priest, and he lifted himself up on his elbows and asked anxiously: 'Are you ill?'

She opened her eyes wide with surprise, as if returning from far away; and she really was beautiful, with her bare arms crossed on her naked breast, slowly shaking her head in negation.

Chapter XVIII

AN UNEXPECTED circumstance arrived to spoil these mornings in the sexton's house. It was all due to Toto's extraordinary conduct. As Father Amaro said, the girl had become a beast to them.

She now showed open aversion to Amelia. As soon as she approached, Toto quickly hid her head under the covers, and on hearing Amelia's voice or feeling her hand on the bed, she twisted and turned frenziedly. Amelia fled from the room, affected with the idea that the devil which possessed Toto, on receiving the odour which she brought from the church on her clothes, impregnated with incense and sprinkled with Holy Water, rolled with terror inside the body of the girl. . . .

Amaro tried, in formidable words, to rebuke Toto, to make her feel her wicked ingratitude to Menina Amelia who came to console her, and to teach her how to speak to her Holy Father in heaven. But the paralytic broke into paroxysms of hysterical tears, after which she suddenly became fixed, tense, staring with the upturned whites of her eyes bulging out of their sockets, while she frothed from the mouth. She inundated the bed with water. It was very frightening. Amaro, as a precaution, recited the exorcisms. And Amelia, from then on, decided, as she said, 'to leave the wild beast in peace'. She would never again try to teach her the alphabet, or the prayers to St Anna.

But, as a matter of conscience, on entering they called to see her for an instant. They did not go into the alcove, but stood at the door and called out 'How are you?' She never replied. They then retired, terrified by those wild bright eyes which devoured them, looking from one to the other, running over their bodies, fixing themselves with a metallic flash on Amelia's dress and on the priest's cassock, as if trying to divine what was underneath, in an avid curiosity which despairingly dilated her nostrils and fixed a livid grin on her lips. But it was her muteness, obstinate and rancorous, which disturbed them above all. Amaro, who had little belief in possession by devils, saw in all this symptoms of dangerous madness. Amelia's fears increased, and she thought it was lucky for them that Toto's helpless limbs kept her nailed to her bed. Otherwise, Jesus, she was capable of entering the room and biting them in one of her fits!

Amaro declared that the whole morning's pleasure was destroyed, after such a terrible spectacle. They then decided that in future they would go up to the room without speaking to Toto.

It was worse. When they crossed the front door to ascend the stairs, Toto leaned over the side of the bed and grasped the edge of the mattress in an anxious effort to see them, to follow them, with her face distorted with despair at her inability to move. And when on entering the room, Amelia heard a dry laugh or a prolonged growl coming from below, it froze her blood.

Now she always went terrified: the idea came to her that God had established there, next to her love for the priest, an implacable demon to hiss at her and hound her. Amaro, wishing to calm her, told her that Our Holy Father Pius IX latterly declared it a sin to believe in possession by the devil.

'But why are there prayers then, and exorcisms?'

'That is the old religion. All that is going to change now. After all, science is science.'

She felt that Amaro was trying to deceive her, and that Toto would destroy all her happiness. In the end Amaro discovered a way of escape from the cursed girl: it was for both of them to enter by the sacristy: they then had only to cross the kitchen to mount the stairs, and the position of Toto's bed in the alcove prevented her from seeing them when they walked cautiously on tiptoe. It was quite safe, as at the hour of the rendezvous, between eleven and twelve on a weekday, the sacristy was deserted.

But it happened that even when they entered on tiptoe and held their breath, their steps, however careful, made the old stairs creak. Then Toto's voice came up from the alcove; a voice hoarse, bitter, rough, bellowing:

'Get out, you bitch! Get out, you bitch!'

Amaro had a mad desire to strangle the paralytic. Amelia paled and trembled.

And the creature howled from inside the room:

'There go the dogs! There go the dogs!'

They took refuge in the room, bolting themselves in. But that desolate voice, which seemed to them to come from the inferno, still reached them and pursued them.

'The dogs are getting on each other! The dogs are getting on each other!'

Amelia fell on the bed, almost fainting with terror. She swore that she could never again return to that cursed house. . . .

'But what the devil do you want?' said the priest furious. 'Where can we go then? Do you want us to lie on the sacristy benches?'

'But what have I done to her? What have I done to her?' exclaimed Amelia, wringing her hands.

'Nothing! She is mad. Poor Uncle Esguelhas has had a great affliction . . . Anyway, what do you want me to do?'

She didn't reply. But at home, as the day of meeting was drawing near, she began to dread the thought of that voice which continually thundered in her ears and haunted her dreams. This fear caused her slowly to awake from the state of torpor into which she had fallen on the first day that she had surrendered her virginity to the priest. She now asked herself if she would continue committing this unpardonable sin. The affirmations of Amaro, assuring her of God's pardon, no longer satisfied her. When Toto howled she clearly saw a lividness cover the face of the priest and a ripple of fear go through his body, as if he felt his guilt and had a terrifying vision of eternal damnation. And if God was going to forgive them, why did he allow the devil, through the voice of the paralytic, to hurl insults at them and mock them?

She knelt at the foot of her bed, offering up endless prayers to Our Lady of Sorrows, begging Her to enlighten her, to tell her the meaning of this persecution of Toto, and if it was Her divine intention to send her a fearful warning in this way. But Our Lady was silent. When praying Amelia no longer, as formerly, felt descend from the sky and enter into her soul that peacefulness, gentle as a summer's breeze, which was like a visitation from Our Lady. She lost all her freshness and became dejected, twisting her hands in despair and feeling abandoned by God. She promised herself never to return to the sexton's house: but when the day arrived, at the thought of Amaro, of the bed, of those kisses which thrilled her whole being, of that fire of passion which penetrated her, she felt helpless and weak against the temptation; she dressed herself, resolving that it would be for the last time; and on the stroke of eleven she left, her ears burning, her heart trembling at the thought of Toto's voice which she was about to hear, her whole being aflame with desire for the man who was going to throw her on the bed.

From fear of the saints, she didn't say her usual prayers on entering the church.

She ran to the sacristy to take refuge in Amaro, to shield herself in the sacred authority of his cassock. She arrived so pale and so upset that he laughed mockingly at her fears, in order to calm her. No, it was nonsense, she wasn't going to spoil all the joy of their mornings because there was a lunatic in the house! He finally promised her to procure another place: and taking advantage of the seclusion of the sacristy, to distract her he sometimes showed her the church vestments and treasures, getting her interested in a new chalice or the old lace of a surplice, proving by the familiar way in which he touched these sacred things

232

that he was still the senhor paroco and had not lost credit with heaven.

It was thus that one morning he produced a cloak for Our Lady, which some days previously had been presented by a rich parishioner of Ourem. Amelia admired it very much. It was of blue satin, representing the firmament, with embroidered stars, and a rich centre pattern from which blazened a gold heart surrounded by gold roses. Amaro unfolded it and took it to the window to show better its heavy shining embroidery work.

'A rich work, isn't it, eh? Hundreds of mil reis. I tried it on the statue yesterday. It becomes her like a jewel. A little long perhaps . . .' Then looking at Amelia, and comparing her tall figure with the stocky figure of the image of Our Lady: 'You're the one it would fit well. Let us try . . .'

She drew back crying: 'No, heavens, what a sin!'

'Nonsense!' said he, coming towards her with the cloak held open, showing its satin lining, white as a morning cloud. 'It's not blessed—it has just come from the dressmaker's.'

'No, no,' said she weakly, her eyes already alight with desire.

Then he got angry. Perhaps she knew better than he what was a sin and what wasn't? She was taking on herself to teach him what respect he owed to the sacred vestments. 'Come on, don't be silly. Let me see how it looks on you.'

He placed it on her shoulders, and fastened it over her breast with its buckle of rich silver work. He then stood back to contemplate this figure all wrapped in the cloak, frightened and still, with a warm smile of heavenly ecstasy.

'Oh, my little girl, how lovely you look!'

Then moving herself with solemn seriousness, she went to the sacristy mirror, an old tarnished mirror in a frame of chiselled oak, with a cross at the top. She looked at herself a minute, wrapped in that heavenly blue silk dotted with brilliant pointed stars forming a magnificent firmament. She felt the rich weight of it. The holiness that the cloak had acquired in its contact with the shoulders of the image penetrated her in a voluptuous sanctity. A fluid, sweeter than earthly air, enveloped her, caressing her body with the ether of paradise. She imagined herself a saint being carried aloft in a procession, or more exalted still, a saint in the sky . . .

Amaro lisped to her: 'Oh, my little one, you are lovelier than Our Lady!'

She gave a quick look in the glass. Yes, she was certainly beautiful. Not as beautiful as Our Lady . . . But with her red lips and her little brown face all sparkling from the reflection of her two black eyes, if she were there over the altar with the organ playing and worshippers all around her, she would make the hearts of the faithful beat quickly . . .

Amaro then came behind her, crossed his hands over her breasts, pressed her whole body to him, and putting his lips to hers gave her a kiss, silent and long, very long . . . Amelia's eyes closed, she leaned her head back, heavy with desire. The priest did not loosen his lips, avidly they sucked her soul. Her breath quickened, her knees trembled: and with a moan she swooned on the shoulder of the priest, colourless, lifeless with joy.

But she suddenly straightened herself up, and blinking her eyelids as if she were awakening from a far-away dream, she gazed at Amaro, while a wave of blood rushed to her cheeks:

'Oh, Amaro, how horrible, what a sin!'

'Nonsense!' said he.

Now all upset, she undid the cloak: 'Take it off me, take it off me!' she cried, as if the silk were burning her.

Then Amaro became very serious. Really one must not play with sacred things . . .

'But it isn't blessed. Of that there is no doubt . . .'

He carefully folded the cloak, and wrapping it in its white cloth, replaced it in the great drawer without saying a word. Amelia watched him, petrified, except for her pallid lips which moved in prayer.

When at last he said to her that it was time to go to the sexton's house she recoiled as if it were the devil calling her. 'Today, no!' she exclaimed imploringly.

He insisted. Such simplicity was really going too far. She knew well it wasn't a sin, as the cloak was not blessed. She was showing a very poor spirit. What the devil, only half-an-hour, only a quarter-of-an-hour!

Without replying, she went slowly towards the door.

'Then you don't want to?'

She turned her eyes to him in supplication: 'Today, no!'

Amaro shrugged his shoulders. And Amelia quickly crossed the Cathedral with head bowed and eyes cast on the flagstones, feeling that she was passing among the indignant saints, whose glances crossed one another to pierce her.

On the following morning, Senhora Joanneira, who was in the dining room, hearing the senhor canon coming up the stairs panting, went out to meet him, and shut herself in with him in the little parlour.

She wanted to tell him of the trouble she had had in the early morning. Amelia woke her up suddenly, crying that Our Lord was about to put His foot on her neck! That she was suffocating! That Toto was trying to set fire to her back! And that the flames of Hell were rising higher than the Cathedral tower—in short, a horror! She found her running round her room in her shift, as if she were mad; a little while afterwards she fell on her side in an attack of nerves. The whole house was in a tumult. The poor little one was now in bed, and had barely touched a spoon of broth.

'Nightmares,' said the canon. 'Indigestion.'

'Ah, senhor canon, no!' exclaimed Senhora Joanneira, who appeared exhausted, sitting down in front of him on the edge of a chair. 'It is something else; it is those visits to that unfortunate child of the sexton!'

Then she poured herself out, with an effusive babble like a dam being opened to set free an accumulated surplus of water. She had never cared to say anything, as she realized it was a great work of charity. But, since they began, the girl was completely changed. Lately, she was full of moods. At one moment she was happy for no reason, another time there were scowls which would turn the milk sour. At night she heard her walking round the house till quite late and opening the windows. There were times when she was almost afraid to see her looking so strange: when she came home from the sexton's she was always as white as chalk, and falling down with weakness. She always had to give her a cup of broth to revive her. She said that Toto was possessed with the devil. And the late senhor precentor (God rest his soul) used to say that, in this world, the two things to which women were most liable were tuberculosis and possession by the devil. It seemed to her then, that she must not consent to the little one's going to the sexton's house, without being certain that it was not going to prejudice her health or do harm to her soul. As a matter of fact, she would like a person of judgment and experience to examine Toto.

'In a word,' said the canon, who had listened with closed eyes to this verbose lament, 'what you want is for me to go and see the paralytic, and find out exactly what is happening there.'

'It would be a relief to me, my precious!'

That word, which Senhora Joanneira, in her dignity as a matron, reserved for the intimacies of the bedroom, touched the canon. He caressed the plump neck of his old friend, promising to go willingly and study the case.

'Tomorrow, Toto will be alone,' remembered Senhora Joanneira.

But the canon would prefer Amelia to be present. He could then see how they both got on together, and find out if there was any evil spirit making trouble between them.

'I will do this for you, because it is you, and I would like to help you

235

—though I really have plenty to do looking after my aches and pains without occupying myself with the affairs of Satan.'

Senhora Joanneira rewarded him with a resounding kiss.

'Ah, you sirens, you sirens!' murmured the canon philosophically.

In his heart he found it a disagreeable task: it would disturb one of his mornings; and it was certainly going to tire him. He would even have to exercise his shrewdness; and apart from that he hated the sight of illness and of everything connected with death. But, a few days later, faithful to his promise, the morning on which it was arranged for Amelia to go to Toto, he unwillingly dragged himself out and made for the shop of Carlos the apothecary; and installing himself in a chair, with one eye on *The Popular* and the other on the door, he waited for Amelia to pass on her way to the Cathedral. His friend Carlos was out; and Senhor Augusto, leaning on his desk, with his head on his closed fist, occupied his leisure time reading Soares de Pasos. Outside, the sun, though it was only the end of April, shone brilliantly on the flagstones of the Square; nobody was about, and the only sound which broke the silence was the noise of hammering in Dr Pereira's house, which was being repaired. Amelia was late. The canon, after considering at length the great sacrifice he was making for his old friend, gradually fell into a doze, with *The Popular* falling down off his lap, when a clergyman entered the pharmacy.

'Oh, Abbot Ferrão, you in town?' said the canon waking up.

'Just a short visit, colleague,' he said, carefully placing two great volumes tied with string on the chair. He then turned and respectfully presented his compliments to the assistant.

His hair was completely white—he must have passed his sixtieth year—but he was robust, with an eternal joy dancing in his bright little eyes, and the enamel of his teeth was still in splendid condition, due to his good health; what disfigured him was his enormous nose.

He then expressed the hope that Canon Dias was there on a visit and not on account of illness.

'No, I'm here waiting. I have an important job on hand, Abbot Ferrão.'

'Ah,' said the old man, impressed by the seriousness of the canon's mission, as he methodically took from his case, stuffed with papers, a prescription for the apothecary. He then gave the canon news of the country. It was at Poyaes that the canon had his farm, Ricoça. On passing there that morning the abbot was surprised to see that the front was being done up. Had friend Dias an idea of passing the summer there?

'No, no, I haven't, but as the men were working on the inside and the front was in such a disgraceful condition I ordered them to set to work on it. It's necessary to have it looking decent as it is on the side of the road where the Morgado of Poyaes passes every day—that windbag, who imagines his is the only mansion for miles around worth looking at. It's worth doing, even if it's only to let that atheist see there are other mansions as good as his! Don't you think I'm right, friend?'

The abbot was just lamenting such a feeling of vanity in a clergyman but, for Christian charity and in order not to annoy the canon, he hurried to say: 'That's right, cleanliness is next to godliness.'

The canon, seeing a skirt and cape pass in the Square, ran over to the door to see if it was Amelia. It wasn't, so he returned and again took up the subject with which his mind was occupied. Seeing that the chemist's assistant had gone into the laboratory, he said in Ferrão's ear: 'I have an important job on hand. I'm going to see a soul possessed by the devil!'

'Ah,' said the abbot, very serious at the idea of such a responsibility.

'Would you like to come with me, abbot? It's a stone's throw from here.'

The abbot politely excused himself. He'd come to speak to the senhor vicar general, and then after he'd gone to ask Silverio for the two volumes, he'd come in here to have a prescription made up for an old man in the village and he'd have to be back in Poyaes at the stroke of two.

The canon insisted. It wouldn't take a minute, and the case seemed strange . . .

The abbot then confessed to his dear colleague that these were things he did not like going into. He always faced them with a feeling of doubt and suspicion, so felt unable to judge them impartially.

'But after all there are strange happenings,' said the canon. In spite of his own doubt, he didn't like this hesitation on the part of the abbot with regard to a supernatural phenomenon in which he, Canon Dias, was interested. He repeated dryly: 'I've got some experience and I know there are wonders.'

'Certainly, certainly there are,' said the abbot. 'To deny that God or the Queen of Heaven could appear is contrary to the doctrine of the Church . . . To deny that the devil could possess a man's body would be a profanity. It happened to Job and to the family of Sarah. It's clear there are wonders, but how rare they are, canon!'

He stopped for a minute to look with his bright discerning eye at the canon, who was pushing snuff up his nose, and then continued in a lower voice:

'And then, haven't you remarked, canon, that it is a thing that only happens to women? It is to them only, whose power of evil is so great that even Solomon himself couldn't resist them, whose temperaments are so nervous and so contradictory that even the doctors don't understand them. It is only to them that these wonders happen. Have you, canon, ever heard of the Virgin appearing to a respectable notary? Have you heard of a dignified judge being possessed by an evil spirit? Yes, this makes one think . . . I think it is some evil in themselves, some illusion, imagination, illness . . . Doesn't it appear so to you? My rule in these cases is to view them very lightly, in fact with indifference.'

The canon who had been watching the door, rushed into the street shouting: 'Psst! Psst! You, there!' and brandishing his umbrella.

It was Amelia passing. She stopped immediately, annoyed with this encounter which was going to make her still later. The senhor paroco must be desperate waiting . . .

'So that,' said the canon from the door opening his umbrella, 'you, abbot, when you smell a wonder——'

'I immediately suspect some scandal.'

The canon contemplated him for a minute with respect. 'You, Ferrão, are capable of giving hints on wisdom to Solomon. To Solomon himself,' he repeated from the street.

'Oh, colleague, oh colleague!' exclaimed the abbot, not pleased with this injustice to the great Solomon.

The canon had prepared a clever story to justify his visit to the paralytic, but during his conversation with the abbot it had fled from his mind as did all which he left in the reservoirs of his memory, and so he said naturally to Amelia:

'Come on, I also want to see Toto.'

She was petrified. The senhor paroco was surely already there! But her protectress, Our Lady of Sorrows, whom she now invoked in her affliction, wouldn't let her be caught in a difficulty. The canon, who was walking along at her side, was surprised to hear her say with a little laugh:

'Good, today is the day for visiting Toto! The senhor paroco told me that perhaps he'll turn up there. He may be there already.'

'Oh, he as well? That's good, that's good. We'll have a consultation over her.'

Amelia, happy at the thought of her cleverness, chatted about Toto. The senhor canon would see: Toto was an impossible creature. Lately she hadn't wanted to talk about her at home, but Toto had a spite against her. And she said such things, she had a way of talking of dogs and animals that made one shiver . . . Ah, it was a duty which was costing her a lot. The girl wouldn't learn her lessons nor take her advice —she was a beast!

'The smell is disagreeable!' grumbled the canon entering.

'What else can you expect! The girl is a pig, it is impossible to teach her to be clean and tidy. The father is also dirty and careless.'

'It's here, senhor canon,' she said opening the door of the alcove which now, carrying out the orders of the paroco, Uncle Esguelhas kept shut.

They found Toto half stretched out of bed, her face alight with curiosity at the strange voice.

'Long live Senhora Toto,' said the canon from the door, making no attempt to go near her.

'Come on and salute the senhor canon,' said Amelia, beginning with unusual charity to settle the bedclothes and tidy the alcove. 'Ask him how he is. Don't sulk.'

But Toto remained as dumb as the image of San Bento at the head of her bed, carefully examining this clergyman, so fat, so grizzly, so different from the senhor paroco. Her eyes, more bulging each day as her cheeks caved in, went as was their custom from the man to Amelia, in a burning anxiety to find out why she brought him there, and if he too was going up to the room with her.

Amelia was now trembling with fear. If the senhor paroco entered and there, in front of the canon, Toto in one of her fits broke out into cries about dogs! With the excuse of giving the house a tidy-up, she went to the kitchen to watch the yard. She would make a sign from the window the minute the paroco appeared.

The canon, now alone with Toto, preparing to make his investigation, asked her who were the three persons of the Blessed Trinity—when she pushed her head forward and asked in a whisper light as a breath of wind: 'And the other?'

The canon didn't understand. Would she speak up! Who was it?

'The other one who comes with her!'

The canon went nearer, cocking his ear with curiosity:

'What other?'

'The handsome one. The one who goes up into the room with her. The one who pinches her.'

Amelia entered: the paralytic shut up immediately, calmly breathing as if she had a sudden alleviation of all her sufferings. The canon, struck dumb with surprise, remained leaning over the bed as if he were testing Toto's lungs. He got up in the end, blew out as if it were the heat of August, slowly shoved snuff up his nose and remained with the box open between his fingers, his little inflamed eyes nailed on Toto's bed.

'Then, senhor canon, what do you think of my patient?' asked Amelia.

He replied without looking at her:

'Yes, she is doing well, she is doing well. She's a little strange, but continue with your instruction of her, she's getting on . . . Good-bye.'

He left muttering that he had some business to attend to, and returned immediately to the pharmacy.

'A glass of water!' he gasped, flopping into a chair.

Carlos, who had returned, rushed to offer him orange-blossom tea, enquiring if his excellency were not well.

'Exhausted,' he said.

The canon took *The Popular* from the table, and there he stayed without stirring, buried in the columns of the paper. Carlos tried to speak to him of the nation's politics, of trade with Spain, of the dangers of the revolutions threatening society, of the laxity of the administration of the council of which he was now a fierce enemy . . . In vain: his excellency answered with grunted monosyllables. Carlos in the end took refuge in a disgusted silence, internally comparing, with a disdain which brought a sneer to his lips, the denseness of that clergyman to the inspired word of another Lacordaire or Malhao. It was because of such as he that Materialism was lifting its hydra head in Leiria, and in fact in the whole world.

It was striking one by the clock in the Cathedral tower when the canon, who had been watching the Square out of the corner of his eye, saw Amelia pass. He gathered up the paper and left the pharmacy without a word, hurrying as quickly as his heavy body would permit him to Uncle Esguelhas' house. Toto trembled with fear at seeing the great pot-bellied figure appear at the door of her alcove again. But the canon laughed ingratiatingly, called her Totozinha, promised her a pinto for cakes and sat down on the edge of the bed with an engaging 'Ah!' saying: 'Now we are going to talk, my little friend . . . It's your little foot that is bad, is it? You poor little girl. We must ask God to cure it. I'll see to that for you.'

She reddened and paled by turns, looking all round, disturbed at having that man alone with her, so near that she felt his strong breath.

'Now, listen here,' he said, getting still nearer to her, making the bed creak with his weight, 'tell me, who is it? Who is it that comes with Amelia?'

She replied breathlessly: 'It's the handsome one, the thin one; they go upstairs to the room and shut themselves in there for hours. They are like dogs.'

The canon's eyes were ready to jump out of their sockets.

'But who is he, what is his name?'

'It is the other, the paroco, Amaro!' she said impatiently.

'And they go up to the room, do they? And what do you hear? Tell me everything, little one, tell me!'

The paralytic then recounted, her consumptive voice hissing with fury, how they both entered, rubbed against one another, then rushed up to the room and were shut in there for hours . . .

But the canon, his dull eyes aflame with lewd curiosity, wanted all the indecent details.

'And listen, Toto, what did you hear? Did you hear the bed creak?'

She nodded her head in assent, her face now ghastly white, her teeth clenched.

'And listen, Toto, you saw them kiss and embrace? Tell me all and I'll give you two pintos.'

She remained with her teeth clenched; her distorted face seemed to the canon like a savage's.

'You don't like her, isn't that so?'

She wildly nodded her head.

'You saw them rubbing against one another?'

'They're like dogs!' she hissed from between her clenched teeth.

The canon straightened himself up, gave a loud puff, then vigorously scratched his tonsure.

'Well,' he said, getting up. 'Good-bye, little one. Cover yourself up well; don't catch cold . . .'

He left; and as he loudly banged the door he said aloud:

'This is the vilest, most abominable thing I've ever known. I'll kill him, though I suffer for it.'

He thought a minute and then made for the Rua das Sousas, his umbrella truculently raised, pushing his heavy body along, with a face of apoplectic fury. In the Cathedral Square, however, he again stopped to think and turning on his heels he entered the church. He was in such a state that, forgetting a habit of forty years, he neglected to genuflect in front of the Blessed Sacrament. He reached the sacristy just as Father Amaro was putting on his black gloves, which he now always used to please his little Amelia.

The canon's disturbed look frightened him.

'What is it, master?'

'What is it?' exclaimed the canon: 'It's the villainy of villainies. It's your villainy!' He stopped, suffocated with anger.

Amaro, who had become very pale, stammered:

'What's that you are saying, master?'

The canon recovered his breath:

'Shut up with your "master". You, sir, have dishonoured the girl, it's you who are the master, a master of villainy!'

'What girl? You must be joking.'

He even smiled, pretending to be sure of himself, but his lips were white and trembling.

'Man, I saw!' bawled the canon.

The paroco, suddenly terrified, recoiled.

'You *saw*?'

In a glance he imagined the canon hidden in some corner of Uncle Esguelhas' house spying on him.

'I didn't see, but it is the same as if I actually had seen,' said the canon in a shaking voice. 'I know all. I've just come from there. Toto told me. You and the girl were shut up in the room for hours together. One could even hear the bed creaking. It is scandalous!'

The paroco, seeing himself cornered, put up a desperate resistance.

'Tell me one thing, what has this to do with you?'

The canon jumped. 'What has it to do with me? What it has to do with me is that I'm going straight from here to put the case before the senhor vicar general!'

Amaro, now livid, went for him with closed fist:

'Ah, you unscrupulous blackguard!'

'Would you dare, would you dare?' said the canon with his umbrella raised in protection. 'Would you dare to lay hands on me?'

Father Amaro controlled himself, passed his hand over his sweating brow and closed his eyes: after a minute he said, speaking with forced calm: 'Listen to this, Senhor Canon Dias. Do you know that I once saw you in bed with Senhora Joanneira!'

'Liar!' growled the canon.

'I saw you, I saw you!' affirmed the other furiously. 'One night on entering the house. You were in your shirt sleeves, she had just got out of bed and was doing up her stays. I saw you as plainly as I see you now. You even called out, "Who is there?" If you say a word, I can prove in front of all the clergy that you have been sleeping with Senhora Joanneira for the last ten years. Now that's where you stand!'

The canon, worn out from his excesses of fury, on hearing these words became like a tormented bull and could only answer faintly: 'What a rogue you've turned out on me!'

Father Amaro, now almost calm, as he was certain of having silenced the canon, said with bonhomie: 'Rogue, why? Tell me now! We are both guilty in the case, that's how it is. And listen, I didn't have to go and bribe Toto. It was all very natural when I entered that house. And if you now begin to talk to me of morality, it will just make me laugh. Morality is for the school and the sermon. In my life I do this, you do that, others arrange what they can. You master, an elderly person, get hold of the mother, I who am young get hold of the daughter. It's sad, but what can one do? It is nature which orders and we are but men. And as clergymen, for the honour of our cloth, we must do all in the dark.'

The canon listened, silently nodding his head in acceptance of those truths. He had dropped into a chair to rest himself after so much useless anger. He lifted his eyes to Amaro and said: 'But you, man, at the beginning of your career!'

'And you, master, at the end of your career!'

Then they both laughed. Immediately each one offered to take back the offensive words that he'd said and they gravely shook hands. Afterwards they talked.

What had made the canon furious was that it was the little girl of the house. If it had been anyone else, he'd even have looked favourably on the matter. But little Amelia! If the poor mother knew, she'd die of grief.

'But there is no need for the mother to know!' exclaimed Amaro. 'This must be a deadly secret between the two of us. The mother has no need to know and I won't tell the girl a word of what has passed between us today. Things will remain as they were and the world will go on just the same. But you, master, must be careful! Not a word to Senhora Joanneira. There must be no treason now!'

The canon, with his hand on his heart, gave his word as a *cavalheiro* and a priest that the secret would remain for ever buried in his bosom.

They again affectionately shook hands.

The tower clock struck three. It was the canon's dinner hour.

On the way out, with a knowing look in his eye he patted Amaro on the shoulder and said: 'Ah, you devil, you have a good eye for the girls.'

'What did you expect—what the devil! One begins in fun——'

'Man,' said the canon sententiously 'it's the one thing in life worth living for.'

'It's true, it's true, master, it's the one thing in life worth living for!'

From that day on, Amaro enjoyed a complete tranquillity of mind. Before then, he had sometimes thought that he had repaid with ingratitude the confidence, the loving kindness which he had received in the Rua da Misericordia: but the tacit approbation of the canon had taken the thorn, as he called it, out of his conscience. Because, after all, the chief of the family, the respectable *cavalheiro*, was the canon. Senhora Joanneira was just a concubine. And now sometimes, in a jesting tone, he addressed the canon as his 'dear father-in-law'.

Another circumstance arrived to add to his happiness: Toto got worse quite suddenly. The day after the canon's visit she spouted up blood; and Dr Cardoso, hastily sent for, spoke of galloping consumption, which would carry her off in a few weeks.

'It is the kind, my dear friends,' he said, 'swish, swish.' It was his way of painting death, which, when in a hurry, finished his work with a swish of his scythe.

The mornings in Uncle Esguelhas' house were now tranquil. Amelia and Amaro hadn't to enter on tiptoe and try to steal up to their pleasure unperceived by Toto. They banged the doors and spoke loudly, knowing that Toto was prostrated with fever, under the sheets wet with sweat. But Amelia, on account of scruples, never missed saying a Hail Mary for Toto's recovery. One day when undressing in the sexton's room, she made a sad face and said: 'Ah it seems to me a sin for us to be here enjoying ourselves and that poor thing below fighting for her life.'

Amaro shrugged his shoulders. What could they do? After all, it was the will of God.

Amelia, resigning herself to the will of God in all things, continued letting down her petticoats.

But she now had frequent scruples which annoyed Father Amaro. Some days, she came there very drawn and worried-looking; she had a mournful dream to relate which had tormented her all night and in which she tried to discover warnings of disaster. She sometimes asked him: 'If I died, would you be very sorry?'

Amaro became furious. It was really too stupid, they had this short time together and she had to spoil it with moanings.

'It is not as easy as you think,' she said. 'I carry a heart as black as the night.'

As a matter of fact, her mother's friends found her strange. For whole evenings she didn't open her lips, she just leaned over her sewing pushing the needle slowly in and out, or, too tired to work, she sat by the table spinning the green lamp-shade round and round, with a vacant look in her eyes, her thoughts far away.

'Oh, girl, leave that lampshade alone!' the senhoras would say irritatedly.

She would laugh and give a weary sigh, then take up the white petticoat which she had been hemming for weeks. Her mother, seeing her looking so pale, thought of calling in Dr Gouvea.

'Don't worry, Mamma, it's just nerves. It will pass . . .'

What proved to them all that it was nerves was the sudden frights she got if a door banged, screaming and almost fainting. On some nights she insisted on her mother sleeping with her for fear of night-mares and visions.

'It's what Senhor Dr Gouvea always says,' observed her mother to the canon: 'she's a girl who needs to marry.'

The canon noisily cleared his throat: 'She's not in need of anything,' he muttered, 'she has everything she wants. She has too much, it seems to me.'

It was the canon's idea, as he said to himself, that the girl was over-flowing with happiness. On the days on which he knew she was going to visit Toto, he never tired of studying her, watching her from the depths of his chair with a heavy, lecherous eye. He now lavished paternal pettings on her. He never met her on the stairs without stop-ping her with a little tickle here and a little tickle there and a prolonged patting of her face. He repeatedly wanted her at his house; and while she chatted with Dona Josepha the canon never ceased walking round her, with the air of an old cock, dragging his bedroom slippers. And Amelia and her mother had endless conversations about this friendship with the senhor canon, concluding that he would certainly give her a good dowry.

'You rogue, you,' he would say when alone with Amaro: 'You knew how to lay your hands on a good thing.' Then opening his little round eyes: 'That's a mouthful fit for a king!'

Amaro, puffed up with pride, answered: 'Not a bad mouthful, master, in fact it's an especially good one.'

It was now Amaro's great delight to hear his colleagues praise the beauty of Amelia, who was known amongst the clergy as 'the flower of the devout!' All of them envied him such a penitent. For this, he insisted on her dressing up well for Mass on Sunday; lately getting angry with her for continually wearing an ugly merino dress which gave her the air of an old woman doing penance for her sins.

But Amelia now didn't feel the necessity to please the senhor paroco in all things, because she had completely awakened from that stupid numbness of soul and body into which Amaro's first embrace had thrown her. The sharp consciousness of her guilt was beginning to appear. In the darkness of a spirit enslaved by exaggerated devotion, reason began to dawn. After all, what was she? The senhor paroco's fancy woman. This truth put nakedly seemed terrible to her. Not that she regretted her virginity, her honour, the loss of her good name. She would have sacrificed still more for him and the delights he had given her. But there were worse things to fear than the reproofs of the world: there was the possible loss of paradise and then, more terrible still, was the vengeance of Our Lord, to be inflicted through, not some punishment which would crush her soul the other side of the tomb, but through the torments which come during life, which could ruin her health, her happiness or her body. She had vague fears of leprosy, of paralysis and other illnesses, of poverty with days of hunger—of all those penalties of which she supposed the God of her catechism had an unlimited supply. As in the days of her childhood, when she forgot to pay to the Virgin her regular tribute of Hail Marys, she feared She would make her fall down the stairs or be caned by the teacher. The thought of all this made her tremble with the fear that God would punish her for sleeping with a priest. He would surely send her such an evil that she would be disfigured for life or have to beg her bread from door to door. These ideas never left her after that day in the sacristy when she committed the sin of concupiscence, wrapped in Our Lady's cloak. She was now certain that the Virgin hated her and never ceased crying out against her act; in vain she tried to mollify Her with an incessant flow of humble prayers. She felt Our Lady disdainfully turning Her back on her, becoming inaccessible to her. Never again would that divine face smile on her; never again would those divine hands open graciously to receive her prayers like felicitous bouquets of flowers. She was now met with a frigid silence, the frozen hostility of offended divinity. She knew the power that Our Lady had in the sky: all that She wanted She obtained as a recompense for her wailings and lamentations at the foot of the Cross; now in Heaven sitting at the right hand side of Her divine Son, who always turned a smiling face towards Her and granted Her requests, while God the Father smiled at Her from the left. Amelia realized well that for her there was no hope and that something terrible was being prepared for her up there in paradise, which would one day fall on her, a dreadful catastrophe, smashing her body and soul. What would it be?

She would have cut off all relations with Amaro had she dared: but she feared his anger almost as much as she feared God's. What would become of her if she had both Our Lady and the senhor paroco against her? Besides, she loved him. In his arms all the terrors of the sky, the idea of the sky itself disappeared: sheltered there against his breast, she had no fear of the divine wrath; her desire, the fury of the flesh, as if it were a strong wine, gave her a feverish courage; it was as if a brutal defiance of heaven wound itself round her body. The terrors came again when she was alone in her room. It was this struggle which made her pale, brought wrinkles of age to her parched lips, gave her that dried-up air which infuriated Amaro.

'But what is the matter with you? It seems I'll have to squeeze the very blood out of your lips,' he would say when at the first kisses he found her so cold and indifferent.

'I'd a bad night—I'm nervous.'

'Those cursed nerves,' Amaro grumbled impatiently.

Later came strange questions which drove him desperate, now repeated every day. If he had said his Mass with fervour? If he had read his breviary? If he had made his meditations?

'Is there anything else you want to know?' he said, furious. 'Hell! Now it's this! You think I'm still a seminarist and you are the examiner, verifying that I fulfil the rules. What nonsense!'

'It's that one needs to be right with God,' she murmured.

It was, as a matter of fact, now her chief concern that Amaro should be a good priest, so that he would be her salvation and liberate her from the anger of God. She counted on the influence of the paroco in the courts of heaven and dreaded that he, through negligence of his devotions, would be the cause of her damnation. She wanted to keep him holy and a favourite of heaven, in order to cull the advantages of his mystical protection.

Amaro said all this reminded him of the scrupulousness of an old nun. He thought it all nonsense, for it took up so much of their precious time in Uncle Esguelhas' house.

'We didn't come here to moan,' he said very dryly. 'Close that door if you please.'

She obeyed; and then after the first kisses in the half-light of the closed window, he at last recognized his Amelia, the Amelia of the first days of love, whose delicious body trembled in his arms in the spasms of passion.

And each day he had a stronger desire for her, a tyrannically persistent desire that those few hours didn't satisfy. Ah! positively as a woman there was no one like her! He'd bet there wasn't anywhere in Leiria, even amongst the gentry. She had silly scruples, but one mustn't take those seriously, the thing was to enjoy it all while one was young.

And he did enjoy it. His life on all sides held comforts and delights: as in one of those salons where all is upholstered, where there are no hard or angular pieces of furniture and the body, no matter where it rests, finds the luxurious softness of a cushion.

Certainly, his greatest delights were in the sexton's house. But he had other joys. He ate well and smoked good cigarettes from an expensive cigarette holder; all his white linen was new and of the best; he had bought some furniture and now hadn't any worries about money, as Dona Maria of the Assumption, his richest penitent, was always there with her purse at his disposal. Lately, a great bit of luck had fallen his way. One night in Senhora Joanneira's house, that excellent senhora spoke about an English family who had passed in a car on the way to Batalha, and expressed the opinion that all the English were heretics.

'They are baptized as we are,' said Dona Joaquina Gansoso.

'Yes, senhora, but it is just a Baptism to laugh at, it's not like our efficacious Baptism, it has no effect.'

The canon then, who loved to torment, declared slowly and solemnly that Dona Maria had uttered a blasphemy. The Council of Trent, in its Canon IV, Session VII, had laid down that anyone who said that the Baptism given to heretics, in the name of the Father, Son and Holy Ghost, was not true Baptism, was blaspheming! And Senhora Maria according to the Holy Council of Trent was from the moment she made that statement excommunicated.

The excellent senhora collapsed with an attack of hysterics. The next day she threw herself at the feet of Amaro, who in punishment for her affront against the Holy Council of Trent, Canon IV, Session VII, ordered her to have said thirty Masses for the souls in Purgatory: and Dona Maria was now paying for them at the rate of five tostões per Mass.

On account of this he could occasionally enter the sexton's house with a mysterious air of satisfaction and a little parcel in his hand. It was a present for Amelia—a silk scarf, a coloured necktie, a pair of gloves. She went into ecstasies at these signs of his affection, and then in the dark room there was a delirious feast of love; while below the consumption continued its ravages on Toto—swish! swish!

Chapter XIX

'IS THE senhor canon in? I want to talk to him. Hurry!'

Canon Dias' servant pointed to the study and ran upstairs to tell Dona Josepha that the senhor paroco had come to see the senhor canon and seemed so upset that surely something terrible had happened!

Amaro pushed open the door of the study, closed it with a bang, and without even bidding the canon good-day blurted out:

'The girl is pregnant!'

The canon, who had been writing, fell in an inert mass against the back of the chair.

'What's that you're saying?'

'Yes, pregnant!'

In the silence, the boards could be heard creaking as the paroco walked agitatedly from the window to the bookcase.

'Are you sure of this?' asked the canon in the end, terrified.

'Absolutely certain. The girl was doubtful for some days. She did nothing but cry. But now it's certain. Women know, they don't make mistakes about these things. All the proofs are there. What am I to do, master?'

'Lord, what a calamity,' said the canon, stunned.

'Just imagine the scandal! The mother, the neighbours! And if they suspect me, I'm lost. I won't wait to hear what they'll say, I'll run away.'

The canon stupidly scratched the back of his neck, with his lip hanging down like a trunk. He could already hear the screams in the house on the night of the delivery. Senhora Joanneira forever in tears; his peace gone for the rest of his life.

'Tell me one thing!' cried Amaro desperately: 'What do you think? Haven't you any solution? I can't think of anything, I'm reduced to idiocy. I'm distracted!'

'Here are the consequences, my dear colleague.'

'Go to the devil! It's nothing to do with morality. It's obvious it was stupid. But now it's done we must find a solution.'

'But what is it you want to do?' said the canon. 'Surely you are not thinking of giving the girl a drug to destroy her.'

Amaro shrugged his shoulders with impatience at such an absurd idea. His master was surely wandering in his mind.

'But what do you want?' replied the canon in a hollow tone, dragging the words from the depths of his throat.

'What do I want! I want to avoid a scandal. What else could I want?'

'How many months is she gone?'

'How many months? But it has just happened, this is the first . . .'

'Then the thing to do is to marry her. Marry her to the clerk!'

Father Amaro gave a jump. 'Damn you, you're right. It's a great idea!'

The canon nodded, affirming that it was a great idea. 'Marry her at once, while there is time! "*Pater est quem nuptiae demonstrant.*" Who is the husband is the father.'

But the door opened and the blue glasses and black bonnet of Dona Josepha appeared. Upstairs in the kitchen she had been in a fever of curiosity, and not being able to contain herself any longer she came down on tiptoe and pasted her ear against the lock of the study door; but the heavy baize folding-door was shut, and some wood was being unloaded in the house next door, so the voices were smothered. The good senhora then decided to enter and bid good-day to the senhor paroco.

But it was in vain that from behind her smoked glasses her little sharp eyes scrutinized the great fat face of her brother and the pale face of Amaro. The two clergymen were as impenetrable as the two closed doors. The paroco spoke lightly of the senhor precentor's rheumatism, of the news going round of the marriage of the senhor general secretary . . . At the end of a pause he got up, said that today they were having pig's ear for dinner, and Dona Josepha had to look at the paroco going off after saying from the other side of the door: 'Well then, master, till tonight at Senhora Joanneira's.'

The canon very seriously continued his writing. Finally Dona Josepha couldn't hold out any longer, and after dragging her carpet slippers round her brother's chair, she ventured to ask: 'Is there some news?'

'Great news, sister,' said the canon shaking his pen. 'Dom John VI is dead!'

'You rude fellow!' she shouted, turning on her heel and disappearing, cruelly followed by her brother's chuckle.

That same night, below in Senhora Joanneira's little parlour—while Amelia above with despair in her heart was banging out the waltz of the *Two Worlds*—the two priests, close together on the old sofa, each with his cigarette between his teeth, under the sombre picture of the monk with his hand vaguely spread out like a claw over the skull, whispered as they concocted their plan. It was first necessary to find João Eduardo, who had disappeared from Leiria; Dionysia, good at following up scents, would search every hole and corner to find where the beast had his lair; then at once, as it was urgent, Amelia would write to him. Just a few words, saying that now she knew that he had been the victim of an intrigue; that she had lost none of the friendship she had had for him; that she felt she owed him reparation; and wouldn't he come and see her. If he hesitated, which wasn't probable (so the canon affirmed), they'd use the job in the civil governor's office as a bait. It would be easy to arrange for that through Godhinho, completely under his wife's thumb, and his wife was Father Silverio's little slave . . .

'But Natario,' said Amaro, 'Natario who hates the clerk, what is he going to say to this turn of affairs?'

'Man!' exclaimed the canon loudly smacking his thigh, 'I'd forgotten! Don't you know what's happened to poor Natario?'

Amaro didn't know.

'He's broken his leg! Fell from his mare.'

'When?'

'This morning. I had the news this evening. I always told him that mare would injure him one day. Now he's done it. It's going to be a long job. I'd forgotten. The senhoras upstairs don't know yet.'

There was desolation above when the news was recounted. Amelia closed the piano. All immediately thought of remedies that they might send; there was a croaking of offers of help—bandages, a pomade made by the nuns of Alcobaça, a half bottle of liqueur made by the monks in the desert near Cordova . . . It was also necessary to secure the intervention of the heavenly hosts and each one got ready to use her influence with the saint to whom she was devoted: Dona Maria, who had lately become interested in St Eleuterio, would ask her intervention; Dona Josepha Dias earnestly recommended the help of Our Lady of the Visitation; Dona Joaquin Gansoso spoke of St Joaquim.

'Amelia, who is your favourite saint?' asked the canon.

'Mine?'

She paled, and a sadness filled all her being, at the thought that she with her sins and her deliriums had lost the useful friendship of Our Lady of Sorrows, and so couldn't count on her influence to put Natario's leg right. It was one of her bitterest crosses, perhaps the worst she had suffered since she had loved Father Amaro.

It was in the sexton's house a few days later that Amaro informed Amelia of the master's plan. He prepared her by telling her that the canon knew all, adding to appease her: 'He knows all as a secret of confession.'

Then he took her hand and looked at her tenderly as if already commiserating with her for the tears she was about to shed: 'And now child, don't get upset at what I'm going to say to you. It is necessary, it will be our salvation.'

However, at the first words of her proposed marriage to the clerk, she was loudly indignant.

'Never, I'll die first!'

What? He'd put her in that state and now he'd like to rid himself of her by passing her on to another. Was she perchance a rag that one used and then threw to a beggar? After ordering the fellow out of the house was she to humiliate herself by calling him back and falling into his arms? Ah, no! She also had her pride! Slaves were still bought and sold, but that was in Brazil!

She then felt sorry for herself. He didn't love her any more, he was tired of her! How unfortunate she was, how unfortunate! She threw herself face down on the bed and broke into a loud fit of crying.

'Shut up, girl, they can hear you in the street!' said Amaro desperately shaking her by the arm.

'Let them hear! What do I care! I'm going to shout through the streets that it was Senhor Father Amaro who put me in this condition and now he's going to abandon me!'

Amaro became livid with rage and had a furious desire to beat her. But he held himself in and only the tremor in his voice showed the state he was in: 'You are forgetting yourself, my dear. Tell me now, can I marry you? No! Well, what do you want? If people see you are in this state, if you have the child in the house, look at the scandal! You'll be lost forever! And if it is known, what will become of me? Suspended, perhaps brought to court . . . How do you think I'm going to live? Do you want me to die of hunger?'

The thought of the probable privations and miseries of the excommunicated priest calmed her and made her feel sorry for him. Ah, it was she who didn't love him and after he'd been so affectionate, so tender with her, she wanted to repay him by exposure and disgrace. . . .

'No, no!' she exclaimed sobbing, and throwing herself into his arms.

They embraced, trembling with sympathy and tenderness for one another: she damping the priest's shoulder with tears and he biting his lips with his eyes blinded with tears.

In the end, he gently pushed her from him and wiped his eyes: 'Yes my love, it is a misfortune which has come upon us and it has to be. If you suffer, imagine what I feel at the thought of you marrying and living with another. Don't let's speak about that. But then it's fate. God had ordered it thus.'

She sat on the end of the bed, shaken with sobs, completely beaten. The punishment had arrived, the vengeance of Our Lady which had been preparing so long for her up there in the depths of the sky. Ah, it was now worse than all the flames of purgatory! She'd have to separate from Amaro whom she now thought she loved much more, and go to live with the other one, the excommunicated one! She could never more enter into the grace of God, after having lived with a man the canons, the Pope, the whole clergy considered cursed. He'd be her husband, perhaps the father of other children . . . Ah, Our Lady's vengeance was too much!

'How can I marry him, Amaro, if he is excommunicated?

Amaro then hurried to put her mind at rest. The fellow wasn't really excommunicated, Natario and the canon had interpreted the canons and bulls wrongly: the striking of a priest, not in his robes of office, was not a motive for excommunication *ipso facto*, according to some authorities. He, Amaro was of this opinion. Moreover the excommunication could be lifted.

'You understand, as the Holy Council of Trent says, and as you know: we bind and we unbind. The boy was excommunicated. Good, we lift the excommunication. He becomes as clean as before. No, this needn't worry you.'

'But how are we going to live, if he has lost his job?'

'You didn't wait for me to explain that. A job will be arranged. The canon will see to that. We have everything thought out, child.'

She didn't reply, feeling utterly crushed and miserable. The tears streamed down her face.

'Now tell me, your mother hasn't noticed anything?'

'No, up to now she has noticed nothing,' she replied with a big sigh.

They remained silent: she wiping her tears and trying to calm herself before leaving; he with his head down, wearily moving the loose floorboard with his foot, thinking of the other grand mornings when all was kisses and smothered laughs; all had changed, even the weather was cloudy, with the threat of rain.

'Can you see I've been crying?' she said, arranging her hair in front of the glass.

'No. Are you going?'

'Mamma will be waiting for me.'

They kissed sadly, and she left.

Meanwhile Dionysia was on the scent round the town trying to track down João Eduardo. Her activities increased as soon as she knew that the rich Canon Dias was interested in the search. Every day, as night fell, she sneaked in cautiously by the back gate to give the news: she now knew that the clerk went first to Alcobaça, to a cousin, an apothecary; after that he went to Lisbon armed with a letter of recommendation from Dr Gouvea and got a job in an attorney's office; but unluckily the attorney died of apoplexy a few days after João began work with him, and no trace could be found of João in the chaos of the capital. Yes, there was a person who was sure to know of João Eduardo and his wanderings: it was the printer Gustavo; but unfortunately, Gustavo, after an argument with Agostinho, had left the *Voice of the District* and disappeared. No one knew where he had gone and unfortunately his mother couldn't give any information as she also had died.

'Oh, good God!' said the canon when Amaro brought him these threads of information, 'oh, hell! In this story everyone has died! This is a hecatomb.'

'You can joke, master, but it is serious. Looking for a man in Lisbon is like looking for a needle in a bundle of straw. It's rotten luck!'

Then Amaro, very worried, as time was going on, wrote to his aunt asking her to enquire all round and see if she could get any news of one João Eduardo Barbosa. He received three pages of scrawl from his aunt, complaining of Joãozinho, her Joãozinho, who was making her life a hell, getting drunk on gin so that no lodger would stay in the house. But she was happier now as poor Joãozinho had sworn on the soul of his mother that from now on he'd drink nothing but lemonade. As to that João Eduardo she asked the neighbours and Senhor Palma, Minister of Public Works, who knew everybody, but she could get no information. Yes, there was a Joaquim Eduardo, in the district, who had an ironmonger's shop; if he wanted to do business with him, yes, he was an honest fellow.

'Blather! blather!' interrupted the canon impatiently.

Then, egged on by Amaro, who continually reminded him what Senhora Joanneira and he, himself, Canon Dias, would suffer with the scandal, he authorized a friend in the capital to employ the police on the job. The reply was long in coming, but it arrived in the end, great with promise. The clever policeman had discovered João Eduardo! He didn't yet know where he lived, as he'd only seen him in a café; but in two or three days he'd send more definite information. The despair of the priests was great when a few days later, the canon's friend wrote to say that the boy the clever policeman, Mendes, took for João Eduardo in the café in the Baixa was a lad from Santo Thyrso who was in Lisbon studying law . . . And there were three sovereigns and seventeen tostões for expenses.

'Seventeen devils!' bawled the canon, turning furiously towards Amaro. 'And in the end of it all, it was you who had the fun, and the comforts, and here am I destroying my health with all this and running into expenses!'

Amaro, who was dependent on the master, bowed his head at these accusations.

But, thank God, all was not lost, as Dionysia was still on the scent.

Amelia received the news with despair in her heart. After the first tears the inescapable necessity impelled her on. After all, what remained to her? In two or three months, with her tiny waist and narrow hips, she would no longer be able to hide her condition. What would she do then? Go, as did Uncle Stork's daughter, to Lisbon to be beaten in the Bairro Alto by the English sailors, or as Joanninha Gomes, who was Father Abilio's mistress, to have dead rats thrown in her face by the soldiers? No. Then she must marry . . .

Then, at the end of the seven months, she could see her baby (it was so frequent) legitimized by the sacrament, by the law and by God Our Father; and her son would have a father, receive an education and not be a poor abandoned creature.

Since the paroco had sworn to her that the clerk wasn't really excommunicated, and that to make sure it would only be necessary to recite some prayers to remove the excommunication, her religious scruples in the matter died like live coals quenched with water. In the end, she began to see that the evil deed of the clerk had arisen from jealousy and love: it was through thinking himself despised by her that he had written the *Communication*; it was in the fury of betrayed love that he had given the senhor paroco that blow—ah, she'd never forgive him for that brutality! But what a punishment he'd had! Unemployed, homeless, without a sweetheart, so lost in the depths of Lisbon that even the police couldn't find him! And all for her. Poor lad! After all, he wasn't ugly . . . They talked of his want of religion; but she always saw him very attentive at Mass and every night he said a special prayer to the St João in an embroidered frame which she had worked for him.

With the job in the civil governor's office they could have a little house and a servant . . . Why couldn't she be happy in the end? He wasn't a boy who frequented cafés, nor a lounger. She was sure she could dominate him and impose her tastes and her religious devotion on him. And wouldn't it be nice to turn out on Sunday for Mass, well-dressed, with her husband at her side, saluted by all. She could, in the face of the whole town, walk out with her child very well-dressed in his little lace cap and his great fringed cape! Who could tell then, if on account of the care and love she'd give her child and the comforts with which she'd encircle her husband, that the sky and Our Lady would not soften towards her? Ah, for this she'd do all. What joy to have again in the heavens that friend and confidant, always ready to cure her pains and relieve her of her misfortunes, busy preparing for her a luminous place in the sky.

She would pass the hours she was at her sewing with these thoughts running through her mind, and even on the way to the sexton's house they came to her. She would spend a minute with Toto, who was very quiet now on account of the fever which was eating her up. When she went up to the room her first question to Amaro was: 'Well, is there any news?'

He frowned and muttered: 'Dionysia is on the scent. Why, are you in a great hurry?'

'Yes, I'm in a hurry, the shame will be mine.'

He didn't answer; there was as much hate as love in the kisses he gave her, that woman who was so easily resigned to leave him and sleep with another!

Black jealousy had filled his mind since he had seen her agree to the hateful marriage. Now that she didn't cry, he began to be furious at her lack of tears, and secretly despised her for not choosing shame with him to respectability with the other. It wouldn't have cost him so much if she had continued to complain and protest noisily about her lot; that would have been a serious proof of her love, a delicious sop to his vanity; but the acceptance of the clerk, without repugnance, without protests of horror, made him indignant and appeared traitorous to him. He began to think that at heart she wasn't averse to the change. After all, João Eduardo was a man in the strength of his twenty-six years, with the attraction of a beautiful moustache. She would have in the clerk's arms the same delights she had had in his . . . If the clerk were an old man eaten up with rheumatism, she wouldn't show such resignation. Then, for priestly vengeance, he felt like breaking up the whole thing, and began wishing João Eduardo wouldn't turn up. Sometimes when Dionysia came with her story, he would say with a sneer: 'Don't tire yourself. The fellow will never appear. Give it up. It's not worth getting a pain in the chest over it.'

But Dionysia had a strong chest; and one night she came triumphant, to say she was now on the fellow's track: the printer, Gustavo, had been seen going into Osorio's tavern. She was going to speak to him the next day. He would surely know all.

It was a bitter hour for Amaro. That marriage for which he had been so anxious in the first days of terror, now that he felt secure appeared the most terrible tragedy in his life.

To lose Amelia forever—and that man whom he'd made her send away, whom he had expelled, now, with one of these malignant twists of fortune which Providence dealt out, would turn up again and claim her as his legitimate wife. The idea that he was going to have her in his arms, that she would give the clerk the same fiery kisses that she'd given him, that she'd cry 'Oh João!' as now she cried 'Oh Amaro!', made him furious. And he couldn't prevent the marriage; everyone wanted it, she, the canon, even Dionysia with her excessive zeal.

What did it serve him to be a man with blood in his veins and the strong passions of a healthy body? He'd have to say good-bye to the girl, see her walk off arm in arm with the other, the husband, watch them play together with the child, his child! And he'd have to look on at the ruin of his happiness with his arms crossed, forcing himself to smile, return to his life of eternal solitude, and again take up the reading of his breviary! Ah! if it were only the age when one could annihilate a man by denouncing him for heresy! Oh, that the world could go back two hundred years and Senhor João Eduardo would find out what it was to mock a priest and to marry Amelia . . .

This absurd idea, on account of the excited state he was in, took such a hold of his imagination that that night he dreamed a vivid dream, which he afterwards recounted, laughing, to the canon. There was a narrow road, beaten on by a burning sun; between great, high, plated doors the populace were crammed; on the balconies, nobles in gorgeous embroidered suits twisted their groomed moustaches; through the folds of mantillas bright eyes shone, lit up by a holy fury. Amidst a great noise made by all the bells of the city churches tolling the funeral knells, the procession of the *auto-da-fé* moved slowly along. In front, the half-naked flagellants with their great white hoods pulled down over their faces tore their flesh, howling the *Miserere*, with their backs all pasted with blood; João Eduardo, mad with terror, rode on an ass, his legs hanging down and his white garment daubed with fiery devils; from his neck hung a card on which was written 'FOR HERESY'. Behind him a frightful servant of the Holy Office prodded the ass; and at his side, a priest held aloft the crucifix, shouting in his ears counsels of repentance. And he, Amaro, walked at the side singing the *Requiem* with his open breviary in one hand and with the other blessing the old ladies, the friends of the Rua da Misericordia, who knelt to kiss his tunic. Now and again, he turned round to enjoy the dismal pomp, and saw the long file of the Confraternity of Nobles: there a big-bellied, apoplectic man, there the face of a mystic with a ferocious moustache and two flaming eyes; each one carried a lighted torch in one hand and in the other held his great wide-brimmed hat, the black feathers of which swept the ground; the arquebusiers' helmets shone; a religious wrath contorted the hungry faces of the mob; and the procession wove its way through the tortuous streets, amongst the clamour of the plainchant, the cries of the fanatics, the melancholy sound of the church bells, and the clink of arms, in a terror which filled the whole town, making for the tiled platform where the flames were already leaping up from the piles of wood.

Great was his disillusion after all that ecclesiastical glory when the servant woke him up early with his shaving water.

It was that very day he was to know about João Eduardo and Amelia was to write to him. He was to meet Amelia at eleven and the first thing he said as he angrily pulled the door open was: 'The fellow has turned up, at least his best friend the printer has, and he must know where the beast is.'

Amelia, who was in one of her most hopeless moods and full of fear, exclaimed: 'Thank God, now this torture will finish!'

'Then you're pleased, eh?' said Amaro with a sneer.

'What else could I be in this terrible fear in which I'm living?'

He made a gesture of impatience, of despair. Fear! that was right hypocrisy! Fear of what? With a mother who gave in to her every wish, who spoiled her. It was just that she wanted to get married. She wanted the other fellow. That little fun just for the mornings wasn't enough for her—she wanted the thing comfortably in her own house! She imagined she was taking him in, a man of thirty with four years' experience of the confessional? He saw through her all right. She was like all the others, she wanted to change her man.

She didn't reply, but turned very pale. Angry with her silence, he went on: 'You haven't a word to say, that's obvious. But what could you have to say, seeing it's the pure truth? After all I've suffered for you—the other man appears and you want to leave me!'

She raised her head and stamped her foot in desperation: 'It was you who wanted it, Amaro!'

'To be sure! Do you imagine that I'm going to die because of you? It's what you want.' Then looking at her disdainfully, making her feel the contempt of a good man: 'You are not even ashamed to show your delight, your anxiety to give yourself to the fellow . . . You're a bitch, that's what you are!'

White as chalk, without a word, she grabbed up her cape to go.

Exasperated, Amaro pulled her back roughly by the arm: 'Where are you going? Look well at me. You are a whore. That's what I'm saying. You are dying to sleep with the other.'

'Well, shut up, I am!' she said.

Amaro, losing control of himself, gave her a blow.

'Don't kill me!' she cried, 'and your child!'

He stood in front of her, his face full of grief, trembling in every limb: that word, that idea of his son, created a pity, a desperate love in him; throwing himself on her, crushing her with his embrace as if he wanted to bury her in his arms, to absorb her completely for himself, he kissed her madly on the cheeks and hair so that his kisses hurt:

'Forgive me, Ameliazinha! forgive me. I was mad.'

She moaned and sobbed: and the rest of that morning there in the room in the sexton's house, there was a delicious feast of love, with that sentiment of maternity joining them as a sacrament, giving a greater tenderness, a continued renewal of desire, which threw them each time more avidly into the arms of one another.

They forgot the time; and Amelia only jumped out of bed when she heard the sound of Uncle Esguelhas' crutch in the kitchen. While she hurriedly arranged herself before the bit of looking-glass which adorned the wall, Amaro stood in front of her, melancholically contemplating her as she passed the comb through her hair—that hair which he would soon never again see her comb; he gave a great sigh, and said tenderly: 'Our happy days are near their end. You must sometimes think of these mornings.'

'For God's sake don't speak of that,' she said with her eyes swimming with tears.

Suddenly throwing herself into his arms, with the old passion of their happy mornings, she murmured: 'I'll always be the same for you— even after marriage.'

'You swear?'

'I swear.'

'By the Sacred Host?'

'I swear by the Sacred Host and by Our Lady!'

'Always when you get the chance?'

'Always!'

'Oh, Ameliazinha! Oh, my love, I wouldn't change you for a queen!'

She went downstairs. The paroco, arranging the bed, heard her talking calmly to Uncle Esguelhas; and said to himself that she was a great girl, capable of taking in the devil himself, and that she'd soon have that booby of a clerk running round at her bidding.

The pact, as Amaro called it, became to them so irrevocable that they calmly discussed the details. The marriage with the clerk they considered one of those necessities which society imposes and which suffocates independent souls; but nature would ooze out by the least chink, like an irreducible gas. Before Our Lord, her true husband was the senhor paroco. He was the husband of her soul for whom would be kept the best kisses, the intimate compliance, the desires; the other would just get the shell. They planned the tricks they'd have to get up to in order to correspond with one another, to arrange secret meeting places . . .

Amelia was again, as in the first days, in the heat of passion. The thought that the marriage would make her white as snow caused her sorrows to disappear and calmed down her fear of the skies. The blow Amaro had given her was like a whipping which livens up a lazy horse: it had revived her fiery passion which now carried her along impetuously.

Amaro was again enjoying life, though sometimes the idea of that man with her day and night worried him. But, in the end, what compensations. All the dangers would magically disappear and so his sexual desires would be still stronger. All those atrocious responsibilities of seduction would be gone, and the girl would become still more desirable.

He insisted, however, that Dionysia should finish her wearisome campaign. But that good woman, sure that the more she multiplied her efforts, the more she would be paid for her work, couldn't get hold of the printer, that famous Gustavo, who, like the dwarf of the romance of chivalry, held the secret of the wonderful tower where the prince lived under a spell.

'Oh, senhor,' said the canon, 'this is beginning to have an ugly look. We've been nearly two months looking for the scamp . . . Man, there is no shortage of clerks. Arrange another one!'

At last, one night when he'd come in to rest in the paroco's house, Dionysia appeared, and exclaimed immediately she opened the dining-room door, where the two clergymen were taking coffee: 'There's news at last!'

'What is it then, Dionysia?

The woman, however, was in no hurry: after asking the permission of the senhores, she sat down, as she was dog tired . . . No, the senhor canon couldn't imagine the walking she had had to do. The cursed printer reminded her of a story they used to tell her as a child, of a deer which was always in view but which the hunters never succeeded in catching. But in the end she had caught up with her prey—as it happened, he was tipsy.

'Finish, woman!' bawled the canon.

'Well, here's the news. Nothing.'

The two clergymen looked at her mystified.

'Nothing what, woman?'

'Nothing. The fellow went to Brazil.'

Gustavo had received two letters from João Eduardo: in the first, on which he had put his address, a street near Poco de Borratem, he said he was going to Brazil; in the second he said he had moved but gave no address. He was to sail for Rio on the next boat, but didn't say where the money was coming from nor what hopes he had of getting a job there. All was vague and mysterious. That was a month ago, and he hadn't written since, from which the printer concluded that he was now on the high seas . . . 'But we will have to pay them out for what they've done to him,' Gustavo said to Dionysia.

The canon slowly stirred his coffee, nonplussed.

'Now, where are we, master?' said Amaro, very pale.

'We are in a nice mess.'

'The devil take the women, and may hell confound them!' said Amaro between his teeth.

'Amen,' replied the canon gravely.

Chapter XX

WHAT TEARS when Amelia heard the news! Her honour, her life's peace, so much bliss, all lost, swallowed up in the sea mists round that boat on the high seas sailing to Brazil.

They were the worst weeks of her life. She went to the paroco every day bathed in tears, asking him what she was going to do.

Amaro, worsted, without an idea in his head, went to the master.

'I did all I could,' said the canon, desolate. 'You'll have to put up with it. You should never have got mixed up in such a business.'

Amaro went back to Amelia with these poor consolations: 'All will right itself. We must put our trust in God.'

It was a good moment for her to count on God, when He, indignant, was crushing her with sorrow! And such indecision in a man and a priest, who should have had the ability and strength to save her, gave her a feeling of despair; her tenderness for him vanished like water absorbed by sand; just a confused feeling remained, in which, under the force of her persistent desires, hatred shone through.

The meetings in the sexton's house became less and less frequent, till in the end they only met every other week. Amaro didn't complain, as now these once joyful mornings were destroyed with moanings; each kiss was followed by a trail of sobs which unnerved him so much that he also had a strong desire to throw himself face down on the bed and weep away all his bitterness.

In his heart, he accused her of exaggerating her difficulties, just to add to his terror. Another woman with more sense wouldn't make such a fuss. But, after all, what was she but a hysterical *beata*, all nerves, all fear, all excitement! Ah, but there was no doubt about it, it had been a great stupidity on his part!

She also thought it had been a great stupidity on her part. She had never imagined that this could happen to her. What! She had rushed madly into love, certain that she would escape all the consequences—and now that she felt her child in her womb, it was tears and alarms and complaints! Her life was dismal: during the day she had to control herself in front of her mother, apply herself to her sewing, talk, pretend to be happy . . . It was at night that her imagination ran wild and tortured her with an incessant phantasmagoria of punishments in this world and in the next: miseries, being forsaken and spurned by honourable people, and not the least of her terrors, the flames of hell.

It was then that an unforeseen event arrived to divert her mind from her anxiety, dwelling on which was becoming a morbid habit. One night the canon's servant appeared, breathless with running, to say that Dona Josepha was at the point of death. The evening before, the excellent senhora had got a sudden sharp pain in her side, but had insisted on going up the hill to the Church of the Incarnation to say her rosary. She returned benumbed with cold, with the pain more acute and a temperature. When Dr Gouvea came he diagnosed pneumonia.

Senhora Joanneira ran immediately to install herself as nurse. Then for weeks in the canon's tranquil house there was a commotion of devoted offers of help: the friends, when they were not rushing to the church to make Promises and to implore their favourite saints, were stuck there, creeping in and out of the room like phantoms, lighting candles to statues, tormenting Dr Gouvea with stupid questions. At night in the parlour, with the wick of the lamp turned down, there was a sound of dismal voices coming from the corners of the room; and during the tea, between each bite of toast, there were sighs, and tears furtively wiped from eyes.

The canon was also there in a corner, utterly crushed by this sudden appearance of sickness and its melancholy accompaniments: the bottles of medicine filling the tables, the solemn entrance of the doctor, the sorrowful faces coming to know if the patient was better, the breath of fever permeating the house, the funereal timbre which the wall clock took on now that the whole house was in a hushed silence, the dirty towels which remained for days in the place where they were dropped, the arrival of each night with its threat of eternal darkness . . . Besides, a sincere sorrow prostrated him: he had lived with his sister for forty years and she had kept him going, habit had made her dear to him; her droll ways, her black bonnets, her fussiness round the house had all become a part of him. Apart from this, who knew but that death on entering the house might, in order to save time, take him also!

For Amelia that time was a relief; at least no one would notice her. Neither her sad face nor the signs of tears on it would look strange now that her godmother was so ill. Besides, her duty as a nurse took up most of her time; as she was the youngest and strongest, now that her mother was worn out by her heavy nightly vigils it was Amelia who passed the long nights at the side of Dona Josepha's bed: she tended her patient with loving care, never relaxing, in the hopes of appeasing Our Lady in Heaven and receiving equal charity when she too was laid low with illness . . . Under the atmosphere of death which the whole house exhaled, she was taken with the persistent idea that she too would die, in childbirth: sometimes when alone, wrapped in her shawl at the side of the sick woman, listening to her monotonous moaning, she softened thinking of her own death which she judged certain, and her eyes filled with tears in a vague pity for herself, her youth and her love. She then went to kneel by the chest of drawers where an image of Christ, in front of which burnt a light, threw on the light wallpaper a distorted form which broke on the ceiling. There she remained praying, asking Our Lord not to deny her entry into paradise ... But the old lady moved with a dolorous sigh; she went to smooth down her pillow, and to soothe her with soft words. Then she would go to the parlour to look at the clock to see if it was time to give her her medicine; often she trembled at hearing from the next room a sound like a trumpet or a wail as of a flute; it was the canon snoring.

At last one morning Dr Gouvea declared Dona Josepha out of danger. There was loud rejoicing amongst the senhoras, each one being certain that it was due to the intervention of her particular saint. Two weeks later there was more rejoicing in the house when Dona Josepha, leaning on the arms of her friends, took two trembling steps across the floor. Poor Dona Josepha, what ravages the illness had made on her! That irritated little voice, in which words had been sent out like poisoned arrows, now came out as a sort of dying sound, when she anxiously asked for the spittoon or the cough mixture. The ever-alert little eyes, searching and malignant, were now sunken in her head, frightened of the light and of the shadows and forms of things. Her body, formerly so rigid, dry as a vine branch, was now buried in the chair, wrapped in shawls and blankets, limp as an old rag.

But in the end, Dr Gouvea, while announcing a long, tricky convalescence, said laughing to the canon, in front of the friends (after he had heard Dona Josepha express a desire to be placed near the window), that with the good care, tonics and the prayers of these senhoras his sister would be soon fit for love.

'Ah, doctor, our prayers won't be wanting,' said Dona Maria.

'And I won't be wanting with the tonics,' said the doctor. 'So there is nothing to do but congratulate ourselves.'

The joviality of the doctor was a certain sign to all of them of Dona Josepha's return to health.

A few days later, the canon, seeing that August was drawing near, spoke of taking a house in Vieira as he did every other year, to take his sea baths. Last year he hadn't gone, this was his year to go.

'And there in the good sea air sister can build up her health and strength.'

But Dr Gouvea disapproved of the idea. The strong piercing air of the sea wouldn't suit Dona Josepha. It would be better for her to go to the farm at Rocoça, in Poyaes, a sheltered spot with a temperate climate.

It was a great disappointment to the poor canon, who was profuse in his complaints. What! go and bury himself at Ricoça the whole summer, the best time of the year! And his baths, my God, his baths?

'Just look,' he said to Amaro, one night in his study, 'look at all I've suffered. During the illness, what an upset, tea never on time, the supper all dried up! With all the worry I've lost weight. And now, when I thought of going and building myself up at the seaside, no, senhor, I've got to go to Ricoça, and do without my baths. This is what I call suffering! And mind you, it wasn't I who was ill. But it is I who have to put up with these things. It means that I'll have to go two years running without my baths . . .'

Amaro suddenly banged the table, and exclaimed: 'Man, a great idea had just struck me!'

The canon looked at him doubtfully, as if he thought that a solution to his sorrows was humanly impossible.

'When I say a good idea, master, I mean a superb idea!'

'Go on, man . . .'

'Listen, you go to Vieira and naturally Senhora Joanneira goes too. You can rent houses next door to each other as you usually do——'

'Well, continue.'

'Then your sister can go to Ricoça.'

'So the poor thing will have to go alone?'

'No,' exclaimed Amaro triumphantly. 'She'll go with Amelia! Amelia will go as her nurse. The two will go alone. And there in that hole which a living soul never enters, they can live without anyone suspecting and there the girl can have her baby! Now what do you think of the plan?'

The canon sat up with his eyes bulging with surprise: 'Man, it's splendid!'

'It will suit everybody! You can take your baths. Senhora Joanneira, far away, won't know what's happening. Your sister can get the benefit of the air—Amelia will have the ideal place to have her baby in secret—no one will go to Ricoça to see them. Dona Maria is going to Vieira also, and the Gansosos. The confinement is expected in November, and none of you will return from Vieira before the beginning of December. When we all unite again the girl will be fresh and unembarrassed.'

'Well, senhor, considering this is the first idea you've had in these two years, it's a grand one.'

'Thanks, master.'

But there was one great difficulty, it was to know how Dona Josepha was going to take it all. The rigorous Dona Josepha, so implacable towards the weaknesses of love that, if she could, she would demand for her erring sisters the old Gothic penalties—letters branded on their foreheads with red hot irons, public whippings, the tenebrous *in pace*— to have to ask Dona Josepha to take part in sheltering a girl who had fallen!

'Sister will bawl at you like a bull!' said the canon.

'We'll see, master,' said Amaro, settling himself back in the chair and swinging his leg, very sure that his prestige amongst the devout would pull him through the difficulty. 'We'll see. When I have recounted some tales to her—when I point out to her that she is in conscience bound to protect the girl—when I remind her that at the hour of death she will have a good action to her credit which will ensure that she doesn't approach the gates of heaven empty-handed—we'll see when I've talked to her!'

'Perhaps, perhaps,' said the canon. 'The occasion is a good one, as poor sister is a bit weak in the head after the illness, and is behaving like a child.'

Amaro got up and vigorously rubbed his hands: 'Well, it's hands to the plough, hands to the plough!'

'And it's better not to waste any time,' said the canon, 'as the scandal might break out. This morning in the house I heard Libaninho telling the girl that her waist was getting bigger.'

'Oh, what a scamp,' muttered the paroco.

'No, he didn't mean any harm. But that the girl is looking fatter is true. As everyone was so busy fussing about Josepha, no one had eyes for her, but now they might notice. It's serious, friend, it's serious.'

So, the next day, first thing in the morning, Amaro went, as the canon put it, to 'land' sister. Before he went up to her he discussed his plan of campaign, below in the study, with the canon: first, he was going to tell Dona Josepha that the canon was in entire ignorance of the calamity which had befallen Amelia, and that he, Amaro, knew of it, not as a secret of confession, as then he couldn't reveal it, but because Amelia and the married man who had seduced her had taken him into their confidence. (A married man it had to be, as it was necessary to prove to the old lady that there was no possibility of a legitimate reparation.)

The canon scratched his head dissatisfied: 'This is not well arranged,' he said. 'Sister knows well that no married men visit the Rua da Misericordia.'

'What about Arthur Couceiro?' exclaimed Amaro, without a scruple.

The canon roared with laughter at the thought of Arthur, poor

Arthur with his houseful of children, his toothless gums, his mournful sheep's eyes, accused of violating virgins! That wasn't a bad one!

'That won't wash, friend, that won't wash! Another, another . . .'

Immediately the two together hit on the same man—Ferreira, Ferreira, the draper! A handsome man, who Amelia admired very much. Every time she went out she went into his shop . . . In the Rua da Misericordia, there had been indignation at his cheek in openly accompanying Amelia along the Marrazes Road when she was on the way to Morenal, about two years ago.

'As you know, you mustn't say directly to sister that it was he, just hint at it.'

Amaro hastened up to the old lady's room, which was over the study. He was there a half an hour, a long dreary half hour for the canon, who could hear faintly from above the creaking of Amaro's boots on the floor-boards and the old lady's hollow cough. And in his customary walk from the bookcase to the window, with his hands behind his back and his snuffbox between his fingers, he kept thinking of all the inconveniences, all the expenses he'd still have to undergo, for the senhor paroco's bit of fun! He'd have to have the girl on the farm for four or five months; then would come the doctor and the midwife, whose expenses he'd naturally have to pay, as well as the baby clothes. And what were they to do with the baby? In the town, the *Roda* had been done away with: in Ourem, as the governors of the Misericordia were low in funds and the abundance of abandoned children scandalous, they'd posted a man at the side of the *Roda* bell to interrogate and raise difficulties; there had been investigations as to parentage, restitution of babies; in fact, the authorities were cunningly combating the excess of abandoned children with the terror of discovery and other annoyances.

The poor master saw in front of him a bristling mountain of difficulties to disturb his peace and destroy his digestion. But at heart the excellent canon was not angry: he'd always had the affection of a master towards his pupil for Amaro; and he had a weakness, partly paternal, partly lustful, for Amelia, and lately he was beginning to feel the vague condescension of a grandfather towards her.

The door opened and the paroco appeared triumphant.

'Of all the thousand-and-one wonders, master! What did I tell you?'

'She's agreed?'

'To all. It wasn't without difficulty. She began by being waspish. I spoke to her of the married man—of the girl being so distracted that she wanted to kill herself—that if she didn't consent to help her by

267

hiding her, she'd be responsible for a great misfortune. I reminded the good senhora that she has one foot in the grave, that God might call her from one minute to another and that if she had this sin on her soul there wasn't a priest who would give her absolution; and that she'd die like a dog!'

'In fact,' said the canon approvingly, 'judging from the result, you seem to have chosen your words well.'

'I told her the truth. Now, make it your business to speak to Senhora Joanneira and get her off to Vieira as soon as possible.'

'Another thing, friend, have you thought of how you are going to dispose of the fruit?'

The paroco scratched his head helplessly. 'Ah, master, that's another difficulty. You can't think how much it has worried me. I'll naturally give it to some woman to bring up, far away from here: I thought of Alcobaça or Pombal. The luck would be if it were born dead, master!'

'It would be one more little angel for the heavenly choir!' muttered the canon, sniffing up his pinch of snuff.

The first thing the canon did that evening was to speak to Senhora Joanneira of their proposed visit to Vieira, downstairs in the little parlour where she was busy pouring quince jam on to saucers to be dried and cut into blocks in preparation for Dona Josepha's convalescence. He began by saying he was going to rent Ferreira's house for her.

'But that is only a bandbox!' she exclaimed at once. 'Where can I put the little one to sleep there?'

'Now that's exactly what I want to talk about. The fact is that this time Amelia isn't coming to Vieira.'

'Not coming?'

Then the canon explained that sister couldn't go alone to Ricoça and he'd been thinking of sending Amelia with her. It was an idea which came to him that very morning.

'I can't go because, as you know, I must get in my baths; and we can't send the poor soul in Christ there alone with no one but a servant.'

Senhora Joanneira fell for a minute into a melancholy silence: 'That's true, but, to speak frankly, it costs me a lot to leave my girl. I could go without my baths, I could go to Ricoça.'

'You! Certainly not, you are coming to Vieira with me. I can't go there alone, you ungrateful woman!' Then taking on a very serious air: 'You can see well that sister has one leg in the grave. She is very attached to Amelia—after all, she is her godmother—and now if she goes to look after her in her illness, and is alone with her there for some months, she has her in her pocket. Remember that Josepha is worth a couple of thousand cruzados. And as she knows I have plenty to live on, the girl will stand a chance of a good dowry. I won't say any more . . .'

Seeing that it was the wish of the canon, Senhora Joanneira gave in.

Upstairs, Amaro was rapidly explaining his great plan to Amelia, and the scene with the old lady: stating that she was immediately ready with offers of help, the poor old thing was full of charity, why she'd even offered to see to the clothes for the baby.

'You may have every confidence in her. She is a saint. So all will be saved, girl. You'll be four or five months there in Ricoça.'

It was on account of this that Amelia moaned: to lose the whole summer in Vieira, the joys of bathing! To have to go and be buried in that great sinister old house, so big that a hollow echo came from every corner! The only time she'd been there for an evening she'd been filled with terror. It was all so dark there. She was certain she was going to die in the godforsaken place.

'Nonsense!' said Amaro. 'You should thank God for inspiring me with this idea to save you. You'll have Dona Josepha, Gertrude, and the orchard to walk about in, won't you? I'll come to see you every day. You are going to like it there. You'll see.'

'Anyway, what can I do but go? I'll just have to put up with it!' With tears streaming down her face, she inwardly cursed that love which had brought her so much sorrow, and forced her now, when the whole of Leiria was off to Vieira, to go and shut herself up in that solitary place, listening to the old lady's cough and the dogs whining in the patio. And mamma, what was he going to say to mamma?

'What else can I say, but that Dona Josepha couldn't be sent alone to the farm? Someone whom they could trust would have to go to take care of her. Don't you worry. Master is down below working on her. I'm going down to them as I've been a good few minutes here with you and we can't be too cautious these last few days.'

Just as he was going down the stairs the canon was coming up. As they passed Amaro said in the master's ear:

'How did it all come off?'

'Everything is settled. And you?'

'I've arranged everything satisfactorily.'

In the darkness of the stairs the two priests silently squeezed one another's hands.

A few days later, after a scene of wailing and weeping, Amelia and Dona Josepha left for Ricoça in a charabanc. With piled-up cushions they had arranged a comfortable corner for the convalescent. The canon accompanied them, put out by all the commotion. And Gertrude was stuck on top, sitting on a cushion, in the shade of the great mountain made by the leather trunks, the baskets, the tins, the parcels, the cotton sacks, the basket in which the cat miaowed and a great bundle tied with string containing pictures of the saints most beloved of Dona Josepha.

Then, at the end of the same week, Senhora Joanneira went to Vieira, in the evening to take advantage of the freshest time of the day. The Rua da Misericordia was completely blocked with the bullock cart, which carried the china, the mattresses, the kitchen utensils; and in the same charabanc which had been to Ricoça now went Senhora Joanneira, also taking a cat in a basket on her lap.

The canon had gone the day before and only Amaro was left to see her off. After a whole lot of fuss, of tearing up and down the stairs a hundred times for a basket which was lost or a bundle which had disappeared, Ruça locked the door and they were ready to start. Senhora Joanneira, already on the steps of the coach, burst out crying.

'Now, my dear senhora, this won't do!'

'Ah, senhor paroco, you can never know how much it costs me to leave my little girl . . . I have the feeling I'll never see her again. Do me the great kindness of going to visit her in Ricoça. Let me know if she is happy there.'

'You may go away with an easy mind, I'll look after her.'

'Good-bye, senhor paroco. Many thanks for all. I can never repay you for all your kindness!'

'Nonsense my dear senhora. A pleasant journey, don't forget to write. Remember me to the senhor canon. Good-bye, senhora, good-bye! Ruça . . .'

The charabanc left, and by the same road on which it rolled along Amaro walked slowly to the Figueira Road. It was nine o'clock: the moon had already risen on a warm, serene night of August. A light luminous mist softened the peaceful landscape. Here and there the door of a house shone out through the shadows of the trees, beaten on by the moon. At the foot of the bridge he stopped to look sadly at the river which ran along over the sand with a monotonous murmur; in the places where the trees bent down there was a thick, impenetrable darkness, and further on the light trembled over the water like a tissue of sparkling filigree. There he remained in that soothing silence, smoking cigarettes and throwing the butts into the river, sunk in a vague sadness which calmed him. Then, hearing eleven strike, he started for the town, passing through the Rua da Misericordia with a heart full of tender memories: the house, with the windows all shut and without the lace curtains, appeared abandoned for all time; the boxes of rosemary were forgotten in the corners of the balcony. How many times had he and Amelia leaned over that balcony! One day there was a fresh carnation and while talking she plucked off a leaf and broke it asunder between her lovely little teeth. All was finished now; and at the side of the Cathedral the screaming of the owls gave a feeling of ruin, of loneliness and of the end of all things. He slowly made for home with his eyes swimming with tears.

As he entered, the servant came to the top of the stairs to say that Uncle Esguelhas had called twice, round about nine o'clock, in great affliction, as Toto was dying and would only receive the sacraments from the hands of the senhor paroco.

Amaro, in spite of having a superstitious repugnance to return on such a sad mission to the house which was saturated with memories of the happy times of his love, went to please Uncle Esguelhas. But the death, coinciding with Amelia's departure and with the sudden dispersion and end of all that up to then interested him or had been a part of his life, moved him strangely.

The door of the sexton's house was ajar and in the dark he bumped into two women who were leaving emitting deep sighs. He went straight to the paralytic's bed: two great wax candles, brought from the church, were alight on the table; a white sheet covered Toto's body and Father Silverio, who was on duty that week, was sitting there reading his breviary, with his handkerchief on his knees and his large glasses on the point of his nose. He got up when he saw Amaro: 'Ah, colleague,' he said very softly, 'we looked for you everywhere. The poor soul in Christ wanted only you. When they came to look for me I was at our usual card party at Novaes. What a scene! She died unrepentant: it was just like the stories we read in books about unrepentant sinners. When she saw me and realized that you weren't coming, what an exhibition! I got such a fright. I even thought she'd spit on the crucifix . . .'

Amaro without a word lifted up a corner of the sheet, but let it fall immediately on the face of the corpse. Then he went up to the sexton's room, where he found him stretched out on the bed with his face to the wall, sobbing desperately; there was another woman there sitting silent and still in a corner with her eyes on the ground, in a vague annoyance at the neighbourly task she was obliged to take on. Amaro touched the sexton on the shoulder: 'You must be resigned, Uncle Esguelhas, it was ordered by God. It is even a relief for the poor girl.'

Uncle Esguelhas turned round and through the mist of tears which veiled his eyes recognized Amaro and wanted to kiss his hand. Amaro drew back: 'Now, Uncle Esguelhas . . . God will have pity on you in your affliction. He will make up to you for all your suffering.'

He didn't listen, being shaken with convulsive sobbing; while the woman very calmly wiped now one eye and now the other.

Amaro went downstairs and offered to relieve the good Silverio of his disagreeable service. He took Silverio's place by the candle with his breviary in his hand.

He stayed there till very late. The neighbour, on the way out, said that Uncle Esguelhas had at last fallen asleep and she'd promised to return with the shroud at the break of day.

The whole house now sank into a silence which the nearness of the great Cathedral seemed to make more dreary: now and again an owl hooted weakly from the walls, or the pounding of the crutch upstairs shook the house. Amaro, taken with an undefined terror, wanted to fly from there, but was held by the force of his awakened conscience; urged on by fear, he precipitated his prayers. Sometimes the book fell on to his knees and then he sat very still, conscious of that body under the sheet, recalling in a bitter contrast those happy hours in which the sun beat down on the yard and the swallows circled and he and Amelia went laughing up to that same room where Uncle Esguelhas now lay sobbing in his sleep.

Chapter XXI

THE CANON had strongly recommended Amaro not to go to Ricoça in the first few weeks, as his sister or the servant might get suspicious. Amaro's life then became sadder and emptier than when he had left Senhora Joanneira's house and gone to live in Rua das Sousas. All his acquaintances were out of Leiria: Dona Maria of the Assumption was in Vieira; the Gansosos were at the foot of Alcobaça with an aunt, the famous aunt who for the last ten years they had been expecting to die and leave them a great fortune. After the service at the Cathedral, the hours, all the long day dragged as heavy as lead. If he had been St Anthony in the sands of the Lybian desert he couldn't have been more separated from all human contact. Only the doleful coadjutor came to visit him. He usually arrived once or twice a week, just after supper, looking thin, dried up, gloomy, with his umbrella in his hand. Amaro detested him; and sometimes, to get rid of him, he pretended to be very occupied with his reading; or, as soon as he felt his slow steps on the stairs, he hurriedly rushed to the table, and said as he entered: 'Excuse me, friend coadjutor, but I have something here that I must scribble.'

But the fellow installed himself, with his odious umbrella between his knees: 'Don't bother about me, senhor paroco, don't bother about me.'

Then Amaro, tortured by that depressing figure which never moved in the chair, threw down his pen, grabbed his hat and muttered: 'I can't put my mind to anything tonight, I'm going to get a little air.'

And at the first corner he brusquely left the coadjutor.

Sometimes, tired of his solitude, he went to visit Silverio. But the good-natured happiness of that obese individual, who spent his time collecting home-made remedies, or observing the fantastic perturbations of his digestion, his constant praise of Dr Godinho, of his children and his senhora, and the obsolete jokes which he had been repeating for the last forty years and the innocent hilarity which they caused him, made Amaro impatient. He left there unnerved, thinking of the evil fortune which had made him so different from Silverio. That, after all, was real happiness: why wasn't he also a good, old-fashioned priest, with small tyrannical ideas, the satisfied parasite of a prosperous family; one of the confident tranquil type who, like a stream beneath a mountain, contentedly rolled their fat bodies, without the danger of overstepping the bounds of respectability and causing trouble.

273

At other times he went to see his colleague Natario, whose fracture, wrongly treated at the beginning, still kept him in bed with a frame on his leg. But there he was nauseated by the aspect of the room, impregnated with the smell of arnica and sweat, with a profusion of rags soaking in glass bowls, and squadrons of medicine bottles on the chest of drawers, between rows of saints. Natario hardly gave him time to enter before he broke into complaints: the stupidity of the doctors! his habitual bad luck! the torturing pains he was suffering! the backwardness of this cursed country with regard to medicine! And as he talked he strewed the dirty floor with spit and cigarette ends. Since he had become ill the good health of others, and especially of his friends, filled him with indignation, and seemed like a personal offence to him.

'And you are always strong? So you can be, you weren't thrown off a mare as I was!' he would murmur with rancour. 'And when I think of that beast of a Brito who never even has a headache! And that glutton of an abbot who boasts that he is never in bed after seven in the morning! Animals!'

Amaro then gave him the news: a letter he had received from the canon, the improvement in Dona Josepha . . .

But Natario wasn't interested in the people with whom he was united socially and in friendship; he was only interested in his enemies, to whom he was bound in hatred. He wished to know what had happened to the clerk, if he was yet bawling with hunger.

'That at least would have been good to see before I took to this cursed bed!'

His nieces then appeared: two little freckled creatures with very sneaky eyes. Their great disgust was that uncle hadn't sent for the *benzedeira* to put virtue back into his foot: it was she who had cured the Morgado of Barrosa and Pimentel of Ourem . . .

Natario became calmer with the presence of 'the two roses of his garden'.

'Poor little things, it isn't for want of their care and attention that I'm not better. But I've suffered, heavens!'

And the two roses, with a simultaneous movement, turned aside and wiped their eyes with their handkerchiefs.

Amaro left more disgusted than ever.

To tire himself, he attempted to take long walks along the Lisbon road. But he no sooner left the movement of the town than his sadness became more intense, in sympathy with that scene of mournful hills and miserable trees; and his life seemed like this same road, monotonous and long, without an incident to brighten it, desolately stretching along till it was lost in the mists of the twilight. Sometimes on his return he entered the cemetery, walking between the rows of cypresses, feeling in that hour at the end of the evening a soothing emanation from the copses of gilly-flowers; he read the epitaphs, then leaning on the gilded railing of the last resting place of the family of Gouvea, he contemplated the embossed emblems, a hat adorned with the family arms and a sword, and following the black letters of the famous ode which decorated the headstone, he read:

> Passer-by, pause a minute to contemplate
> These mortal remains,
> And if you are overcome with grief
> Leave here your sighs
> With João Cabral da Silva Maldonado
> Mendonca de Gouvea,
> Youthful member of the aristocracy, bachelor-at-law
> Son of the illustrious Cea
> Ex-administrator of this council,
> Exalted by the Church of Christ
> Of virtues a singular mirror.
> Passer-by, believe in this.

Then the rich mausoleum of Moraes whose widow, now forty and rich, and living as the mistress of the handsome Captain Trigueiros, had ordered a pious verse to be engraved.

> Wait amongst the angels, O my spouse
> For the half of thy heart
> Who remains in the world, so lonely
> Devoting all her life to the task of praying for thee.

Sometimes, at the end of the cemetery, near the wall at the side of the pauper's grave, he saw a man kneeling and weeping pitifully at the foot of a black cross, shaded by a willow tree. It was Uncle Esguelhas, with his crutch beside him on the ground, praying at Toto's grave. He went over to speak to him, and, in an equality which that place justified, they walked along familiarly, shoulder to shoulder, conversing. Amaro good-naturedly consoled the old fellow; asking him of what use life would have been to the unfortunate Toto, who would have had to spend her whole time in bed.

'But she at least had life, senhor paroco. And I, look at me now, alone day and night!'

'Each one has his loneliness, Uncle Esguelhas,' said Amaro sadly.

The sexton then sighed, and asked after Dona Josepha, and Menina Amelia.

'They are over there in the farm.'

'It must be very sad and lonely for them, poor things.'

'Crosses of this life, Uncle Esguelhas.'

They silently continued their walk between the rows of boxbushes enclosing the plots full of the blackness of the crosses and the whiteness of the new headstones. Amaro sometimes recognized a grave that he himself had sprinkled and consecrated: where now were these souls which he had commended to God in Latin, distracted, quickly gabbling the prayers in order to hurry to Amelia?

He returned home sadder; and his long endless night began. He tried to read: but at the end of the first ten lines yawned with boredom. He sometimes wrote to the canon. At nine he took tea; and afterwards it was a walk without end backwards and forwards round the room, smoking packets of cigarettes, pausing at the window to look at the blackness of the night, now and again reading the news or an advertisement from *The Popular*, and again taking up his walk with yawns so deep that the servant heard them in the kitchen.

In order to entertain himself on these melancholy nights, and because of a feeling of excessive laziness, he tried to compose some verses, putting his love and the story of his former happy life into the lyrical form which he remembered from his student days:

> *Dost thou remember those hours of delight*
> *Oh my bewitching angel, beloved Amelia,*
> *When all was laughter and adventure*
> *And life ran so smoothly and so calm?*

> *Dost thou remember that night of poesy,*
> *When the moon shone brightly in the heavens*
> *And with our united souls, oh Amelia,*
> *We lifted up a prayer to God?*

But in spite of all his efforts he couldn't exceed these two verses, though he had produced them with promising facility. It seemed as if his brain contained just these isolated drops of poetry and released them at the first pressure, nothing then remaining except the dry prose of his carnal temperament.

And this empty existence so subtly relaxed the machinery of his will and actions, that whatever work with which he could fill the weary, loathsome hollowness of his endless hours was as odious as the weight of an unjust burden. He preferred the tediousness of idleness to the tediousness of occupation. Doing only the essential duties which he couldn't neglect without censure and without giving scandal, little by little he rid himself of all his intimate zealous practices: his mental prayers, his regular visits to the Blessed Sacrament, his spiritual meditations, the rosary to Our Lady, the nightly reading of his breviary, the examination of his conscience; all these works of devotion, these secret means of sanctification, were progressively replaced by endless walks up and down the room from the washbasin to the window, and by smoking packets of cigarettes till he made his fingers black. His morning Mass was rapidly gabbled, his parish duties performed with silent repugnance, which negligence made him to perfection the *indignus sacerdos* of the ritualists; he had in ample totality the thirty-five defects and the seven half defects which the theologians attributed to the bad priest.

The only thing which remained to him, apart from his sentimentality, was a tremendous appetite. And as his servant was an excellent cook, and as before she left for Vieria, Senhora Dona Maria of the Assumption had left him a capital of one hundred and fifty Masses at a cruzado each, he banqueted, treating himself to chickens and jelly, and regaling himself with a piquant Barraida wine which the master had chosen for him. And there he remained at the table, for hours and hours sunk in oblivion, with his legs stretched out, smoking cigarettes and drinking coffee, lamenting that he hadn't his Ameliazinha at hand. And what is she doing there, poor Ameliazinha? he thought, yawning with tedium and inertia.

Poor Ameliazinha was there in Ricoça bemoaning her fate.

On the journey in the coach Dona Josepha tacitly made her feel that she mustn't expect either the old friendship, or pardon for her offence; and that was how matters stood when they installed themselves. The old lady became intractable; she cruelly abandoned the familiar 'tu' and addressed her as Menina; she drew back sharply if Amelia attempted to arrange her cushion or put her shawl straight; there was a reprehending silence when she passed the evening in the room, sewing; and at every moment there were sighing allusions to the sad burden with which God had loaded her at the end of her days . . .

Amelia inwardly blamed the paroco, as he had promised that her godmother would be all charity, all complicity; and then he had treacherously delivered her to the ferocity of this fanatical virgin.

When she saw herself in that great barrack of a house in Ricoça, in a freezing room, painted in canary colour, drearily furnished with a canopied bed and two leather chairs, she cried all night with her head buried in the pillow; tormented by a dog underneath her window, which, no doubt disturbed by the light and the movement in the house, howled till daylight.

One day she went to the other end of the farm to see the caretakers. Perhaps they were nice people, and it would be a distraction for her to talk to them sometimes. She met the woman, tall and mournful as a cypress, laden with black crêpe, the large black dyed kerchief on her head well pulled down over her forehead, giving her the air of a penitent in a procession; her whining voice had the sadness of a funeral knell. The man appeared still worse, bearing a striking resemblance to an orang-outang, with two enormous ears sticking out from his skull, a bestial protruding chin, dirty gums, a body with the joints dislocated from consumption, and a sunken chest. She hastily left them and went to see the orchard. It was very neglected: the paths were smothered with damp weeds, and the shade of the trees, which were very close together in low sunken ground, surrounded by high walls, gave one a sensation of fever and sickness.

It was preferable to pass her days shut up in the great house: endless days in which the hours moved with the lingering pace of a funeral march.

Her room was at the front; and from the two windows she had a sad view of the country all round, a monotonous undulation of barren lands with a stunted tree here and there. There was an oppressive air in which vapours from the adjoining swamps and lowlands seemed to wander, and from which not even the warm September sun could dissipate the atmosphere of malarial fever.

In the mornings she went to help to get Dona Josepha out of bed and arrange her on the sofa; afterwards she came to sit beside her and sew, as formerly, in the Rua da Misericordia, she had sat beside mamma; but now instead of friendly chats she had the stubborn silence of the old lady and her incessant cough. She thought of sending to town for her piano; but she no sooner mentioned it than her godmother exclaimed with acidity: 'You are mad, girl. I'm not well enough to listen to piano playing. What nonsense!'

Gertrude also was no company for her; in the hours in which she was free from attendance on the old lady, and had finished her work in the kitchen, she disappeared. She was a native of that very district, and passed her spare time chatting with her old neighbours.

Amelia's worst hour was when night was falling. After saying her rosary, she remained near the window gazing stupidly at the light fading away in the west, watching all the fields disappear little by little in the same grey tone; a silence seemed to descend and spread over the earth, and then the first small star tremblingly lit up and shone; and before her there was then only an inert mass of shadowy darkness reaching unbroken to the horizon, where there still remained a long strip of fading orange colour. There was nothing in all this to fix her mind, so her thoughts wandered longingly far away, to Vieira: at that hour her mother and friends met to walk on the beach; the nets were gathered up, and already lights were beginning to appear in the houses; and it was tea-time, the hour of the happy games of lotto, when the boys of the town came in bands to their friends' houses with guitars and flutes and improvised *fados* for the evenings. And she was here, alone!

It was then time to put the old lady to bed, to say the rosary with her and Gertrude. They lit the tin lamp, placing an old shade in front of it to keep the glare from the invalid's eyes; and all the evening, in the dreary silence, one heard only the sound of Gertrude's spindle as she sat in a corner spinning.

Before retiring for the night, they went to lock up all the doors, as they lived in constant fear of burglars; then began for Amelia hours of superstitious terrors. She was unable to sleep, feeling at her side the blackness of those old uninhabited rooms, and all round her the dark silence of the country. She heard inexplicable noises: it was the floor in the corridor creaking under innumerable steps; the light of the candle which suddenly flared up as if from an invisible breath; or in the distance, at the side of the kitchen, the silent thud of a body sounded on the soft earth. She piled up prayer upon prayer as she shivered under the bedclothes; but if she slept, the visions of her nightmares continued the terrors of her waking hours. Once she woke up suddenly and heard a moaning voice coming up over the high bars of the bed, saying: 'Amelia, get ready, your end is drawing near!' Terrified, she jumped out of bed and ran across the corridor in her shift to take refuge in Gertrude's bed.

But the following night, as she was trying to sleep, the warning voice returned, calling: 'Amelia, remember your sins! Get ready, Amelia!' She gave a scream and fainted. Happily Gertrude, who hadn't yet gone to bed, heard her sharp cry, which pierced the heavy silence of the great house, and ran to her assistance. She found her stretched across the bed, her hair fallen down from the net and trailing on the ground, and her hands cold as death. She went down to call the caretaker's wife and till dawn they worked at high pressure to bring life into her benumbed body. From that day on, Gertrude slept beside her: and the voice from over the bars of the bed did not return.

But the thought of death and the fear of hell never left her night or day. About this time, a pedlar in holy pictures came to Ricoça; and

Dona Josepha bought two prints entitled *The Death of a Just Soul* and *The Death of a Sinner*.

'It is good that each one should have a living example before her eyes,' she remarked.

Amelia, from the beginning, had no doubt that the old lady, who counted on dying in the same state of glory as the 'Just Soul', wished to show her, the 'Sinner', the terrifying scene which awaited her. She hated her for such a malicious trick. But her frightened imagination didn't hesitate to give her another explanation to the print: it was Our Lady who had sent the pedlar there, to put before her vividly in *The Death of a Sinner* the picture of her last agony; she was now certain that all would be in this manner, line for line: her guardian angel running away sobbing, God the Father hiding His face from her with repugnance; the skeleton of Death grinning and showing its ghastly teeth; and the glittering mass of demons with an arsenal of instruments of torture, taking hold of her, some by the legs, others by the hair, and dragging her with jubilant cries to the flaming cavern which shook from the roars of terror let loose from the Eternal Sufferings of the damned. And she could just see in the depths of the sky, the great scales, with one of the plates, on which were her prayers, not weighing as much as a canary's feather, high in the air, and the other plate holding the sexton's iron bed and her tons of sins falling down, with its chains strained to the uttermost.

She then sank into a hysterical state of melancholy which aged her; she spent her days dirty and untidy, not wishing to care for her sinful body; all movement, all action was repugnant to her; her prayers were a dreary task, as she judged them useless; and she pushed the clothes she was making for her baby to the bottom of an old chest, because she hated that being which she felt moving in her womb, looking on it as the cause of her perdition. Yes, she hated it—but not as much as the other, the paroco, who was its father, that cursed priest who had tempted her, destroyed her life, and condemned her to the fire of hell! How desperate she felt when she thought of him. He was there in Leiria in peace and tranquillity, eating well, confessing others, perhaps making love; and she was here alone, with her womb weighed down and her soul doomed with the sin that he had put there, and which was dragging her to the bottomless pit of hell.

This excitement of her spirit would certainly have killed her, if it hadn't been for the Abbot Ferrão, who just then began regularly to visit the sister of his friend the canon.

Amelia had often heard him talked about in the Rua da Misericordia: it was said there that Ferrão had extraordinary ideas, but that it wasn't possible to deny his virtuous life or his priestly ability. He had been abbot there for many years; bishops had succeeded one another in the diocese, and he remained there forgotten in that poor parish, with dues always unpaid, in a house with a leaking roof. The late vicar general, who never lifted a hand to help him, though very liberal with his praises, said to him:

'You are one of the greatest theologians of the realm. You are pre-destined by God to be a bishop. You will yet wear the mitre. You will take your place in the history of the Church of Portugal as a great bishop, Ferrão!'

'Bishop, senhor vicar general! That's a good one! It would be necessary for me to have the audacity of Affonso d'Albuquerque or of João de Castro to accept, under the eyes of God, such great responsi-bility!'

And there he stayed, amongst the poor, in a village with little land, living on a piece of bread and a cup of milk, with a clean cassock on which the patches made a map, travelling miles in all sorts of weather if one of his parishioners had a toothache, passing hours consoling an old woman who had lost a goat . . . And always in good humour, always with a cruzado in the bottom of his trouser pocket for some needy neighbour; a great friend of the children, for whom he made toy cork boats; and never failing to stop when he met a pretty maid (which was a rare occurrence in that district) and to exclaim: 'God bless you, you lovely girl!'

Even when he was young, the purity of his life was so celebrated that he was known in the parish as 'the virgin'.

He was also a perfect priest in his religious zeal, passing hours oɪ ecstasy at the foot of the Blessed Sacrament; accomplishing with fervent delight the smallest duties of his devout life; purifying himself for the work of the day with deep mental prayer, and meditations on faith, from which his soul issued more agile, they having served him as a fortifying bath; preparing himself for sleep with one of those long and pious examinations of conscience, which are so effective that St Augus-tine and St Bernard performed them in exactly the same manner as Plutarch and Seneca; and which are a laborious and subtle correction of the smallest defects, the meticulous perfectioning of active virtue, conceived with the fervour of a poet who dreams a beloved poem. And all his spare time he spent buried in a chaos of books.

Abbot Ferrão had one sole defect: he liked to go shooting! But he generally abstained, because it took up so much time and, more important still, because he thought it cold-blooded to kill poor birds who went round innocently on their urgent domestic business. But sometimes on the clear winter mornings when the dew was still on the heather, a man could be seen passing with lively gait, a gun on his shoulder, followed by his setter: all eyes were on him. When the temptation conquered him, he furtively seized his gun, whistled to his dog Janota, and with the ends of his coat flapping in the wind, there went the illustrious theologian, the mirror of piety, across the fields and valleys. And a little while after—pum, pum! a quail or a partridge fell to earth. And then the holy man returned with the gun under his arm, and the two birds in his pocket, walking flat against the wall, reciting his rosary to the Virgin, and replying to the 'good-days' of his parishioners, whom he met on the road, with lowered eyes and a very criminal air.

The Abbot Ferrão, in spite of his old-fashioned ways and big nose, pleased Amelia; she liked him from the first time that he visited Ricoça, and her affection for him increased when she saw that Dona Josepha received him coolly, though she knew that her brother the canon had a great respect for his learning.

As a matter of fact, the old lady, after receiving some hours of religious instruction from him, condemned him with one sole phrase: 'He is slack!' she said, with the authority of her experience as a devout member of the faithful.

He hadn't really understood her. The good Ferrão, having lived so many years in that parish of five hundred souls, who were all, both mothers and children, cast in the same mould of simple devotion to Our Lord, Our Lady and St Vincent, patron of the district, and having little experience of confession, now suddenly found himself having to deal with a complicated fanatical soul from the town, an obstinate, finicky churchgoer full of petty scruples; and as he listened to that extraordinary list of mortal sins he murmured, astonished: 'How strange, how strange . . .'

He perceived from the beginning that he had before him one of those morbid religious degenerates, whose state the theologians describe as 'scrupulous illness', a disease from which the majority of Catholics of today suffer; but after hearing certain revelations of the old lady he feared that he was in the presence of a madwoman; and instinctively, with the singular horror that priests have for mad people, he recoiled in his chair.

Poor Dona Josepha! The first night she arrived at Ricoça (she recounted), as she began the rosary to Our Lady, she suddenly remembered that she had forgotten to put on her red flannel petticoat, which was so efficacious for pains in the legs. Thirty-eight consecutive times she began her rosary, but the red flannel petticoat always came between her and Our Lady. She then desisted, exhausted. And immediately she felt lively pains in her legs, and a voice inside her told her that it was Our Lady who was giving her pins and needles for vengeance . . .

The abbot jumped: 'Oh, my dear senhora!'

'Ah, but that isn't all, senhor abbot!'

There was another sin which was tormenting her: sometimes, when she was praying, she felt the phlegm coming up; and, still having the name of God or the Virgin in her mouth, she had to spit it out; lately she had been swallowing the phlegm, but she had been thinking that the names of God and the Virgin entered her stomach wrapped in the spittle and then passed into the faeces! What must she do?

The abbot, who had been listening dumbfounded, wiped the sweat from his forehead.

But that wasn't the worst: her most serious fault was that the previous night as she was praying to St Francis Xavier, feeling so calm, so full of virtue—suddenly, she couldn't think how it happened, she began to picture how St Francis Xavier would look naked, in his skin!

The good Ferrão remained motionless, stunned. Then in the end, seeing her looking anxiously at him, waiting for his comfort and counsels, he said: 'And have you been feeling these terrors and doubts for a long time . . . ?'

'Always, senhor abbot, always!'

'And have you mixed with people like yourself who are also subject to these disturbances of mind?'

'All the people I know, dozens of friends, the whole world. The devil doesn't only pick me out—he assaults all!'

'And what remedies are usually given for these anxieties of the soul?'

'Ah, senhor abbot, those saintly priests in the town, the senhor paroco, Senhor Father Silverio, all, all succeed in freeing us from these troubles of the soul. And with much virtue and ability . . .'

Abbot Ferrão remained silent a minute: he felt so sad, thinking that through the whole realm hundreds of priests deliberately led their flocks into that darkness of soul, keeping the faithful in abject terror of the heavens, representing God and the saints as not less corrupt than Caligula and his libertines.

He would have liked to bring to that gloomy fanatic brain, stocked with phantasmagorias, a higher, nobler light. He told her that all her disturbances came from an imagination tortured by the terror of offending God; but Our Lord was not a fierce, angry tyrant, but an indulgent father and friend; that it was necessary to serve him by love and not by fear; that all these scruples, such as Our Lady giving her pins and needles, the name of God falling into her stomach, came from the disturbances of a sick mind. He advised her to have confidence in God, to follow a good regime in order to regain her health, and not to tire herself with excessive praying.

'And when I return,' he said, as he got up ready to depart, 'we will continue our conversation on this subject and we must try to calm your soul.'

'Thank you, senhor abbot,' responded the old lady dryly.

And when a little while after Gertrude entered with her hot-water bottle, Dona Josepha exclaimed very indignantly, almost crying: 'Ah, he's no good at all, no good at all! He didn't understand me, he is dense. He is a freemason, Gertrude. What a disgrace for a priest of God!'

From that day on she didn't reveal any more of the terrible sins which she continued committing; and when he, considering it his duty, attempted to recommence the education of her soul, she declared that, speaking frankly, as she confessed to Senhor Father Gusmão, she thought it might be indelicate to receive moral direction from another.

The abbot flushed.

'You are right, my dear senhora, you are right, one must be very delicate in these matters.'

He left. And after this, when he came, he went into her room to ask after her health, to talk about the weather, the season, the amount of sickness which was about, some church feast which was coming; then hurriedly took his leave and went out on the terrace to talk to Amelia.

Seeing her always so sad, he began to take an interest in her; the abbot's visits were, in that solitary place, a distraction for Amelia; and thus they began to get so friendly that on the days on which he was expected she put her cloak over her shoulders and went by the Poyaes road as far as the blacksmith's to meet him. The abbot was a tireless talker, and his conversations, so different from the gossiping of the Rua da Misericordia, pleased her: as the sight of a large valley with trees, plantations, water, orchards and the sound of ploughing, delights eyes accustomed to the bare walls of a city garret. Their usual conversation was in fact similar to one of these weekly journals such as *The Family Treasure*, or *Evening Lectures*, containing a bit of everything— moral doctrine, accounts of voyages, anecdotes of great men, dissertations on farming, good jokes, sublime delineations of the characters of the saints, a verse here and there, and even hints on housekeeping, one of which was very useful as it taught Amelia how to wash flannels without shrinking them. He was boring only when he talked of his flock, their marriages, baptisms, illnesses, and disputes.

'Once, my dear senhora, I was passing by the Corrego das Tristes, when a flock of birds . . .'

When he began like that Amelia knew that for at least an hour she would hear of the exploits of his dog Janota, fabulous tales of shots with the gun, recounted in mime, with imitations of the voices of the birds, and the pop, pop of the gun. She loved his descriptions of the savage hunts of which he had read with gluttonous enjoyment: the hunt of the Nepal tiger, of the lion of Algiers and of the elephant, ferocious stories which drew the girl's imagination far away to the exotic countries where the grass is as high as pine trees, where the sun burns like red-hot iron, and where from behind each tree shine the eyes of a wild beast. And afterwards, apropos of tigers and Malaya, he remembered a curious story of St Francis Xavier, and there he was, that terrible talker, spilling out a description of the customs of Asia, the arms of India, the famous rapier thrusts of the circus of Diu!

It was during one of these conversations in the orchard—which the abbot began by enumerating the advantages which the canon would gain by converting the orchard into tillage, and finished by commenting on the courage and dangers of the missionary's life in Japan and India—that Amelia, then in the full intensity of her nocturnal terrors, spoke of the noises which could be heard in the house and the frights which they caused her.

'Oh, what a disgrace!' said the abbot laughing: 'A senhora of your age to be afraid of goblins!'

Then, drawn by the senhor abbot's good nature, she spoke about the voices which she heard at night coming up from behind the bars of the bed.

The abbot became serious: 'My dear senhora, these are fancies which you must dominate at all costs. Strange things have certainly happened in the world, but God never speaks to people like that, nor would he permit the devil to do so. These voices that you hear do not come from over the bars of the bed, they come from yourself, and if your sins are great, it is your conscience which is troubling you. So that if Gertrude or a hundred Gertrudes, and a whole battalion of infantry, sleep at your side, you will continue to hear them—even if you were deaf you would hear them. What is necessary is to calm your conscience with penance and purification . . .'

They had gone up to the terrace, talking on the way: and Amelia, feeling tired, sat down on one of the stone benches, and remained looking out across the farm, far away, where she could see the roofs of the cowsheds, long rows of laurel trees, the threshing floor, and in the distance the fields, flat and smooth with vivid tones from the light rain of the morning: now in the evening all was clear and placid, without a breeze, with great still clouds which the setting sun touched with tender, rosy tints. She thought of the wise words of the abbot, the rest she would enjoy if each sin which weighed on her mind like a heavy stone disappeared under the action of penance. Then came to her desires of peace, of a repose in harmony with the fields which she saw stretching out in front of her.

A bird sang, and was still; and after a moment trilled out so vibrantly, so happily, that Amelia laughed as she listened.

'It's a nightingale,' she said.

'The nightingale doesn't sing at this hour,' said the abbot. 'It is a blackbird. Here is a being who has no fear of phantoms, nor of voices— what ecstasy, the mischievous little villain!'

It was in fact a triumphant trill, the delirium of a happy blackbird, which suddenly gave to the orchard an atmosphere of sonorous festivity.

Then Amelia, beside that glorious quavering of a contented bird, suddenly, without reason, in one of those nervous fits which attack hysterical women, burst out crying.

'Now then, what's the matter, what's the matter?' said the abbot very surprised.

In his privilege as an old man and a friend, he took her hand and tried to calm her.

'Oh, how unhappy I am!' she murmured between her sobs.

He then said very paternally: 'There is no reason for you to be so. No matter what the affliction or worrries, a Christian soul always has consolation at hand. There is no sin which God will not pardon, nor pain that He will not calm. Remember this. What you mustn't do is keep your trouble to yourself: that is what disheartens and makes one weep. If I can be of any use, if I can in any way quieten your mind, come to me.'

'When!' said she with a strong desire to seek refuge in that holy man.

'Whenever you like,' he said smiling. 'I have no special hours for giving consolations. The church is always open, God is always present.'

Early the next day, before the old lady got up, Amelia went to his house; and for two hours she was prostrated in front of the little pine-wood confessional, which the good abbot, with his own hands, had painted a dark blue, with extraordinary little angels' heads, which had wings instead of ears, a work of high art of which he was secretly vain.

Chapter XXII

FATHER AMARO had just finished his dinner and was smoking, with his eyes fixed on the ceiling, in order not to see the long lean face of the coadjutor, who had been sitting there for the last half hour, motionless and spectral, every ten minutes asking a question, which in the silence of the parlour fell like the melancholy strokes of the Cathedral clock at night.

'You, senhor paroco, don't subscribe to *The Nation*?'

'No, senhor, I read *The Popular*.'

The coadjutor was again silent, laboriously collecting his words for the next question. In the end, it came out slowly: 'You never again heard of that scoundrel who wrote the *Communication*?'

'No, senhor, he went to Brazil.'

The servant entered at that very moment to say that there was a person downstairs who wished to talk to the senhor paroco. It was her way of announcing the presence of Dionysia in the kitchen.

She hadn't appeared for several weeks; and Amaro, curious, left the parlour, shutting the door behind him, and called the matron to the top of the stairs.

'Great news, senhor paroco! I came running because it's serious. João Eduardo has turned up!'

'Listen to that!' exclaimed the paroco. 'And I had just this minute been talking about him. It's extraordinary. What a coincidence!'

'It's true, I saw him today. I was amazed . . . And I've already got information about him. He is tutor to the sons of the morgado.'

'Which morgado?'

'The Morgado of Poyaes. Whether he lives there, or whether he just goes there in the morning and comes home at night, I don't know. What I do know is that he has returned. He is a regular dandy, all dressed up in a new suit. I thought it better to warn you because you may be certain that one of these days he'll go looking up Ameliazinha there in Ricoça. It's on the road to the morgado's. What do you think?'

'The vile beast!' muttered Amaro rancorously. 'Now that one doesn't want him he appears. Then he never went to Brazil in the end?'

'It appears not. It wasn't his shadow I saw, it was he himself, flesh and bones. I just chanced to see him as I came out of Fernandes' shop, looking so foppish. It's better to tell the girl, senhor paroco, otherwise she may plant herself at the window . . .'

Amaro gave her the two placas that she was expecting, and a quarter of an hour later, having got rid of the coadjutor, he walked towards Ricoça.

His heart beat wildly when he saw that great yellow house, newly painted, and the large side terrace, in line with the orchard wall, decorated with rows of noble stone vases placed along the parapet. Here he was at last, after many long weeks, going to see his Ameliazinha! And he was already transported with joy at the thought of her passionate exclamations as she fell into his arms.

On the ground floor were the stables of the aristocratic family who formerly inhabited the house, now abandoned to the rats and the toadstools, receiving light from narrow iron-railed windows that had almost disappeared under myriads of spiders' webs. He entered by an immense dark patio, where during long years mountains of wooden wine barrels had piled up in a corner; and the noble flight of steps, which led up to the living apartments on the right, was flanked by two stone lions, benign and somnolent.

Amaro went up to a salon with a panelled oak ceiling, unfurnished, and with half the floor strewn with dry beans.

Feeling embarrassed, he clapped his hands.

A door opened. Amelia appeared for a minute, in a white petticoat and with her hair uncombed. On seeing him she gave a little cry and rushed away, banging the door. He remained disconsolate in the middle of the salon, with his umbrella under his arm, thinking of the pleasant familiarity with which he had entered the Rua da Misericordia, where the door seemed to open of itself and the paper on the walls to become brighter with the joy of his coming.

Feeling a little annoyed, he was just about to clap his hands again, when Gertrude entered.

'Oh, senhor paroco! Enter senhor paroco! He has arrived at last! It is the senhor paroco, senhora!' she cried, in the joy of at last receiving a pleasant visit, a friend from the town, in that lonely, deserted Ricoça.

She took him up to Dona Josepha's room, at the end of the house, an enormous apartment, where on a little sofa, lost in a corner, the old lady passed her days tightly gathered into her shawl, with her feet wrapped in a rug.

'Oh, Dona Josepha! How are you? How are you?'

She was unable to reply, having been taken with a fit of coughing at the excitement of the visit.

'Just as you see me, senhor paroco,' she murmured in the end, in a very weak voice. 'I'm just alive, dragging on from day to day. And you, senhor? Why haven't you come before?'

Amaro excused himself, vaguely muttering something about parish duties. He now understood, as he looked at her yellow sunken face, with the hideous black lace kerchief on top, what sad hours Amelia must be passing there. He asked for her, said he had caught a glimpse of her, but that she had run away . . .

'It was because she wasn't dressed fit to appear,' said the old lady. 'Today is the day of the *barrella*.'

Amaro wished to know how they entertained themselves, how they passed their days in that solitary place.

'I am here. The little one is there.'

After each word, she appeared to break down with fatigue, her hoarseness increasing.

'Well, senhora, do you feel that the change has done you no good?'

She nodded her head saying yes, she felt so.

'She is just talking, senhor paroco,' interrupted Gertrude, who had remained by the side of the sofa, enjoying the presence of the senhor paroco. 'Let her talk. She is exaggerating—she gets up every day and takes her little walk as far as the parlour, eats her wing of chicken; she will completely recover here. It is just as Senhor Abbot Ferrão says: "Health flies with all speed, but returns with slow paces." '

The door opened. Amelia appeared, her face scarlet. She was in her old merino wool dressing-gown and her hair had been hurriedly arranged.

'Excuse me, senhor paroco,' she muttered, 'but today was the day of the *barrella*.'

He gravely pressed her hand: they remained as silent as if they were miles apart. She fixed her eyes on the ground and remained tremblingly twisting the edge of the cloak which she had thrown loosely over her shoulders. Amaro found her different, her cheeks a little swollen and wrinkles of age at the corners of her mouth. In order to break the strange silence he asked her also if she felt well.

'I'm doing all right. It is a little sad here. And as Senhor Abbot Ferrão says, it is too big a house for us to feel at home with one another.'

'None of us came here to enjoy ourselves,' said the old lady without raising her eyelids, in a hard metallic voice which had now lost all signs of fatigue.

Amelia turned pale and dropped her head.

Amaro, seeing in a flash that Dona Josepha was torturing Amelia, then said with much severity: 'It's true that you didn't come here to enjoy yourselves. But nor was it for the purpose of being miserable. Because if a person is ill-humoured and makes other people's lives unhappy, it is a terrible want of charity; there is no worse sin in the eyes of Our Lord. A person who acts thus is unworthy of the grace of God.'

The old lady became very excited and burst into tears, moaning: 'Ah, what a trial God has in store for me at the end of my days!'

Gertrude tried to soothe her. 'Now senhora,' she said, 'you'll make yourself worse going on like that. All will come right with the help of God. You will soon again have health and be able to enjoy life. What nonsense!'

Amelia went to the window to hide the tears which rushed to her eyes. And the paroco, in consternation at the scene which he had raised, began to say to Dona Josepha that she was not supporting this sickness of hers with true Christian resignation. Nothing angered Our Lord more than to see his creatures revolting against the pains and the burdens which he had sent them. It was a rebellion against His just decrees . . .

'You are right, senhor paroco, you are right,' murmured the old lady very contrite. 'Sometimes I don't know what I'm saying . . . It's due to my illness.'

'Good, good, my dear senhora, you must resign yourself and try to see all through rose-coloured glasses. It is the sentiment which God appreciates most of all. I know it is hard to be buried here.'

'It's just what the Senhor Abbot Ferrão says,' broke in Amelia, returning from the window: 'Godmother feels strange here. It is difficult for her to change her life after so many years.'

Then noticing the repeated quoting of Abbot Ferrão's words, Amaro asked if he were in the habit of visiting them.

'Yes, he has been great company for us,' said Amelia. 'He comes here almost every day.'

'He is a saint!' exclaimed Gertrude.

'To be sure, to be sure,' murmured Amaro, dissatisfied at such lively enthusiasm. 'A person of much virtue.'

'Of much virtue,' sighed the old lady. 'But——' She checked herself, not daring to express the opinions which she in her experience as a devout churchwoman had formed of him. She then exclaimed hopefully: 'Ah, it is the senhor paroco who must come here to help me to bear this heavy cross of sickness . . .'

'I must come, my dear senhora, I must come. It would be good to entertain you a little, to give you news. And apropos of news, I had a letter from our canon yesterday.'

He took the letter from his pocket and read some parts of it. The master had already had fifteen baths. The beach was black with people. Dona Maria was ill with a boil. The weather was marvellous. Every evening they took a lovely walk to see the nets being gathered in. Senhora Joanneira was well, but was always talking of her daughter.

'Poor mamma,' moaned Amelia.

But the old lady wasn't interested in the news, she groaned about her hoarseness. It was Amelia who asked about the friends of Leiria, Senhor Father Natario and Senhor Father Silverio . . .

It was already getting dark: Gertrude went to get the lamp ready. Amaro stood up: 'Well, my dear senhora, till I come again. I'm sure to turn up from time to time. There is nothing for you to worry about. Wrap yourself up well, eat all you can, and trust in the mercy of God who will never abandon you.'

'The mercy of God won't be wanting to us, no, it won't be wanting to us, senhor paroco . . .'

Amelia held out her hand to say good-bye there in the room; but Amaro said jokingly: 'If it's not too much trouble, Menina Amelia, I'd be grateful if you'd accompany me to the front door, as I might lose myself in this big house.'

They both left and entered the salon, where the light still entered by the three large windows.

'The old lady is making your life bitter, child,' said Amaro stopping.

'What else do I deserve?' she answered, dropping her eyes.

'It's shameful. I must speak severely to her. My Ameliazinha, if you only knew what it has cost me——'

As he spoke he attempted to embrace her.

But she drew away from him, very perturbed.

'What's this?' asked Amaro astonished.

'What is it?'

'Yes, this strange behaviour. You don't want to give me a kiss, Amelia. You're ridiculous!'

She raised her hands towards him in anxious supplication, and said with her whole body trembling: 'No, senhor paroco, leave me! It is finished. We have sinned quite enough . . . I wish to die in the grace of God. Never speak to me of such a thing again! It was disgraceful. Finish it. Now I want to save my soul.'

'You're being absurd! Who put this into your head? Look here——'

He again went towards her with open arms.

'Don't touch me, for the love of God!' she cried, running quickly towards the door.

He gazed at her a minute in silent anger.

'Good, just as you like,' he said at last. 'Anyway, I want to warn you that João Eduardo has returned, that he passes here every day, and that it is better for you not to go near the window.'

'What difference does it make to me whether João Eduardo, or anyone else, passes here?'

He interrupted, and said with bitter sarcasm: 'That's plain, the great man now is Senhor Abbot Ferrão!'

'I owe him much, that I must say . . .'

Gertrude entered at that moment with the lighted lamp. And Amaro, without taking leave of Amelia, departed, with his umbrella truculently raised, and grinding his teeth with rage.

But the long walk to the town calmed him. After all, the behaviour of the girl was just due to a fit of virtue, an attack of scruples. He could just imagine her there alone in that great house, bitter because of her treatment by the old lady, impressed by her talks with that moralist Ferrão, far away from himself; and that pious reaction had come because of her terrors of the next world and her desire for innocence. It was all talk! If he began to go to Ricoça, in a week he would regain all his dominion over her. Ah, he knew her well! He just had to touch her, to wink an eye at her—and she would give herself to him immediately.

He passed a disturbed night, desiring her more than ever. And the next day, at one o'clock he started off to Ricoça, carrying a bouquet of roses.

The old lady was happy to see him. Ah, the very presence of the senhor paroco made her feel better! And if it wasn't for the distance, she would ask him to do her the favour of coming every morning. After his other little visit she had prayed with more fervour . . .

Amaro smiled, inattentive, with his eyes nailed to the door.

'And Menina Amelia?' he asked in the end.

'She's gone out. She takes a little walk now every morning,' said the old lady acidly. 'She's gone to the abbot's house. He is everything to her now.'

'Ah!' said Amaro with a livid smile. 'A new devotion, eh? The abbot is a very worthy person.'

'But he's no use, he's no use!' exclaimed Dona Josepha. 'He doesn't understand me. He has very queer ideas. He instils no devotion in me.'

'He is a man of books,' said Amaro.

Then the old lady leaned forward on her elbows, and lowering her voice, said, with her large lean face lit up with hate: 'This is between ourselves, but Amelia has behaved very badly! I can never forgive her. She goes to confession to the abbot. It is indelicate, seeing that you, senhor paroco, are her confessor, and that she has received nothing but kindness from you. She is ungrateful, and false!'

Amaro turned pale: 'You don't say so, senhora?'

'It's true! She doesn't deny it. She is proud of it. She is a disgrace, she is a disgrace! When one thinks of the kindness we are doing her!'

Amaro disguised the indignation which took possession of him. He even laughed. It was necessary not to magnify the case. There was no ingratitude. It was a question of faith. If the girl thought that the abbot could direct her better she was quite right in opening her heart to him. What they all wanted was that she should save her soul, it didn't matter with whom. She would be quite well in the abbot's hands.

Then quickly drawing his chair near the old lady's bed: 'So now she goes every morning to the abbot's house?'

'Nearly every morning. She'll soon be here now, she goes after breakfast, and returns about this time. Ah, I've been so upset over it all!'

Amaro walked nervously about the room, then turned and gave his hand to Dona Josepha: 'Well, my dear senhora, I can't stay any longer, I just came to pay a quick visit. Well, till one day soon.'

And without listening to the old lady, who was anxiously inviting him to stay to lunch, he went down the stairs at the speed of a falling stone, and walked furiously in the direction of the abbot's house, with the bouquet of roses still in his hand.

He hoped to meet Amelia on the road; and in a short time he saw her just past the blacksmith's, crouching down at the side of the path, sentimentally picking wild flowers.

'What are you doing here?' he exclaimed, coming up close to her.

She jumped up with a little cry.

'What are you doing here?' he repeated.

At the sound of his angry voice she put her hand to her mouth and gasped. The senhor abbot was inside the forge with the smith.

'I heard up there,' said Amaro with flaming eyes, grabbing her arm, 'that you confess to the abbot?'

'Why did you want to know? I confess to him. It's nothing to be ashamed of.'

'But you confessed all, all?' he asked through his teeth, which were clenched with rage.

She became very upset, and answered: 'It was you who told me many times, that the greatest sin in this world was to hide anything from one's confessor.'

'You fool,' he shouted.

His eyes devoured her; and through the cloud of anger which filled his brain and made the veins on his forehead throb, he thought her prettier than ever—with a roundness in all her body which gave him a burning desire to embrace her, and with her lips, which he would like to bite till he drew the blood, vividly red from the pure country air.

'Listen,' he said, conquered by an invasion of brutal desire. 'Listen—let's finish with this. Confess to the devil if you like—but you must be the same for me!'

'No, no!' she said determinedly, drawing away, and getting ready to run into the forge.

'I'll pay you out, curse you!' hissed the priest between his teeth, as he turned round and went down the road, with despair in his heart.

He didn't slacken his steps till he reached the town, carried on by an impulse of indignation. Under that sweet peace of the middle of autumn, he thought out ferocious plans of vengeance. He arrived home worn out, with the bouquet of roses still in his hand. But in the loneliness of his room, little by little the feeling of his impotence came to him. What could he do after all? Go round the town saying that she was pregnant? It would be denouncing himself. Spread the rumour that she was Abbot Ferrão's mistress? That would be absurd: an old man of nearly seventy, of a loyalty approaching the ridiculous, with a whole life of virtue at the back of him . . . But to lose her, never again to hold in his arms that beautiful snow-white body, never again to hear muttered those tender words of love which moved his soul more than thoughts of heaven . . . It couldn't be!

And was it possible that she, in six or seven weeks, had forgotten all? Surely on those long nights in Ricoça, alone in bed, thoughts of the mornings in the sexton's house would cross her mind. Of that he was certain: he knew from his experience with so many penitents in the confessional, who had revealed persistent obstinate temptations which, once they had sinned, never left the flesh in peace . . .

Yes: he must importune her, and try in every possible way to light in her again that desire which burnt stronger and more tumultuously than ever in him.

He spent the whole evening writing her an absurd letter of six pages, full of passionate pleadings, of abstract arguments, of interjection marks and threats of suicide.

He sent it by Dionysia early the next day. The answer, brought by a boy working on the farm, didn't arrive till night. Voraciously he tore open the envelope. There were a few bare words: 'I beg of you to leave me in peace with my sins.'

But he persisted: the next day he was again in Ricoça visiting the old lady. He found Amelia in Dona Josepha's room. She was very pale; but during the half hour he was there her eyes never left her sewing; there he remained in a sombre oppressive silence in the depths of the armchair, heedlessly replying to the old lady, who that morning was in a very talkative mood.

And the next week it was the same: when she heard him enter she hurriedly shut herself up in her room, and only appeared when the old lady sent Gertrude to say that the senhor paroco was there and would like to speak to her. She came then and gave him her hand, which he always found so hot; then sitting by the window and taking up her eternal sewing, she stitched with a taciturnity which rendered the priest desperate.

He wrote her another letter. She didn't reply.

He swore he would never again return to Ricoça; he would scorn her, but after having passed a night tossing on the bed, without being able to sleep, with the same vision of her nudeness intolerably imprinted on his brain, in the morning he again left for Ricoça, colouring when the road ganger who saw him pass every day, took off his oilskin cap to him.

One afternoon of drizzling rain as he entered the great house, he ran into Abbot Ferrão, who was just coming out of the door, opening his umbrella.

'Hello, you here, senhor abbot!' said he.

The abbot replied naturally: 'You shouldn't be surprised at that, senhor, you yourself come here every day.'

Amaro, not being able to contain himself, said, trembling with anger: 'And what has it to do with you, senhor abbot, whether I come here or not? Is the house yours?'

This unjustified rudeness offended the abbot: 'It would be better for everybody if you didn't come——'

'And why, senhor abbot, and why?' cried Amaro, losing control of himself.

Then the good man shivered. He had just committed the gravest fault a Catholic priest could commit: what he knew of Amaro and his love affairs was a secret of confession; showing that he disapproved of that persistence in sin was treason against the mystery of the sacrament. He bowed very low, and said humbly: 'You are right, senhor. I ask your pardon. I spoke without reflecting. A very good afternoon, senhor paroco.'

'A very good afternoon, senhor abbot.'

Amaro didn't enter Ricoça. He returned to town in the rain which was now beating down heavily. And the minute he entered the house he wrote a long letter to Amelia, describing the scene with the abbot, and piling accusations against him, stressing the fact that he had indirectly betrayed a secret of confession. But with this letter as with the others, he had no answer.

Then Amaro began to convince himself that so much resistance couldn't come just from repentance or terror of hell. There is another man there, he thought. And devoured by black jealousy he began to walk round Ricoça at night: but he could see nothing; the great house remained dark and sleeping. On one occasion, when he was near the orchard wall, he heard a voice on the Poyaes road, sentimentally singing the waltz of the *Two Worlds*, and the glowing point of a lighted cigar shone out in the darkness in front of the advancing figure. Frightened, he sought refuge in the ruins of an abandoned cottage at the other side of the road. The voice became silent; and Amaro, peeping out, saw a form which appeared to be wrapped in a light cloak, stopping, and gazing up at the windows of Ricoça. A furious jealousy took possession of him, and he was about to jump out and attack the man, when he saw him tranquilly resuming his journey, with his cigar held high and humming:

> *Dost thou hear the echo far away in the mountains,*
> *The sound of bronze which causes horror . . . ?*

It was in fact João Eduardo, who whenever he passed Ricoça, whether during the day or the night, stopped a moment to take a melancholy look at the walls of the house which 'she' inhabited. Because, for all his disillusionment, Amelia remained for the poor boy the 'she', the well-beloved, the most precious thing on earth. Neither in Ourem, nor in Alcobaça, nor in the places through which he had wandered and suffered hunger and cold, not even in Lisbon, where he arrived like the keel of a wrecked boat washed up on the beach, was the tender longing for her, the sweet pain caused by the thought of her, for one minute out of his mind. During those bitter days in Lisbon, the worst days of his life, when he was a clerk in an obscure office, lost in that city which to him seemed like a vast Rome or a Babylon, and in which he felt the hard egotism of the noisy bustling throng, he set himself to develop this love more, so that in the end it became a tender companion to him. He thought himself less isolated through having in his mind that image with whom he held imaginary dialogues, on his endless walks along the Caes do Sodre, accusing it of the sorrows which were ageing him.

And this passion, being for him the undefined justification of all his miseries, made him interesting in his own eyes. He was a martyr of love; this consoled him, just as thinking himself a victim of religious persecutions had consoled him in his former despair. He wasn't just an ordinary poor devil whom chance, stupidity, want of friends, bad luck and a patched coat fatally maintained in the privations of dependence: he was a man with a great heart, whom a catastrophe, partly amorous, partly political, a domestic and social drama, had thus forced, after heroic struggles, to travel from one notary's office to another with a lustre bag full of deeds. Destiny had fashioned him like several heroes

296

of whom he had read in sentimental novels. And his pallet of rough straw, his meals costing four vintens, the days on which he had no money for tobacco, all were attributed to his fatal love for Amelia and to the persecution of a powerful class, so that, with the most human of instincts, he gave to his trivial miseries a noble origin. When he encountered those whom he thought happy individuals procuring hackney-carriages, young men whom he met with pretty girls on their arms, well-dressed people going to the theatre, it made him feel less sad as he thought that he also possessed a great inner luxury, his unhappy love. And when at last he chanced to obtain the certainty of employment in Brazil and the money for his passage, he idealized his banal adventure as an emigrant, telling himself that he was going to travel the high seas, exiled from his country because of the combined tyranny of the priests and the authorities and because he loved a woman!

Who would have thought then, as they saw him packing his clothes into his tin trunk, that a few days later he would be again a few miles away from those same priests and authorities, gazing with love-lit eyes at Amelia's window! It was that odd Morgado of Poyaes (who wasn't really a morgado nor of Poyaes, but just a very rich eccentric from the foot of Alcobaça, who had bought the ancient property belonging to a noble family of Poyaes, and as he possessed the land the people round about bestowed on him the honour of a title); it was that saintly *cavalheiro* who had saved him from sea-sickness and the risks of emigration. He met him accidentally in the office where he was still working on the day before his proposed voyage. The morgado, a client of his old employer Nunes, knew the history of his famous article *Communication*, and of the scandal in the Cathedral Square; and since then had felt an ardent sympathy for him.

The morgado had in fact a fanatical hatred of priests, carried to such an extent that he never read an account of a crime in the paper without deciding (even when the culprit had been found and sentenced) that a cassock must be at the bottom of it. It was said that this rancour came from the troubles he had had with his first wife, a celebrated religious fanatic of Alcobaça. He no sooner saw João Eduardo in Lisbon and learnt of his intended voyage, than he immediately got the idea of bringing him to Leiria, installing him in Poyaes, and making him responsible for the education of his two little children, as a cutting insult to all the priests of the diocese. He looked on João Eduardo as an unbeliever; and this suited his plan of educating his boys in atheistical ideas. João Eduardo accepted with tears in his eyes: the salary, the position, the family, the home, were all magnificent . . .

'Oh, senhor morgado, I will never forget what you are doing for me!'

'I'm doing it for my own pleasure!—and to annoy those dirty scoundrels. We leave tomorrow!'

They had no sooner alighted from the train in Chão de Macas, than he exclaimed to the stationmaster, who didn't know João Eduardo, and had never heard his history: 'Here I'm bringing him, I'm bringing him in triumph! He's coming to smash the faces of all the clergy . . . And if there is any damage to be paid for, well, I'll be the one to pay!'

The stationmaster wasn't surprised, because the morgado was known in the district as a madman.

It was there in Poyaes, the day after his arrival, that João Eduardo discovered that Amelia and Dona Josepha were in Ricoça. He knew it through the good Abbot Ferrão, the only priest to whom the morgado spoke, and whom he received in his house, not as a priest, but as a *cavalheiro*.

'Senhor Ferrão,' he used to say, 'as a *cavalheiro* I respect you, but as a priest I abominate you!'

And the good Ferrão smiled, knowing that underneath his ferocious ridiculous impiety, the man had the heart of a saint and that he was a father to all the poor of the district.

The morgado was also a great lover of old books, and a tireless arguer; sometimes the two of them had fierce disputes over history, botany, systems of hunting. When the abbot, in the heat of the argument, put up a contrary opinion: 'The senhor presents this to me as a priest or as a *cavalheiro*?' the morgado would exclaim, rising on his toes and prancing round the abbot.

'As a *cavalheiro*, senhor morgado.'

'Then I accept the objection. It is a wise one. But if it was as a priest, I'd break your bones.'

Sometimes, thinking to annoy the abbot, he brought João Eduardo forward, and patting him affectionately on the back, as if he were a favourite horse: 'Now look at this fellow! He's already damaged one of you. And he still has to kill two or three. And if they take him it's I myself who will have to save him from the gallows!'

'That won't be difficult, senhor morgado,' said the abbot coolly taking his pinch of snuff, 'as there are no gallows in Portugal.'

It was then that the morgado became indignant. There were no gallows? And why? Because they had a democratic government and a constitutional king! If the priests had their wish they'd have a scaffold in every square and a burning stake at every corner!

'Tell me one thing, Senhor Ferrão, do you want, here in my house, to defend the Inquisition?'

'Oh, senhor morgado, I don't even want to talk about the Inquisition.'

'No, because you are afraid! You know right well that it's like driving a knife into your stomach!'

And all the time as he spoke he shouted and jumped round the room, making a breeze with the flapping of the sides of his ample yellow dressing-gown.

'An angel at heart,' said the abbot to João Eduardo. 'Capable of giving the shirt off his back to a priest if he thought he was in need of it. You are very well off there, João Eduardo. And take no notice of his little manias.'

The Abbot Ferrão had begun to be fond of João Eduardo: on hearing from Amelia the famous story of *Communication* he wanted, according to a favourite expression of his, 'to open up the man here and there'. He talked to him for whole afternoons in the laurel avenues of the estate, in the house where João Eduardo was tutor and librarian; and beneath 'the priest exterminator', as the morgado called him, he found a poor sensitive fellow with a sentimental religion and longings for domestic bliss, and a great lover of work. Then an idea came to him one day as he was coming out from his devotions to the Blessed Sacrament, and so appeared to him to have come from the skies, to be the will of Our Lord: it was to marry him to Amelia. It wouldn't be difficult to induce that weak affectionate heart to pardon her sin; and the poor girl, after so much anguish, would conquer her passion; that passion which had entered her soul like a breath of Satan, taking away her will, her peace, her maidenly modesty and which would drive her, in the end, to the bottomless pit of hell. For the rest of her life she would find peace and contentment in the company of João Eduardo, a pleasant sheltered corner for the years to come and a sweet refuge from her past. He spoke to neither of them about this idea which moved his heart, as now she was carrying the child of another man in her womb. But he lovingly worked towards that end, especially when he was with Amelia, to whom he recounted his conversations with João Eduardo: some clever thing the latter had said, how carefully he was developing the minds of the morgado's sons.

'He's a good fellow,' he would say. 'He would make an ideal husband and father. He is one of these men to whom a woman could safely entrust her life and happiness. If I were a married man and had a daughter, I'd give her to him.'

Amelia would blush, and remain silent.

She couldn't now put up the old formidable objection of the impious *Communication* against these persuasive eulogies. Abbot Ferrão had waved that aside in a few words: 'I read the article, my dear senhora. The boy didn't write against the priests, he wrote against the Pharisees!'

And to soften this severe judgment, the least charitable which he had made for many years, he added: 'It was in fact a grave fault on his part. But he has repented. He has paid with tears and hunger.'

And that touched Amelia.

It was just at this time that Dr Gouvea began to come to Ricoça to see Dona Josepha, who had become worse when the cold days of autumn arrived. At first Amelia shut herself up in her room when the hour of his visit approached, trembling at the idea that her condition might be discovered by old Dr Gouvea, the family doctor, a man of known severity. But in the end it was necessary for her to appear in the old lady's room in order to receive, as nurse, instructions about the patient's medicine and diet. And one day as she was accompanying the doctor to the door, she froze with fright when she saw him stop, turn towards her and say smiling, as he smoothed down his great white beard, which fell down over his long velvet jacket: 'I was right when I told your mamma that you should marry!'

The tears sprang to her eyes.

'It's all right, it's all right, child, I don't think any worse of you for this. You have been true to nature, who ordered you to conceive, not to marry. Marriage is just an administrative form . . .'

Amelia listened to him without understanding, with large round tears running slowly down her cheeks. He patted her neck very paternally: 'I would like to say that as a naturalist, I rejoice. I think you have fulfilled your destiny as a woman. Now for the important thing.'

He gave her advice as to health and hygiene. 'And when the event arrives, if you are in any difficulty, send for me.'

He turned to go down the stairs, but Amelia, frightened, stopped him and begged: 'Please, senhor doctor, don't tell anyone in the town.'

The doctor stopped: 'Now that is a stupid thing to say. But never mind, I forgive you. It's what I might have expected from you. No, my girl, I won't tell anybody. But why the devil didn't you marry that poor João Eduardo? He would have made you as happy as the other one and you wouldn't have had to beg people for secrecy. Anyway, that is a secondary detail for me: the essential thing is what I've just told you—send for me. Don't depend too much on your saints. I understand more about these matters than St Bridget, or whoever she is. You are strong, and must give a healthy lump of a boy to the state.'

All these words, which she only partly understood, but which she vaguely knew to be true and in which she felt a kindness like that of an indulgent grandparent, and above all that science which promised her health and security, and to which the grizzly beard of the doctor, a beard like God the Father's, gave an air of infallibility, comforted her and increased the serenity that she had enjoyed since her confession in the little chapel at Poyaes.

Ah, it was certainly Our Lady, who at last looking with pity on her torments, had sent her from the skies that inspiration to deliver all her troubles into the hands of Abbot Ferrão! It seemed to her that she had left there, in that dark blue confessional, all her bitterness, all her terrors, the black tatters of remorse which had oppressed her soul. At each one of his consolations, so persuasive, she felt the dark clouds which had been shutting out the sky from her disappear; now she saw nothing but a clear blue; and when she prayed, Our Lady no longer turned away her face, indignant. And the abbot was so different in confession. His method was not to represent God as a rigid, inflexible, ill-tempered being; in his God there was something feminine and maternal which passed through the soul like a caress; and instead of bringing before one's eyes the sinister spectacle of the flames of the inferno, he showed the sky as a vast region of compassion and pity, with the door wide open and innumerable paths leading to the seat of eternal bliss, so easy and so sweet to tread that it was only a very obstinate sinner who would refuse to make the attempt. In that tender interpretation of the other life, God appeared as a kind, smiling grandfather; Our Lady as a sister of charity; the saints as hospitable comrades. It was a religion of love, all bathed in grace, in which one tear shed in sincerity was sufficient for the remission of a life of sin. How different from the sullen doctrines which from childhood had caused her to pass her life in fear and trembling! As different as was that little village chapel from the vast mass of stone masonry of the Cathedral. There, in the old Cathedral, those great thick walls shut out all human and natural life: all inside them was dark, melancholy, penitent, the faces of the statues were severe and forbidding; none of the bright things of this world ever entered there, neither the blue sky above, nor the birds, nor the rich fresh air of the fields, nor the merry laughter of animated lips; the *enxota-caes* was posted there at the door to prevent the little children entering; the few flowers there were artificial; even the sun was exiled, and all the light there was came from the dismal branched candlesticks. And here, in the little chapel in Poyaes, what familiarity there was between nature and the good God! Sweet perfumed air from the wild-woodbine entered the wide-open door; the joyful cry of little children at play echoed through the white-washed walls; the altar was like a combined garden and orchard; daring little sparrows warbled at the very feet of the pedestal bearing the cross; and sometimes a grave bullock poked in his nose with the same familiarity as the bullocks in the stable of Bethlehem, or a wandering sheep came in, rejoicing to see one of his race, the Paschal Lamb, sleeping contentedly at the foot of the altar with the Holy Cross between his feet.

Besides this, the good abbot, as he said himself, didn't expect the impossible. He knew well that to drag up that guilty love, which had dug its roots into the very depths of her being, was not just a moment's work. He only wanted her to seek refuge in the thought of Jesus when thoughts of Amaro assaulted her mind. With the colossal force of Satan, who had the power of a Hercules, a poor girl couldn't fight hand to hand; the only thing she could do when she felt his attack was to take refuge in prayer, and leave him to tire himself out fuming and howling around that impenetrable refuge. Each day, with the care of a nurse, he helped her in the purification of her soul: it was he who pointed out to her, like a prompter in the theatre, the attitude she must adopt on Amaro's first visit to Ricoça; it was he who came to her with a few words of comfort, as a cordial, when he saw her vacillating in her slow reconquest of virtue; if at night she was agitated by memories of her former passionate pleasures, the following day he lectured her familiarly, pointing out to her that the heavens had in store for her much greater joys than those she had experienced in the sexton's dirty room. He proved to her, with the subtleness of a theologian, that the paroco's love for her was nothing but bestiality; and that sweet as was the love of a man, the love of a priest could only be a momentary explosion of suppressed desires. When they began to examine the paroco's letters, he analysed them phrase by phrase, revealing to her all they contained of hypocrisy, egotism, rhetoric and carnal desires.

It was thus that he slowly turned her against the priest. But he taught her to esteem legitimate love, purified by the sacrament; he knew well that she was all woman and full of sexual desires, and that to throw her violently into mysticism would only be to distort for a time the natural instincts, and therefore would not result in a durable peace. He didn't attempt brusquely to uproot her human love, and make her a nun; he desired only that her propensity for love should be directed towards a lawful spouse and the useful harmony of a family, and not wasted here and there in casual affairs. At heart the good Ferrão, with his priestly mind, would certainly have preferred the girl to separate herself absolutely and entirely from all the egotistical interests of individual love, and pass the rest of her life as a sister of charity, or nurse in a charitable institution, and so turn her affections to the broader love of all humanity. But he saw that poor Ameliazinha had a beautiful, weak body, and that it would be unwise to frighten her with the idea of such noble sacrifices. She was a woman, and all woman she must remain; to limit her natural inclinations would be to limit her fulfilment. The mystical idea of Christ with his limbs nailed to the cross would not be sufficient for her; she required an ordinary man with a moustache and a tall hat. Patience! At the least he must arrange for her a legitimate union blessed by the sacrament.

It was thus, by every day directing her thoughts and actions, that he tried to cure her of her morbid passion, and he proceeded with the persistence of a missionary who has a sincere faith in his mission, joining the subtlety of an advocate to the able and paternal morality of a philosopher—a marvellous cure of which the good abbot was secretly a little vain.

And great was his joy when it finally appeared that her passion for Amaro was no longer fiery and active; it was dead, embalmed, packed in the depths of her memory as in a tomb, already hidden under the delicate flowering of a new virtue. Or so thought the good Ferrão—seeing that she could now allude to the past with a tranquil look, without the rush of hot blood which formerly scalded her cheeks at the very mention of Amaro's name.

As a matter of fact, the thought of the senhor paroco didn't disturb her as much as it had done formerly. She had been brusquely separated from the false religion of the *beatas*, which had nurtured her love for Amaro. Free from the terror of nightly fears and the enmity of Our Lady, and under the penetrating influence of the abbot, she succeeded with new peace of mind in reducing her turbulent, fiery passion to a few dying embers. At the beginning the paroco occupied her mind like an enchanting, powerful idol covered with gold: but how many times, since she became pregnant, in her hours of religious terror or in her hysterical fits of repentance, had she shaken up that idol and the little of it that was gold had remained in her hands, and the dark worthless form which was left couldn't dazzle her. It was thus that the abbot had entirely overthrown her passion, without a struggle or a tear on her part. If she still thought of Amaro, it was because she was unable to keep the sexton's house out of her mind; but what now tempted her was the pleasure and not the priest.

And being naturally a good girl, she was sincerely grateful to the abbot. As she had said to Amaro that afternoon, she owed all to him. She had the same feeling towards Dr Gouvea who came regularly every second day to see the old lady. They were her two good friends, like two fathers which the heavens had sent her: one guaranteeing her health and the other, grace.

She took refuge behind these two protectors, and in the last weeks of October enjoyed a kindly peace. The days were serene and warm. It was pleasant to sit on the terrace in the evenings of those calm autumn days. Dr Gouvea and Abbot Ferrão often met there; they appreciated each other. After visiting the old lady, they went on the terrace, and then began their eternal arguments on religion and morality.

Amelia, with her sewing dropped on her knees, listening to her two friends at her side, those two giants of science and of holiness, became lost in the charm of the evening, looking over the fields where the leaves of the trees had already begun to wither. She thought of her future; it now appeared to her secure and without difficulties: she was strong, and the actual birth, with the doctor present, would be just about an hour of pain; afterwards, free from embarrassment, she would return to the town and to mamma. And then another hope, which grew out of the abbot's constant conversations about João Eduardo, danced in her imagination. Why not? If the poor boy still loved her and would pardon her . . . As a man he wasn't repugnant to her, and it would be a splendid marriage now that he had secured the morgado's friendship. It was even said that João Eduardo was going to be made manager of the whole house. And she saw herself living in Poyaes, driving along the road in the morgado's carriage, called to dine by a bell, served by a servant in livery . . . She remained motionless for a long time, lost in the sweetness of that prospective delight, while at the end of the terrace the abbot and doctor disputed over the doctrine of Grace and Conscience, and the irrigation waters in the orchard murmured monotonously.

It was just at this time that Dona Josepha, worried at the paroco's long absence, sent a special message by the caretaker, begging the favour of a visit from him. The fellow returned with the alarming news that the senhor paroco had left for Vieira, and wouldn't return for at least two weeks. The old lady cried with disappointment. And Amelia was unable to sleep that night because of the annoyance she felt at the idea of the senhor paroco diverting himself in Vieira, without a thought of her, chatting with the senhoras on the beach, and going about from one jolly evening party to another.

During the first week of November the rains came. In those short days, as the water poured down from the heavens, Ricoça, under that tempestuous sky, seemed drearier than ever. Abbot Ferrão, laid low with rheumatism, couldn't come. Dr Gouvea, when he'd finished his half-hour visit, trotted away in his little old gig. Amelia's only distraction was to place herself at the window in order to watch João Eduardo pass along the road; she saw him three times, but on catching sight of her he dropped his eyes, or sheltered more under his umbrella.

Dionysia also came frequently. Dr Gouvea had recommended a Michaela, a woman with thirty years' experience, as midwife; but Amelia, fearing to have more people in on her secret, decided to have Dionysia only; and besides this the latter always brought her news of Amaro, which she heard through his servant. The senhor paroco was finding Vieira so good that he had decided to stay there till December. This disgraceful decision filled her with indignation: she had no doubt but that the priest wished to be far away at the time of the anguish and danger of her delivery. Also it had been decided some time before that he would arrange to send the child to a foster-mother at the foot of Ourem, who would bring it up in the village; now the time was drawing near and nothing had been settled definitely with the woman; and the senhor paroco was picking up shells on the seashore!

'It's shameful, Dionysia,' Amelia exclaimed furious.

'Ah! to me it appears very wrong on his part. *I* can't talk to the foster-mother. It's evident that it is very serious. It is the senhor paroco who must take charge of this.'

'It's infamous!'

She had neglected to continue with the making of the baby's clothes —and here she was on the eve of its arrival, without a rag in which to cover it and without money with which to buy them! Dionysia had offered her some for which she had lent a woman money, but Amelia shrunk with horror at the thought of her baby being wrapped in another's clothes, fearing that it might bring disease or ill-luck. Her pride kept her from writing to Amaro.

Also the old lady's ill-humour had become unbearable. Poor Dona Josepha, deprived of the devout help of a priest (a real priest, not an Abbot Ferrão), felt her old soul undefended and exposed to the audacities of Satan: the strange vision which she had had of the naked St Francis Xavier returned with frightening insistence, but now it included all the saints: she saw the whole heavenly court boldly casting off tunics and habits and dancing sarabands in their skin: and the old lady was dying from the importunity of these unholy spectacles, engineered by the devil. She sent for Father Silverio, but it appeared as if rheumatism was attacking all the priests of the diocese, as he also had been in bed with it since the beginning of the winter. The Abbot of Cortegassa, in answer to an urgent message which she sent him, arrived: but it was just to give her a new recipe which he had just discovered on the cooking of Biscayan *bacalhau*. This lack of a virtuous priest threw her into fits of ferocious temper, which caused her to shower abuse on Amelia.

And the good senhora was seriously thinking of sending to Amor for Father Brito—when one evening, just after supper, the senhor paroco appeared unexpectedly.

He arrived looking splendid, burnt brown from the sun and the sea air, with a new coat and patent leather boots. And speaking at length of Vieira, of the acquaintances there, the fish he had caught, the grand games of lotto, he brought a lively breath of the sea wind which seemed to blow right through the melancholy sick room and leave a strong impression of the happy life at Vieira. Dona Josepha's eyelashes were wet with tears from the joy of seeing the senhor paroco again and hearing him speak.

'And your mamma is well,' he said to Amelia. 'She has already had thirty baths. The other day she won fifteen tostões at a chance game which had been arranged. And what have you people been doing?'

Then the old lady broke into bitter complaints. She had been so lonely! The weather was so wet! She had felt the want of her friends so much! Ah! There she was losing her soul in that miserable place . . .

'Well,' said Amaro, crossing his legs, 'I liked it so much there that I'm seriously thinking of returning this week.'

Amelia, who couldn't contain herself, exclaimed:

'Heavens, listen to that! Again!'

'Yes,' he said. 'If the senhor precentor gives me a month's leave, I mean to spend it there. The canon will put up a bed in the dining-room for me, and I can do a little bathing. I am so weary of Leiria, and all its worries.'

The old lady was disconsolate, What, go away again! Leave her there with her terrors and her sorrows!

He replied with a loud laugh.

'The senhoras have no need of me. They have another priest to look after them, one that they like better.'

'I don't know,' said Dona Josepha with acidity, 'if *others*,' she accented the word with rancour, 'don't want the senhor paroco: but I for one am not well suited with the priest here, I'm losing my soul. From the people who come here I derive no benefit, nor do I feel any honour in their visits.'

Amelia hurried to defend the abbot. 'Moreover Senhor Abbot Ferrão has been ill with rheumatism. The house is like a prison without him.'

Dona Josepha gave a laugh of scorn. And Father Amaro, standing up to go, lamented the absence of the good abbot: 'God help him! The poor holy man—I must go and see him when I have time. Well, Dona Josepha, you may expect me again tomorrow, and together we must try to put that soul of yours in peace. Don't trouble to see me out, Menina Amelia, I know the way now.'

But she insisted on accompanying him. They crossed the salon without a word. Amaro put on his new black kid gloves. On arriving at the top of the stairs he raised his hat ceremoniously: 'My dear senhora——'

Amelia became petrified when she saw him calmly descend the stairs—taking as much notice of her as if she were of no more importance than one of those stone lions below, sleeping with its nose between its paws.

She went up to her room and throwing herself face downwards on the bed, sobbed with rage and humiliation. Oh, the shame of it! And not one word about their child, about its foster-mother, or its clothes! Not one look of interest towards her body which he had disfigured by pregnancy! Not one angry complaint when she showed him how much she despised him! Nothing! He just drew on his gloves, pulled his hat to the side and went. What an insult!

The next day he came earlier. He was a long time shut up in the old lady's room.

Amelia, impatient, walked up and down the salon with eyes like burning coals. He appeared in the end, as on the evening before, putting on his kid gloves with a very prosperous air.

'Well then?' she asked in a trembling voice.

'Yes, here I am, my dear senhora. I was giving Dona Josepha a few spiritual instructions.'

He took off his hat, and bowing very low, said: 'My dear senhora——'

Amelia, now livid, murmured: 'Disgusting!'

He looked at her as if thunderstruck: 'My dear senhora,' he repeated. And, as before, he slowly descended the wide stone stairs.

Amelia's first impulse was to denounce him to the vicar general. Afterwards she spent the night writing him a letter of three pages, full of accusations and complaints. But the only reply she had was a verbal message, delivered by Joãozinho of the farm, saying that perhaps he would come on Thursday.

She had another night of tears: while in the Rua das Sousas Father Amaro was rubbing his hands with glee at the success of his famous strategem. And it wasn't really his idea; it had been suggested to him in Vieira, where he had gone to make merry in the company of his master, and to disperse his griefs in the fresh air of the beach; it was there that the famous strategem had come to his mind, one night at a happy gathering, as he was listening to a dissertation on love by the brilliant lawyer Pinheiro, a university first and the pride and glory of his native town of Alcobaça.

'In this, my dear senhoras,' said Pinheiro, smoothing down his hair, long as a poet's, to the semi-circle of senhoras who hung on his golden words, 'in this I am of the same opinion as Lamartine.' (With him it was alternately the opinion of Lamartine or Pelletan.) 'I say with Lamartine: a woman is the same as a shadow: if we run after her she runs away from us; if we run away from her she runs after us!'

Some of the company called out a convincing 'very good'; but one senhora of ample proportions, mother of four delicious angels, all Marias (as Pinheiro used to say), wanted an explanation, because she had never seen a shadow running.

Pinheiro gave her a scientific one: 'It is very easy to observe, my dear Dona Catharina. Place yourself on the beach, with your back to the declining sun, then if you walk forward you pursue your shadow, which always runs on in front of you.'

'A very interesting physical exercise!' murmured the public notary in Amaro's ear.

But the paroco wasn't listening to him; the famous strategem was already dancing in his brain. Ah! as soon as he returned to Leiria he would have to treat Amelia like a shadow and run away from her so that she would follow him. And here now was the delightful result: three pages of passionate declarations, all stained with tears.

He appeared on the Thursday. Amelia was waiting for him on the terrace, from where she had been looking out for him with binoculars since the early morning. She ran to open the little green orchard gate for him.

'So you are here!' said the paroco, walking up behind her to the terrace.

'It's true, I am alone here.'

'Alone?'

'Godmother is sleeping and Gertrude is in town. I've been here all the morning in the sun.'

Amaro went right into the house without answering; he stopped in front of an open door, and looking at the great canopied bed with the big abbatial leather chairs at the side, asked: 'Is this your room?'

'It is.'

He entered familiarly, with his hat still on his head: 'It's much better than the one at the Rua da Misericordia. And a lovely view . . . Is that the morgado's estate over there?'

Amelia shut the door, and going directly to him said with flaming eyes: 'Why didn't you answer my letter?'

He laughed.

'That's a good joke! And why didn't you answer mine? Who began this? It was you. You said that you didn't want to sin any more. Well, I also don't want to sin more. So that finishes the matter.'

'But it's not that!' she exclaimed, pale with indignation. 'It is that you must think of the child, of its foster-mother, of its clothes. You can't abandon me now!'

Affecting a serious air, he said with resentment: 'I beg your pardon. But I pride myself on being a *cavalheiro*. I guarantee that all will be arranged before I return to Vieira.'

'You are not returning to Vieira!'

'No! Who says so?'

'I, it is I who don't want you to go!'

She put her hands forcefully on his shoulders, detaining him, leaning on him, and there, without even noticing the unlocked door, she abandoned herself to him, as before.

Two days later Abbot Ferrão appeared, quite recovered from his attack of rheumatism. He told Amelia of the morgado's generosity, how every day he sent him a chicken cooked with rice, in a special contrivance containing hot water. But it was João Eduardo who had showed him the greatest kindness: every spare hour he had he passed at the side of his bed, reading aloud to him, helping him to turn, remaining with him till one o'clock in the morning, caring for him like a nurse. What a boy!

And suddenly taking both Amelia's hands, he exclaimed: 'Tell me, have I your permission to tell him all? I will ask him to pardon you and forget . . . And if this marriage takes place and you are happy again——'

'It's so sudden—I don't know—I must think . . .' she muttered, blushing furiously.

'Well think. And may God enlighten you!' said the old man fervently.

It was that same night that Amaro had arranged to enter by the little orchard gate, Amelia having given him the key. But unluckily for him, he had forgotten the caretaker's pack of hounds. Amaro no sooner put his foot inside the orchard than the sharp barking of the dogs broke the silence of the dark night. The senhor paroco flew along the road, his teeth chattering with terror.

Chapter XXIII

THE NEXT morning, Amaro had no sooner finished reading his post than he sent a message telling Dionysia to come quickly. But the matron had gone to the market, and therefore didn't turn up till after he had returned from Mass and finished his breakfast.

Amaro wanted to know immediately and for certain, when the event would take place.

'The delivery? Between fifteen and twenty days. Why, is there any fresh news?'

There was; the paroco then read her, in confidence, a letter he had beside him.

It was from the canon, who wrote from Vieira, saying that Senhora Joanneira had already had thirty baths and wished to return! 'I,' he added, 'nearly every week miss three or four baths, with the idea of spreading out the time, because my woman here knows that without my fifty I won't move from Vieira. I've already taken forty, so you see how things are. Besides, it has turned really cold here. Already many people have gone away. Let me know by return of post how things are developing.' And in a postscript he added: 'Have you thought of the destiny of the fruit?'

'Twenty days, more or less,' repeated Dionysia.

Amaro immediately wrote a letter to the canon, for Dionysia to take to the post: 'All will be ready in not more than twenty days. By all the means in your power hold up the return of the mother! Tell her that her little one hasn't written, or gone to see her, because your excellent sister is ill all the time.'

And crossing his legs: 'And now Dionysia, as our canon says, what is to be the destiny of the fruit?'

The matron opened her eyes wide with surprise: 'I thought that you, senhor paroco, had settled all that. I thought you were arranging to have the child brought up at a distance from here.'

'Of course, of course,' interrupted the paroco impatiently. 'If the child is born alive it is evident that we must give him to someone to bring up, and that it must be a person living at some distance from here. But what I want to know is, who is going to be the foster-mother? That is what I want you to arrange for me. Now it is time to see to that.'

Dionysia appeared very embarrassed. She never liked suggesting foster-mothers. She knew a good one, strong, with plenty of milk, a dependable person; but unhappily she had just been taken ill, and had gone to hospital. She also knew of another, in fact she had just had some business with her. She was one Joanna Carreira. But she wouldn't do because she lived in Poyaes at the foot of Ricoça.

'Who wouldn't do!' exclaimed the paroco. 'It doesn't matter about her living near Ricoça. When the girl is better she and Dona Josepha will return to town. That will be the end of Ricoça for them.'

But Dionysia was still considering, slowly scratching her chin. She also knew of another. This one lived near Barrosa, a good distance away. She brought the children up in her house, that was her job . . . but she didn't want to talk of her.

'The woman is weak, ill?'

Dionysia went up close to the paroco and whispered in his ear: 'Ah, my dear young man, I don't like to accuse anybody. But, it has been proved, she is a "weaver of angels"!'

'A what?'

'A "weaver of angels"!'

'What is that? What does that mean?' asked the paroco.

Dionysia stammered out an explanation. They were women who received babies to be brought up in their houses. And without exception the babies died . . . There had been one very well known who had been a weaver, and as the babies went to heaven—that was how the name came into use.

'Then the babies always die?'

'Without fail.'

The paroco walked slowly up and down the room rolling his cigarette.

'Tell me all about it, Dionysia. The women kill them?'

Then the excellent matron declared that she didn't like to accuse anybody! She wasn't a busybody. She didn't know what happened in other people's houses. But all the babies died . . .

'But who would think of giving a baby to a woman like that?'

Dionysia laughed in pity at his innocence. 'They take them there, yes, senhor, by the dozen!'

These was a short silence. The paroco continued his walk from the washbasin to the window, with head bent.

'But what advantage is it to the woman if the children die?' he asked suddenly. 'She loses the money for their keep.'

'The advantage is that she receives a year's money in advance, senhor paroco, reckoned at ten tostões a month, or a quartinho, according to the circumstances.'

311

The paroco, now leaning against the side of the window, drummed slowly on the pane.

'But what do the authorities do, Dionysia?'

The good Dionysia silently shrugged her shoulders.

The paroco then sat down, yawned, and stretching his legs said: 'Just what I expected. I see that the only thing to do is to talk to that woman who lives near Ricoça, Joanna Carreira. I'll arrange that.'

Dionysia then spoke of the baby clothes which she had bought for him, of a very cheap second-hand cradle which she had seen at the carpenter's; and she was just leaving to take the letter to the post, when the paroco got up and laughed scoffingly: 'Oh, Dionysia, that thing about the "weaver of angels"—it's all made up by you, isn't it?'

Then Dionysia was offended: the senhor paroco knew well that she wasn't the kind of woman who made up stories. She had known the 'weaver of angels' for the last eight years, and had seen her in town and spoken with her almost every week. Last Saturday she saw her coming out of Grego's tavern. Had the senhor paroco ever been to Barrosa?

She awaited his reply, and continued: 'Well then, you know the beginning of the townsland. There is a fallen down wall. Then there is a road going down. At the end of this is a little stream and an over-flowing well. In front, standing all alone, is a little house with a porch. That is where she lives: she is called Carlota. This is just to prove to you that I am telling the truth, my friend!'

The paroco stayed indoors the whole morning thinking, walking up and down his room, strewing the floor with cigarette ends. Here he was at last facing that fatal problem, which up to now had just been a distant preoccupation: the disposition of his child.

It would be a serious thing to give it to a woman in the village whom he didn't know. The mother, naturally, would often want to visit it, and the foster-mother might talk to the neighbours. The boy would come to be known as 'the paroco's son'. Some other priest, who was envious of him, or who coveted the parish, might denounce him to the senhor vicar general. Then, a scandal, sermons, enquiries; and if he wasn't suspended, he might be sent far away into the mountains, to live among the shepherds, like poor Brito . . . Ah, if the 'fruit' was stillborn! What a natural and final solution! And what happiness for the child! What future could it have in this hard world? It would be illegitimate, the son of a priest. He was poor, the mother was poor. The boy would grow up in misery, without a proper home, collecting animal droppings for manure, sore-eyed and neglected. Going from one want to another he would experience all forms of human misery in this Vale of Tears: days without bread, freezing nights without a blanket to cover him, the brutality of the tavern, and in the end prison. A pallet of straw during his life, and at death the pauper's grave. And if he died now he would be a little angel whom God would welcome into paradise.

He continued walking sadly up and down his room. Really the name was very apt, 'weaver of angels'. It was true that whoever prepared a baby for life with the milk of the breasts was just preparing it for work and tears. It would be better to twist its neck, and send it directly to heavenly bliss. Look at him! What kind of a life had he had in his thirty years! A dreary infancy in the house of that chatterbox of a Marqueza d'Alegros; and afterwards in that house in Estrela, with his ignorant uncle, fat as a roll of lard: and then the cloistered life of the seminary, the continual snow of Feirão, and there in Leiria, so many worries and troubles. If his skull had been battered in when he was born, he would now be an angel with two white wings, singing in the courts of heaven.

But after all there was nothing to be got from philosophizing: he must go to Poyaes and speak to the foster-mother, Senhora Joanna Carreira.

He went out and slowly walked along the road. At the foot of the bridge, the idea suddenly came to him to go, just for curiosity, to Barrosa, to see the 'weaver of angels'. He wouldn't talk to her: he would just examine the house, the face of the woman, and the sinister aspects of the place. Besides, as paroco, as an ecclesiastical authority, he ought to investigate this seat of criminal practice carried on at the side of the road. It was evidently a profitable trade and allowed to go unpunished. He could denounce it to the senhor vicar general or the civil governor's secretary. He still had time, it was only four o'clock. A horse ride would be very pleasant on that calm bright afternoon. He hesitated no longer, and went to hire a mare at the Inn of the Cross. A short time after, driving hard, he rode straight along in the direction of the Barrosa road.

When he arrived at the sloping road of which Dionysia had spoken, he dismounted and walked along, leading the mare by the reins. It was a delightful afternoon; a large bird leisurely described semicircles high up in the sky.

In the end he came to the overflowing well, at the side of which were two great chestnut trees in which the birds still warbled. In front of him on some flat land was the house with the porch, very isolated: the declining sun beat on the only window at the side, lighting it up with the splendour of burning gold; a very thin line of smoke from the chimney rose into the clear calm air.

A wonderful peace extended all round; on the dark mountain covered with low pines the whitewashed wall of the little chapel of Barrosa stood out bright and gay.

Amaro began to picture to himself the appearance of the 'weaver of angels': without knowing why, he imagined her very tall, with two ugly witches' eyes staring out of a large yellow face.

He tied his mare to the staple in front of the house, and looked in through the open door. The kitchen had an earthen floor, and a great wide hearth; it opened on to a flagged patio full of bundles of grass, into which two young sows were pushing their snouts. The white china shone on the dresser. At the side of the fireplace hung great copper pans, shining brightly, and giving an air of prosperity. In an old cupboard, whose doors were half open, piles of white linen could be seen: and there was so much neatness that a welcome seemed to spring from the cleanliness and orderly appearance of the house.

Amaro then clapped his hands loudly. A dove beat its wings, panting with fright inside its basketwork cage, hanging from the wall. He then called loudly: 'Senhora Carlota!'

Immediately a woman came in from the patio, a sieve in her hand. Amaro, surprised, saw a very pleasant-looking creature of about forty, with a full bosom and broad shoulders, a very white neck, two large hooped earrings hanging from her ears, and black eyes which reminded him of Amelia's, or, when not lit up, of the calmer eyes of Senhora Joanneira.

Astonished, he muttered: 'I believe I've made a mistake. Is it here that Senhora Carlota lives?'

He hadn't made a mistake, it was she; but with the idea that the horrible form that wove the angels must be hidden away in some dreary corner of the house, he asked: 'Do you live alone here?'

The woman looked at him suspiciously, and said in the end: 'No senhor, I live here with my husband.'

Just at that moment the husband came in from the patio. He was repulsive looking, almost a dwarf, with his head, which was buried in his shoulders, wrapped in a kerchief. His yellow face resembled bright oily wax, on his chin were the curly hairs of a miserable black beard, and under the deep forehead, without eyebrows, were two red eyes streaked with blood, heavy from insomnia and drunkenness.

'We are at your service, senhor, if there is anything we can do for you?' he said, keeping very close to his wife's skirts.

Amaro entered the kitchen, muttering a story which he laboriously invented. It was one of his family who was expecting her delivery. The husband couldn't come himself to talk to them, because he was ill. He

314

would like a foster-mother to live in the house with them, and they had said . . .

'No, in someone else's house, no. Here in our house,' said the dwarf, still stuck to his wife's skirts, and looking sideways at the priest with his horrible blood-streaked eyes.

'Ah, then I have been informed wrongly. I'm sorry; but what these people want is someone to live in the house.'

He went out, slowly walking towards his mare: he then stopped and buttoning up his coat, asked: 'But do you take children to bring up in your house?'

'It depends on what the arrangement is,' said the dwarf, who had followed.

Amaro settled the spur, gave a pull to the stirrups, delayed as if undecided, and after walking round the mare turned and asked: 'But would it be necessary to bring the baby here?'

The dwarf turned round, and exchanging a look with his wife, who had remained at the kitchen door, said: 'We could go to fetch it.'

Amaro patted the mare on the neck, and without lifting his head, remarked: 'But if it is at night, and in this cold weather, it would be enough to kill the child.'

Then the two, speaking together, affirmed that it would do the child no harm—provided it was well wrapped up—and that they would take the greatest care with it.

Amaro vigorously spurred his mare, called out a good afternoon and trotted away along the low road.

Amelia now began to go about terrified. Day and night she thought only of those hours of labour which were approaching. She suffered much more than during the first months: she had fits of dizziness, and an ugly taste in her mouth which seemed to poison all her food: all these symptoms Dr Gouvea observed with a grave frown of dissatisfaction. Besides, at night, she was disturbed by bad dreams. Now they were not religious hallucinations: these had immediately ceased on the appeasement of all her pious terrors. Now she had no more fear of God than if she were already a canonized saint. They were other fears, dreams in which her delivery was represented as something frightful: now it was a horrible monster which issued from her womb, half woman and half goat; now it was a poisonous snake which came from her, like an endless ribbon, rolling itself in coils which reached the ceiling: she awoke so troubled and nervous that she lay prostrate, unable to rise.

But, in spite of all her terrors, she was anxious to have the child. She shivered with fear at the idea that her mother might one day appear at Ricoça. She had written to her daughter complaining that the senhor canon was keeping her too long in Vieira; she also spoke of the bad weather there, and the dreariness of the now deserted beach. Besides, Dona Maria of the Assumption had returned; luckily for Amelia, she had taken the journey home on a frosty night and had, according to news received from Dr Gouvea, been in bed for weeks with bronchitis. Libaninho had been to Ricoça, but left disappointed at not having seen Amelia, who was confined to her room with a feigned attack of migraine.

'If this is delayed another few weeks the whole thing will be discovered,' she said whiningly to Amaro.

'Have patience, child, nature can't be forced.'

'Oh how you've made me suffer!' she sobbed, 'how you've made me suffer!'

He remained silent and resigned; he was now very kind to her, very tender. He came to see her almost every morning, but avoided the afternoons as he didn't want to meet Abbot Ferrão.

He calmed her about the foster-mother, saying that he had spoken to the woman at Ricoça recommended by Dionysia. He described her as being as strong as an oak tree with barrels of milk, and teeth white as ivory.

'But she lives so far away that it will be difficult for me to go there often, to see my child,' moaned Amelia.

For the first time she became very enthusiastic about being a mother. She was in despair because she couldn't finish the baby clothes herself. She wanted the boy—because she was sure it would be a boy!—to be called Carlos. She already pictured him a man, a cavalry officer. She thrilled at the thought of seeing him crawl . . .

'Ah, if it wasn't for the shame of it, how I would love to rear him myself!'

'He'll do very well where he is going,' said Amaro.

But what tormented her and made her shed tears every day was the thought that he would be illegitimate.

One day she told the abbot of a wonderful plan with which Our Lady herself had inspired her: it was to marry João Eduardo at once—but first he must sign a paper legally adopting her Carlinhos! In order that the little angel should not be illegitimate, she would even marry a common labourer. She squeezed the abbot's hands in frenzied supplication. She begged him to induce João Eduardo to agree to be a father to Carlinhos! She attempted to kneel down at the feet of the senhor abbot, her friend and protector.

'Oh, my dear senhora, calm yourself, calm yourself. That also is my earnest desire. And we must arrange it so, but later on,' said the good abbot, embarrassed at so much excitement.

A few days later, she had another mania: she suddenly discovered one morning that she mustn't betray Amaro because he was the father of her Carlinhos. She talked so convincingly of her wifely duties towards the paroco that the abbot blushed in spite of his seventy years.

The abbot, who was ignorant of Amaro's visits to her, said reprovingly:

'My dear senhora, what are you saying? What are you saying? You are forgetting yourself . . . How shameful! I thought you had finished with all that madness.'

'But he is the father of my child, senhor abbot,' she said, looking very seriously at him.

For a whole week she wearied Amaro with puerile tenderness, reminding him every half hour that he was the father of her Carlinhos.

'I know that, I know that, my girl,' he said in the end, impatiently. 'Thank you, but I don't need to boast of the honour.'

At that she cried, curling herself up on the sofa. A whole series of caresses were necessary to calm her. She made him bring a little stool and sit by her side; she kept him there like a doll, contemplating him, slowly scratching his tonsure, she wished him to have a little photo taken of Carlinhos so that both of them could wear it round their necks; and if she died, he must bring Carlinhos to the grave, make him kneel down, join his little hands together, and make him pray for mamma. She then drew him down beside her on the pillow and patting his face said: 'May God help me and my poor little child!'

'Keep quiet, there's somebody coming!' said Amaro furious.

Ah, those morning in Ricoça! He looked on them as an unjust penance. When he entered the house he had to go and see the old lady and listen to her complaints. Afterwards there was that hour with Amelia, who tortured him with her fits of sentimental hysteria—stretched on the sofa, big as a barrel, her face all puffed out, her eyes bulging.

One of these mornings, as Amelia was complaining of cramp, he took her arm and walked her up and down the room; she dragged her feet along, looking enormous in her old dressing-gown. They suddenly rushed to the window as they heard the trot of a horse coming along the road; but Amaro drew back quickly, leaving Amelia gazing out with her face pasted against the glass. In the road, gracefully mounted on a bay mare, passed João Eduardo in a white coat and high hat; at his side trotted his two little pupils, one on a pony, and the other strapped on a donkey; and behind, at the distance prescribed by courtesy and respect, a servant in uniform, with high boots and enormous spurs. His livery, being much too big for him, bulged in grotesque folds at the sides; he had a scarlet rosette in his hat. She stood there impressed with the grand show, following them with her eyes till the lackey's back disappeared round the corner of the house. Without uttering a word she came and sat down on the sofa. Amaro, who continued walking up and down the room, said with a sarcastic little laugh: 'The idiot, with his lackey as a rearguard!'

She became very red, but didn't reply. And Amaro disgustedly left the room, slamming the door, to go and tell Dona Josepha about the stupid procession and to revile the morgado.

'An excommunicated man with a servant in livery!' exclaimed the good senhora, pressing her head between her hands. 'What a disgrace, senhor paroco, what a disgrace for the nobility of these times!'

From that day on, Amelia didn't cry when the senhor paroco missed a morning in coming to see her. She now waited with impatience for the visit of Senhor Abbot Ferrão, in the afternoon. She took possession of him, making him sit on a chair by the side of the sofa; and then like a bird slowly encompassing its prey, she led up in devious ways to the fatal question—had he seen João Eduardo.

She wanted to know what he had said, if he had spoken of her, if he had seen her at the window. She pestered him with questions about the morgado's house, the furniture of the salon, the number of lackeys and horses, if a servant in livery served at the table.

And the good abbot patiently satisfied her curiosity, happy to see her forgetting the paroco and occupying her mind with João Eduardo; he now felt sure that he would be able to bring about the marriage; she avoided all mention of Amaro, and once when the abbot asked if the senhor paroco still came to Ricoça, she replied: 'Yes, he comes every morning to see godmother. I don't appear as I'm in this indecent state.'

All the time she was not lying down she spent at the window, very neat and well arranged from the waist up—as that was all of her that could be seen from the road—and very untidy and rumpled from the waist down. She was waiting for João Eduardo, his pupils and the lackey; and from time to time she had the joy of seeing them pass to the measured steps of the thoroughbred horse, above all João Eduardo on his bay mare, worth a fortune. As he passed Ricoça, he made the mare trot, while he rode with his whip held horizontally and his legs á Marialva, as the morgado had taught him. But it was the lackey above all who enchanted her: with her nose to the window pane, her eyes greedily devoured him, until the poor old man, with his back bent, the collar of his coat dropping down to the nape of his neck and his legs shaking, disappeared round a bend in the road.

And how delicious for João Eduardo were those rides on his bay mare with the morgado's sons. He never failed to go through the town: the sound of the horses' shoes on the flagstones made his heart throb with pleasure: he passed in front of the apothecary's Amparo, in front of his old office, where Nunes looked out at him from his desk, placed near the window; he passed in front of the arcade and in front of the senhor administrator, who was there on the veranda with his binoculars fixed on the house of Telles; and his only disappointment was that he and his bay mare, the morgado's sons, and the lackey, couldn't ride right through to Dr Godinho's writing-room which was at the back of the house.

One day after one of these triumphant rides, about two o'clock in the afternoon, he was returning from Barrosa. Having arrived at the well he turned to go into the main road, when he suddenly caught sight of Father Amaro going down the cart track on a mean-looking nag. João Eduardo immediately wheeled his mare back on to the cart track, which was so narrow that in spite of the fact that they were both scraping against the hedge, their knees rubbed as they passed one another. Then João Eduardo, menacingly flicking his whip from the height of his precious mare, worth fifty moedas, could look down disdainfully on Father Amaro who ferociously spurred on his slow-going beast. At the top of the road, João Eduardo stopped and turning round in his saddle saw the paroco dismount at the isolated house, where a short time before the morgado's children, as they passed, had laughed at the dwarf.

'Who lives there?' João Eduardo asked the lackey.

'One Carlota. Bad people, Senhor Joãozinho!'

On passing Ricoça João Eduardo, as always, slowed down his bay mare. But he didn't see the pale face beneath the scarlet kerchief on the other side of the window. The blinds were half down; and at the gate, with the handles in the earth, was Dr Gouvea's gig.

The day had arrived at last. That morning one of the farm boys of Ricoça delivered an almost unintelligible note from Amelia to Amaro saying: 'Dionysia at once, the thing is arriving!' He was also ordered to call Dr Gouvea. Amaro went himself to give the message to Dionysia.

A few days before, he had told her that Dona Josepha herself had suggested a foster-mother, and that he had settled with her, a fine woman, strong as a chestnut tree. And now they quickly arranged that

319

that same night Amaro would wait at the little orchard gate with the foster-mother, and that Dionysia would bring him the baby well wrapped up.

'At nine o'clock tonight, Dionysia. And don't keep us waiting!' urged Amaro, as he watched her bustling about getting ready to depart.

Afterwards he returned home and locked himself into his room, to be alone face to face with his dilemma, which he felt was something definite staring at him, questioning him: what was he to do with the baby? There was still time for him to go to Poyaes and settle things with the other foster-mother, the good foster-mother, whom Dionysia knew; or he could hire a mare and go to Barrosa to arrange the matter with Carlota . . . And there he was, in an agony of indecision about those two roads in front of him. He wanted to get the thing clear in his mind, to discuss the case as if it were a point of theology, weighing the pros and the cons: but instead of two arguments, his mind audaciously forced two pictures before his eyes: the child growing up and living in Poyaes, or the child strangled by Carlota, in a corner of the Barrosa road.

And as he was walking up and down in his room, sweating with anguish, Libaninho's voice piped from the stairhead: 'Ah dear friend paroco, open the door, I know you are at home!'

He could do nothing but let Libaninho enter, shake hands with him, offer him a chair. But luckily Libaninho was in a hurry. He was just passing, and called in to know if his friend had any news of those two saints in Ricoça.

'They are very well, very well,' said Amaro, forcing himself to smile and look pleasant.

'I couldn't go there, as I've been so busy! I've been called up as a soldier. Don't laugh, my friend, I'm doing a great deal of good there. I go amongst the soldiers and talk to them of Christ's wounds.'

'I suppose you are going to convert the whole regiment,' said Amaro, nervously pushing the papers on his table, feeling like a wild animal caught in a trap.

'It won't be for want of trying on my part, senhor paroco, if I don't. Look, here are some scapulars that I am taking to one of the sergeants. They were blessed by Father Saldanha, they are full of grace. Yesterday I gave similar ones to a lance-corporal, a perfect boy, a love of a boy. I myself put them under his vest—a perfect boy!'

'You should leave all these cares to the colonel of the regiment,' said Amaro opening the window, smothering with impatience.

'Heavens, that unbeliever! If I left things to him he'd unbaptize the whole regiment. Well good-bye, friend. You are so yellow, man! You are in need of a purgative, I know how it feels to be like that.'

He turned to go out, but stopped as he reached the door: 'Ah, tell me, friend, tell me: have you heard anything?'

'Of what?'

'It was Father Saldanha who told me. He said that our precentor declared (the exact words of Saldanha) that it is evident there is a scandal going on about one of the clergymen of the parish. But he didn't say who it was or what was its nature. Saldanha tried to sound him, but the precentor said he had only received a vague complaint, no name being mentioned. Who do you think it is?'

'Ah, it's Saldanha's idle talk.'

'Ah, friend! with the help of God it is only talk. Wouldn't our enemies be pleased if it were true? When you go to Ricoça remember me to those two saintly women.'

He leapt down the stairs, rushing to bring grace to the battalion.

Amaro was terrified. It was surely he. The story of his infatuation for Amelia had reached the ears of the vicar general in some roundabout way. And now there would be that child, brought up a few miles from the town, another living proof of his guilt! It appeared to him extraordinary, almost supernatural, that Libaninho, who had only visited him twice in the last two years, should appear with such terrible news, and just at the very moment when he was battling with his conscience. It was as if Providence, under the grotesque form of Libaninho, came to warn him, to murmur: 'Don't allow the creature to live—it will be the means of your disgrace! You are already under suspicion!'

It was certain that God, through pity, didn't want another bastard, another unfortunate in the world—and that instead He wished to claim His angel.

He hesitated no longer: he left for the Inn of the Cross stables and from there hired a mare and rode to Carlota's house.

He left the place at four o'clock.

When he returned home he threw his hat on the bed, and felt relieved in all his being. It was finished now! He had spoken to Carlota and the dwarf; he had paid a year in advance; now he just had to wait for the night . . .

But in the loneliness of his room all kinds of morbid imaginings began to assault his mind: he saw Carlota strangling the baby until it was purple in the face; he saw the police arriving later to order the disinterment of the body, then Domingos of the administration with a book on his knee, writing an account of the crime, and he, in his cassock, dragged to the San Francisco prison, in irons, beside the dwarf.

He had an urge to mount a horse, return to Barrosa, and undo all the arrangements. But a feeling of inertia detained him. After all, he thought, there was nothing to force him to give the child to Carlota. He could take it, well wrapped up, to Joanna Carreira, that good woman of Poyaes.

In order to escape from the thoughts which were tormenting his brain, he went to see Natario who had now risen from his bed. Immediately he appeared Natario roared from the depths of his armchair: 'Have you seen him, Amaro? The idiot, with the lackey following up the rear!'

From the time that João Eduardo had begun to ride round the town on his bay mare with the morgado's sons, Natario had been mad with impatience at the thought of being tied there to the chair and unable to continue his campaign against his enemy, to drive him, by a bit of trickery, from the house of the morgado, and deprive him of his mare and lackey.

'But I'll still do it, if God only restores to me the use of my leg . . .'

'Leave the man alone, Natario,' said Amaro.

'Leave him alone! When I have a magnificent idea! I'm going to prove to the morgado that João Eduardo was a religious fanatic! What do you think of it, friend Amaro? I have documents to prove it.'

Yes, he thought it would be a delightful way of getting at the fellow, who well deserved it, if only for the impudent way that he surveyed decent people from the top of his mare. Amaro reddened, still feeling indignant as he thought of the meeting that morning in the cart track at Barrosa.

'It's plain!' exclaimed Natario. 'Why are we priests of Christ? To raise up the humble and pull down the mighty from their seats.'

From there Amaro went to see Dona Maria of the Assumption who was also recovering. She told him the story of her bronchitis, and enumerated her latest sins: her worst being that in order to distract herself a little during her convalescence, she had had her couch moved near the window, and a carpenter who lived in front had stared at her; and because of the influence of evil spirits, she was unable to drag herself away from the window and immoral thoughts had come into her mind . . .

'But you are not giving me your attention, senhor paroco.'

'What a thing to say, my dear senhora!'

He busied himself pacifying her scruples: for the salvation of the idiotic soul of that old lady brought him more profit than all the rest of the parish.

It was already dark when he arrived home. Escolastica grumbled about him being late, the dinner was all burnt. But Amaro only took a glass of wine and a forkful of rice, and gulped it down standing, looking out of the window and dreading the night which was relentlessly approaching.

As he entered the parlour to see if the street lamps were yet alight, the coadjutor appeared. He came to talk about the Baptism of Guedes' son, which had been fixed for the next morning at nine.

'Shall I bring a light?' the servant called out from inside, as soon as she heard the visitor.

'No!' Amaro shouted immediately.

He was afraid that the coadjutor would notice the lividness of his face, or that he might install himself there for the evening.

'They say there was a very good article in *The Nation* of the day before yesterday,' observed the coadjutor gravely.

'Ah!' said Amaro.

He took up his customary walk from the washbasin to the window, stopping every now and then to drum on the pane; the street lanterns were now alight.

Then the coadjutor, offended at the dark room and that eternal pacing like a wild beast in a cage, got up and said with dignity: 'Perhaps I am in the way.'

'No!'

The coadjutor satisfied, again sat down, with his umbrella between his knees.

'It gets darker earlier now,' he said.

'It does . . .'

In the end Amaro got desperate and said he had a terrible headache, and would go and lie down; and his visitor left, after reminding him of the Baptism of his friend Guedes' baby.

Amaro left immediately for Ricoça. Luckily the night was dark and warm, though threatening rain. He now had a hope which made his heart beat furiously: it was that the baby would be born dead! And it was quite possible. When Senhora Joanneira was young she had two stillborn children; and the excitement in which Amelia had lived must have affected the pregnancy. And if she also died? Then that idea, which had never before occurred to him, suddenly filled him with pity and tenderness for the beautiful girl who loved him so much, and who now, on account of him, was screaming out with the pains which were tearing her body. And yet, if both died, his sin and the fruits of his sin would be buried forever in the dark abyss of eternity . . . He would again become the tranquil man he had been before he came to Leiria, occupied with his parochial duties, passing a life now washed and clean as a white page.

He stopped in front of the broken-down cottage at the side of the road, where the person who was to take the baby from him would be waiting: he didn't know if it would be the man or Carlota; and a feeling of dread came to Amaro at the thought that it might be the dwarf, with those wicked eyes streaked with blood. He shouted into the darkness of the house: 'Hello!'

It was a relief when the clear voice of Carlota answered: 'I'm here!'

'Good, wait there, Senhora Carlota.'

He felt happier: it seemed to him that he had nothing to fear if he left his child nestling against that ample, fecund bosom of forty years, so clean and fresh.

He then went and walked round Ricoça. The whole house was silent, invaded with layer upon layer of the thick darkness of that sad December night. Not a vestige of light issued from Amelia's room. Not a leaf rustled in the heavy air. And Dionysia didn't appear.

The waiting tortured him. Someone might pass and see him on the road. But he found the idea of going to hide in the broken-down cottage with Carlota repugnant. He was walking along the side of the orchard wall, when he turned and saw a light shining through the glass door of the terrace.

He ran at once to the little green gate, which opened almost immediately; and Dionysia, without a word, put a bundle in his arms.

'Is it dead?' he asked.

'Dead? Alive! A fine lump of a boy!'

She slowly closed the gate, at which the dogs, hearing the noise, suddenly began to bark.

The contact of his child against his breast dispelled all Amaro's ideas like a strong wind. What! go and give his son to that woman, that 'weaver of angels', for her to throw him down a ditch, or to take him to her house and drop him into the cesspool? Ah! no, he was his son!

But what then was he going to do? There wasn't time to go to Poyaes and arrange with the other foster-mother—Dionysia had no milk—it was impossible for him to take the baby to town. Oh! what a passionate desire he had to smash down the door of the house, run to Amelia's room, put the infant in the bed, all well wrapped up, and have all three remain there, under the shelter of heaven! But no, he was a priest! Cursed be the religion which so crushed him!

A little whine came from the bundle on his arm. He ran to the broken-down cottage and almost knocked into Carlota, who immediately took possession of the child.

'Yes, here he is,' he said. 'But look here. Now it is serious. Everything is changed, I don't want him to be killed. He is to be brought up.

The arrangement we made before doesn't hold now, he must be brought up! He must live. You have a fortune here. Treat him well!'

'Without a doubt, without a doubt,' said the woman, anxious to get away.

'Listen—the child hasn't enough clothes on him. Wrap my coat round him.'

'He's all right, senhor, he's all right.'

'To the devil with you, he's not all right! He is my son! He must have the coat round him! I don't want him to die of cold!'

He dragged the baby from her, and resting him on his chest folded the cloak around him; then the woman, already very impatient, seized the child and hurried down the road with him.

Amaro stood there motionless in the middle of the road, gazing after the bundle till it disappeared in the blackness of the night. Then, the crisis over, all his nerves relaxed and like a weak, sensitive woman, he broke down and cried.

He stayed a long time walking round the house. But all remained in the same obscurity, in the same terrifying silence. Afterwards, sad and weary, he returned to the town. He reached his house just as the Cathedral clock was striking ten.

At that same hour in the dining-room at Ricoça Dr Gouvea, after the heavy labours of his day, was tranquilly eating the roast chicken which Gertrude had prepared for him. Abbot Ferrão was also there, sitting near the table; he had come provided with the sacraments, in case any danger should arise. But the doctor was satisfied: during eight hours of labour the girl had shown great courage; the delivery had passed off well, and she had brought forth a beautiful boy of whom its father could be proud.

The good Abbot Ferrão with priestly modesty cast down his eyes during the recital of these details.

'And now,' said the doctor, cutting the meat off the breastbone of the chicken, 'now that I have introduced the child into the world, you senhores (and when I say you senhores, I mean the Church), take possession of him and don't let him out of your hands till death takes him. On the other side, though not quite so voraciously, the State never loses sight of him: and so the poor unfortunate passes his life from the cradle to the grave, between the priest and the police.'

The abbot leant forward and noisily took a pinch of snuff, in preparation for the controversy.

'The Church,' continued the doctor serenely, 'begins before the poor little creature knows that he is alive, to impose religion on him . . .'

The abbot interrupted him, half serious, half laughing: 'Oh, doctor, I would like to remind you, even though it is only in pity for your soul, that the Holy Council of Trent, Canon XIII, lays the penalty of excommunication on anyone who says that Baptism, when it is imposed before the recipient has arrived at the use of reason, is null and void.'

'Take note, abbot: I, and others who think as I do, are used to all that sweet talk of the Council of Trent.'

'It was an honourable assembly!' the abbot interrupted, already scandalized.

'A sublime assembly, abbot, absolutely sublime. The Council of Trent and the Convention were the two most prodigious assemblies that the world has ever witnessed.'

The abbot made a face of repugnance at the irreverent comparison between the holy authorities on doctrine and the assassins of the good king Louis XVI.

But the doctor proceeded: 'Afterwards, the Church leaves the child in peace for a little time, while he is teething and going through his attack of worms . . .'

'Go on, go on, doctor!' murmured the abbot, listening patiently, with his eyes closed; as much as to say: 'Go on, go on and bury that soul of yours in fire and darkness!'

'But when he shows the very first signs of reason,' continued the doctor, 'when it is necessary, in order to be distinguished from the animals, for him to have some notion of himself and of the universe, then the Church enters and explains all! All! So completely, that a little imp of six, who doesn't yet know his A.B.C., has a science, vaster and more conclusive than the scientists of London, Berlin and Paris put together. The crafty villains don't hesitate one moment in telling him how the universe and the planetary systems came into being; how man and the animals appeared on the earth; how the different races came about; how the geological revolutions proceeded; how the different languages were formed; how writing was invented . . . He knows all: he has a complete and immutable rule with which to direct all his actions and form all his judgments; he has even the certainty of all the mysteries; even though he be as blind as a bat he can see all that passes in the profundity of the skies and in the interior of the globe; he knows, as well as if he had been present at the spectacle, what will happen after death. There is no problem which has not been decided for him. And when the Church has filled the little monkey with wisdom, she sends him to learn how to read. What I would like to ask is: why?'

The abbot was speechless with indignation.

'Tell me now, abbot, why do you senhores send him to learn to read? The whole science of the world, *res scibilis*, is in the Catechism; and memorizing it, the boy has the science and conscience of all things. He knows as much as God . . . In fact, he is God himself.'

The abbot jumped.

'This is not discussing,' he exclaimed, 'this is not discussing! These are only taunts from Voltaire! These things should be treated with more respect.'

'Why taunts, abbot? Let us take an example: the formation of languages. How are they formed? It was God who, angry at the Tower of Babel——'

But the door of the dining-room opened, and Dionysia appeared. A short time before, in Amelia's room, the doctor had reprimanded her sharply, and now the matron spoke, shrivelled up with fright.

'Senhor doctor,' she said, in the silence which her appearance had caused, 'Menina Amelia has awakened and says that she wants her baby.'

'They have taken the child away, haven't they?'

'Yes, the child has been taken away,' said Dionysia.

'All right, that's enough.'

She turned to shut the door, but the doctor called to her: 'Look here, tell her that we'll bring her baby back tomorrow. That tomorrow she will have him without fail. Lie. Lie like a Trojan; the senhor abbot here will give you permission. She must be kept calm, she must sleep.'

Dionysia left. But the controversy wasn't resumed immediately: faced by the mother who had returned to consciousness after the fatigues of her labour and called for her child, the child that they had taken far away forever, the two old men forgot the Tower of Babel and the formation of languages. The abbot, especially, seemed very moved. But the doctor, remembering that these were the consequences of the situation of the priest in society, continued without pity.

The abbot lowered his eyes, busied himself with his snuff, and remained silent, as if in these sad circumstances he wanted to ignore the fact that there was a priest mixed up in the business.

The doctor then, following up his idea, talked against the preparation for and education of the priesthood.

'Here, abbot, we have an education entirely dominated by the absurd: resistance against the most just demands of nature, and resistance to the most elevated powers of reason. To prepare a priest in this way is to create an abortion, who must pass his unfortunate existence in a desperate battle against the two most irresistible forces of the universe: the force of Matter and the force of Reason!'

'Whatever are you saying?' exclaimed the abbot astounded.

327

'I am speaking the truth. In what does the education of a priest consist? First: in preparing him for celibacy and virginity; that is, for the violent suppression of his most natural feelings. Secondly: in seeing that all knowledge and ideas which might shake his faith in the Catholic religion are kept from him; that is, the forced suppression of the spirit of investigation and of criticism, with regard to all science both physical and metaphysical.'

The abbot sprang up, stung with pious indignation: 'Then you, senhor, deny the science of the Church.'

'Jesus, my dear abbot,' the doctor calmly went on, 'Jesus, and His first disciples and the illustrious St Paul, represented in parables, in epistles, with a prodigious flow of words, that the products of the human spirit were useless, peurile, and even pernicious . . .'

The abbot rushed up and down the room like a pricked bull, knocking against the furniture, pressing his hands against his head in desolation at those terrible blasphemies; not being able to contain himself, he shouted: 'You don't know what you are saying! Pardon, doctor, I humbly ask your pardon. You, senhor, almost made me commit a mortal sin. But this is not discussing: this is talking with the levity of a journalist.'

He then gave a heated dissertation on the learned men whom the Church had produced, its great Latin and Greek scholars, and all the philosophy created by the Holy Fathers through the ages.

'Read St Basil!' he exclaimed. 'There you will see what he says of the works of profane authors, the study of which is the best preparation for the study of the sacred works. Read *The History of the Monasteries in the Middle Ages*! It is there that you will find science and philosophy.'

'But what philosophy, what science, senhor! For philosophy you have half a dozen conceptions in a mythological spirit, in which mysticism is substituted for social instincts. And what science! The science of the commentator, the science of the grammarian. In later times new sciences were born of which the ancients had been ignorant, and for which the ecclesiastical teaching offered neither base nor method; instead it established immediately an antagonism between them and Catholic doctrine. In the early days of science the Church tried to suppress it by persecution with fire and the dungeon! You needn't wriggle, abbot. Fire, yes, fire, and the dungeon. But now that that is impossible you oppose it with vituperations and bad Latin. And all the time in your seminaries and your schools you continue with your old-fashioned education, the education of the times before science, which you ignore, which you despise, taking refuge in your scholastic divinity. I'll thank you not to press your hands on your head. You disapprove of all modern ideas, in their principles and methods, you are hostile to the spontaneous development of human knowledge. You, senhor, cannot have the face to deny this! Look at the Syllabus in its Canon III actually excommunicating Reason—and in its Canon XIII——'

The door was opened timidly; it was Dionysia again.

'The girl is sobbing, she says that she wants her baby.'

'Bad, bad!' said the doctor.

And after a minute's thought: 'How does she look? Is she flushed? Is she agitated?'

'No, senhor, she is well. But she is crying, and all the time talking of her baby. She says that she must have him today, she insists on that.'

'Talk to her, distract her. See if you can get her to sleep.'

Dionysia retired; and the abbot said anxiously: 'If she is so troubled, doctor, could it do her harm?'

'It could do her harm, abbot, it could,' said the doctor as he went to look in his medicine bag. 'But I'm going to give her something to make her sleep. Now it is true, the Church of today is an intrusion, a fraud, abbot!'

The abbot again put his hands up to his head.

'We needn't go any further than here for an example. Now look at the Church in Portugal. It is encouraging to watch its state of decadence.'

He stood up on tiptoe and waved largely round the room with the flask in his hand. 'Formerly the Church was the nation; today it is just a small minority tolerated and protected by the State. It used to dominate in the law-courts, in the councils of the crown, in the disputes of the peasantry, on the seas; it made wars and dictated peace; today a deputy of the government has more power than all the clergy in the kingdom. At one time it was the master of all the learning in the country; today all that it knows is a little dog-Latin. It was rich, possessing entire districts in the country and whole streets in the town, today it depends for its miserable daily bread on the minister of justice, and begs for alms outside its chapels. Its members were at one time recruited from amongst the nobility and the most important people in the realm; today in order to keep up its numbers, it must go in shame to look for boys to train for the priesthood, amongst the abandoned children of the Misericordia. It was the depository of the traditions of the nation, of the united ideal of the country; and today, without communication with the national thought (if such a thing exists) it is a stranger in the land, a citizen of Rome, from whom it receives its law and its spirit.'

'Well, if it is as you say, so prostrated, it is another reason for loving it more!' said the abbot, as he sprang up with his face blazing.

But Dionysia appeared once more.

'What's wrong now?' said the doctor.

'Menina Amelia is complaining of a weight on her head. She says there are flames dancing in front of her eyes . . .'

The doctor then, without a word, followed Dionysia. The abbot, now alone, walked up and down the room ruminating on bristling arguments which he could prove with texts, and the words of the most famous theologians, with which he would confound the doctor. But half an hour passed, the candle had burnt down to its socket, and the doctor didn't return.

Then the ominous silence of the house, where the only living sound seemed to be the noise of his steps on the boards as he walked up and down the room, began to affect the old man. He slowly opened the door and listened; but Amelia's room was at the other end of the house, where the terrace was; and not a stir, not a vestige of light came from there. He again took up his lonely walk around the room, feeling an indefinite sadness taking possession of his mind. He also wanted to go and see the patient; but his character, his priestly office prevented him approaching the bed of a woman in or after childbirth, unless she was in danger of death and in need of the sacraments. Another longer and drearier hour passed. Then, creeping along on tiptoe, and blushing in the darkness at his own audacity, he walked to the middle of the corridor: he was terrified to hear a confused, soft noise of feet moving excitedly on the floor as if in a struggle. But not a sigh, not a moan. He stole back to the dining-room, and opening his breviary began to pray. He heard the sound of Gertrude's carpet slippers as she ran quickly to get something. A distant door banged. Then a tin water jug was dragged across the floor. At last the doctor rushed in.

At his appearance the abbot turned pale with shock: his tie was missing, his shirt collar was torn; his waistcoat had no buttons; the turned cuffs of his shirt sleeves were all splashed with blood.

'What is the matter, doctor?'

The doctor, with his face glowing from the heat of the battle, picked up his case of instruments without answering, but as he turned to leave the room he remembered the anxious question of the abbot: 'She has convulsions,' he said.

The abbot then stopped him at the door, and very grave, very dignified, requested: 'Doctor, if the patient is in danger, I beg of you to remember me. It is the soul of a Christian in agony, and I am here.'

'Certainly, certainly . . .'

The abbot was again alone, waiting. All were sleeping in Ricoça,

330

Dona Josepha, the caretaker and his family, the farm, all the country around. In the dining-room, the wall wagger, enormous and sinister, with its dial plate a hideous face representing the sun, and the sculptured figure of a pensive owl over its case, struck midnight; then one o'clock. Every few minutes the abbot stole halfway down the corridor: it was the same sound of feet crossing and recrossing the room in a struggle, followed by a frightening silence. He took refuge in his breviary, meditating on this poor girl, who there in that room was perhaps approaching the moment in which eternity would be decided for her: without her mother, without her friends; the vision of her sin must be passing through her terrified memory: before those eyes, already growing dim, would appear the sad face of her offended God: her poor miserable body would be wracked with pain: and in the darkness, which was already falling on her, she would feel the hot breath of Satan. How fearful was the end of time and the end of the flesh. He then prayed fervently for her.

But then he thought of the other, who was responsible for half her sin, and who now in the town was stretched on his bed, snoring tranquilly. And he also prayed for him.

He had a small crucifix laid on his breviary. And contemplating it with love, he became tenderly sunk in the certainty of its power against which all the science of which the doctor had spoken, and the vanities of reason, were as nothing! Philosophies, ideas, earthly glories, generations and empires passed: they were as the ephemeral sighs of human passion; the only thing which had lasted and would last was the cross: the hope of man, the trust of the desperate, the support of the weak, the refuge of the vanquished, the greatest force of humanity, *crux triumphus adversus demonios, crux oppugnatorum murus* . . .

Then the doctor entered, very flushed, and trembling from the violent battle which he was having with death; he had come to look for another flask; but without saying a word he opened the window in order to feel for a minute a gush of fresh air against his face.

'How is she?' asked the abbot.

'Bad,' said the doctor, going out.

The abbot then fell on his knees, and muttered the prayer to St Fulgencio: 'Senhor, give her above all patience in her suffering, and afterwards pity.'

He remained there, leaning on the edge of the table, with his face in his hands.

At the sound of steps in the room he turned his head. It was Dionysia, sighing deeply as she gathered up all the napkins which she found in the drawer of the sideboard.

'What's the news, senhora, what's the news?' asked the abbot.

'Ah, senhor abbot, she is lost. After the convulsions, which were horrifying, she fell into that sleep, which is the sleep of death . . .'

Then looking round into all the corners to make sure that they were alone, she whispered excitedly: 'I didn't like to say anything—you know that the senhor doctor had a fearful temper! But to bleed a girl in that condition is to kill her. It's true she only lost a little blood . . . But a woman should never be bled under those circumstances. Never, never!'

'But the senhor doctor is a very clever man!'

'He may be as clever as you like, I also am no fool. I have twenty years of experience. No one ever died under my hands, senhor abbot. Heavens, to bleed in convulsions! It's shocking!'

She was indignant. The senhor doctor had tortured the poor creature. He had even tried to give her chloroform . . .

But Dr Gouvea bawled for her from the end of the corridor, and the matron ran off, her bundle of napkins in her hand.

The hideous clock, with its pensive owl, struck two, then three . . . The abbot then, slowly succumbing to the fatigues of age, closed his eyes for a moment. Then brusquely resisting, he went near the window to get a breath of the heavy night air, gazed a minute at the dark sleeping village; and returned to his seat, murmuring, with head bent and hands placed on his breviary:

'Senhor, turn Thine eyes of pity towards that bed of agony . . .'

It was then that Gertrude appeared, very agitated. The senhor doctor had sent her down to wake up the boy and tell him to tackle the horse to the gig.

'Oh, senhor abbot, the poor creature! She was doing so well, and then this suddenly happens! It was all because they took her baby from her. I don't know who is the father, but what I do know is that it is a sin and a crime!'

The abbot didn't reply, he was muttering a prayer for Father Amaro.

The doctor then entered with his case in his hand: 'You can go in now if you like, abbot,' he said.

But the abbot didn't hurry, he stared at the doctor with a question dancing on his half-opened lips, and then said timidly: 'You have done all, is there no other remedy, doctor?'

'None.'

'We, doctor, we are forbidden to approach the bed of a woman who has brought an illegitimate child into the world, unless she is in her last extremity.'

'It is her last extremity, senhor abbot,' said the doctor, as he buttoned up his greatcoat.

The abbot then gathered up his breviary and his cross; but before he left, thinking it was his duty as a priest to put before the doctor, this rationalist and man of science, the certainty of the eternal mystery, which was revealed at the hour of death, he murmured: 'It is in this moment that one feels the terror of God, the vanity of human pride . . .'

The doctor, who was busy fastening his case, didn't reply.

The abbot then went out, but on reaching the middle of the corridor he returned, and said in a very disturbed tone: 'Oh, excuse me, doctor —but I know you have often seen that after the aids of religion, the dying, on receiving special grace, recover. The presence of the doctor may then be useful.'

'I'm not going yet, I'm not going yet,' said the doctor, smiling in spite of himself, at seeing the presence of Medicine called to aid the efficacy of Grace.

He went down to see if his gig was ready.

When he returned to Amelia's room, Dionysia and Gertrude were sprawling on the floor at the side of the bed, praying. The bed itself, the whole room, had been turned into a field of battle. The two candles were burnt to their sockets, Amelia was motionless, with her arms lying stiff at her side, her shrunken hands a dark purple—and the same colour, though redder, covered her rigid face.

And leaning over her, with the crucifix in his hand, the abbot was crying out in a voice of anguish:

'Jesus, Jesus, Jesus! My child, think of the grace of God! Have faith in the divine mercy! Repent on the bosom of Our Lord! Jesus, Jesus, Jesus!'

In the end, seeing that she was dead, he fell on his knees and murmured the *Miserere*. The doctor, who had remained at the door, slowly withdrew, crossed the corridor on tiptoe, and descended to the road, where the boy was holding his horse by the reins.

'The rain won't be long in coming, senhor doctor,' said the lad, yawning with sleep.

Dr Gouvea turned up the collar of his greatcoat, arranged his case on the seat; and a few minutes later the gig was rolling noiselessly down the road under the first shower of rain, cutting the darkness of the night with the clear red light of its two lanterns.

Chapter XXIV

FROM SEVEN o'clock the next morning, Father Amaro was posted at his window, with his eyes nailed to the corner of the street, watching out for Dionysia. He was in such a state of excitement that he didn't notice the fine rain beating in on his face. But Dionysia failed to appear, and he had to leave for the Cathedral, embittered and ill, to baptize the son of Guedes.

It was a maddening torture for him to see those happy people, who on that drear December day filled the grave Cathedral with the noise of domestic rejoicing and paternal felicity, which they vainly endeavoured to restrain. There they all were: papa Guedes resplendent in his white coat and white necktie, the godfather full of his own importance, with a great camellia on his chest, and the senhoras in their gala attire. Standing out amongst them all was the stout midwife, carrying with pomp her mountain of starched lace and blue ribbons, from amongst which her two little brown cheeks were barely visible. At the end of the Cathedral, with his thoughts far away in Ricoça, and in Barrosa, Father Amaro hastily gabbled through the ceremony: he blew the Sign of the Cross over the cheeks of the infant in order to drive out the devil, who had already taken up his abode in that tender flesh: he laid salt on the little mouth so that all his life the child would loathe the bitter taste of Sin and nurture himself only with the divine desires of Truth; then the priest then took saliva from his mouth and put it into the earholes and up the nostrils of the baby, so that he should never listen to the solicitations of the flesh and never breathe the alluring perfumes of earthly things. And standing all round, with great wax candles in their hands, the godfather and godmother and the guests, wearied with all that quickly muttered Latin, were only occupied with the baby, fearing that he might respond with some impudent irreverence to the tremendous exhortations which his Holy Mother the Church was making to him.

Father Amaro, then, lightly putting his finger on the little white bonnet, urged the baby, there in that great Cathedral, to renounce for life the devil with all his works and pomps. The sacristan Mathias, who gave the ritual replies in Latin, renounced them for him—while the poor little baby opened his tiny mouth in search of his mother's nipple. Then the paroco went in the direction of the baptismal font, followed by the whole family and a crowd of sanctimonious old women who had collected, and a band of street boys hoping for a distribution of coins. But the anointing of the baby was a scene of confusion: the midwife excitedly fumbled at the ribbons of the gown, which had to be undone for the oil to be put on the little bare shoulders and chest; the godmother rushed to her aid, letting her candle slip and spilling the grease down the dress of one of the senhoras, a neighbour of the family, who frowned angrily.

'*Franciscus, credis?*' asked Amaro.

Mathias hurried to affirm, in the name of Francisco: '*Credo.*'

'*Franciscus, vis baptizari?*'

'*Volo,*' responded Mathias.

Then the shining water fell on the little head, round and soft as a tender melon; the baby kicked with impatience.

'*Ego te baptizo, Franciscus, in nomine Patris . . . et Filii . . . et Spiritus Sancti . . .*'

At last it was over! Amaro ran to the sacristy to take off his vestments; while the midwife, looking very serious, Papa Guedes, the doting senhoras, the old women and the expectant beggars, departed to the jingle of the bells; sheltering under their umbrellas, and splashing in the mud, carrying in triumph Francisco, the new Christian.

Amaro tore up the steps of his house, as he had the feeling that Dionysia would be there waiting for him.

Sure enough, there she was, sitting in his room looking completely worn out and dirty from the night's struggle and the mud of the road. He no sooner entered than she began to moan.

'What's happened, Dionysia?'

She broke into sobs and didn't reply.

'She is dead!' exclaimed Amaro.

'We did all we could to save her, my son, we did all we could!' cried the matron in the end.

Amaro dropped on the bed, as if he also were dead.

Dionysia shouted for the servant. They poured water and then vinegar on his face. He revived a little and pushed them away with his hand. He was ghastly white, but did not utter a word; turning his face down on the pillow he sobbed desperately, while the two women fled in consternation to the kitchen.

'It looks as if he was very fond of Menina Amelia,' Escolastica began, speaking in an undertone as if she were in a house where someone was dying.

'He visited there so often. He was a lodger there for a long time. Yes, they were like brother and sister . . .' said Dionysia, still weeping.

They then spoke of diseases of the heart (Dionysia had told Escolastica that poor Amelia had died of a burst artery); Escolastica also suffered from heart trouble, caused by her husband's ill-treatment; her infirmity took the form of fainting fits . . . Ah, she also had her worries!

'Would you like a little drop of coffee, Senhora Dionysia?'

'Listen, to tell you the truth, Senhora Escolastica, I could do with a little drop of geropiga.'

Escolastica ran to the tavern at the end of the road, and returned with a glass of geropiga hidden under her apron: and the two of them sat at the table, one dipping pieces of bread in her coffee, and the other draining her glass to the last drop, both agreeing with sighs, that in this world there was nothing but trouble and tears.

It struck eleven: and Escolastica was thinking of taking a bowl of broth to the senhor paroco, when he called from inside. He was dressed in a high hat and buttoned-up overcoat, and his eyes were as red as two burning coals.

'Escolastica,' he said 'run to the Inn of the Cross and tell them to send me a mare. Hurry.'

He then called Dionysia; and sitting down in front of her, almost touching her knees, with a face as livid and rigid as marble, he listened in silence to the history of the night: the sudden convulsions, when Amelia became so violent that she, Gertrude and the senhor doctor could hardly hold her down; the blood, the fits of dejection, which weakened her; and then the anxiety of the asphyxy which made her whole body turn as purple as the tunic of one of the images in the Cathedral . . .

But the boy from the Inn of the Cross had arrived with the mare. Amaro took a little crucifix from underneath some white linen in a drawer and gave it to Dionysia, who was returning to Ricoça to help with the preparation of the body for burial.

'Put this crucifix on her bosom, it was she who gave it to me.'

He went down and mounted the mare; immediately he reached the Barrosa Road he spurred the animal to a gallop. The rain had stopped, and from behind the leaden clouds a weak ray of the December sun was reflected on the grass and the wet stones.

When he arrived at the overflowing well, from where he could see Carlota's house, he had to wait in order to let pass a large flock of sheep, which took up the whole road. The shepherd, with his goatskin thrown over his shoulders and his gourd hanging from his neck, suddenly reminded him of Feirão and his life there, fragments of which passed quickly through his mind: those landscapes clouded in the grey mountain vapours; Joanna laughing stupidly as she swung on the bell rope; his suppers of roasted kid in Gralheira with the abbot, sitting in front of the huge fire, with the wood blazing up the chimney; the long days in which he sat lonely and desperate in his house watching the endless falling of the snow. And now came to him an anxious desire for the solitude of the mountains, for the life of the shepherds, far removed from men and towns, buried there with his sorrow.

The door of Carlota's house was shut. He knocked, and receiving no answer he called her name all round the stables and the patio, where he heard the geese cackling. There was no response. He then made for the village, leading the mare by the reins; he stopped at the tavern where a very fat woman was sitting at the door knitting a stocking. Inside, in the darkness of the shop, two men, with their glasses of wine beside them on the table, played a heated game of *bisca*, loudly smacking their cards on the table; a young boy, with the yellow face of fever, sadly looked on at the play.

The woman told him that Senhora Carlota had just left after having purchased a quartilho of olive-oil. She must have gone to Michaela's house in the Church Square. She called inside, and a young girl with a squint appeared from the shadows at the back of the huge wine barrels.

'Run to Michaela, and tell Senhora Carlota that there is a senhor here from the town who wishes to see her.'

Amaro returned to Carlota's house, and sat outside on a stone to wait for her, holding his mare by the reins. But the silence and the closed house brought terror to his heart. He got up and put his ear to the key-hole, hoping to hear from inside the cry or whine of a child. But the house had the silence of an abandoned cave. He calmed himself with the thought that Carlota had taken the child with her to Michaela's. He really should have asked the woman at the tavern if Carlota had a baby in her arms. He looked at the house, so well white-washed, with muslin curtains on the upper windows, a rare luxury in that poor locality; he remembered the tidiness of the home, the neat arrangement of the bright china in the kitchen. His baby was surely well cared for and had a clean cradle . . .

Ah, he must certainly have been mad yesterday evening, when he had left there, on the kitchen table, four gold sovereigns, the price in advance of one year's keep, and when he had said so cruelly to the dwarf: 'I count on you!' Poor little mite! But Carlota understood clearly last night in Ricoça, that he now wanted his baby to live, to be brought up with care and affection! He wouldn't leave him there any longer, under the horrible eye of that dwarf, all streaked with blood. He would take him that very night to Joanna Carreira of Poyaes.

The sinister stories of Dionysia about the 'weaver of angels' were just stupid gossip. The baby was now well and happy in Michaela's house, drinking from those fine healthy breasts . . . Then he knew that he wanted to leave Leiria, and bury himself in Feirão. He would take Escolastica with him, and he would bring up and educate his son as his nephew, experiencing again through him all the emotions of those two years of romance; and there he could pass his life in sadness, but in peace, thinking always of Amelia, until he went like his predecessor, Abbot Gustavo, who also had brought up his nephew in Feirão, to his eternal rest in the little cemetery, to sleep peacefully under the wild flowers in summer, and the clean white snow in winter.

Carlota then arrived: she was so astonished when she recognized Amaro that she stood still without attempting to pass the gate. There was a frown on her forehead and her beautiful face looked very grave.

'The baby?' exclaimed Amaro.

She was silent for a minute, and then replied calmly: 'Don't talk to me about that . . . It caused me such a lot of sorrow. Yesterday, two hours after I'd brought him here—the poor little angel began to turn purple, and died here in front of my eyes . . .'

'You liar!' shouted Amaro. 'I want to see him.'

'Come in, senhor, if you would like to see him.'

'But what did I say to you last night, woman?'

'But what could I do, senhor? He died. Well——'

She opened the door very simply, without either anger or fear. Amaro saw in a glance, at the side of the hearth, a cradle covered with a red petticoat.

He turned and went out without a word; then jumped immediately on his mare. But the woman, suddenly becoming talkative, said that just now she had gone down to the village to order a decent little coffin. As she could see that the baby had come from nice people she didn't want to bury him just wrapped up in an old rag. But anyway, as the senhor was there, it seemed only right that he should leave a little money for the expenses of the funeral—two mil reis if possible.

Amaro stared at her a minute with a brutal desire to strangle her; but in the end he put the money in her hand. He was trotting along the road when he heard her running after him, calling 'psst, psst'. Carlota wished to return his coat which he had wrapped round the baby the evening before: it had done good service, the baby had arrived home as warm as crinkly pork. Unfortunately . . .

Amaro, without even listening, furiously spurred the mare's flanks.

When he arrived in the town, after dismounting at the door of the Inn of the Cross, instead of going to his house he went straight to the bishop's palace. He now had one sole idea; which was to leave that cursed town, and never again look on the faces of those *beatas*, never again enter the door of that hateful Cathedral.

As he was going up the large stone steps of the palace, he remembered with disquietude what Libaninho had said the evening before of the senhor vicar general's indignation over the obscure complaint. But Father Saldanha, the confidential friend of the palace, was so affable, as he showed him into his excellency's library, that he again felt at ease. The senhor vicar general was very pleasant, expressing great concern at the paleness and agitation of the senhor paroco.

'I've just had a terrible shock, senhor vicar general. My sister in Lisbon is dying. I came here to beg your excellency for a few days leave.'

The senhor vicar general affected great sympathy: 'Ah, certainly, I will grant it—ah! we must all be one day passengers in the boat of Charon! *Ipse ratem conto subigit, velisque ministrat, et ferruginea subvectat corpora cymba.* None of us will escape. I am so sorry for you, so sorry. I will remember you in my prayers.'

And very methodically, his excellency took out a pencil and made a note of it.

Amaro, on leaving the palace, went directly to the Cathedral. He shut himself into the sacristy, which was deserted at this hour: and after thinking a long time with his head between his closed fists, he wrote to Canon Dias:

My dear master,
It is with a trembling hand that I write these lines. The poor girl is dead. I am leaving here, as you must see that it is impossible for me to remain. It would break my heart. Your excellent sister is arranging the burial. You understand that I could not do so. I am very grateful to her . . . Good-bye till, if God so wills, we meet again one day. My intention is to go far away in the mountains to some poor parish of shepherds, to finish my days there in tears, meditation and penance. Do what you can to console the unfortunate mother. Never, while I have a breath in my body, will I forget all I owe you. Good-bye again, I am so distracted that I don't rightly know what I am saying.
The friend of your heart,
Amaro Vieira.
P.S. The baby died also, and is already buried, A.V.

He placed the letter in a mourning envelope; and after arranging his papers, went to open the great wrought-iron door, and gazed for a minute at the yard, the shed, the sexton's house. The mists, resulting from the first rains, gave to that corner of the Cathedral the dreariness of winter. He walked slowly under the sad silence of the great gloomy walls, and peeped into Uncle Esguelhas' kitchen: there he was, sitting at the hearth, with his pipe in his mouth, sadly spitting into the ashes. Amaro tapped lightly on the window; and when the sexton opened the door he glanced at the interior of that house which he knew so well, the curtain which shut off Toto's alcove, the stairs which led up to the room. The paroco was suddenly affected with so many memories and longings that his throat choked with sobs and he couldn't speak for a minute.

'I came to bid you good-bye, Uncle Esguelhas,' he murmured in the end. 'I'm off to Lisbon as my sister there is dying . . .'

And continuing with lips trembling with emotion: 'All the troubles come together. Do you know that poor Ameliazinha died suddenly . . .'

The sexton was shocked, astounded.

'Good-bye, Uncle Esguelhas. Give me your hand, Uncle Esguelhas. Good-bye.'

'Good-bye, senhor paroco, good-bye!' said the old man with his eyes overflowing with tears.

Amaro fled to his house, restraining himself from sobbing out loud in the street. He said immediately to Escolastica that he was leaving that night for Lisbon. They were sending him a mare from the Inn of the Cross, as he had to catch the train from Chão de Macas.

'I only have enough money for the journey. But all the towels and sheets and other things here I'm leaving to you.'

Escolastica, crying at the thought of losing the senhor paroco, wanted to kiss his hand in order to show her appreciation of his generosity; she also offered to help him to pack his clothes . . .

'I'll see to all that myself, Escolastica, don't you trouble.'

He shut himself into his room. Escolastica, still weeping, went to examine and to gather up the small amount of linen in the cupboard. But Amaro shouted for her a few minutes after, as two men with harp and fiddle were posted in front of his window, playing the waltz of the *Two Worlds*, out of tune.

'Give a tostão to those men,' said the priest furious, 'and send them to hell! Tell them that there is someone sick here!'

And till five o'clock Escolastica didn't hear a sound coming from the room.

When the boy from the Inn of the Cross came with the mare, she knocked gently on the door, thinking that the senhor paroco was sleeping. She was still crying at the thought of his departure. He immediately ordered her to enter. He was standing in the middle of the room with his cloak over his shoulders, about to tie up his canvas bag which was to go on the crupper of the horse. He gave her a pile of letters to be delivered that same night to Dona Maria of the Assumption,

Father Silverio, and Father Natario. He was going down the stairs, followed by the servant sobbing aloud, when he heard the familiar sound of a crutch below, and Uncle Esguelhas appeared looking very agitated.

'Come in, Uncle Esguelhas, come in.'

The sexton shut the door and said, after a minute's hesitation: 'I hope you will excuse me, senhor paroco, but—on account of all the trouble I had forgotten something. Some time ago I found this in the room, and I thought that——'

He put a little gold earring in Amaro's hand. Amaro recognized it at once: it was Amelia's. She had looked everywhere for it; it had no doubt fallen out on one morning of love on the sexton's bed. Amaro, choking with emotion, embraced Uncle Esguelhas.

'Good-bye, good-bye, Escolastica. Think of me sometimes. Remember me to Mathias, Uncle Esguelhas . . .'

The boy roped the bag to the saddle, and Amaro departed, leaving Uncle Esguelhas and Escolastica both weeping at the door.

After passing the irrigation dam, at a turn in the road, he had to dismount in order to arrange one of his stirrups: he was in the act of remounting, when Dr Godinho, the general secretary and the senhor administrator of the council, all very good friends, now appeared; after having had a walk together they were returning to the town. They stopped to talk to the senhor paroco, whom they were surprised to see there with his bag on the crupper, and with all the appearances of making a journey.

'It's true,' he said. 'I am going to Lisbon.'

The secretary and the administrator sighed with envy at his luck. But when the paroco spoke of his sister dying, they were politely sad; and the senhor administrator said: 'You must be very grieved, I understand . . . Besides, this other trouble in the house of your friends in the Rua da Misericordia—poor Ameliazinha, dying so suddenly . . .'

The secretary said: 'What? Ameliazinha, that pretty girl who lived in the Rua da Misericordia? Dead?'

Dr Godinho also heard the news for the first time, and appeared shocked.

The senhor administrator had been told by his servant, who had heard the news from Dionysia. He had heard that it was heart trouble.

'Well, senhor paroco,' said the secretary, 'forgive me if I upset your religious sentiments, which, by the way, are also mine. But God committed a horrible crime—He took from us the prettiest girl in the town! What eyes, senhores! And then that provoking virtue of hers——'

Then, in a sympathetic tone, all lamented this blow which must have affected the senhor paroco so much.

He answered very gravely: 'I am sincerely grieved—I knew her so well. She had some very good qualities, and would, without a doubt, have made a model wife. I really am very sad about it.'

He silently shook hands all round, and while these *cavalheiros* continued their walk home, Father Amaro trotted along the road which was already growing dark, in the direction of Chão Macas station.

The next day at eleven o'clock, Amelia's funeral procession left Ricoça. It was a bitter morning: the sky and the whole countryside were covered with a dark grey fog, and a freezing cold rain was falling. It was a long way from the farm to the chapel at Poyaes. A choir boy walked in front, with the cross raised. He moved quickly, with long strides, splashing his feet in the mud; Abbot Ferrão, in a black stole, recited the *Exultabunt Domino*, as he sheltered under the umbrella which the sacristan at his side, with the hyssop, held up for him; four labourers from the farm, with their heads lowered against the slanting rain, carried the coffin, lined with lead, on a bier and Gertrude, with the hood of her long cloak over her head, walked under the caretaker's huge umbrella, saying her rosary. At the side, the mournful valley of Poyaes was buried in grey leaden clouds and a deep silence; and the priest in his enormous voice bellowed out the *Miserere*, passing quickly along by the deep crevices where the little streams bubbled, overflowing with water.

On reaching the first houses of the village, the men who were carrying the coffin stopped exhausted; and at that moment a man with his umbrella raised, who had been waiting under a tree, came out and silently joined the funeral. It was João Eduardo, in black gloves, and laden with crêpe. He had two deep black furrows under his eyes, and the tears streamed down his face. Immediately from behind him came two servants in livery to join the procession, with their trousers well tucked up and great wax candles in their hands; they were two lackeys whom the morgado had sent to honour the funeral of one of those senhoras of Ricoça, friends of the abbot.

Then, on seeing those two men in livery, whose presence gave an air of nobility to the procession, the choir boy raised the cross higher and stepped out more valiantly; the four men, forgetting their fatigue, straightened the poles of the bier: the sacristan boomed out a tremendous *Requiem*. Women stood at the doors making the Sign of the Cross and admiring the white surplices and the gold plated ornaments of the coffin as it was borne up the steep muddy road, followed by groups of men and women under umbrellas, while the dreary rain beat down relentlessly.

The chapel was situated on the side of a hill, amongst a grove of oaks; the bell rang out the funeral knell: and the procession disappeared into the dark chapel, as the sacristan hoarsely intoned a canto of the *Subvenite sancti*. The two servants in livery, carrying out the instructions of the senhor morgado, did not enter the chapel.

They remained at the door, under an umbrella, listening, and stamping their cold feet on the ground. The sound of plain chant issued from the open door; afterwards a deafening murmur of prayers; and then suddenly the dismal Latin obsequies, in the great loud voice of the priest.

Then the two men, weary of it all, crossed the chapel yard, and went down to Uncle Seraphim's tavern. Two cowmen from the morgado's estate, who were silently drinking their glasses of wine, stood up immediately the servants in livery appeared.

'Sit down, boys, and enjoy your drink,' said the little old lackey who accompanied João Eduardo on his rides. 'We are here on a dreary task. Good day, Senhor Seraphim.'

They shook hands with Seraphim, who, as he measured them out two *aguardentes*, enquired if the dead girl was Senhor Joãozinho's sweetheart, and if she had died, as was said, from a burst vein.

The old lackey laughed: 'What burst vein! Nothing whatever burst. What burst out was a big baby from her inside.'

'The work of Senhor Joãozinho?' asked Seraphim, opening wide his rascally eyes.

'I don't think so,' said the other with importance. 'Senhor Joãozinho was in Lisbon. It was the work of some *cavalheiro* of the town. Do you know who I suspect, Senhor Seraphim?'

But Gertrude arrived, out of breath, shouting that the procession was nearing the cemetery and that the senhores were wanted. The lackeys moved immediately and caught up with the funeral as it was entering the cemetery and the last verse of the *Miserere* was being sung. João Eduardo, with a candle in his hand, was now immediately behind Amelia's coffin, almost touching it, and staring with eyes clouded with tears at the velvet pall with which it was covered. The chapel bell rang desolately without ceasing. The rain still fell, though not so heavily. And hushed in the melancholy silence of the cemetery, with steps muffled by the soft earth, all made for the corner against the wall where Amelia's grave, freshly dug, showed up black and deep amidst the wet grass. The choir boy stuck the pole of the plated cross in the earth, and Abbot Ferrão advanced to the edge of the dark hole, murmuring the *Deus cujus miseratione*. Then João Eduardo, ghastly pale, suddenly

343

tottered, and the umbrella fell from his hands; one of the liveried servants rushed forward and caught him by the waist; they tried to drag him away from the side of the grave, but he resisted, remaining there with teeth clenched, desperately holding on to the sleeve of the servant, watching the grave-digger and the two boys tying the ropes round the coffin and letting it slip slowly down into the soft earth. There was a creaking sound of badly nailed boards.

'*Requiem aeternam dona ei, Domine!*'

'*Et lux perpetua luceat ei,*' muttered the sacristan.

The coffin struck the bottom with a dull thud: the abbot sprinkled a little earth on top, in the form of a cross; and slowly shaking the hyssop over the velvet pall, the earth, and the grass at the side, he cried:

'*Requiescat in pace.*'

'Amen,' responded the cavernous voice of the sacristan and the piping voice of the choir boy.

'Amen,' said all in a murmur, which rustled and was lost amongst the cypresses, the grass, the tombs and the cold fogs of that sad December day.

Chapter XXV

AT THE end of May 1871 there was great excitement at the hotel restaurant, Casa Havaneza, in the Chiado, Lisbon. People arrived out of breath, and pushed their way through the crowds which were filling up the door, standing on tiptoe and stretching their necks between rows of hats, trying to get a glimpse at the railings of the balcony, where a placard with telegrams from the Havas Agency was hung; individuals with faces full of astonishment left in consternation, exclaiming to more peaceful friends who were waiting for them outside:

'All is lost! All is burning!'

From inside came the babble of the throng which pressed against the counter, as excited arguments went on; and along the avenues in the Loreto Square, in front of the residences by the Chiado, right out to the Magalhaes, on that hot day at the beginning of summer, there was a terrific buzz of voices full of emotion, where the words, 'Commune! Versailles! Incendiaries! Thieves! Crime! International!' were heard on all sides, ejaculated with fury, above the noise of the hackney-cabs and the newspaper boys screaming out the latest editions.

Every hour telegrams arrived announcing the successive episodes of the revolutionary battles which were being waged in the streets of Paris: telegrams sent out in terror from Versailles, telling of the palaces which were burning, the streets which were in ruins; the mass shootings in the barrack-yards and amongst the mausoleums in the cemeteries; vengeance wreaked even in the dark sewers; the fatal madness which was disgracing the uniforms and blouses; and the resistance, which with the furore of agony mixed with the methods of science, sought to exterminate the aristocratic class with paraffin-oil, dynamite and nitro-glycerine! A violent spasm, an end of a world—which a telegram of twenty or thirty words revealed in a flash.

The people in the Chiado indignantly resented the ruin of Paris. They recalled, with exclamations of regret, the edifices which had been burnt down. The Hôtel de Ville, 'so beautiful', the Rue Royale, 'so luxurious'. There were individuals so furious with the destruction of the Tuileries that one might have imagined that it belonged to them; those who had been in Paris for one or two months broke out in invectives, claiming the rights of a Parisian to the wealth of the city, scandalized that the insurrectionists had not respected the monuments on which they had placed their eyes.

'Just think of it!' exclaimed one fat man. 'The Palace of the Legion of Honour, in ruins! And less than a month ago I was there with my wife. Disgraceful! what villainy!'

But the shouts were louder when the minister received another telegram, still more desolate: the whole boulevard, from the Bastille to the Madeleine, was in flames; and the Place de la Concorde, and the Avenue des Champs Elysées to the Arc de Triomphe. And thus had the revolutionaries insanely demolished all that system of restaurants, café-concerts, public dance-halls, gambling-houses and nests of prostitution! Then right from Lorento Square to Magalhaes ran a wave of fury. So flames had reduced to ashes that highly convenient centre of feasting! Oh, how infamous! It was surely the end of the world! Where could one eat better than in Paris? Where could one meet other women of such experience? Where else could one see that prodigious file of carriages returning from the Bois, in the dry bitter days of winter, when the victorias of the *cocottes* rode resplendent at the side of the phaetons of the Bourse? How abominable! They forgot the libraries and the museums: but their regret for the ruined cafés and brothels was sincere. It was the end of Paris, it was the end of France!

A group of politicians had collected outside the Casa Havaneza; they uttered the name of Prudhon, who at that time in Lisbon had begun to be vaguely cited as a bloody monster; and invectives were hurled against Prudhon. The majority of people thought that it was he himself who had lit the fires. But an esteemed poet, author of *Flowers and Sighs*, stated that in spite of all the stupid things that Prudhon had said, he was a delightful stylist. Then the athlete Franca bawled: 'A stylist! An empty head! If I had that plunderer here in the Chiado I'd smash every bone in his body!'

And he would have done, as after a few glasses of brandy Franca was a wild beast.

Some few young men, however, whose dramatic instincts had been aroused by the romantic element of the catastrophe, applauded the bravery of the Commune. Vermorel opening his arms to form a cross and crying amidst the shower of bullets which pierced him: 'Vive l' Humanité!' The old man Delacluze, with the fanaticism of a saint, dictating from his bed of agony orders for the violence of the resistance . . .

'They are great men!' exclaimed a young man excitedly.

The serious people near muttered. Others left, turning pale as they saw in imagination their houses in the Baixa dripping with paraffin oil and that same Casa Havaneza a prey to the socialistic incendiaries. Then all the groups were filled with the fury of authority and repression: it was necessary that society, attacked by the International, should take refuge in the force of its religious and conservative principles, surrounding itself with bayonets! Citizens with small haberdashery shops spoke of 'the scoundrels', with the impudent disdain of a La Tremouile or an Ossuna. Individuals picking their teeth decreed vengeance. Vagrants became furious against the workers who wished to live as princes. They spoke with devotion of property, of capital.

On the other hand, there were verbose young men, excited individuals, who declaimed against the old world, the old ideas, shouting threats against them, proposing to destroy them in tremendous articles.

And it was thus that a torpid stagnated set of people hoped, with the help of a few police, to keep back a social revolution; and some youths with a smattering of learning decided, with a few sheets of foolscap, to destroy a social system of eighteen centuries. But no one showed more excitement that a clerk of the hotel, who from the top of the steps of the Casa Haveneza brandished his walking stick, and advised France to restore the Bourbons.

Then a man dressed in black, who had emerged from a tobacco shop, and was passing through the groups of people, stopped, as an astonished voice behind him called out:

'Oh, Father Amaro! Oh, you rogue!'

He turned round: it was Canon Dias. They heartily embraced one another, and in order to converse tranquilly walked along to the Camões Square and stopped there next to the statue.

'And you, when did you arrive, master?'

He had arrived the evening before. He had a lawsuit against the Pimentas of Pojeira, because of a claim they were making on his farm. It had been appealed to the High Court of Justice, and the question was going to be settled in the capital, so he had come in order to watch the case.

'And you, Amaro? In your last letter, you said that you wanted to leave Santo Thyrso.'

It was true. The parish had advantages; but Villa Franca had become vacant, and in order to be nearer the capital, he had come to speak about it to the Senhor Conde of Ribamar, his conde, who was already arranging the transference for him. It was the condessa, above all, to whom he owed so much!

'And Leiria? Senhora Joanneira, is she better?'

'No, the poor woman. Do you know, at the beginning we had a devil of a fright. We thought that she was following Amelia to the grave. But no, it was anasarca, a form of dropsy.'

'God help her, the sainted woman! And Natario?'

347

'He has aged a lot. He also has had his trouble. There has been much gossip about him.'

'And tell me now, master, Libaninho?'

'I wrote to you about him,' said the canon laughing.

Father Amaro also laughed; and for a few minutes the two priests stopped, holding their sides.

'Yes, it's the truth,' said the canon at last. 'The thing was really scandalous. Because in the end they caught him in the act with the sergeant, in circumstances which left no doubt whatever ... And at ten o'clock at night in the poplar avenue. He was very imprudent. But the thing was soon forgotten, and when Mathias died we gave him the position of sacristan, a good post for him. Much better than his office job. And he will fulfil his task with zeal!'

'Yes, he will fulfil it with zeal,' agreed Father Amaro very seriously. 'And how is Dona Maria of the Assumption?'

'Man, things are being muttered—a new servant—a carpenter who lived in front. The fellow has fallen on his feet.'

'Is it really true?'

'Yes, he has fallen on his feet all right. Cigar, watch, gloves! It has its funny side, hasn't it?'

'It's divine!'

'And the Gansosos are just the same,' continued the canon. 'They now have your old servant Escolastica.'

'And the beast of a João Eduardo?'

'Haven't I written to you about him? He is still there in Poyaes. The morgado is suffering from liver trouble. They say João Eduardo has tuberculosis. I don't know. It was Ferrão who told me.'

'How is he, Ferrão?'

'He's well. Do you know whom I met the other day? Dionysia.'

'Yes, and so?'

The canon whispered a word in Father Amaro's ear.

'Really, master?'

'In the Rua das Sousas, a few steps from your old house. It was Dona Luiz da Barrosa who gave her the money to start the establishment. Well, here you have all the news. You seem stronger, man! The change has done you good!'

And putting himself in front of him, he said mockingly: 'Oh, Amaro, you wrote and told me that you wanted to retire to the mountains, enter a monastery, spend the rest of your life in penance ...'

Father Amaro shrugged his shoulders:

'What could you expect, master? In those first moments—you can imagine how I suffered! But it has passed now.'

348

'All passes,' said the canon. And after a pause he added: 'Ah, but Leiria is no longer Leiria!'

They walked along for a minute in silence thinking of the past, of the jolly games of lotto at Senhora Joanneira's, the jokes at tea, the pleasant walks to Morenal, the *Adeus* and the *Miscreant*, sung by Arthur Couceiro, and accompanied by poor Amelia, who now slept in the cemetery at Poyaes, under the wild flowers . . .

'And what do you think of what is happening in France, Amaro?' the canon asked suddenly.

'It's horrible, master—the archbishop and a crowd of priests shot! A nice game!'

'A dirty game,' muttered the canon.

'It seems as if the same ideas are spreading to our little corner of the earth,' said Amaro.

The canon agreed. They then spoke indignantly of that dirty rabble of freemasons, republicans, socialists and people who wanted to destroy every respectable institution—the clergy, religious instruction, the family, the army, capital . . . ah! society was threatened by these unchained monsters! The repressions of former days were necessary, the dungeon and the scaffold, to inspire men with a respect for the faith and its priesthood.

'Ah, that is what is wanting,' said Amaro. 'The fact is they don't respect us! On the contrary, they do nothing but discredit us. These fiends are destroying the veneration which the people had for the priests of God.'

'They calumniate us, infamously,' said the canon ponderously.

Then two senhoras passed in front of them; one, whose hair was already grey, had a very noble air; the other was a little creature, thin and pale, with black shadows under her eyes, her sharp elbows tight against her obviously sterile body. She wore an enormous puffed skirt, a large chignon and very high heels.

'Odds bobs!' said the canon in an undertone, tapping his colleague on the sleeve. 'Eh, Father Amaro, that young one is the kind you like to confess.'

'That time is gone, master,' said the paroco laughing, 'now I only confess married women!'

The canon abandoned himself for a minute to a little hilarity; but presently returned to his ponderous air of priestly obesity, as he saw Amaro take off his hat and make a profound bow to a *cavalheiro* with a grizzly moustache and gold-rimmed spectacles, who had entered the Square from the direction of Loreto, with his pipe grasped firmly in his teeth and his sunshade under his arm.

It was the Senhor Conde of Ribamar. He advanced towards the two priests with a friendly air; and Amaro, with head still uncovered, and striking an attitude of respect, proudly presented his friend, Senhor Canon Dias of the Cathedral of Leiria, to the conde. They spoke for a moment of the season, which was already hot. Then Father Amaro commented on the latest telegrams.

'What does your excellency think of what is taking place in France?'

The statesman waved his hands in a despair which overshadowed his face. 'It is almost too painful to talk about, Senhor Father Amaro, too painful. To think of half a dozen ruffians destroying Paris—my Paris! Did you know, senhores, that it has made me ill?'

The two clergymen, with faces of consternation, united in their sympathy for the grief which had so prostrated the statesman.

And then the canon asked:

'And what does your excellency think will be the result of this?'

The Senhor Conde of Ribamar stated deliberately, in words which, being overburdened with ideas, issued very slowly from his brain: 'The result? That is not difficult to foresee. When one has some experience of History and Politics, one can see the result of all this distinctly. As distinctly as I now see you two clergymen.'

The two priests hung on the prophetic words which flowed from the lips of the member of the government:

'The insurrection being suppressed,' continued the senhor conde, looking straight in front of him with his finger in the air, as if following, pointing out, the future historical events into which the pupils of his eyes, aided by his gold-rimmed glasses, penetrated; 'the insurrection being suppressed, in two or three months the monarchy will again be restored. If you gentlemen could have seen, as I did, a reception in the Tuileries and again in the Hôtel de Ville in the time of the sovereign, you would have to admit that France is profoundly imperialist, and entirely imperialist. We will have Napoleon III, or perhaps he will abdicate and the empress will become regent during the minority of the royal prince. This is what I have said from the beginning would be the most prudent solution. And, as an immediate consequence, the Pope of Rome would again become the temporal, as well as the spiritual ruler. I, to speak the truth, and I have many times stated these views, do not approve of the restitution of the papal power. But I am not here to say of what I approve or disapprove. Happily I am not the dictator of Europe. It would be an undertaking beyond my age and my capabilities. I am here to say what I have learnt definitely from my experience of politics and of history. Well, what do I predict? Ah! The empress on the throne of France, Pius IX on the throne of Rome, and it is thus we will have democracy crushed between those two sublime forces. And believe me, senhores, you have in front of you a man who knows his Europe and the elements of which modern society is composed. You also may believe that after this example of the Commune, we will never again hear republicanism spoken of, nor social questions, nor the people, and that for at least the next hundred years!'

'May Our Lord Jesus Christ grant that it be so, senhor conde!' said the canon fervently.

But Amaro, radiant, delighted at finding himself there in a Lisbon Square in intimate conversation with an illustrious statesman, asked still another question, putting into his words the anxiety of a frightened conservative: 'And does your excellency think that these ideas of republicanism, of materialism, could spread here amongst our people?'

The conde laughed; and said, as he walked between the two priests, till they arrived near the railings which surrounded the statue of Luiz de Camões: 'Don't worry about that, my dear senhores, don't worry about that! It is true that there are one or two hotheads here who find fault, and make ridiculous assertions about the decadence of Portugal, stating that we are blind to all going on around us, that we are becoming besotted and stupid, and that our present state cannot last for another ten years, etc., etc. A lot of ridiculous nonsense!'

He had been standing with his back against the railings of the statue, but now leant forward in a confidential attitude.

'The truth is, my dear senhores, that other countries envy us. I don't say what I am going to say in order to flatter your reverences: but while we have respectable clergymen like you, senhores, Portugal will maintain with dignity her place amongst the nations of Europe! Because religion, my dear senhores, is the base of order!'

'Without doubt, senhor conde, without doubt,' said the two priests with enthusiasm.

'Just look around you, senhores! What peace, what movement, what prosperity!'

And he made a large gesture which took in the whole of the Loreto Square, in which at the end of that serene afternoon the entire life of the city was concentrated. Empty hackney cabs rode slowly round; senhoras passed in pairs, with full chignons and high heels, in listless, weary movements, their faces, pale as chalk, testifying to the decadence of the race; now and then a young member of the aristocracy trotted on a miserable lean horse, with his face still green from his night of wine; on the benches people were stretched in the torpor of despair; a bullock-cart went by shaking unsteadily on its high wheels, a symbol of an agriculture and a peasantry generations behind the times; habitués of the bull-rings and the halls of the *fado* singers slouched along, with their cigarettes between their teeth; a passerby, weary of life, read on the posters the announcement of obsolete operas; the miserable faces of the workers were the personification of decaying industries . . . And all this decrepit world moved slowly under the brilliant sky of a rich climate, between the mournful voices of the street urchins calling out tickets for lotteries and public games of chance, newspaper boys offering the local paper, all passing sluggishly through the Square, where two dreary façades of the church stood out, and shining brilliantly amongst the long row of houses were the signboards of three pawnbrokers and the gloomy doors of four taverns; and opening on to the Square with the poisonous air of a fetid sewer, were the alleys of a district of crime and prostitution.

'Just look,' the conde continued, 'look at this peace, this prosperity, this contentment . . . My dear senhores, I am not really surprised that we are the envy of Europe!'

And the representative of the state, the two representatives of religion, all three in line, near the railings of the monument of Camões, their heads raised, were filled with delight at the certainty of the glory and grandeur of their country; there at the foot of that pedestal under the cold bronze gaze of that old poet, erect and noble, with his fine strong horseman's shoulders, his epic over his heart, his sword held firm; surrounded by the Portuguese historians and heroic poets of the past, a past gone forever, a memory almost lost.